RISE OF THE BEAST

THE TRIBULATION BEGINS

JOCOLBY PHILLIPS

Rise Of The Beast: The Tribulation Begins

Published in Brambleton, Virginia, by Christian Warrior Fiction Publishing LLC.

Publisher's Note: This novel is a work of fiction. Names, characters, places, and incidents are either products of the author's imagination or used fictitiously. All characters are fictional, and any similarity to people living or dead is purely coincidental.

Library of Congress Cataloging-in-Publication Data

ISBN: 978-1-7360017-2-1 (Paperback)

978-1-7360017-9-0 (Ebook)

To my grandparents, Johnny and Johnnie Mae Phillips. Your commitment to serve God changed the lives of generations of your family and countless others who will read this book. Thank you for giving your life to Christ and instilling the love of God in your family. I look forward to our family reunion in Heaven one day.

Prologue from Rapture

JOHN BARNES READIED the navigation system looking for a valley about five kilometers away from the secret US base's northern ridgeline. The sun began to set, and they needed to be on the ground before darkness to maximize the night. As he grew angry that they were lost, he saw the destination arrow populate on the GPS screen.

Barnes directed the pilot as they hovered to an open spot in an arctic forest about half-mile away from the pre-selected location. "Put us down there."

Barnes ordered, "You will wait here until we return. Give me the keys."

The pilot said, "Are you serious? You're leaving me without a way to stay warm."

Barnes laughed, throwing the man an extra assault pack. "I suggest you make yourself comfortable in that sleeping bag; it's supposedly rated for survivability for this harsh climate."

Barnes led his group of hired special operatives into the darkness. "Ruck up, boys, we got six kilometers to cover in this terrain before sunup."

❧

Christopher and Jackson were hanging out in the operations center, watching a special news report from Israel regarding the recent terror attacks. The news tied two mysterious men to the growing number of Christian rallies worldwide being led by former Jewish men.

Jimbo said, "All is well out there. I was a little nervous, considering I had to take down the north ridge passive security system due to the limited number of folks here now. We don't have enough to monitor or respond to a significant threat. The terrain located on the north ridge of the mountain is very restricted, so I accept risk there. It would take someone with strong mountaineering skills to get to the top."

Jackson said, "I am glad the missile field and that large north granite face are a good half kilometer away from us. If that face ever falls in an earthquake or something, it's going to create a monster avalanche. Still, I guess that was the point of building the base in this location, right, Jimbo?"

"You're right; when we let our nukes go, Mother Nature will take this place over."

Christopher said, "I'm heading to bed guys. Today has been a long day. Now that we got the report that our former teammates safely arrived in Anchorage and all is clear on the security front, it's lights out for this soldier."

Jackson said, "Yeah, I think I'm turning in too."

Jimbo said, "Well, I'm going to do a final check with Max to make sure he's good to go. I will see you guys in the morning."

Jackson said, "Goodnight, don't let the polar bears bite."

Christopher said, "The fun never stops, does it, Jackson?"

"It never stops for me."

The march through the forest and up the mountain had been more robust than John Barnes had expected. Thankfully, he had enough people with mountaineering experience to make it to the top of the north ridge slightly ahead of schedule. He had about forty-five minutes of darkness left. This was enough time to place the charges along the ridgeline to destroy the quiet base below.

The lack of response to the team climbing up the ridgeline made him wonder if this was, in fact, the right place. Barnes shuddered at the thought of reporting to Draven that the American base had been a decoy.

Barnes got nods from all thirteen of his people. "Okay, guys, let me know when you have all your charges in place. We'll move back down the mountain to our last rally point and then set off the charges. We'll fly by to make sure the job was done; worst case, we land and do some cleanup."

After all the charges had been placed, the UE Special Activities Group (SAG), the special operations arm of the UE, made it back down the mountain about 800 meters from the ridgeline summit.

Barnes retrieved the radio transmitter detonator from his assault pack. "Well, men, nothing to do now but start us a well-paid war."

He pushed the detonator.

~

As UE One made its way across the Atlantic to the *Palazzo Caelum*, Draven happily accepted a phone call from John Barnes, saying the "secret" US base had been destroyed.

Draven ordered an immediate military strike against Uruguay, specifically targeting former UN Secretary-General Maximilian Aguilar and strategic locations in Lagos, Nigeria, the United States, and several other countries and cities.

"I want one-megaton nuclear weapons used against Aguilar's home in the Uruguay capital, the Nigerian leader's home outside of Lagos, Los Angeles, New York City, and DC. The remainder of the nuclear weapons I have under my control will be reserved in case our forces encounter heavy resistance in the days ahead," Draven said.

Gabriella jumped from her seat and, before she knew it, had slapped Draven Cross. A man of unmatched power who held her life in her hands.

"How could you? How could you? You have killed millions of innocent people, you monster!" Gabriella screamed as Evan and security forces pinned her to the ground.

"Let her go, gentlemen! Let her go! I would have been worried if that had not been her response. She lost her father figure in President Rodgers, closest friends within the Omega team, and her homeland. I understand your emotion. The vitriol directed at me is misplaced but understandable. I am sure in time Gabriella will apologize and come to understand why the actions of today were necessary," Draven said.

"I will never forgive you. You're pure evil."

Gabriella stormed out of the conference room aboard UE One, collapsing near the press pool seats.

She wept bitterly for friends who were now gone. She cried for a beloved country that would never be the same, and she wept for herself. Gabriella realized the isolation that surrounded her, as Draven had proved to be an evil dictator and perhaps something more sinister. As she stared out into the dark waters of the Atlantic Ocean below her, she attempted a prayer.

"God, please help me to find You. I am all alone. Help me, and please don't forget me."

ꕥ

Christopher was having a hard time sleeping. He kept having dreams of being back in the Special Forces selection course, falling asleep. The penalty of which being caught asleep led to your dismissal from the selection course. Every time he would fall into a deep state of sleep, he'd be told to wake up.

Christopher had donned his heavy winter jacket and pants. He prepared to make his way outside when he noticed that Jimbo and Jackson were missing. Christopher thought they were in the operations center, probably drinking coffee. Yet, when he left the living quarters, he saw Jimbo and Jackson outside talking.

Christopher grew concerned. "What's going on?"

Jackson said, "Oh, man, I hope we didn't wake you. We finished getting dressed out here, so we didn't. It's funny neither one of us could sleep. I was telling Jimbo it's like the Holy Spirit kept slapping me in the face. I can understand how the disciples must have felt when Jesus asked them to pray all night. I am so tired right now; I could sleep all day."

Jimbo said, "Yeah, I keep dreaming my mom was coming in to wake me up for school. I never got into a deep sleep. Let's head up to check on Max and then do an early morning security sweep. Then rack out for a few more hours of sleep."

Christopher said, "I like the way you think."

Jackson said, "Amen to sleep and the patrol."

As the three men neared the operations center, Christopher heard the loud cracking of rock and what seemed like explosions and felt his heart skip. His instincts went into fight mode despite Christopher not seeing the enemy his body felt.

Max burst out of the operations center about forty meters in front of them, yelling to run.

Jimbo said, "My God, an avalanche."

As the men scrambled toward two snowmachines, Christopher stopped and looked in horror as two ICBM nuclear weapons streaked the early dawn sky with their fiery tails.

Christopher screamed as Jackson and Jimbo frantically tried to start the snowmachines. "We're at war!"

Jimbo shouted, "Let's go!"

Jackson raced ahead on a snowmachine catching up to Max, allowing him to jump on with him. Christopher and Jimbo were fast on Jackson's heels as the men rocketed toward the trail that led to the helicopter pad. However, the two snowmachines were no match for the impressive display of power unleashed in the avalanche.

Christopher felt the cold air racing in front of the avalanche and the deafening roar of the snow and debris mere meters behind them. As the first wave of snow mass tumbled over Jackson, he tried to scream something, but the noise of the destruction upon them was too great. Christopher fought to remember his mountaineering training, what to do in an avalanche. He recalled he needed to "swim" to say above the surface of the snow, if possible. However, as the snow engulfed him, Christopher felt as if he were covered in cement. He was sure these were his final moments, and fear stole his breath with the thought he remained at war with God. Christopher was surrounded by darkness, and the only sound now was his labored breathing. Pain flooded his body. He enjoyed the silence that invaded his mind and almost laughed at the thought that his impending death was going to be better than he had envisioned. As the blood from a head wound flowed across his face, Christopher prayed three words. "I surrender God."

Chapter 1

DESPITE THE CHAOS that the disappearances levied on the world, the night had been another boring shift at the NORAD operations center for Major Walters and Sergeant Smith. Major Walters liked no surprises when he was senior watch officer.

Major Walters said, "Sergeant Smith, I thought I told you to get that faulty launch alarm fixed last week."

Sergeant Smith said, "That's the strange thing. I did, Sir."

Beads of sweat rose on the major's forehead as he prepared to notify the Pentagon and White House, while ordering Sergeant Smith, "Bring your display up on the main screen."

As Major Walters attempted to quell the chaos growing in the NORAD command center, General Alpharan, the NORAD commander, entered the command center ahead of his morning update. The general stopped and watched multiple missile tracks racing over the North Pole towards the US.

General Alpharan demanded, "Tell me what's going on."

The uncertainty of the situation hung in the cracking voice of the major. "Sir, we have multiple inbound nuclear-ICBMs from China and Russia. I notified the Pentagon and the White House."

General Alpharan already knew the fate of the country and the very complex where he stood. He said the only thing that came to mind with multiple nuclear-armed missiles tracking directly for Cheyenne Mountain, "God help us."

Screams and panic in the operations center were overtaken by the massive explosion of the first nuclear warhead striking the mountain. The subsequent strikes ensured the famous US military installation became a tomb for all those inside.

❧

The White House chief of staff announced that a nuclear missile would strike Washington D.C. in three minutes. The notion that America was under attack gripped President Rodgers's mind. According to his staff, Los Angeles and Cheyenne Mountain were gone, along with the Vice President and senior military advisors. Rodgers thought about the time wasted worrying about his pursuit of the Oval Office. The thought that the White House was his highest achievement brought sadness.

The frantic and tense shouts among officials in the Oval Office, intermixed with the constant din of phones ringing, faded away for President Rodgers as he reflected on his and the nation's demise.

The snake charmer Draven Cross had lured the country to sleep with hypnotic promises of peace. A challenging thought for the seasoned fighter pilot to accept. America had lost the war with Draven before it had even started. The President grew angry at the realization that he would be the last President of the United States of America as Secret Service dragged him toward the Presidential bunker.

President Rodgers attempted to hold a relaxed posture. He wanted to portray strength and calm. He laughed to himself for trying to be presidential, considering these were his final moments, and there would be no late-night talk show pundits or political rivals judging the mistakes leading to the nation's demise. President Rodgers closed his eyes shortly, savoring the vision of the snow-filled White House lawn in his mind before the Secret Service enclosed him in the underground bunker. His wife's words haunted him. Janet had often spoken of a type of peace God provided that went beyond understanding for those that place their trust in Him. President Rodgers never understood what Janet meant until now.

The tremor in the President's daughter's voice brought him back from reflection. The crisis was now real and painful. He watched Susan push into the Presidential Bunker, fighting a stream of officials fleeing like rats jumping from a sinking ship into the abyss of the open ocean. President Rodgers realized his greatest failure was fighting Janet's Christian beliefs and bringing disillusion to Susan. He knew his daughter shouldn't be here, and tears flowed.

Susan Rodgers screamed, embracing her father. "Daddy, I'm scared!"

A loud crack suffocated the noise-filled room, announcing a one-megaton nuclear warhead explosion above the White House.

President Rodgers whispered, "Honey, I am too, but let's think about seeing Mom and Jesus soon."

ॐ

On the Palazzo Caelum flight, the new Unified Earth Organization (UE) headquarters nestled along the Tiber River near Rome, Draven Cross fell into a dream-like state. It had to be a dream, he thought, as the executive suite of UE One aircraft faded away. The darkness surrounding him was alive and carried a sense of dread and hopelessness, almost pressing the life from Draven, making the experience painfully real.

The living darkness consumed everything except a faint light radiating on a horizon, providing Draven's perception of being in the middle of a vast plain. Despite Draven's efforts to walk toward the radiance, it moved farther away. There were snarls and screams coming from the darkness surrounding Draven, causing him to panic and cry for help. A mocking laugh from the familiar voice of his spirit guide, the Prince of this World, silenced the nightmarish sounds of Draven's environment.

The Prince of this World spoke to Draven in a near-continuous message. "The time has come for you to assume control over this world and start destroying my enemies. The enemy representatives are reaping a great harvest of souls. Place the blame for the world's problems on the witnesses and their God, then isolate and eliminate the followers of the God of Israel."

Draven murmured as he was thrust back into his suite. "Yes, I will."

As UE One completed its taxi at *Aeroporto Internazionale di Roma–Fiumicino,"* outside of Rome, Draven Cross felt prepared to exploit the World War he started. He intended to use the conflict to solidify a one-world government overseen by himself.

A knock on Draven's suite door caused him to jump from his bed. "What is it?"

Gemma said, "Sir, we have arrived in Rome. Are you feeling well?"

"I've never been better; I need five minutes. Ensure the headquarters' staff is ready to provide me an update on the war immediately upon my arrival."

Draven laughing in pride, slammed the door in his executive assistant's face.

❧

An eerie silence rested over the sunny, remote, Alaskan forest. The warmth of the sun revived Jackson as he pulled himself out of a gap between his snowmachine and a fallen white spruce tree.

Thank you, Jesus, that was some ride.

While Jackson was bruised up and felt the sting of a few cuts that would require some attention, his pains faded. Seeing Max, Jackson's heart sunk. The body was contorted by a spruce tree trunk pinning him in the snow. Jackson could do nothing for Max, but time was of the essence if he wanted to find Christopher and Jimbo alive. The problem was everything looked the same, one thick layer of snow and mowed down spruce trees for as far as he could see.

Jesus, I need you; there is no way I can do this by myself.

Jackson started walking in what he thought was the direction of travel the men had been on as they attempted to escape the avalanche. He pressed his lips tight and sighed deeply over the path he was taking. Jackson's sense of direction was based on a glance at the now smaller mountain face behind him. He had walked for about three hundred meters when he saw a snowmachine skid protruding from the snow, about 20 meters ahead of him. The waist-high snowpack made the short journey endless as Jackson struggled to move.

Jackson's breathing labored, and he felt more wounded than first assessed as his right leg throbbed with waves of pain with each step. He reached the skid and dug frantically, praying that his friends would be alive. As Jackson cleared away the snowmachine's front, a large arm came toward him; it had to be Jimbo given the appendage's mass.

A wave of adrenaline surged within Jackson, knowing that Jimbo was nearby and alive. "Hold on, buddy!"

Jackson dug for another ten minutes before he cleared away enough snow to pull Jimbo's massive upper body upright.

Jimbo was a pale-bluish color and shivered continuously. "Jackson, I think my left arm is broken."

Jackson handed Jimbo his parka that he had lost during the avalanche. "A broken arm is a small issue; at least you're alive. We need to find Christopher now."

Jimbo squinted at the bright sun reflecting from the snow. "Where's Max? We could use his help."

Jackson gave a solemn look and head shake for his answer.

Jimbo realized that Max was dead, and the only help available was Jackson and himself. He returned his thoughts to Christopher, saying, "He can't be far; I know the tree line was close to us as we started to tumble in the snow."

Jackson walked in a large circle around the snowmachine again, praying, *Jesus, guide me to him; I need you.* He rose and fell several times as the snow's depth gave way to the unsure surfaces below. Hot tears streamed down Jackson's face. The fact of not finding Christopher after nearly completed a full circle around the snowmachine crushed his soul. Nearing Jimbo, he sunk to his waist at a bent over spruce, whose crown bowed and arched out of the snow, feeling a semi-squishy object around his feet.

Jackson quickly moved snow around his feet where he felt the squishy something. "I think I found him."

By the time Jimbo had gingerly traced Jackson's path, Jackson had cleared enough snow to see Christopher's legs. The avalanche had pinned Christopher on his back.

"Oh man, we got to get him from under that snow!" Jimbo screamed, lurching into the small excavation site, grabbing one leg to pull Christopher.

Jackson ordered, "On the count of three, pull."

Jimbo pulled with one arm. Jackson did the same pulling with every ounce of grit he had within him, only to barely moved Christopher's legs.

Jackson said, "Again, Jimbo, put your back into it."

The men pulled on Christopher again; this time, he budged slightly from his icy prison.

Jackson pleaded. "One more pull, Jimbo, and we should have him free; give it all you got."

The final pull was enough to spring Christopher free and sent Jimbo and Jackson flying back into the fresh powder around them. Jackson jumped up to look at Christopher while Jimbo writhed in pain from jarring his broken arm.

Jackson pointed to the crimson snow in the void Christopher left, shouting to Jimbo. "It looks like he took a solid knock to his head; look at the blood. Get over here quick. I'm barely getting a pulse and only shallow breathing."

ର

Jimbo's medical training as a US Air Force Special Operations para-rescuemen blared in his mind, reminding him that Christopher was in a dire situation. The ashen face of Christopher pushed Jimbo's concern for his new friend beyond the pain of his broken arm as he frantically attempted to save his friend.

Jimbo ordered Jackson, "I need you to start a fire ASAP. Check my snowmachine; hopefully, the fire starter is still in the seat cargo hold."

Jimbo watched Jackson make his way back along the men's path between Jimbo's snowmachine and Christopher's location. Jackson found the cargo hold latch stuck, and after three solid kicks, the seat cover flew open, revealing the fire starter and a wad of cotton balls for kindling. Jackson held up the precious items for Jimbo to see as he started back to Christopher and him. However, before reaching Jimbo and Christopher, Jackson cut a new path toward a nearby downed spruce section. Jackson pointed to the fading Alaskan sun that only provided a few precious hours of sunlight in this late-winter season. Jimbo assumed he was going to get a lifesaving fire going soon.

Jimbo yelled, "Get the fire going and then get over here and help me with Christopher."

Jackson wanted to smart off and say something snarky per his nature in stressful situations. He stopped himself, realizing both men were working to save their friend's life. He was glad the fire starter was military-grade, which gave him a better shot of starting a fire in the damp, cold environment around him. Jackson cleared an area to the ground with the seat cover, knocked the snow from the overhead branches to stop melting, and piled up some dry tinder from the tops of a downed tree. He then laid the cotton balls on a piece of kindling and struck the fire stick.

Nothing happened. Jackson struck the fire-starter again and watched white-hot sparks set the cotton balls and the dry tinder ablaze. While the small stack of kindling smoldered, Jackson broke off a few larger limbs from nearby to grow the campfire. After five minutes more effort of gathering wood from nearby fallen trees, Jackson had a decent blaze.

Jackson grew concerned with how long Christopher had been unresponsive. "Jimbo, how's Christopher doing?"

"We need to get him warm."

Jackson nodded. "Alright, let's get to it."

Jimbo had taken Christopher's and his cargo belts off and latched them together. He looped one end under Christopher's right arm and hooked the other loop over his own neck and across his chest.

Jackson's belt was shorter, so he made a single loop under Christopher's left arm. Securing his grip on the loose end of the belt, Jackson gave the nod to Jimbo. "Okay, we pull together to lessen the chances of hurting him further. If you need to rest, just shout out."

As they yanked, Christopher jerked along the snow begrudgingly, making the fifty meters to the campfire seem like a desert mirage, close but out of reach.

Jimbo's face in the fading light was fire-hydrant red.

Jackson encouraged, "Dig deep, Jimbo, we're almost there, a few more meters."

With the sun now set and only faint glimmers of sunlight and hope remaining, both men pulled Christopher toward the fire, where they collapsed in exhaustion. Jackson fought waves of physical pain and tears back as he thought a friend he loved like a brother might die. The crackle of the fire and the rich smell of spruce pushed him beyond his limits in the effort to save Christopher.

⁂

Comfort seemed to not exist aboard the UE executive aircraft as every part of Gabriella pinged with an ache or pain. She slept little on the overnight flight to Rome. The pain of losing her father figure in President Rodgers and her assumed loss of friends Christopher and Jackson in Omega stung deeply. Now, a new era had dawned on the world, and she faced the challenge of being a spy with no country. It was too late for Gabriella to persuade President Rodgers that Draven Cross was America's greatest threat. Now, she had to survive and find a new purpose in life. Her friend's deaths would not be in vain.

Gabriella had minimized her presence at the new headquarters since slapping the world's de facto ruler upon his announcement to start World War III with a nuclear attack on the United States. While grateful that no one mentioned the incident with Draven, Gabriella noticed huddled whispers as she walked through the headquarters. As she watched a devastated world engulfed in war via an intermittent television feed, the insignificance of the event between Draven and her was apparent.

A UE soldier purposefully strode toward Gabriella after making eye contact with her. "Dr. Costa, the Secretary-General has called a security meeting in five minutes in the large conference room."

"Thank you." Gabriella made her way toward the conference room on the opposite side of the state-of-the-art UE Command Center.

Gabriella wondered if her execution drew near. She fought back a sensation of nausea rushing over her, heightening the urge to run out of the headquarters and never look back. She stopped in a woman's lavatory to gain her composure or at least vomit in a proper location. Gabriella was unsure which outcome would happen first.

She splashed water on her face. Then took an apprehensive look into each stall, relieved to find herself alone before committing to something she was embarrassed to do: pray aloud. Leaning back on the countertop, she called out to God, all while doubting if He was listening, "God, I'm trying to believe in Your existence, but I am unsure of Your effect on this world. There is a part of me that wants to accept You, but I need more; I need something to clearly point me to You. Please help me find my purpose in working for Draven."

Just as Gabriella finished the "prayer," she heard a toilet flush and a steel door open, which was a shock as no one was in the lavatory moments ago. Gabriella watched an elegant woman emerge and wash her hands. The woman wore a tailored, navy-blue suit beset with a pearl necklace and pearl-studded earrings. Her appearance was enhanced by her radiant brunette locks and stunning gray eyes.

The mysterious woman moved closer. "Gabriella, God is always willing to listen to you. Until recently, you shunned speaking to Him. You had a purpose before you were born, and if you fully commit yourself to serve God, you will find meaning in your life. Unfortunately, your rejection of God has brought you to this season of tribulation. God has always been here, patiently waiting for you to accept Him. If you trust in *Him*, you will find the strength for the days ahead. Despite your analytical doubts, before this time of trouble passes here on Earth, you will powerfully serve the Kingdom of God."

Gabriella was speechless as the stranger commented on her inner struggles.

"A final word, stop trying to formalize your path to accepting God. You have all the information needed to make the right decision. Make a choice before it's too late." The stranger smiled at a stunned Gabriella as she promptly left the lavatory.

Gabriella watched in awe as the woman departed the lavatory before her logical mind re-engaged and sought questions from the mysterious woman. Gabriella rushed out after the woman mere seconds later, but there was no trace of her anywhere in the command center.

Gabriella thought, "I'm going crazy."

Outside of the bathroom, the sharp voice of Evan Mallory forced Gabriella into the present. "Everyone is waiting for you. I suggest you get your mind back in the game before your loyalty is questioned."

"Sorry, I felt a little off and had to gather myself for a moment before the meeting. Let's go." Gabriella walked through, still searching for the woman in the navy suit. She whispered, "God, thank you, I think?"

Evan questioned, "What was that you said?"

Gabriella entered the conference room. "Nothing, just feeling better."

⁂

There was a whisper of tension in the conference room amongst the UE senior staff that reminded Gabriella of her high school's gossip-filled hallways. Except for the bullies, here were not mere-drama filled teens, but rather power-driven killers, led by the deputy UE Secretary-General Evan Mallory and would-be ruler of the world Draven Cross. As Gabriella entered, everyone tracked her movement, meaning the word had spread of her slapping Draven.

Draven sensing and relishing the discomfort of Gabriella's presence pushed tension to a crescendo, saying, "Let me clear the air for everyone. I accepted Gabriella's heartfelt apology for her understandable loss of emotional control. Gabriella, would you like to add anything?"

What arrogance, she thought. Gabriella hoped her face had not given away her true feelings.

"Yes, sir, I want to reiterate to the entire staff that my lack of emotional control won't happen again."

Draven beckoned Gabriella to approach the head of the conference table for a hug. "Oh, dear, my grace knows no bounds. You were forgiven before we even landed."

Gabriella felt faint. She was overcome with the thought of embracing the man who had destroyed her homeland. Gabriella felt out of her body as she walked into his open arms.

Draven displayed grace and charisma in these moments that drew people to him. "Now, let us focus on the business of ruling the world."

Gabriella returned to her seat next to Evan Mallory, feeling dirty and in need of a shower.

General Vivaan Ahuja, the UE armed forces commander and former Indian defense minister, positioned himself to brief the room. "Sir, UE forces are preparing for a global counter-offensive as I speak against the attack by the alliance of President Rodgers. In coming days, we anticipate the fiercest battles within the United States, Australia, Western Europe, and China."

General Ahuja silenced a nameless staffer attempting to ask a question. "Please hold all questions to the end."

Draven brought on nervous laughter from the room by saying, "Surely, I can ask questions, correct, Vivaan?"

Gabriella was sure that General Ahuja looked displeased by the distractions to his brief. His displeasure brought a little comfort to her as she fought back a raging headache and another wave of nausea listening to the brief's propaganda.

General Ahuja curtly answered, "Yes, sir," focusing his briefing on how the late President Rodgers was to blame for the war. "As I was saying, American forces have demonstrated a strong resilience, despite the eastern seaboard command and control nodes being effectively neutralized."

Gabriella fought a temple pulsating headache at the lies that General Ahuja perpetrated. It was as if Draven had sold the entire UE staff on the notion that President Rodgers and not himself aboard UE One had ordered the attack against the US and other nations. She did not attempt to hide her malice at the reference that President Rodgers was deranged in trying to kill Draven. *Was it possible that no one else remembered Draven ordering the US attack?*

General Ahuja continued the war update, "A primary goal in these opening moments of the conflict is finding the remaining resistance leaders: the Australian Prime Minister and NATO Secretary-General. Suppose we can find these leaders before they muster significant ground forces. In that case, I anticipate large portions of the world rapidly transitioning to full UE control."

Draven interrupted the brief. "And what will we do with the Australian and European resistance leaders when they are detained?"

A perturbed General Ahuja said, "Sir, they will be scheduled for execution for starting a third World War, including crimes against humanity for the causalities in Sydney and Brussels respectfully."

Draven said, "Excellent, Evan, let's make this a global spectacle. I want these men's death to serve as an example to those that go against peace."

Evan said, "I will make the arraignments."

Draven observed. "Respectable briefing, Vivaan. How soon will this war conclude?"

General Ahuja stoically remained in front of the interactive telescreen at the center of the room. "Sir, I will do all I can to make your wishes a reality. However, the truth is the global resistance organized by the late President Rodgers was well-armed. We will likely require two or three additional months to gain control of the entire world."

Gemma's harrowed entrance into the conference room broke Gabriella's concentration on her aching head. Whatever the message, it caused Draven to swear and slam his fist on the table. Draven stood and pressed a remote, causing Ahuja's briefing to disappear. A grainy and broken All-News-Network broadcast replaced the presentation.

"Vivaan, shut up, and sit down. Evan, can you explain to me what you're doing about these pests?" Draven asked, venom dripping from his words.

As the headline rolled across the screen, TWO WITNESSES PROCLAIM WORLDS DOOM AT HANDS OF UE SECRETARY-GENERAL.

"Well, sir, I plan—"

Draven cut him off. "Be quiet; I will give you the plan."

Despite it only being four o'clock in the afternoon, the day gave way to the lurking dangers of Alaska at night. In other circumstances, Jackson would have been amazed by the quiet and beauty of the star-filled sky silhouetted by the Aurora Borealis's glowing colored bands. He knew the clear sky meant temperatures would drop sharply. If the men were to survive the night, staying warm was their only hope. The "smaller" problem of how they would make it back to civilization would have to wait.

Jackson was in the best health out of the three men and took the task upon himself to ensure they all survived the night. A quick inventory of the resources on hand indicated that maintaining a fire would not be an issue. The biggest problem would be hydration, despite being surrounded by a vast sea of frozen water. *Food*, Jackson laughed with the thought, *food is luxury at this point.*

Jackson said, "Hey, listen, Jimbo, I'm going to head back to my snowmachine to see what I can scavenge to help us get through the night. I know you said you kept some survival supplies on the snowmachines, so what can I hope to find?"

Jimbo adjusted his injured arm. "If you're lucky, a canteen and a couple of emergency thermal blankets per machine."

After stabilizing Christopher, Jackson's mind finally allowed him to appreciate Jimbo's injuries. "I don't remember seeing any of that stuff earlier, but let's hope I find them. But, before I go, I'm going to set your broken arm. Hand me your T-shirt."

Jackson's mind wandered as he started splinting Jimbo's arm. "Do you think there's a nuclear war raging across the world right now that we helped start?"

Jimbo said, "I would like to think that's not happened, but we both saw two nuclear missiles streak across the sky earlier. We both know that means other countries with nukes launched theirs. I'm glad my folks started a relationship with Jesus before this started; I'm not sure I will ever see them again."

Jackson felt a lump rise in his throat with Jimbo's mentioning of family. The sting of losing his wife Sarah and daughters, Sadie and Katie, in the wake of Rapture still hurt. He finally said. "Well, that's not my best splint, but given the situation, it will have to work. I mean, for that big thing you call an arm, I really needed a couple of sequoia trees."

Jackson contemplated another snarky response as he helped Jimbo strip down to his underwear, matching the attire of Christoper as Jimbo prepared to share body heat near the warmth of the fire wrapped in their outer clothing layers.

Jackson smarted off. "Make sure you rotate him when he's done cooking on that side. You know—"

Jimbo cut Jackson's harassment short by throwing a rock at him. "Ha, ha, funny guy, get going and find what we need. Go, man, not another funny word, go."

Jackson conceded to the critical task at hand, turning on his headlamp as he began retracing the trail leading to the snowmachines. "Alright, I'm going."

❧

Draven seethed in the conference room, angered by Gemma's message and the sporadic newsfeed detailing Reuel and Eliyahu's anti-Draven news. After signing the peace-treaty between Isreal and the UE, these two men entered the public eye. They proclaimed themselves to be representatives of Isreal's God. Only recently, the men provided their respective names, Reuel and Eliyahu, after months of silence on the topic. However, the media often called them the Two Witnesses for ease of broadcasting and flippantly gave them a formal title, "God's Ambassadors to the UE," as they proclaimed daily to represent the Biblical God.

The flawless public face of Draven Cross cracked as he threw a water pitcher against a distant wall, causing staffers to wilt and cower in his wrath shadow. Draven's aspirations were being undermined by the two fanatics and the rising Christian movement. "I need everyone in this room to listen, especially you, General Ahuja. This is the reason President Rodgers started the war." Draven emphasized his anger by pointing to the large screen. "These are the real enemies of humanity. We cannot have peace here on Earth if we are tied to these archaic notions that God is upset and demands we live within humanity's constructs of God-centered living. General, you will provide the soon-to-be empowered regional ambassadors every resource the UE has available. I have a special measure to deal with any insurgencies that arise."

Draven ordered, "I also want to know what essential services are lacking *right now* and the plan to fix the problems."

Hushed and panicked side conversations broke out amongst a group of people that, mere months ago, were some of the most respected and celebrated in their chosen professions.

Draven demanded. "Well, someone better answer quickly."

A bearded, pale, wiry young man from the global health and food program agency hesitantly spoke, "Sir, there are many pressing needs, from clean water distribution to food supplies. Honestly, there are more issues than I believe we have resources. In my opinion, the most pressing need is reliable communications to reach the masses. As you can see from this, All-News-Network feed, global satellite communications have been affected by the war."

The entire room turned its gaze toward the young man.

Draven asked, "Your name?"

"Ken Gothard, sir."

"Ken Gothard, you earned a significant promotion." Draven turned his accusing eyes to the director of the global health and food program agency. "Director Agnes Blomqvist should have spoken instead of you."

Draven prepared to use the simple misstep as an event to cause fear on his staff as he watched a stunned Agnes Blomqvist attempt to defend herself.

Agnes Blomqvist said, "Sir, I was going to provide you a detailed update."

Draven said, "Today, Agnes, you will serve as a point of instruction for everyone. The world expects, and more importantly, I demand quick solutions. I will not tolerate hesitancy and cowardice. Security escort Ms. Blomqvist from the headquarters, her service to the UE is terminated. Kenneth, you will now sit at the head table and try to have a longer career, shall you? This meeting is adjourned."

Agnes Blomqvist lost what dignity she had remaining after the public beratement. She repeatedly shouted as the muscular security guards dragged her in disgrace from the UE headquarters. "How can you treat me like this? You're an evil man."

Draven seemed to enjoy the spectacle he had created as he regained his regal appearance. "Ms. Blomqvist's failure shall serve as a constant reminder for all of you. I expect results, not excuses. Vivaan, Evan, and Gabriella, I want to see you in my office in five minutes."

As Gabriella stood to meet the others in Draven's office, the scene she had watched, where Draven lost emotional control for the first time, left little doubt that Draven was at best a cold-hearted dictator. She even saw traits that would have made Jackson say aloud that the man was the devil himself. Gabriella sensed her new purpose would be finding a way to thwart his efforts and stay alive at the same time.

ℴ

Chapter 2

WALKING THROUGH THE cold night illuminated by the dancing ribbons of the northern lights, Jackson's soul was heavy with the realization that he had a part in millions of lives lost when the two nuclear-armed missiles launched. Jackson dreaded facing the world he failed. Maybe it would be better if he never found out what was going on and met his fate out in this icy landscape. The Holy Spirit's presence washed over him in this moment of despair. Jackson felt the Holy Spirit place in his mind a comforting thought, *Then call on Me when you are in trouble, and I will rescue you, and you will give Me glory.* "Lord, thank You for Your provision. We need You to get us out of this mess. Please spare Christopher's life, so he can receive Your gift of salvation."

The calming presence of the Holy Spirit gave him the strength to keep moving, and soon his headlamp shone on Jimbo's snowmachine. After digging around the vehicle for ten minutes by hand, Jackson wished his focus had been on the task in front of him and not giving Jimbo a hard time. His comedy routine caused him to forget the seat cover intended for digging.

Nevertheless, his stiff and numb hands were rewarded, as he found two emergency thermal blankets buried in the snow, but no canteen, meaning he would need to search near his snowmachine. Jackson furrowed his brow with the thought of seeing Max's body again. With a deep sigh, Jackson set out, hoping to find a canteen and more thermal blankets.

Twenty minutes later, and after more hard digging, Jackson was on his way back to the campfire with a canteen and four thermal blankets. These were enough to get the men through the night; however, each step shot waves of searing pain up Jackson's right leg. He tried not to think about what the pain might mean for his survival.

The crackle of wood in a fire and the gradual warmth of flames as he moved closer drew Jackson toward the campsite like a moth lost in a snowstorm. The comfort of the heat from the roaring fire paled in comparison to seeing Christopher Barrett sitting up on his own. He stared for a moment at his brother-in-arms shivering, wrapped within Jimbo's oversized outer layers of clothes before rushing Christopher and falling on his neck in a deep embrace.

Jackson unashamedly let his tears fall, melting the snow around Christopher and him, as he mumbled, "I thought I'd lost you."

Christopher strained. "You know how stubborn I can be; plus, I needed to make sure you live to see Jesus's second coming in a few years."

Jackson wisecracked. "Good job warming up the human Popsicle, Jimbo. I'm thrilled to see you have more clothes on than when I left."

Jimbo shook his head, smiling in the glow of the firelight. "I see your witty personality is always running full speed."

Handing a warmed cup of water to Christopher, Jackson responded. "As it should be, laughing helps you keep your sanity in tough situations." Jackson winced and grabbed his right leg as he moved to settle in near the fire.

Christopher asked in a raspy voice. "Jackson, what's wrong with you? Are you okay?"

Jackson grabbed a couple of thermal blankets and prepared to take the weight off his leg and mind, listening to his friends debate the next survival step. "I'll be fine; just been pushing hard trying to save your bacon. All I need is some rest."

Christopher and Jimbo gave each other a worried look, as Jackson's pained face indicated everything was not okay.

Christopher moved on to the next crisis. How to get out of this remote forest with everyone in less-than-ideal health. "So, let me ask the obvious. How are we getting out of here?"

Jimbo said, "The quickest option would be getting the snowmachines up and running. The only problem is we might run out of gas before reaching the nearest ranger station for help."

Christopher wanted to bring the quiet Jackson into the conversation. "What do you think, Jackson?"

Jackson was too tired to debate with men and pretended to be asleep and seemingly at peace with the situation at hand.

Christopher said, "It figures he would fall asleep right now. Well, the only thing we can do is stay warm and keep this fire going through the night. Who knows what tomorrow will hold for us."

Draven's personal space was extensive, consuming the *Palazzo Caelum*'s entire fourth floor. The extravagance of the area spoke of the ego of the man fighting for control over the world. Gabriella felt anger rising. She noticed Draven's oversized, rosewood desk, perhaps the only surviving piece of furniture from the historic UN building.

It was clear that Draven had spared no expense in designing the UE's new headquarters. His office ceiling had been painted with a sizeable all-seeing-eye image, with Draven's name underneath it. *How long had this been planned*, Gabriella puzzled, soaking in the new UE Headquarters' intricate details for the first time.

The most eye-catching item was an iron sculpture mounted to the wall behind Draven's desk with the name "Sigil of the Light Bearer," embossed in golden letters attached to a plaque beneath the sculpture. As Draven, Evan Mallory, and General Ahuja briefly fawned over the opulent office, Gabriella began feeling uneasy.

Her pulse quickened, and a presence of heaviness pressed in on her as she sat down at an oval meeting table. She sensed that it was not the stylish and modern fixtures of this new office that brought on these feelings, but rather the darkness the atmosphere seemed to exude.

Draven began the meeting with his deputy, minister of defense, and intelligence chief. "Here is what I expect you all to understand. The world must never doubt my control over any situation. That means if we need to generate a crisis to provide a solution for lasting global peace, then that's what will occur. Understand? The aftermath of the conflict will usher in my one-world government and the beginning of peace on Earth."

Gabriella was reading Evan and General Ahuja's faces. They told the story that they believed everything that Draven said without question. It didn't explain how Draven could start World War III, and everyone thought it was due to President Rodgers. The feeling of living darkness in this office was likely a better reason for his manipulative abilities.

Draven turned to General Ahuja. "I want you to have your propaganda experts create a social media campaign that depicts these resistance elements espousing warmongering. Place emphasis on the resistance forces committing attacks against women and children. You think you can handle that?"

General Ahuja assured him. "Yes, Sir. I believe I follow your desires."

Draven said, "Excellent. Evan, you have been called to be my image-bearer; start living up to that responsibility. These Two Witnesses and the baffling yet growing number of Jewish men spouting off Christian tenants worldwide are overshadowing my accomplishments. I want you to use the world religions' unification under the Interfaith banner to draw people under my control. Provide the world a spiritual counter to these lingering Christian sects popping up everywhere. You must be the conductor of my symphony, not the lead violinist. Do you understand?"

Evan nodded that he did, but it was clear to Gabriella—and apparently Draven—that Evan was unsure of what was expected.

Draven clarified himself. "To make myself crystal clear, Evan, I gave General Ahuja the daily duties of running the UE military to free you up to promote my image. I expect you to release your prized Interfaith creation to a proxy. I've heard the former Catholic church has a few capable Cardinals without a day job."

General Ahuja added, "Sir if I might inject a concern I have?"

Draven rolled his eyes. "What is your concern, Vivaan?"

"In the first moments of the war, resistance leaders launched anti-satellite weapons against various space-based communications platforms. This created a significant degradation in our abilities to command and control our forces or communicate with your desired global audience."

Gabriella found it telling how Draven enjoyed placing others in positions where they did not have the answers, but he did. She watched as he belittled these two senior leaders into compliance. She only hoped to contain her penchant for standing up for herself, especially against a chauvinist like Draven; her failure could be deadly.

Draven responded, "Your ignorance is why the world will not remember you, general. Thankfully, I have the answers to problems the world faces. We will convert the ICBMs gained from the former nuclear nations into space-launch vehicles, as many as needed. Then I expect you to deliver a massive CubeSat farm into low Earth orbit; the CubeSats will serve as the backbone for a new global communications network. I have ten clean storage warehouses filled with a CubeSat type and size required to bridge our communication needs until long-term solutions are developed."

"So, sir, these small satellites will give us all of our lost space-based capabilities?" General Ahuja asked.

Draven pressed his deriding of the general, "What a simple-minded way of thinking. The satellites provide an interim continuous global communications coverage platform. I will provide you points of contact to move the satellites from the warehouses near the Port of Felixstowe to testing and launching locations. You have six weeks from this moment to get the system operational. My needs for the space-based global navigation systems will diminish with the soon completed war. My last statement is correct, I believe, General Ahuja."

"I will not display my ignorance of these CubeSats here, but I will move forward as directed. Regarding your inquiry into the hostilities' conclusion, I will have the mission completed as quickly as possible."

Draven relished a final slight against General Ahuja, "You have displayed plenty of ignorance today. Ensure, general, that you don't fail in delivering a swift conclusion to this war. You're dismissed."

Gabriella felt sick to her stomach, mad and confused at this point in the meeting. Draven had belittled everyone in the room except her, though she was sure she was next. Draven was such a petty and cold-heart individual; she questioned her sanity for ever believing his dribble about world peace.

Steepling his hands and staring coldly, Draven said, "Now, my plans for you, Gabriella. I have a few enemies I need to eliminate, and you will oversee the program that will accomplish that goal."

Gabriella held her repulsion in check, steeling her mind for what questionable task awaited.

ℰ

Now alone with Evan and Draven in the cavernous office, Gabriella couldn't shake the feeling of a third and ominous presence. Evan and Draven's expressions of glee regarding a mystery program aimed at UE enemies repulsed Gabriella. *These were enemies likely without much cause or reason,* she thought. She had to take charge of her destiny. The plan to thwart Draven started now.

Gabriella began to shape her destiny. "Sir, I want to take an active role in directing intelligence support for the war effort and what's to come. I am requesting to operate away from the headquarters."

Draven smirked. "I am impressed. I foresaw trouble with you, considering the incident aboard UE One. Tell me, where do you want to start?"

Gabriella was glad to see Draven's willingness to allow her to shape intelligence support. "I think China would be ideal, considering it remains a focal point for our efforts. I can establish an intelligence network to identify potential enemy locations that, in the long term, we can leverage for other applications."

Evan enthused. "Can we discuss the program mentioned in New York?"

Draven's voice dripped in sarcasm. "Yes, Evan. Based on Gabriella's request, I can think of no one better to oversee the Sentinel Program through all phases of its implementation."

Gabriella rolled her eyes and crossed her arms, not willing to give Draven the satisfaction of matching Evan and his enthusiasm over the topic du jour.

Gabriella was tired of the pressing feeling in Draven's office and his presence. "Sir, I am anxious to get started on my new found purpose. Perhaps, we could cover the Sentinel program another time."

Draven shook his head. "No, we will not. While I love the enthusiasm to support me, I assure you what I have to say will benefit you *and* supports global peace."

The combination of Gabriella's fighting spirit and growing by the second anxiety of being in Draven's office pushed her to say something she regretted instantly. "I hardly call anything we're doing here as promoting peace, but what do I know."

Draven snapped, inching close to the seated Gabriella. "I hope we will not have a problem with your loyalty. I tolerate your slights, as I tolerate Evan and General Ahuja's ignorance because now you're needed. However, you're not indispensable. You can suffer the same fate as Agnus Blomqvist. You need to quickly understand all I do is for the good of the world. Your talent will save your life only so many times. Tell me you grasp my actions as peaceful before we move forward."

Gabriella knew she had gone too far by verbalizing the emotions of a rough few months and being unsettled in her present environment. Being overly emotional is dangerous for a spy, a point emphasized during her career at the Agency. She had to pull it together. *Remember, your purpose here,* Gabriella thought.

Gabriella took a deep breath. "My apologies, Sir. I understand your vision."

Draven rebuked. "Your hesitancy with my methods will change with time, dear, but never let emotion cloud your judgment. Emotion is a dangerous thing for a spy."

Gabriella shivered with Draven's last statement. *Is it possible he knows my thoughts and is now just toying with me, like a cat with a mouse*? She was grateful he turned his attention to other matters than her attitude.

Draven continued, "I will keep this short for both of you. As Gabriella correctly assessed, there are many pressing matters. The Sentinel Program's three stages will integrate with Evan's Interfaith movement. Step one is the identification and neutralization of threats. Step two will be marking those faithful to me with the identification system. The final stage of the program will be total government control of society. I envision such control of the world that no one will be able to buy or sell a loaf of bread without my knowledge."

Gabriella noticed a devilish smile rise on Draven's face as he prepared to discuss another security topic. "Gabriella, your spy network will allow me to rid the world of religious fanatics and dissidents against my government. I have a tailorable biological weapon that can target specific genetic markers. China and America will serve as perfect testbeds. Do you have any objections to my plan?"

Gabriella couldn't respond aloud; she merely nodded and thought, *How had this man developed all these capabilities without detection from the United States or other governments? Is there no limit to his power?*

Draven sighed. "Well, I can tell by the mindless stare, you have reached your mental capacity load, Gabriella."

Draven moved to his desk, buzzing Gemma's intercom. "Prepare for me to deliver a speech in an hour and ring the President of the ANN. I require his services," Draven commanded as he hand-waved Gabriella and Evan out of his office.

~

Gabriella was glad to be out of the uncomfortable presence of Draven and the unseen presence. As she stepped off the elevator on the third floor of the *Palazzo Caelum*, which held the UE executive staff's suites, she took a moment to be grateful for her office that resembled a small studio hotel room. The suites' isolation was terrific, as her administrative staff was in an office across the hallway. She entered her personal space, finally alone, and made a beeline for the bathroom. Gabriella stepped onto the marble floor and turned on the multi-jet shower, seeking comfort.

As Gabriella let the hot shower water envelop her, tears began to flow. Her mind whirled with the faces of lost friends and the suffering that the war caused. The pain cascaded over her like a torrent. She sat on the shower floor with her head buried in her knees, rocking back and forth, under the warm water. "God, is this what you want me to do? Is fighting against Draven my purpose? I need an answer!" she screamed.

The only responses heard were Gabriella's sobs and the steady downpour of water. She sat in the shower until the water turned cold, emerging battered, and lost. Gabriella knew that her analytical mind found comfort in trying to solve a challenge in moments like this. Today's problem, learning all she could about the mysterious biological weapon Draven had developed before leaving for China.

Before solving the bioweapon problem, a more practical dilemma faced Gabriella as she stared down at her dirty clothes. Gabriella realized the only clothes she had with her were the dirty ones crumpled on the floor. Maybe she'd get lucky, and Gemma had her luggage delivered to the office. Gabriella placed a robe on and started searching her office space for luggage. Her three large pieces of luggage sat in a small nook in her office that contained a refrigerator and hot plate to her delight.

Changing into clean clothes boosted Gabriella's spirit. As she dried her hair and reapplied some makeup, the only thing better at this moment would be some food. However, the desire to find a way to slow down Draven and his plans were more urgent now.

Gabriella sat at her desk and opened her personal laptop. The laptop contained a partition that allowed her to run non-attribution software, denying access to her identifiable information, most notably in this case, her location. She furiously typed, bringing up Cross Industries homepage. Once there, Gabriella opened a hacking application and began manically searching for biotechnology programs.

Gabriella pondered the data on the screen. *"It seems Cross Industries invested heavily in biotechnologies. One of the company's most profitable sites in the last fifteen years has been the national security applications lab in Inverness, Scotland."*

A loud knock on Gabriella's office door caused her to slam her laptop shut. "Yes, come in!" Gabriella exclaimed nervously, knowing she had been tempting fate in her recent internet adventure.

"Hello, I wanted to check to see if your luggage had arrived and if you felt like grabbing a bite to eat with me?" Gemma asked.

"I thought you had a hand in my bags being here. Thank you so much. I can't even tell you how great it feels to be clean and wearing clean clothes. And yes, I want to get some food; I think you read my mind."

"Great, we can chat about the slap heard around the world."

"Yeah, about that, let's go." Gabriella chuckled, glancing back at her laptop, wondering what nightmare she would find when she returned.

⸙

With the pain in his leg increasing, Jackson had gotten only a few fitful hours of sleep. Jackson had moments of feeling like he was back in the Omega selection course between the lack of sleep and pain. He'd been happy to see Christopher's strength slowly returning along with his friend's innate sense to lead. The Alaskan night felt endless as staying warm consumed the men's existence. Christopher and Jimbo had shared fire watch duties, preserving the life-sustaining fire through the bitterly cold night. Now, a new day was dawning, despite the darkness that still pervaded the early morning, a product of being located in the far northern latitudes of the planet. Soon, Jackson would wake Christopher for a final shift before the sun. Before the last fire watch hand over, Christopher had said to Jackson that hearing how he and Jimbo had made efforts to save his life buoyed his spirit. Jackson had to argue with Christopher, who demanded that they sleep longer. Christopher, refusing to go back to sleep immediately, had expressed sensing a new beginning surrounding his life. Jackson understood Christopher's sentiment but dared not call it hope and optimism. His unbelief in God was why he missed the Rapture and was suffering through the chaos consuming the world. Jackson reminded Christopher that the three of them shared a lack of belief in the redeeming work of Jesus; hence they were nearly freezing to death in Alaska.

Christopher smarted off, snapping Jackson from his daydream. "Good job, soldier; I'm glad to see you did not fall asleep on guard duty. I would hate for you to be 'recycled' to the next training course because you couldn't stay awake."

Jackson chuckled. "I wish all of this were only a training course. There's not much I wouldn't do right now for a strong cup of coffee."

Jimbo yelled. "Would you two keep it down? I'm trying to sleep over here!"

All three men immediately started laughing at their collective efforts to make light of the dire situation.

Jackson said, "I will never get used to it being dark so late in the morning up here; it makes me feel crazy."

Jimbo answered, "It's 0705 by my watch, and we have at least another three hours of darkness before the sun appears for the day."

"It's crazy—" Christopher was cut off by Jackson.

Jackson stood looking for the unknown in the dark forest surrounding the men. "Shhh… listen. Do you guys hear that? It sounds like some sort of large vehicle, and it's getting louder."

The men were unarmed and in no real shape to fight. But if trouble was heading their way, the look Jackson saw in Jimbo, and Christopher's eyes told him every man was going to fight until the end.

The snapping and cracking of spruce trees were deafening as a military-type, small support vehicle emerged and blinded the men with its bright headlights.

Jackson waved a large branch in the direction of an unseen driver. "Hey, do you mind turning those lights off?"

Christopher questioned, "What are you going to do with that branch?"

Over the roar of the approaching vehicle, Jimbo yelled. "I was thinking the same thing!"

Jackson's sense of protecting others kicked in as he glanced at his wounded and weak friends. If an enemy had found them, he was not going down without a fight.

"I'm ready to fight; what about you two."

The vehicle powered down, leaving the campfire as the only light illuminating the men. The men watched as the cab opened and a man wearing the Park Rangers' distinctive tan campaign hat emerged.

The park ranger explained, "Sorry I spooked you folks, but I've been tracking your fire for the last several kilometers. I got a signal in my station that an avalanche had occurred in this area yesterday. I figured I had better see if there were any survivors considering the war raging against our country. Honestly, when I set out, I didn't expect survivors; your fire gave me hope. My name is James Stinson."

Jimbo said, "Sir, I'm glad you followed your hunch. The government site was destroyed in the avalanche, and we are the only survivors."

Christopher added, "Yes, Sir, we're grateful you've come up here. We were in some real trouble."

"I am glad to give you guys a lift back to the station and get you back on your feet. I'm sure you've had enough of roughing it in the Alaskan wilderness," Ranger Stinson said.

Jackson didn't introduce himself. Instead, he grabbed Jimbo's detached snowmachine seat cover and headed off into the darkness. "We need to head back to my snowmachine and properly take care of Max. Plus, I need to find something important."

Jackson's demeanor had switched quickly. Christopher watched as Jackson's silhouette faded and only the beam of his headlamp provided any indication of him. He was worried about his friend.

Jimbo called out as he smothered the lifesaving campfire, "Hey, wait, Jackson, we can ride with the Ranger."

&

As Christopher stared at the hole in the darkness Jackson's headlamp was creating, his attention turned back to the salvation at hand. "My apologies, Sir; let me properly introduce my team and myself. I am MAJ Christopher Barrett U.S. Army, and this is Chief Master Sergeant Jim (Jimbo) Petty, Air Force. The gentleman that left is Army Sergeant Major Jackson Williams."

Ranger Stinson said, "I am pleased to meet you. And I want to thank each of you for your service to our nation. You're needed now more than ever."

Christopher asked, "What do you mean?"

Ranger Stinson said, "You boys are missing the fight; America is being overrun. Let's get loaded up, so we can help your friend."

"What do you mean? Overrun by who?" Christopher asked.

Ranger Stinson updated the men as they headed to his large vehicle. "The news trickling in via shortwave radio points to UN, I mean, UE forces."

Christopher and Jimbo looked at each other in grim silence as they loaded into the cab with Ranger Stinson. They knew all too well that the missiles launched from the now destroyed secret government site were linked to the war. Christopher's thoughts turned to Gabriella. She was one of his closest friends, the only other person besides Jackson left he knew before the Rapture. *I hope she is all right.*

❧

While grateful to be rescued, Jackson was angered by the fact that death had invaded his life yet again. Grim deaths were becoming as common as seeing the sunrise. Despite barely knowing Max, it was a harsh realization that death was ever-present, seemingly stalking him from the shadows. He thought *This is strange. I've been surrounded by death—I've even glorified death professionally—so why do I care about the passing of strangers now.*

Jackson got his answer as he finished the relatively short trip to his snowmachine, burning up and limping. The Holy Spirit spoke into his heart, "*A new command I give you: Love one another. As I have loved you, so you must love one another. By this, everyone will know that you are my disciples if you love one another.*"

Jackson was ashamed that he had not committed more scripture to memory, an important reason to find Rev's Bible and journal.

Jackson had already begun attempting to free Max from the fallen tree as the lights of Ranger Stinson's tracked-vehicle illuminated the level of work remaining in the grim task. He didn't turn to face the men as they approached.

"Hey, we've brought some tools; step back so we can help you," Christopher said.

Jackson continued to frantically dig around Max using the snowmachine seat.

"Jackson, move back, we have shovels, and a chain saw. What's wrong with you?" Christopher shouted, reaching for Jackson's shoulder.

Jackson shrugged Christopher off and threw the snowmachine seat into the dark forest. He walked away from the other men coming to rest on a fallen tree and stared at the effort to free Max's body from a snowy grave.

The men intuitively understood they needed to give Jackson a moment to process whatever he was going through and turned their attention to freeing Max's body.

As the chain saw pierced the quiet of the forest, Jackson broke down into deep, uncontrollable sobs. He cried in deep and soulful spurts with the thoughts of losing his family in the disappearances and his missed opportunity to find Jesus and lead them away from the disaster. Jackson worried about Christopher and Gabriella's souls. He felt empathy for the countless people who didn't know Jesus as they faced death in a war-ravaged world. The sting of death resonated with Jackson personally, despite a military career where he employed death on his nation's enemies. The fact that any moment he could lose his life or someone he cared for, like Christopher, was impressed upon him during the recovery of Max's body.

"God, please don't forget Christopher. I understand that our choices placed us in the middle of this nightmare. I know there is no guarantee to see, but please give him the chance to accept your salvation. Please watch over Gabriella and all those like her," Jackson pleaded as tears rolled down his face.

Jackson tried to pull himself together as he watched the silhouette of Christopher drawing near to him.

"Hey, brother, is everything alright?"

"Yeah, you know me; I'm concerned for you guys. With all the dying going on right now in the world, this is a tough time to be alive," Jackson said, losing his ability to control his emotions.

Christopher placed an arm over Jackson's shoulder. "I know you've been through—and lost—a lot over the last year, but you're always telling me that God is looking out for us. You still believe that, don't you?"

Jackson merely nodded.

"Look, I'm going to help these guys finish up with Max, but I got something I need to talk to you about when we get the chance. Hang in there, brother, you're never alone," Christopher said, walking back to help wrap up Max's body so they could bury him closer to the Ranger Station and thawed ground.

Jackson's head swirled as he stood to help prepare the transport of Max's remains after his self-induced pity party. His legs buckled, causing him to fall. The shock of the cold snow against his body stole his breath. Jackson could faintly hear Christopher's shout right before his eyes closed, and the world went black.

ꟹ

Jackson awoke to the sun illuminating a cabin bedroom. The smell of freshly brewed coffee and sizzling bacon pushed sleep from his mind. Visions of his childhood at his family's homestead in Alabama drifted into his mind with each whiff of breakfast. *I must have died. I'm in Heaven.* The thought only lingered until Jackson felt the sharp pain in his right leg elevated and bandaged.

"Hey, bring me some of that coffee and bacon you guys have out there!" Jackson yelled.

His bold spirit lit up as Christopher, Jimbo, and Ranger Stinson walked into the bedroom. He received a playful slap on his right shoulder by Christopher, who said, "Welcome back. You once again cheated the grim reaper."

Jimbo shook Jackson's hand. "If Ranger Stinson discovered us a few days later, the infection that was growing in your system would have won."

"I'm not going anywhere without a fight. How did you guys know I had an infection in my leg?" Jackson asked, now sitting up in the bed.

Jimbo explained, "After we picked you up and got you back here to the ranger station, I examined you. You were burning up, so I figured your body was trying to fight off something. When I saw your right leg, it was red, hot to the touch, and you had infection tracks, racing away from a part of the tree that had pierced your leg. Ranger Stinson helped me clean the wound. I gave you antibiotics and hooked you up with a saline drip bag to rehydrate you. My hope was with rest, hydration, and the antibiotics, any infection would be fought off."

"You've been out for almost three days," Christopher added.

An emotional Jackson said, "I am grateful for the efforts to take care of me from all of you guys."

Christopher asked, nodding to Jimbo and Ranger Stinson. "Hey, guys, can you give us a minute?"

Jimbo said, "You got it, buddy. We'll get breakfast ready."

Jackson leaned back on the bed's headboard, placing his hands over his face, overcome with emotion, and embarrassed by being so sensitive.

Jackson confided, "I'm sorry for all this crying, but I don't know how we're going to make it to Jesus's glorious appearance."

Christopher announced, "You're right. There is no way we can make it on our own; it will take a miracle. When that avalanche rushed over me, I knew it was the end. God had won, and I had lost. All these years of fighting God and He was my only hope at that moment, and I didn't even know Him. My last words, so I thought, were I surrender God. Yet, God spared me, Jackson, and I want to believe it was so I can live out my days fighting not against Him but for Him. I am ready to receive Jesus as my Lord and Savior."

Jackson didn't say anything. He only wept more and sobbed loudly.

Christopher repeated, "Jackson, did you hear me? I want you to lead me in the prayer to accept Jesus into my life."

Jackson pulled Christopher into a big hug. "Yeah, I heard you, and I'm crying with joy because my prayer is being answered. I don't have the words."

Christopher's tears splashed the wooden floor as Jackson prayed. "Dear heavenly Father, you told us in Your word that a shepherd will leave his flock of ninety-nine to find one who was lost. And, when discovered, the lost sheep will celebrate its return with friends and family. I know today that all of Heaven is praising this moment. Christopher has moved from foe to friend. Thank you, Father. Christopher, repeat the following with me: Lord Jesus, I've pushed You out of my life for too long. I know that I am a sinner and that I need You in my life. No longer will I not answer Your calls in my life; I will answer Your voice. By faith, I humbly receive Your gift of salvation. I trust You as my Lord and Savior now and forever. Jesus, I believe You are the Son of God who died on the cross for my sins and rose from the dead on the third day. Thank You for accepting my sins and the punishment I deserved and instead gave me the gift of eternal life. Father, in Jesus's name, we pray. Amen."

Christopher and Jackson's tears told the bittersweet story of the moment. As they smiled and embraced, knowing the cost of the decision both men had made by accepting Christ Jesus's salvation amid the tribulation.

Jackson asked, "How do you feel?"

Christopher proclaimed. "For the first time in a long time, I actually have a sense of peace with a decision I've made. I don't feel angry or like God is against me."

Jackson gave Christopher some advice on his new life. "Over time, the transformation in how you see the world will be all the proof you need to know your salvation is real. I feel like I am learning who I am every day. Not to be corny, but I have a new life now. Hey, did you guys find my backpack with Rev's Bible and journal?"

Christopher replied, "Yeah, Jimbo stepped on it as we were dragging you to the ranger's vehicle."

"I am surprised it survived if the living mountain stepped on it," Jackson joked. "Do me a favor and grab it. I hope my phone is still there. We should reach out to Gabriella."

Christopher said, "Man, why didn't I think of that? I should have checked your bag for the communicator; I could have already called Gabriella. I lost my phone during our adventure with the avalanche. Let me grab the bag. I want to share this good news with Gabriella and find out what's going on in the world."

CHAPTER 3

AT ANY OTHER time in history, the UE headquarters cafeteria would have easily won multiple interior design awards. As Gabriella and Gemma exited the elevator below the main level, they entered into a dining space constructed into a natural cave with a stunning view of the Tiber River at the far end. The rough-hewn rock ceiling accented with bright recessed lights provided a relaxing and stimulating mood as the light danced off the rock walls.

Rows of long tables with thick, white linen coverings lined the center of the ample space. The atmosphere was filled with curries and various spices intermixed with light chatter from the few employees eating in the spacious dining hall. There were various food stations along one wall of the cave, paying tribute to multiple nations' culinary treasures. The entire cafeteria bathed in the aromas of different spices and sauces as the food was dished out to the eager UE employees lined up at various stations. You could pick from the Italian station's local delicacies or spicy curries at the Indian booth and hearty comfort foods at the American canteen, and many more. Two sixty-foot tall glass doors separated the main cave from a grand wooden deck with several round tables that overlooked the Tiber with Rome in the distance.

Gabriella could imagine the smiles and joy emanating from elegant balls and wedding receptions. Ornate spaces like this one would have been coveted and sought after in the former world. The venue's emptiness against the backdrop of smoke rising above Rome and piercing sounds of war broadcast on the large televisions reminded her that the world was far from idyllic and closer to hellish.

Gemma gleefully turned to Gabriella. "So, where in the world do you feel like eating?"

Gabriella had remorse in her voice as she realized that America would never be the same. "There's no place like home."

Gemma agreed, heading off for the British food station. "Ahh, comfort food can be nice. Fish and chips will be my sample fare for today. Why don't you grab your food, and I'll meet you at a table of your choosing?"

Gabriella nodded and walked over to the near-empty American food line. The new world order's reality filtered into Draven's artificial reality in more ways than just the television. She read a large signboard at the head of the line, "no burgers, chicken, or fries due to supply shortages." The sign made her think about the outside world from a practical perspective and things to come for her away from the UE headquarters. The lack of food at the center of the world's political, economic hub meant that most of the world starved.

Gabriella's appetite waned, but she was now up to order.

"What can I get you, ma'am?" asked the sullen cafeteria worker.

Gabriella ordered, "I will take two hot dogs, a bag of chips, and a bottle of water."

The cafeteria worker unapologetically denied Gabriella's food dreams. "The limit is one hot dog due to the number of buns we have available. I don't have any chips as the man in front of you took my last bag and no bottled water. The cafeteria worker, turning to return to the kitchen area to help the only other worker, added, "I'll give you a cup, and you fill it at one of the potable water tables."

Gabriella gathered her disappointing hot dog and a cup for water and walked over to an already seated Gemma.

Gabriella inquired, "How's the fish and chips? And I am really puzzled as you have chips, but I couldn't get fries or potato chips."

After inspecting Gabriella's food choices, Gemma said, "An offense to the King. I think this fish is well past ripe. The chips aren't half-bad. You mean they didn't have chips or, as you yanks say, fries?"

Gabriella commented, grabbing one of Gemma's chips. "I was rationed to one rubbery hot dog, no fries, no potato chips, and no bottled water. Gemma, I'm not sure everyday people will make it another year at this rate if *we're* running out of common items. I plan to find out on my own starting tomorrow."

"What do you mean you're going to find out starting tomorrow?"

Gabriella explained, "You got time for a brief walk down to the gardens."

Gemma glanced at her watch. "I have enough time to hear how you've come to this decision."

Discarding their poor excuses for a meal in a trash bin as they left the UE cafeteria, the two friends made their way to the nearby UE gardens. The gardens had been patterned after the Jardins du Château de Versailles, only smaller. The chill of Italy early winter nipped at the women driving the conversation to begin quickly.

Gabriella said, "I'm getting out of here so I can help people. We both know that Draven is a monster; look at this war. I need to try to stop him for my friends and for my country."

Gemma pushed back. "I don't know, love. I think you're playing a dangerous game. I agree Draven is a dictator in the making. But how do you plan to support him and fight against him? It looks like a losing campaign on your end."

Gabriella said, "Gemma, you will help me from here. I can communicate my plans, and you can watch my back; you know, let me know if Draven is growing suspicious. What do you think?"

Gemma turned to walk back to the main headquarters building. "I love you like a sister, as you're all I have in this world now. But I'm scared, Gabriella. The Draven you're seeing is only the tip of his cruelty. You're angry and hurt from losing Christopher, Jackson, President Rodgers, and even America, as you know it. Nevertheless, going after Draven is foolish. I have worked for him long enough to know he has no concern about arranging fatal accidents for people that challenge him. Look, we can discuss this more tonight. I hate to rush, but I need to get back to my post. Draven is due to give his speech in ten minutes."

Gabriella wanted to defend her actions and highlight the virtue of standing up against such an evil man but instead settled for a less confrontational question. "Hey, before you go. A quick question. Do you know who is setting up our apartments here on campus and where I'll be located?"

Gemma giggled. "Of course, I do, and you're staying with me; that is when you're here. Let's link up at the end of the day. You still owe me details on what brought on that infamous slap."

Gabriella saw potential in having Gemma feed her inside information to undermine Draven. The thought brought a flush of shame to her, as she remembered getting Gemma tipsy at a previous dinner to find out more about Draven and his plans. Gabriella now cared for Gemma deeply. It felt strange for a trained spy to experience remorse for using someone. Gabriella thought, walking towards the main building; w*ell, Draven's speech is my cue to finish snooping into Cross Industries.*

Spending the past week in a Beijing hotel room, Gabriella was flooded with emotion. She remembered the sense of failure hanging over her with the realization that years ago, Draven should have faced the light of justice. Now, a soul-crushing weight rested on her shoulders to limit his damage. Tears rolled down Gabriella's face as she thought of the intelligence failure by the US and others around the world to collect on Draven's activities. She had spent hours between trying to find the leader of the Chinese UE resistance movement and exploring Cross Industries' secret files on her laptop. Gabriella discovered Draven developed a bioweapon named Pyretos that he now meant to unleash on the world. The face of the prisoner Draven's lab used as Pyretos test subject still haunted her. Remembering the severe febrile seizures racking his body and the unnatural constriction of his limbs, and the foaming at his mouth was horrific.

Gabriella wiped her face and wrung her hands through her raven-colored hair, preparing to leave her hotel. After days of failed attempts to uncover the UE resistance movement in China, success had found her finally yielded a meeting. The joy she sought after gaining a linkup location with a potential ally against Draven was fleeting. Thoughts of

Gemma questioning her attempts to slow down Draven away from the UE headquarters, which were unresolved, clouded her thinking. Gemma thought it was prudent for Gabriella to let her emotions settle before making such a rash decision. However, Gabriella knew with Christopher and Jackson now gone that she could trust no one besides herself to stop Draven Cross. Gabriella hoped Gemma would come to understand why she chose this path.

While the view from her hotel room was not glamorous, the ride to Yingcui Lake was unnerving at best. The post-Rapture world, now crippled by a world war, was leaving deep scars on humanity. The sounds of battle filled the acrid Beijing air as the UE loyal government fought against people filled with years of animosity and the specter of increasing personal restrictions under the UE. The once-populous Chinese capital city felt vast and isolated, a byproduct of the disappearances and all that followed as her rideshare passed through the streets. Gaunt faces confirmed Gabriella's fears that food shortages were far worse outside the UE capital of Rome. She wondered how the war-ravaged buildings and frail, squalid people constituted living. The pain etched on these strangers' faces signaled an unfathomable level of human suffering, and it all fell at the feet of Draven. Gabriella's dejection with the world's suffering level left her ill as the rideshare arrived at the park entrance to her link-up point.

Smoke filled the midday sky, casting a foreboding shadow over the idyllic Yingcui Lake. Tourists and locals ignored glancing at the scenery as Gabriella did; survival was a more significant concern than leisurely strolls in a once-popular park. It seemed even nature recoiled from the world as no bird's song could be heard. Gabriella walked toward a small pagoda overlooking the lake where a large man sat, who she assumed was her contact.

Gabriella said, "I was told you could help me stop a mutual enemy."

The man remained silent, studying Gabriella like a lioness right before making a final pounce on its prey.

Undeterred, Gabriella pressed. "You are Abdulkerim Hoshur, leader of the Jiātíng Jiàohuì. If you're not, be warned I am not alone, and you will not leave here a free man."

The mystery man laughed. "Gabriella, you are alone and were unwise to show up here. You risk a lot with someone you know nothing about."

Gabriella was now annoyed. "Okay, can you stop the super-spy routine? You know who I am, and I know who you are. I want the same thing you do. So are you going to help me?"

The man stood up and whistled as three other men rushed to the pagoda and grabbed Gabriella, binding her arms and legs. As the whistling man wrapped a course scarf around Gabriella's mouth, he said, "I am Abdulkerim Hoshur. Your next choices will determine if that is the last name you ever hear."

❧

Christopher felt a sense of relief, and the park ranger cabin in a remote Alaskan wilderness had become a balm for his soul. By the time Christopher returned to Jackson's bedroom, Jimbo had brought in a pot of coffee and a plate of bacon and eggs, placing the items on a bed tray.

Jimbo stood, embracing Christopher. "I want to welcome you to the family. I was happy to hear the news that you've accepted Jesus as your Lord and Savior."

"Thanks, Jimbo. It's something I should have done years ago…" Christopher trailed off as he thought about what his indecision cost him, namely his relationship with his wife, Erin.

Jimbo commented, "Look, we all made that mistake. It took the Rapture and the ensuing chaos to wake up a lot of us."

Jackson prompted Christopher, "Yeah, don't focus on the past, but the new future you have in Jesus Christ. Now, hand me that fancy quantum phone; I want to call Miss Sassy Pants, aka Gabriella."

Christopher handed Jackson the quantum communicator and watched him dial her. The phone rang, but no answer. Christopher knew that sending a text message to Gabriella or voicemail was of little value, as the customized devices would destroy any unauthenticated communication received after fifteen minutes. Christopher silently prayed that Gabriella was alive and would call back after seeing the missed call notification.

Jackson hesitantly said, "No answer, I'm sure she's in a meeting or something. She'll call back later."

Christopher looked at Jackson, unsure that either of them believed that Gabriella would ever call him back.

❧

Gabriella tried to remain calm as she bounced around the back of a panel van and take in her surroundings. The van had a greasy scent, similar to her expectations for a diner kitchen. Her captors talked in hushed tones mixed between Mandarin and some other language. She hoped she wouldn't see the maroon beret of a UE soldier when the doors opened. As the vehicle stopped, she began to tremble; Gabriella willed herself into showing strength no matter what happened next. Relief came for a moment, as the face of Abdulkerim was the first she saw when the van doors opened. She quickly flushed with anger and thrashed against the bonds holding her arms in place.

Abdulkerim turned to Gabriella. "I will remove your restraints, but if you attempt to run or cause a scene, I will restrain you once again. Do you understand me?"

Gabriella nodded.

One of Abdulkerim's men untied Gabriella's arms and feet and removed her mouth gag. Gabriella promptly slapped Abdulkerim, causing him to stagger into large barrels that smelled like old soy sauce.

Abdulkerim said something in a language she knew was not Mandarin, causing all the men to laugh.

Gabriella said, "You think that's funny. You will have to kill me before I let you hurt me."

Abdulkerim was now holding his face. "Relax. No one here will hurt you if you are who you say you are. I need you to report two men we captured to the UE as traitors. If you do that, then we can discuss other matters."

Gabriella shook her head. "Are you crazy? They will report me once they're detained. You didn't really think this out, did you, big boy?"

Gabriella scanned the area for a potential escape but didn't find one. Though she did understand the source of the putrid-sweet smell overwhelming her senses. She was in an alley behind what she assumed was a restaurant.

Abdulkerim said, "Take your phone and call the Beast at the UE; tell him you caught two senior officers helping the resistance. I assure you if you do this, your life will be spared. Refuse and suffer their fate.

Gabriella hesitated as Abdulkerim's men dragged two blindfolded and gagged UE officers out of the old restaurant. Abdulkerim's men stood behind the blindfolded and bound UE officers with pistols to their heads.

Abdulkerim racked a round into the chamber of his pistol. "Make the call."

ꟹ

In a moment of daydreaming moments before a virtual meeting in his office, Draven reflected on how he stood at the head of the global media elite. Draven relished the moment from a few days ago, where he took control of the world's largest media organization to create his propaganda. He had spoken with the President of the ANN, Martin Sorenson. He told Sorenson that the UE now controlled his company. Smiling, Draven replayed the conversation in his mind.

Draven said, "Martin, listen, I don't have much time to discuss this matter as I am due to give a speech in a few moments. The bottom line is I am taking over the ANN to serve my communications needs. This is effective immediately."

"You have a lot of gall calling me, Cross, and telling me you're taking over my business to be your propaganda machine. I don't see this deal going through; good luck with your speech," Martin Sorenson said, laughing as he prepared to hang up.

"Listen, Martin. Suppose you value your pathetic existence that you call a life and the lives of your contemptible wife and progeny. In that case, you will comply with my simple request."

"Now, you listen here—" Sorenson was cut off by Draven.

Draven stated, "I will not listen to anyone beneath me. After my speech, you will announce to the world that you will serve my vision of peace by bringing the largest media network in the world under UE leadership. I would hate for the world to find out about your penchant for trafficking young women around the world for unspeakable purposes."

Silence hung on the other end of the phone.

A dejected Martin Sorenson replied, "You will get what you want, Cross."

"I always do, Martin, and never call me solely by my last name again. I am Secretary-General Cross to you," Draven said, hanging up the phone on Sorenson.

Draven came back into the present as Gemma told him the regional ambassadors were online awaiting him. However, he also had an urgent call from Gabriella.

Draven scolded Gemma. "Make the ambassadors wait. Give me the phone. Ah, Gabriella dear, how are things in China?"

Gabriella said, "I've got some troubling news. I have detained, with support from UE loyal forces, two traitors."

Draven said, "You do work fast, don't you? Place me on speaker, so I can solve this matter quickly for you."

Gabriella responded, "Go ahead, sir. You're on speaker now."

"Gentlemen, you have forfeited your right to live; betrayal of the UE comes at a high price. Gabriella, kill them."

The loud retorts of two handguns caused Draven to pause momentarily. He was impressed with Gabriella's progress. "My goodness, you are efficient. Keep up the excellent work."

Draven transitioned from the horrible scene with Gabriella in China with as much thought as a person ordering lunch at a deli. "Okay, Gemma, put me through with the ambassadors. Gabriella made my day.

"Good day, gentlemen. I will be brief. Regarding the war topic, I am heartbroken that yet another senseless global war has started. The cause comes from deluded men who believed the time before the disappearances were the only way humanity should live. The former President of the United States of America, along with several conspirators, preemptively attacked the UE. Thank you for your loyalty and those under your stewardship who fight to preserve humanity and our unified vision for peace. I am happy to announce that UE forces have detained two of the masterminds behind this war, the former Australian Prime Minister and the NATO Secretary-General. These two men will face a public trial, where I will let the citizens of the world decree their fate."

Draven feigned emotional exhaustion. "The two mentally ill 'witnesses' Reuel and Eliyahu who attacked me months ago in Jerusalem—continue to spread their messages of doom and religious hatred. I have a plan in the works for these men and their followers. I will end this war soon and guide us to a bright new future. Good day, gentlemen."

Draven entered an elevator for his office. "Gemma, find John Barnes and his team. I have some unfinished business with Martin Sorenson that requires his skill set."

⁂

War was a distant thought in Pattaya, Thailand, only brought to mind if a go-go bar had the news on versus music videos. John Barnes was lost in this hedonistic amusement park. He had been fulfilling all of his lustful desires since destroying the American black site in Alaska and gaining his revenge on Christopher Barrett and the Omega Group.

Barnes was not new to Pattaya and all it offered. However, things had been dialed-up a notch since his last visit right before the disappearances. The lines for the prostitutes and brothels were packed now. The women had become bolder, and the advertisements for carnal desires more pronounced. He did not understand why the previous attempts at restraint in Pattaya were now gone, but he loved every minute of this new world.

As Barnes was lying in a humid room with two women, his phone rang. The display flashed an unknown number registry, but he guessed who was calling: Draven Cross.

"Barnes here," he said, pushing the legs of a young woman off him to stand so he could close an open window that overlooked the neon-illuminated depravity below him.

"Please hold for the Secretary-General," came the distinct and sensual voice of Gemma Sutherland.

Before his dirty mind could act upon hearing Gemma's voice, Draven's stern tone filled Barnes's phone. "John, job well done in Alaska. I am even glad you failed to prevent two nuclear weapons from launching.

The nuclear weapons only add to my message about the late President Rodgers. Look, I need you to take care of a couple of things for me."

Barnes lit a cigarette and smiled at the two women who had awoken and now were beckoning him to rejoin them. "I'm listening."

Draven continued, "I require your talent to dispatch Martin Sorenson, the soon-to-be-late President of the ANN. Ensure his death looks like a murder-suicide, which provides a plausible reason for his family's deaths. Unfortunately, he was not in New York City when one of the nuclear weapons struck, but he is near you in Sydney. When we conclude this conversation, check your phone for the address."

Barnes agreed, "Consider it done."

Draven ordered, "After you're done in Sydney, I want you and your men to head for Inverness, Scotland. You will oversee the loading of a weapon at the Cross Industries National Security Laboratory. The agent at the lab will ensure the prompt conclusion to the war I am seeking. For your sake, I hope your time in Pattaya hasn't softened your military acumen."

Barnes assured his leader. "No, sir. We will get the mission done. I'll call the airfield now to get our jet ready. I want to thank you for the jet—"

Draven cut off John Barnes. "Excellent, I will be in touch when I need you."

A shiver ran through John Barnes for a moment, with his cell phone now silent. He realized he had not told Draven where he was, but the man had known his exact location. He checked his watch and then flashed a mischievous smile to the two women, dismissing the thought of Draven as he ran and jumped into the bed.

☙

Hours later and half-the-world away, John Barnes relished the cool pre-dawn breeze and view of Sydney harbor that the lavish Point Piper suburban home of Martin Sorenson afforded him. He wiped the sweat from his brow as the sun rose behind the home and illuminated the distant Sydney Opera house and Harbor bridge.

Sorenson, realizing the fate awaiting his family and himself, cried loudly.

Barnes spoke over Martin Sorenson's sobs. "Martin, I must confess you've had a view to die for."

After a brief scream from the late Mrs. Sorenson, followed by the muffled report of a silenced handgun and breaking glass and furniture in the home, Barnes yelled. "Hey, boys, let's wrap things up in there! We have a long flight to Scotland and need to return to the airport in an hour."

A UE SAG soldier reported to Barnes, "We're done, boss. Sorenson's family is an afterthought."

Barnes commanded, "Make sure the guys don't steal anything. This needs to look like a murder-suicide when it's investigated and reported in the news." Barnes then walked over to Martin Sorenson, who wailed at the feet of the UE SAG soldier who had been holding him while his family was killed.

Barnes ordered, "Get him on his knees."

Sorenson cried out, asking who Barnes and his men were and why they killed his family.

John Barnes calmly put on his tactical gloves. He took the instrument of Sorenson's family execution from one of his men. He wrapped Sorenson's ungloved right hand around the weapon while pushing it to his right temple and whispering. "Draven Cross sends his regards."

With Sorenson's finger, Barnes pulled the trigger.

What Christopher thought were going to be his final words as the avalanche overtook him, that he surrendered in his war-with-God, were troubling him. He couldn't deny that making good on his "deathbed" conversion was positive. But, doubts about the future and survival filled his mind. He forced a conversation with Jackson, Jimbo, and Ranger Stinson to slow the rising doubts about God's faithfulness invading his mind. Christopher attempted a thought-provoking question.

Christopher turned to Jackson. "Where are we on the Tribulation timeline?"

Jimbo added, "Yeah, I was kind of curious myself."

Ranger Stinson mumbled, attempting to leave the room. "I'll give you guys some privacy."

Jackson stopped the man that had been so kind to Christopher, Jimbo, and himself. "Ranger Stinson, there is nothing private about what God is doing. In fact, it's crucial that everyone possible understand what's coming so they can give their lives to Christ Jesus while there is still time. I wish I would have paid more attention before the Rapture to God's warnings of these days."

Ranger Stinson smiled as he dragged a chair into the room. "Okay, I'm willing to listen."

Jackson reached into his backpack for Rev's journal and Bible, pulling out his most treasured possessions. He assumed everyone realized the challenge ahead. "Fellas, we're in more trouble than a cow in a butcher shop."

Christopher laughed as he leaned against the wall near the bedroom window. "Let me translate for you guys. As I've been around Jackson long enough to understand Southern. Things are going to get rough."

Jimbo and Ranger Stinson laughed but quickly stopped when they noticed the deadpan look on Jackson's face.

Jackson proclaimed, "As much as the college boy here likes to make fun of my wonderful Southern tongue, I am dead serious here, guys. The world has only begun to experience God's judgment for rejecting Jesus and his gift of salvation."

Christopher stifled a laugh. "I'm sorry, Jackson, go ahead."

Jackson explained, "I'll keep this brief. The war that we had a part in starting means that God, for sure, has opened the second seal. The next judgments, third and fourth seals as described in *Revelation 6: 3-8,* complete the riders of the apocalypse. "

Christopher asked, "So, how long do we have until the next judgment?"

Jackson responded, "I'm not sure. There is nothing provided in the Bible for the time between judgments. I assume that if the second seal deals with a great war, then the natural byproducts of a war, which the third and fourth seals comprise, will follow quickly."

Jackson continued, "I believe the rider of the first horse, a white horse, is the Antichrist who is driven by a conquering spirit. An evil spirit that has been around since God declared his redemptive plan for fallen humanity in *Genesis 3:14-15,* the section of scripture that announced Jesus's future birth and redemptive death. Satan, throughout history, has always had to be ready to have his Antichrist deceive the world.

"The Bible describes the Antichrist as the ultimate deceiver. Sounds like a trendy man we've all seen on TV a lot lately, doesn't it?"

Jimbo agreed, "I get it, Jackson, how you could think that Draven, whom I'm guessing you're talking about here, would be the Antichrist. I'm sure he's not the first charismatic political leader that has deceived many. His schemes are not new phenomena in human history."

Jackson nodded. "You're correct, Jimbo, but I'm sticking to my guns on Draven; he's the devil in my mind. Anyways, the third seal will bring famine and economic collapse. The starving faces we hear about on the radio news will only get worse in the days ahead. The fourth seal is the natural culmination of wars, famines, and economic ruin: death. Millions of people will die, many never knowing Christ Jesus during the next two judgments."

Jackson, reading the facial expression of the other men in the room, added, "That's a lot to take in, so let's take a break. I'm going to try and put some weight on this leg and get some fresh air. I think I might try to call General Havid and see how Isreal is making out in this war."

The scene that unfolded behind the old dumpling restaurant between Abdulkerim' s group and the UE officers unsettled Gabriella. She was questioning if too many years in D.C. office jobs had made her unfit for fieldwork. Gabriella fought to find her composure. She watched a crimson trail follow the two dead UE officials as they were hauled toward an empty field near the restaurant. Abdulkerim Hoshur was not a token extremist group leader; his demonstrated willingness to exact violence on the UE made Gabriella unsure of the wisdom of seeking him out.

"Gabriella, your face tells me you didn't expect this outcome. I am a man of my word and a man at war," Abdulkerim said.

Gabriella responded, "As you said, you're a man of your word. Would you agree that I am a woman of my word?"

Abdulkerim nodded. "Yes, you are. So what do you want? And please call me Kerim."

Gabriella said, "I want to stop the UE. I want revenge for my friend's deaths. I want Draven Cross to suffer for destroying America. That is what I want."

Kerim studied Gabriella for a moment. "You have a lot of wants but not a clear purpose. We are not going to be able to help each other. Those men died not for my revenge, but because they opposed my God and His people."

Gabriella took offense as she stared down Kerim. "Oh, so you're one of those groups, religious terrorists."

Kerim's eyes narrowed. "Gabriella, I am not a terrorist. The man who ordered the death of his own officials is a terrorist. I use my resources and talents to support the God of Heaven, not my own revenge. If you want my help, then you need to understand what I am about."

Gabriella sassed. "Fine. Warrior-monk. How do I gain a better understanding of your group of religious, not-terrorist fighters?"

Kerim admired the fiery personality of Gabriella. "Spend some time with me, and then we can both decide on the next steps."

Gabriella questioned herself for contemplating accepting the risk but saw a great potential ally. "I will give you two days, and then I'll find someone else to help me bring down the UE."

❧

CHAPTER 4

WATCHING THE TWO Witnesses' daily sermons from the temple mount consumed General Havid, like many people around the globe. Each "sermon" stirred such condemnation of the sin and lust that dominated not only the world but the hearts of every person listening. It was common for the power of personal conviction in the daily messages to trigger an emotionally-disturbed man from the audience to harm the speakers. The result was the individual giving his life in the effort.

Havid had noticed a message pattern or what he thought might be a pattern for each of the respective men. Reuel proclaimed God's faithfulness to Israel throughout the nation's history and Jesus Christ's messiahship. Eliyahu focused on impending judgment and directly challenged the Beast, who governed the world, which everyone knew was a direct assault on Draven Cross. As a man who had made his living in the military, there was something incredibly appealing when Eliyahu spoke. Any message directly attacking Israel's real enemy stirred a great passion in the general's heart for serving Jesus Christ.

Today's message seemed particularly foreboding, as the two men spoke on the devastating war that raged around the world and the man—or Beast as they described Draven Cross—at the heart of the war. The general turned his television up as the witness named Reuel spoke.

Reuel chided as he sat against the ancient temple wall. "Israel, open your ears and hear what the LORD your God has to say to you. How long will you ignore God's call for you to return from playing a harlot with Satan and his Beast? This war is only the start of your sorrows. Millions of you under my voice are doomed to eternal separation from the true and living God unless you repent from your sins and accept Jesus Christ as your Lord and Savior. Have you forgotten so easily how God delivered you from your enemies' attacks a few short years ago? Your ancestors showed equal contempt for the great I AM by creating an idol of gold, despite witnessing His delivering hand at work."

General Havid laughed as the crowd took a collective three steps back as Eliyahu began to speak. Everyone knew the power the man of God commanded.

"Israel, hear the message of the God of Abraham, Isaac, and Jacob that you may live and not die. '*When the Lamb opened the second seal, I heard the second living creature say, "Come!" Then another horse came out, a fiery red one. Its rider was given the power to take peace from the Earth and to make people kill each other. To him was given a large sword.*' Can you not see the truth of God being fulfilled before your eyes, the Beast who runs this world in the name of peace is waging war.

"Know, Israel, that our very presence is a testament to the power and mercy of the God of Heaven. We are a sign to this rebellious generation. Hear my words and submit your lives to God before it is too late. As the LORD, the God of Israel lives whom I serve. No matter how you cry out, there will be neither dew nor rain except at my word."

Eliyahu stopped speaking as a man broke through the barricades and security forces to challenge his message.

"How can you take away our rain? How can you love God and kill his people? You are the Beast here. You should die!" the man shouted as he ran across the 300-meter gap between the crowd and the witnesses at the temple wall, drawing a handgun from his jacket.

Onlookers screamed and moved farther back as security forces shouted but dared not chase the man.

Reuel stood and joined Eliyahu as the crazed man ran closer in an attempt to get a killing shot on the two men. Just as the man came within twenty-five meters of the Two Witnesses, he raised his gun, taking aim.

The ANN anchor seemed encouraged that the gunman might accomplish what others had failed to do. The impossible task of silencing the representatives of Heaven, as the newscaster emphatically exclaimed, "I think he's going to take them down."

General Havid compassionately winced and closed his eyes momentarily at the sound of gunshots. He feared to watch the imminent death of the Two Witnesses, who remained unmoved. The anchor's exclamation at the retort of gunshots caused the general to open his eyes, expecting to see the two men of God dead.

The dejected and visibly angry news anchor said, "I don't know what just happened, but the attacker seemed to hit a wall of flame and instantly consumed near the Two Witnesses. Another victim of these men is now dead. It seems that these two fanatics have no mercy. The world will be a better place once those two are dead."

The two men proclaimed in unison, "We will not be moved and cannot be uprooted until the true and living God proclaims it so. Woe to the inhabitants of Earth for the Wrath of the Lamb is yet to come."

After this announcement, the two men returned to the Wailing Wall, as security forces in full riot gear appeared to extinguish the smoldering corpse and collect the remains of the would-be assassin.

General Havid sat back in his chair, inspired by the display of God's provision for those he entrusted for a task. He felt an overwhelming sense of calm and then felt the presence of the Holy Spirit, as a thought permeated his heart and mind. *I will save you from the hands of the wicked and deliver you from the grasp of the cruel.*

As a past Torah studies student, the General knew the message well; it was *Jeremiah 15:21.* The Holy Spirit's message motivated him to use his skills as a former Israeli special operations operative to thwart Draven Cross's plans.

The general concluded his thought, "Thank you, LORD. I know what must be done for the days ahead," as his office phone rang with an unknown number.

Gabriella's two days had turned into almost a month of following Kerim around, expecting to witness a terror group's operations; however, she found a man on a mission she did not fully understand but appreciated.

She chuckled to herself as she bounced alongside Kerim in a dilapidated utility truck returning from an ammo resupply run for resistance fighters outside of Guǎngzhōu along the Pearl River.

Kerim broke the silence. "I thought you were only giving me two days. You've covered most of eastern China over the past month. I think you like us."

"It has been a pleasant surprise to see you're not bloodthirsty madmen. However, I have more questions now than answers. I know you want to bring down the UE, but I am struggling to find the God you say drives you to help people. What is your story? Why do you believe in God?"

"I guess I could ask why you don't believe in God after the last year. I will give you the short version."

"Thank you for not boring me to death."

Kerim smiled. "You have a lot of will for a woman."

Gabriella challenged. "I think you meant to say I have a lot of strength as a person, but continue with your story."

Kerim laughed. "The Jiātíng Jiàohuì or 'the church' you have seen was not always militant. While the Chinese government has feared the Jiàohuì, we are revered by many as one of the strongest resistance movements dating back to before the disappearances. Now we are comprised of post-Rapture believers in Jesus; the group was built upon the legacy of secret Christian gatherings under the former Chinese Communist Party rule to help protect Christ's followers from Draven."

Kerim continued his story as they pulled up to the safe house. He rolled down his window—Gabriella followed suit—allowing the swampy air to fill the truck cabin before saying, "I am Uyghur by birth. I have lived every day up to this very moment under some form of oppression. Growing up, it was the Chinese Communist Party; now it's Draven Cross. I was forced into the People's Liberation Army, as many are from my province. The worst part was not the physical torture or the painful experiments I underwent; it was the Chinese government's deliberate attempt to dehumanize me. They tried to shame where I came from and who I was as a person.

"I was allowed minimal contact with my parents in Ürümqi because we were the wrong ethnic group and always considered a threat. However,

I still found a way to send them money or write to them, a must, as I was their only child.

"We were not devout to the Islamic faith, which is common in Xinjiang province when I was growing up. My parents adhered to the traditions to keep from being outcasts, but we did not believe in Islam. My parents had gotten involved with the house church right before the disappearances, during an outreach meeting by a Taiwanese-American Christian missionary couple who secretly held meetings in my parent's neighborhood. However, they went to Heaven before the Rapture. As they often did in Xinjiang, the Chinese government conducted a raid to keep rebellions in check and searched for Christian missionaries like those who led my parents to Christ. My mother was on a list to be detained, and my father fought against the soldiers. He and my mother were shot during the struggle."

Kerim fought back the tears, composing his perceived emotional weakness before continuing. "When I found out what had happened to them, I began preparing to escape from the PLA."

Before Gabriella could respond, a woman approached the truck in the fading evening light. Gabriella tried to understand the frantic tones between the woman and Kerim.

Kerim picked the woman up from the ground, shouting to Gabriella, "Follow me!"

Gabriella raced behind Kerim into a dirt-floored, cinderblock building. The safe house had a single room and a couple of dirty mattresses on the floor. There were bloodstains on two of the walls, and the room carried the smell of spoiled meat amplified by the humid night air.

Kerim found a fuse box and turned on the lights, which consisted of two exposed LED bulbs. He ordered, "Gabriella open that wooden box in the corner and bring me the first aid kit and some water."

Gabriella grabbed the items. "What's going on, Kerim? Who is this woman?"

"She's a local named Li Wei that was attacked by UE soldiers. Attacks like this are why I fight."

Gabriella did not know what to say, but she knew that the UE had to be stopped and was convinced Kerim was the man for the job.

Jackson was glad he reached General Havid. He briefed the general on all that occurred upon their return to Alaska. The general was relieved that they had survived the first moments of the war and shared Christopher and Jackson's fears for Gabriella's life. General Havid also mentioned that the Two Witnesses demonstrated God's power daily, which Jackson longed to view for himself. Now, as Jackson looked out into the expanse of the Alaskan wilderness, he desired to punish Draven Cross for his attack on the US and the suffering he caused.

Christopher said, "Hey, did you get in touch with the general?"

Jackson jumped. "Man, you scared me."

Christopher joked. "Sorry about that, but I figured you had finished your call. It must have been a tough one with General Havid if I got the jump on you."

Jackson replied, "Nah, it was actually a good call. The general promised to help determine if Gabriella is safe or not. He also wants us to get started being a thorn in the devil's side."

Christopher said, "By the devil, I'm guessing you're talking about Draven, and by a thorn, you mean attacking the UE."

Christopher joined Jackson in his staring contest with the endless forest in front of the ranger station.

Jimbo wondered as he and Ranger Stinson joined the men on the porch. "You guys aren't planning something without us, are you?"

Jackson shook his head. "Nope, but we do need to start planning. We need to get out of Alaska and to my family homestead in Alabama. President Rodgers sent us here because he chose to stand against Draven, and so did Gabriella. The fight won't end until we die, or Jesus comes back."

Jackson continued, "Draven's attempts to rule the world will bring death everywhere, widespread hunger, and conflict against all that oppose the UE, and his efforts will intensify until Christ Jesus returns."

Jimbo rubbed his hands through his hair, glancing at the other men. "That is a sobering picture for the future."

Ranger Stinson's voice quivered, "How do I get saved?"

Jackson answered, smiling, "Asking how means you're over 90 percent there; let me help you reach the rest of the way."

"No, let us help you," Christopher happily challenged. He and Jimbo gathered around Jackson to help Ranger Stinson pray to receive the salvation of Jesus Christ.

As the twilight of the evening and the arctic chill it brought invaded the Ranger Station porch, the three brothers in arms and faith finished praying for the salvation of Ranger Stinson. The older man kneeled, surrounded by his new brothers-in-Christ, overcome with emotion.

Jackson referred to the ranger by his first name for the first time. "Are you okay, James?"

Ranger Stinson's voiced cracked, and his hands trembled before saying, "Yes, I feel hopeful considering everything, thanks to you three."

Jimbo encouraged, "Welcome to the family. No matter what comes in the days ahead, you have made a decision that will last for all eternity."

Ranger Stinson rejoiced over his salvation as the three warriors he had grown to know prepared to depart. "Jimbo, knowing that I am at peace with God is a good feeling, and good feelings have been hard to come by lately. I'm going to go start dinner."

Christopher announced, "I've led many missions to rescue someone or prevent the latest D.C. crisis, but I've never felt as satisfied as I do right now, after helping that man find Jesus. What a feeling, thank you, Jesus!"

Jimbo and Jackson looked at each other and smiled at the new Christian fire they both had and now saw manifested on their beloved friend and leader.

"I agree; it's been an awesome day for Ranger Stinson and you. Shoot, for all of us. I hate to be the party pooper, but we need to leave for Alabama tomorrow. Something tells me that if the war has been going as reported, the UE is near winning. The UE's victory will mean traveling freely about the world will be harder than woodpecker lips," Jackson remarked, causing Christopher and Jimbo to erupt with laughter.

Jackson asked, "What's so funny?"

Christopher replied with tears rolling down his face, "Nothing, I mean, you and that southern tongue crack us up, that's all."

Jackson shot back, "Are you sure you're from Texas? I think you spent too much time in them fancy East Coast schools; I know people in Texas talk like me."

Christopher laughed and slapped Jackson on the back as he and Jimbo followed their noses and stomachs into the Ranger Station. "Yeah, I'm from Texas, not the part of Texas where I've ever heard sayings like yours. Let's eat, country boy."

Jackson pulled out his phone. "Yeah, yeah, I'm going to call Gabriella one last time. It can't hurt. I'm hoping she's been busy with old Mr. Cross. From the news, we know that devil-in-disguise is pulling overtime."

Jackson felt dejected that his numerous attempts to reach Gabriella had failed, nor had she returned a call from him. He was beginning to resign himself to the fact that she was gone.

Christopher yelled to Jackson from the cabin. "Hey, are you going to eat?"

Jackson put his hands to his face. "Yeah, I'm coming in soon. I'm worried about Gabriella. I think we let her down. Maybe we should have tried to get her out of the UE."

As Jackson stared into the star-filled night sky, Christopher walked out onto the porch.

Jackson challenged Christopher with a question. "You remember that night in our apartment when Gabriella first told us about the assignment to spy on Draven and how she fought us? She would sooner argue with the devil than admit she had made a bad choice in working for him. Look, you know Gabriella well enough to know that she would never let us convince her of anything she didn't want?"

Christopher laughed. "Knowing Gabriella, she has likely given Draven an earful by now. We don't know if she's alive or not, so let's not get worked up over the unknown. Have you tried to reach Charlie about picking us up in Anchorage tomorrow?"

Jackson said, "No, but that's a good point. I hope Charlie is still alive. I'll call him now. Thanks for checking on me."

Christopher said, "I will always be here for you, brother. Don't stay out here too long; you need to eat and get some rest. We have a long day of travel tomorrow."

ꕥ

Gabriella sat quietly as Li Wei changed into some clean clothes Kerim provided her. While Kerim busied himself warming two cans of soup for the disheveled trio atop a metal grate over a fire. Gabriella felt pressure to report back to the UE; weeks had passed since the fateful phone call with Draven that pushed her to want to follow Kerim and the Jiàohuì. Gabriella pulled her dead phone from her pocket, once a lifeline to dear friends, now a leash to a brutal master. She wrapped her arms around her legs and rocked back and forth on the cold earthen floor as tears streamed down her face, not noticing Li Wei approaching her.

Li Wei wondered aloud, "Why do you cry? You lost your lover?"

The woman's broken English forced Gabriella to strain to understand her, which stopped her pity session.

Gabriella said, "I'm sorry. No. I'm upset not for my lover but for losing my country, friends, and my sense of purpose. Do you understand me?"

"Yes, my name Li Wei. I lost family too. My son disappeared with the other children. He was our only child. So, my husband cannot take the loss and kill himself, leaving me. The war starts, and I want to die."

Gabriella got up and embraced Li Wei as Kerim entered with hot soup, whose vegetable aroma mingled with the earthen, safe house floors, drawing Gabriella's memory to her grandfather's vineyards in Italy. Kerim spoke to Li Wei in Mandarin and got her to take a bowl. Gabriella explained the conversation they were having before Kerim entered as he handed her a bowl of soup. She enjoyed the comforting lentil soup, which warmed her soul and heart with its flavor.

Kerim took the remaining soup and joined the women on the floor. "I am committed to helping you, Gabriella, to enact your revenge against Draven. UE soldiers attacked Li Wei earlier today as she was looking for food. I will get her connected with one of the resistance cells in the city tomorrow. What is your next move?"

Gabriella thought about that for a moment. "I plan to return to Rome and find out more of Draven's plan. The best way you can help me destroy Draven is by attacking targets I provide you. In return, I will send you updates on Christians that need assistance. Sound like a deal?"

Kerim nodded. "We have a deal. I can drop you off near the UE headquarters in the city tomorrow. I'm sure they will be happy to see you."

"I'm not sure they will."

ℰ

Gabriella had not prepared herself for the mental switch from operating with people fighting against the UE to serving in the lion's den. It was here back at the UE headquarters that Gabriella felt like a hollow, fake impersonation of herself. What Gabriella expected was scrutiny upon her arrival back in Rome but instead was deemed a hero. According to Evan, the UE's tenuous control over China was attributed in part to her efforts to covertly identify resistance cells. Gabriella felt sick to know that the unfortunate resistance members detained were suffering and that Draven gave her credit. It had been a whirlwind day being back at UE headquarters. Draven had given a speech earlier that nearly convinced her that the UE would solve the devastation the war was creating. However, she knew the truth behind the conflict.

It was odd that Gemma had not attempted to speak with her, and she hoped the time away, and her efforts to undermine Draven had not cost her a friendship. As she clicked her office television off in preparation to close out a first day that felt as if it were stretched into three, Evan knocked and entered. "I see you don't wait for an answer before entering an office, Evan," Gabriella sassed.

Evan scanned Gabriella's office. "I'm your superior. Why would I need to ask your permission to enter your office?"

Gabriella asserted, "What if I was changing? You do know that our offices contain full bathrooms."

Evan did not reply but stared at Gabriella with longing eyes, which told the story that he was entertaining the proposition of interrupting a changing Gabriella.

Gabriella grew disgusted by Evan's presence. "Evan, what do you want? I was going to my apartment."

Evan said, "You will be accompanying me to the Apostolic Palace tonight, ahead of my announcement of the first Interfaith conclave."

Gabriella exclaimed. "What is the Interfaith conclave, and what does it have to do with me?"

Evan held Gabriella's office door open for her. "Let's go, Gabriella; I will explain once we reach the Vatican. Some things are clearer when you have the right atmosphere."

Gabriella glanced around to see if she needed anything. She looked at her quantum phone, which still needed a charge, but it was pointless as the people she longed to hear from were gone.

Gabriella worried that the lustful Evan might have had other desires on his mind. "Let's get this over with, Evan; I'm exhausted. Who else is going with us?"

"Gemma is waiting for us in the car. I think I am the luckiest man in the UE. I'll be surrounded by beautiful women in a beautiful setting," Evan said, closing Gabriella's door behind her.

Gabriella mumbled, "I'm going to be sick."

Evan asked, "What did you say?"

"Nothing, I feel a little sick to my stomach. Likely something I ate."

Evan pushed the garage floor on the elevator. "Well, the night air will do you some good."

As Gabriella rode in a three-car caravan through the streets of Rome toward the Vatican City, the fading light could not hide the devastation from the global war. The car's view matched what she had experienced in China. The streets of Rome reinforced Li Wei's horrific story of ongoing suffering. A tale that countless others could recreate in the world caught in the wake of the disappearances. There was no place of refuge, no city left unscarred by the terror of the global war and the disappearance of millions of people. UE soldiers and equipment lined the streets in their distinctive beige uniforms and now maroon helmets, replacing the former UN's iconic blue. The soldiers operated checkpoints along the roads and could be seen protecting Rome's historical sites from looters.

A group of dead people was lying near a row of businesses. The UE deemed them looters, but Gabriella knew the truth. People were resorting to any means necessary to survive. Civility and decency were gone, and survival was all that people outside of the UE bubble cared and thought about each waking moment.

It was hard for Gabriella to grasp the details of the destruction she saw, given the vehicle's speed. The emptiness of the usually bustling *Campo de' Fiori* marketplace indicated how bad things were.

Rome's militarization was a reflection of the rest of the world. The devastation of such a beloved city focused Gabriella on the drastic change the world had undergone in the year since the disappearances. The absence of skilled workers throughout all levels of government led to deaths and disorder. Draven's military might was fueled by the chaos gripping the world, as no government on the planet could challenge the UE. The carnage of the disappearances, now intermingled with a world war, placed wounds on the world that Gabriella believed never would heal.

Crossing the *Ponte Vittorio Emanuele II* bridge, Evan exclaimed, "It's breathtaking, divine inspiration at its best," as he pointed to the towering St. Peter's Basilica.

Gabriella agreed with Evan's assessment of the scene before her. Still, she remained silent, reflecting on what the Vatican and Rome meant to her. St. Peter's Basilica was illuminated against a purple and rose-colored sunset sky. The church's image provided a momentary vision of beauty against the backdrop of devastation, a view that Gabriella relished and hated at the same time. Despite her struggle in believing in God, Gabriella had always sensed there was something beyond herself, something divine if she were honest, when her family visited St. Peter's Square during her childhood.

The once-special hold that Rome and the Vatican held in Gabriella's heart seemed distant; this short trip only magnified remorse and lost feelings. As the vehicles came to a stop, Evan quickly exited the car to greet two gentlemen. Gabriella instinctively glanced out her window, looking for the gelato vendor that she dragged her father to countless times. She could still taste the creamy delights that ruined many meals to the dismay of her mother. Now, the busy and seemingly always open gelato store was shuttered, with the glass broken out and its quaint tables in disarray.

Gabriella whispered, "Wow, the world has changed."

Gemma asked, "What did you say, Gabriella?"

"Nothing, this trip is just bringing up a lot of memories."

"Much has changed—" Gemma was cut off by Evan returning to their vehicle.

Evan ordered, "Ladies, enough with your makeup. Let's go."

Gabriella and Gemma rolled their eyes at the chauvinist assumption by Evan Mallory. The women were greeted by two gentlemen, one wearing Cardinal's garments, the other a business suit, as UE security agents flanked the awkward gathering.

"*Buonasera, signora.* I am Cardinal Lorenzo Conti."

Gabriella responded in flawless Italian, "*Buona sera a te, Eminenza,*"

Cardinal Conti gushed, "*Lei parla Italiano*? How impressive for a young American."

"Yes, Gabriella is quite impressive. Now, Cardinal Conti, or should I say Camerlengo," Evan remarked, as the group walked toward the Apostolic Palace entrance.

Cardinal Conti stopped with Evan's words, lagging behind the group that entered through massive golden overlaid doors held by two Swiss Guards.

The man in the business suit cried out and rushed back to Cardinal Conti. "*Tua eccellenza, stai bene.*"

Gabriella listened to the man's concern, who was either an aide or security guard, perhaps both, as he asked if the Cardinal was okay.

Cardinal Conti lamented. "I am fine, Giuseppe. Please, Mr. Mallory, do not call me such a revered name. I am one of only a few Cardinals left from the college. I am unworthy of such a title and serve only as steward until we can conduct conclave."

Evan turned back to embrace the Cardinal. "I meant no offense, Your Eminence. I am merely addressing you in the title befitting of your excellent service. However, I think by the end of the night, you will see a more significant role for yourself than a Procter for the conclave."

Gabriella and Gemma looked at each other with mutual concern over Evan's exorbitance to the Cardinal.

Cardinal Conti asked for clarification, "What do you mean, Mr. Mallory?"

"Let's journey to the Basilica cupola. A discussion of this magnitude deserves a view to match."

Gabriella felt a twinge of child-like wonder race through her veins as she stared at the masterpiece of Michelangelo, the Sistine Chapel roof, as Giuseppe led the small group through the breathtaking Sistine Chapel and into St. Peter's Basilica. Evan held up his hand at the doors of an elevator marked Cupola Tours.

Evan stated, "Ladies and gentlemen, due to the sensitive nature of the conversation to be had with Cardinal Conti, I ask that the UE security contingent remain here. I understand, Your Eminence, that Giuseppe, as the Inspector General of the Corps of Gendarmerie of Vatican City, will accompany us to the top. Gemma and Gabriella will complete our ensemble."

Cardinal Conti conceded, "As you wish, Signor Mallory."

Evan held the elevator doors open for Gemma and Gabriella and remained in the gap until Giuseppe and Cardinal Conti was in the elevator. As the elevator stopped on the first level of the Basilica, bypassing the first two hundred plus steps, the group found themselves inside the dome. They were now next to the impressive mosaics embedded in the dome's design. Gabriella's head swirled not only from the dizzying height but also from the grandeur.

Gabriella squealed, "This is amazing, Gemma, don't you think?"

Gemma agreed, "It's lovely."

Cardinal Conti led the group around the inner dome, followed by Giuseppe, Evan, Gemma, and Gabriella to a narrow winding staircase. The path was identified by a simple sign, which said Cupola with an arrow pointing up the stairs.

Giuseppe spoke in English for the first time that evening, announcing the uncertainty of the path ahead. "Please walk slowly and carefully. There is not much room along the stairs to the top," he said in his heavily accented safety address.

Gabriella found Giuseppe's assessment of the path to the Basilica cupola accurate. The wrought-iron steps wound up a spiral staircase, which in the final ascent required holding on to a hemp rope to complete the climb. However, the view the cupola commanded was worth every shaky step. The purple haze of the sunset mingled with the smoke rising from various quarters of Rome, casting a shadowy outline of the Apennine Mountains that dominated the distant horizon. St. Peter's Square, now illuminated in its full majesty, added a regal and surreal effect to Gabriella's view.

Given her present company, it was a bittersweet feeling to witness such a divinely postcard-worthy view with Evan Mallory. Gabriella wished her mother could have been here with her. The world's sorrow overtook being atop St. Peter's Basilica as Gabriella watched only parts of Rome shine in the new night. The other half of the city remained in darkness. The cruelty of the days in which she lived once again soured her view of the world.

Gemma invaded Gabriella's thoughts and personal space. "Selfie with my long-lost bestie."

Gabriella responded, "Gemma, you would ruin this moment and view with a selfie?"

Gabriella could see Gemma's real motive for the photo. She took the opportunity with Evan and Cardinal Conti chatting across the Basilica to tempt fate by asking Gabriella about her exploits. "How can you not savor this surreal moment? I don't know how many moments I will get with you as you slink around fighting against our mutual boss."

Gabriella felt the pain and anger in Gemma's words but was in no position to explain all that had occurred in China, the reason why she had been gone and would leave again.

As Gabriella began a response to Gemma, Evan announced. "Now, if I could have your attention, Cardinal Conti. I think you will agree this view was worth delaying our conversation until this moment."

Cardinal Conti nodded his head.

Evan continued, "Your Eminence, let me ask you, what do you see right now?"

Cardinal Conti lamented. "I see much suffering. I see the world in need of hope."

Evan refocused Conti's doubts. "Yes, there is much to feel melancholy about nowadays. However, I am here to give you a chance to guide the world into a new era of faith. I want you to lead the Interfaith movement, starting from right here"—Evan held his arms wide in a dramatic flair—"the center of the spiritual world. You will be the first Pontifex Maximus of the Interfaith religious movement. I will entrust you to bridge a growing faith with the Secretary-General's vision for this fallen world. What do you say to such an honor?"

Gabriella watched as Cardinal Conti slowly moved to the cupola's guardrail, soaking in the view and the question before him. In some way, she hoped that he would decline the offer to align himself and the distinguished organization he still represented with Draven Cross.

Cardinal Conti turned away from the group. "When you arraigned this meeting for this evening, I wondered what the most powerful man in the world wanted from me. I now realize Signore Cross's demand was beyond my comprehension."

ર્

Cardinal Conti watched as lights flickered to life across Rome breaking the void of darkness over half of the city. He contemplated the invitation to lead the Interfaith religion. *Perhaps, this was the purpose of me being left behind as the most senior Cardinal in the church,* the Cardinal thought as he turned to face Evan Mallory and his UE associates.

Cardinal Conti faced his wide-eyed aide. "Giuseppe, prepare, I *quarti papali* per me."

Gabriella understood that the Cardinal had ordered the former Pope's quarters to be prepared for himself. Meaning Conti had accepted the position Evan offered.

Evan attempted to decipher the Cardinal's Italian conversation, pressed, "So, are you accepting this great honor, Cardinal Conti?"

Cardinal Conti extended his hand to Evan. "At first, I attended what you called the World Religious Leader Conference out of a sense of obligation to the church. I felt a wound of shame as the most senior cardinal left behind from the college. I have always felt that God was more than the church's concept. It was not until hearing your message and the Secretary-General's vision that I realized I was at the conference because of destiny. Yes, Mr. Mallory, I accept the Secretary-General's offer. I will lead the world's first truly united religion, Interfaith."

Gabriella had witnessed numerous historic handshakes during her career, but this was the first that sent chills into her soul.

Evan said, "Great news. We can go over the specific details of your role in the coming days. Your first event will be an Interfaith conclave mass in St. Peter's Square in two days; the details will be provided ahead of the event."

Cardinal Conti asked, "What do you mean the details will be provided? Am I not now the leader of the Interfaith religion?"

Evan turned to Gabriella, Gemma, and Giuseppe. "Everyone, could you give Cardinal Conti and me a few moments alone?"

Giuseppe looked past Evan to discern the desires of the Cardinal.

Cardinal Conti replied to his friend and protector's questioning eyes, telling the man he would be fine. "*E, giusto, prego va il mio amico*,"

Gabriella could see Giuseppe's hesitance and the agitated look on Evan's face for all of them to depart. So, she spoke in Giuseppe's native Italian, assuring him of the Cardinal's safety. "*La su eminenza sara indennita, ci ha lasciati va.*"

Giuseppe turned and half-smiled at Gabriella. He then directed a heavily accented English warning to Evan. "If you harm him, you will not leave here alive."

❧

Evan produced a slight smile across his face. He then beckoned Cardinal Conti to join him near a lighted section of the cupola. Evan wanted to make sure that Conti did not lose sight of him as he conveyed the Prince of this World's message. "Cardinal Conti, let me make clear your conditions of employment as the face of the Interfaith religion. You're merely the spokesman and manage the daily ceremonial matters regarding the world's new faith. I am your source of power."

Evan began to chant in a primitive sounding language in front of the Cardinal, working himself into a deep trance, as a howling wind engulfed both men. "Now, witness and worship the power given to me."

Cardinal Conti cowered on the ground. "What is happening?"

From the wind, a sinister voice rose, "This is my chosen one's image-bearer, who I've given my spirit. Follow him and worship me, the Prince of this World, the true and living god."

Gabriella, Gemma, and Giuseppe heard what only could be described as animal growls and snarls at the bottom of the cupola. The group rushed back up the winding staircase to find a visibly shaken Cardinal Conti.

Giuseppe rushed to the Cardinal's side with his pistol drawn. "*La vostra eminenza, e voi giusto*!"

"I am fine, Giuseppe; I had my first encounter with the spirit of god, that is all. Mr. Mallory, I am in the Secretary-General's and your service."

An extremely confident Evan Mallory commanded, "Glad to know there are no questions. Ladies, let's go; our work is done here."

As Cardinal Conti waved goodbye to Gabriella and Gemma, they both gave each other a glance of concern as they left the Vatican, unsure whose work had been accomplished.

❧

Gabriella left the Vatican wondering what had occurred between Evan and Cardinal Conti and on whose behalf. The same feelings she got when in Draven's office she felt at the Vatican and now on the ride home, which scared her. Returning to the *Palazzo Caelum* campus seemed to take longer, and a sense of dread flooded her mind.

Gemma noticed Gabriella was visibly upset. "Are you okay?"

Gabriella replied, "Yes, I'm fine. I'm just tired; it's been a really long few days."

Evan countered as the vehicles arrived at the UE headquarters, "You should be invigorated. We are making the world a better place every day. Future generations will revere our leadership model."

Gabriella did not respond to Evan's declaration of the UE's greatness but instead continued looking out of her window. As the vehicles stopped at the grand entrance to the headquarters, Evan sprung from the car before the guards could open his door, causing Gemma and Gabriella to look at each other again in curiosity at the newfound pep that had overtaken Evan.

Gemma questioned, "I wonder what's gotten into him?"

Gabriella said, "I'm afraid to know."

A hesitant UE security guard hovered around the group of senior officials. "Ma'am, the Secretary-General wanted to see you upon your return in his office. Do you think you could pass that message to Deputy Mallory? He seemed in a hurry."

Gabriella brushed the young guard away with a quick, "Thanks."

Gemma took off her heels and walked toward the living quarters complex. "Well, I'll see you in the morning. I'm going to bed before someone asks for my services. Good luck, love."

Gabriella said, "Gemma, we need to talk."

Gemma responded without breaking stride. "We will tomorrow. Our apartment is 5C, and the door code is the last four digits of your employee number. Nighty-night."

Gabriella said, "Thanks."

Evan demanded, "Gabriella, let's go. Let's not keep the Secretary-General waiting."

Gabriella chose a non-verbal reply as she took more purposeful strides to close the gap between herself and Evan.

As he and Gabriella made their way to a bank of elevators that lead to the command floors, Evan gushed. "My spirit-guide has provided me the topic for tonight's meeting with Draven."

Gabriella sighed. "Yeah, I'm guessing it's about concluding the war. More importantly, I hope it doesn't take long; I'm exhausted."

Evan carried an edge in his tone. "Yes, the war is the obvious topic, but you have not seen the details I have seen. Tonight, you will understand the real power that flows between Draven and me."

Gabriella mused as the elevator doors closed. *I wonder what the name of that power is.*

Gabriella was glad that Draven was not in his office. She was not one for being sensational, but Draven's office had a darkness to it that seemed to live. It took another ten minutes—which at this hour felt like an eternity—for her and Evan to find the Secretary-General on the command center's main floor receiving an update from General Ahuja via teleconference.

"That's excellent news, General. I'm glad to see that Barnes and the Special Activities Unit is paying dividends. Look, Vivaan, I have pressing matters to attend here. Expect authorization to launch the attack as soon as the conditions are ripe," Draven ordered, as the massive screen went black before General Ahuja could respond.

In a better mood than expected for dark-thirty in the morning, Draven pronounced, "Ah, two of my most important senior staffers. I've been told by a trusted spiritual advisor that your expedition to the Vatican met with great success."

Evan said, "Cardinal Conti is as pliable as I hoped. He will serve us well."

Draven produced a wicked smile. "Evan, I can sense the trip was also very beneficial personally. We will talk about that more in private."

"However, I will not belabor the point—" Draven was cut off by Gabriella's loud yawn.

Evan mansplained, "Please excuse Gabriella's abruptness, sir. She does not share the strength our passion for peace provides and has been tired all evening."

Draven displayed an almost unnerving nonchalance as he discussed the inconvenience of having to wait to kill countless people. "Perk up, Gabriella; this will not take long. The bottom line is we have to delay the culmination of the war. Texas's weather is not conducive to releasing the agent, and the enemy has temporarily slowed my plans in China. We are shipping a replacement drone container as we speak from the Inverness laboratory to our forces in China."

Gabriella wanted to slap Draven again for using Pyretos but guessed that another outburst of such anger would not be as easy for Draven to dismiss.

Draven continued, "The only thing I require of you over the next week or so is intelligence updates on the locations of the resistance leaders, to include these religious fanatics leading these Christian rallies around the world. Consider this directive to be the opening of the Sentinel Program, as you will facilitate the unleashing of Pyretos on these contemptible enemies of peace."

Gabriella merely nodded, daring not to verbalize what would likely be one of the biggest mass murders in human history, given what she knew about Pyretos.

"One final intelligence challenge for you. Did Barnes meet with success in ridding the world of the Omega team?"

Through water-filled eyes, Gabriella answered, "All battle damage assessments and satellite collection of the former American site indicate the base was destroyed."

Draven relished the pain he saw his question brought Gabriella as he lit a cigar. "The lack of energy exuding from you is draining me. You're dismissed."

Afraid her anger would manifest into something more damaging to her position, Gabriella curtsied, "Thank you, sir."

The gesture drew an intense stare from Draven and a disappointed shaking of his head from Evan.

What is wrong with you, Gabriella, antagonizing a mad man willing to kill people indiscriminately? I need sleep, or I'm going to snap and get myself killed, she thought, walking to her office suite.

As Gabriella entered her office to close out a final update before heading to her apartment for some much-needed rest, tears flowed yet again. It was exhausting to pretend to support such suffering that the UE exacted. Gabriella felt alone fighting a battle she could not win, thoughts that brought on deep sobs. Honestly, Gabriella wanted to sleep so deep as to never awake to this nightmare again.

For the first time in weeks, she stared at her sophisticated mobile phone and decided to plug it in for a charge before settle down on her office sofa. Gabriella laughed at her attempt to change fate, hoping her friends would reach her, a thought that settled deep in her mind as sleep finally overtook her weary body.

CHAPTER 5

AS THE UE C-17 Globemaster's rear ramp dropped at Dallas-Fort Worth International Airport, a driving rainstorm greeted John Barnes, accompanied by the sounds of war and General Vivaan Ahuja. Barnes took the apathetic face of the General to be a living manifestation of his current surroundings.

Barnes yelled over the storm and roaring fighter jets racing toward unknown missions from the now militarized airport. His tone belied an expectation of receiving a commendation for his efforts. "Good afternoon, sir; as promised, I've delivered the drones."

General Ahuja remained short-tempered with Barnes on the brief ride to the converted Dallas-Fort Worth international airport passenger terminals. "I anticipated nothing less, as your failure would have been your demise. Your orders are to protect the drones until we launch our coordinated strike within the next ten days. A combination of weather and pressure being exerted by our American foes hinders the drones' employment here in Texas. The attack on your second element in China adds to the operational delay considering the loss of drone containers in the attack."

Barnes sighed as he watched the off-loading of two forty-foot shipping containers holding the UE's solution to quickly concluding the month-long war. "General Ahuja, why do we need to guard the drones? We have air superiority and control of the greater Dallas area."

General Ahuja derided Barnes. "Why am I not surprised by the lack of perspective in your question, Mr. Barnes? You, sir, are not the warrior-scholar that historically has filled the ranks of such select American special operations units you once were a member. Did you not hear anything? I said we are at war. Look around. The planes in the air, the facilities, and equipment, the people working here, including you and your team, are primarily Americans. Would you not agree? Therefore, anyone of the people you see could be working with the resistance. Stay alert, for failure will not be tolerated."

The Western Wall, colloquially known as the Wailing Wall, now served as the base of operations for the Two Witnesses and had become a site of mourning for all that dared threaten their lives. While General Havid had convinced the Israeli government to stay away from the men, the general public grew more enraged with their presence by the day. General Havid increasingly was torn between his love of country and declared love for Christ Jesus. The separation from his beloved homeland to focus on fighting Draven Cross was undeniable.

Jerusalem grew more debauched by the day, rivaling the carnality of famous hedonistic cities around the world. The general was not naïve. Tel Aviv and even Jerusalem always had their seedy underbellies. However, now brazen advertisements for adult entertainment, prostitution, and anything that brought instant gratification to one's senses were everywhere, and it sickened him. The only pleasure General Havid found, beyond studying the Bible, was listening daily to the Two Witnesses for the Kingdom of God.

As the general sat in his office working past nine at night, he wondered when these men ate, drank, or slept. The general chuckled that something so fundamental to the human experience had escaped his observation of the Two Witnesses for this long. It was in this moment of thought on God's Witnesses that his eyes were "opened." The two men had moved to a stone archway at the northern end of the Western Wall plaza and were speaking to a third man, who provided the men bread and water.

"Get me the park police now; some fanatic has gotten too close to the Two Witnesses!" General Havid screamed into his intercom, alerting his assistant.

The general ran out to his assistant's desk, snatching the phone handset from him to hear firsthand how someone had breached the inner cordon surrounding the men.

"This is Minister Havid, explain to me—" He was cut off by the apparent shocking answer from the park police officer at the site.

"What do you mean they are talking to the air and eating and drinking? I'm watching the men on my screen speaking with a third man." The general barked as he gestured for his assistant to bring up the security feed on the office lobby's adjacent monitors.

"Sir, I respectfully think you need to get some sleep. Those two men are talking to themselves and eating; it's likely someone threw the food at them earlier," General Havid's aide asserted.

General Havid felt foolish until the calming voice of the Holy Spirit spoke within his heart, "*They cannot see because they do not believe these men represent the God of Israel. Let this sight bring peace to your soul.*"

"Praise to God, like the servant of the Prophet Elisha, I was blind, but now I can see," the general said, hanging up on the likely confused park police officers.

"Are you okay, sir? Should I call your driver to take you home?" the concerned assistant questioned.

"I'm fine, my young friend, and yes, please send for my driver," General Havid responded to the wide-eyed young man. Under his breath, the general mumbled, "I long to get home to praise God for what I've seen."

As the first rays of a new day broke through Christopher's window, he got dressed, donning one of the heavy jackets Ranger Stinson provided the men to brave the cold embrace of the Alaskan morning on the front porch of the cabin. He felt a strong urge to reach out to God—his new friend and old foe—for guidance. The backdrop of God's majestic handiwork in the Alaskan wilderness seemed like the best setting.

Christopher sought the God of the Universe for the first time in a long time. "Dear Lord, I am grateful that I can reach out to you now and not feel shame or anger. I am asking for your guidance on where my life should go. How should I serve you now?"

Heaven's response was as gentle as a distant bird's song. For the first time since the fateful Afghanistan mission months ago, Christopher heard the familiar still, quiet voice that had tormented him and now brought comfort: The Holy Spirit.

He smiled as the Spirit of God spoke into his heart. *"Ask, and it will be given to you; seek, and you will find; knock, and the door will be opened to you. For everyone who asks receives; the one who seeks finds; and to the one who knocks, the door will be opened."*

"I am sorry, Lord; I am so new to following Your lead. I ask You to guide the men that follow me. Make our paths clear," Christopher pleaded.

"If any of you lacks wisdom, you should ask God, who gives generously to all without finding fault, and it will be given to you," came the response of the Holy Spirit to Christopher.

Christopher opened his eyes, trying to understand the message that was being written on his heart. He believed that the answer was when he needed something or felt unsure, ask God, and He would help him. "Thank you, Lord, for never giving up on me."

As he stepped out on the porch, nursing a steaming cup of black coffee, Jackson asked, "Who are you thanking out here?"

Christopher shot back. "I was thanking my newfound savior for helping me answer a question."

Jackson teased. "I might be a monkey's uncle because I am still shocked—grateful—but shocked you are talking to my God."

Christopher said, "As hairy as you are, I have zero doubts you're part animal. And God is for everyone. If you wanted to be useful, you could have brought me some coffee. I'm glad to see you're off the crutches and spry this morning."

Jackson snickered. "My hairy body is the definition of manliness, first off. Secondly, you can get your own coffee; remember not getting me a plate of breakfast back in D.C. I remember things when it comes to food, college boy."

Christopher said, "I offered you a plate; look, we need to get going."

Jimbo interrupted the conversation, "You're right; we do need to get going. It's already ten in the morning."

Christopher said, "Good morning, Jimbo. I need to grab a few things, and we can head out."

Jackson called out to Christopher, "Hey, wait, you'll never believe who's calling me right now. You're going to want to hear this phone call."

ᯓ

As Gabriella worked late into the Italian evening in her executive office suite, pouring herself into finding ways to mitigate the harm Draven sought every day, she pondered over the one person she trusted and valued now that her closest friends were gone: Gemma. Gabriella wanted to assure Gemma she was fighting for the side of good.

Since Gabriella ended her day with deep sleep in her office, she was grateful that the sofa bed was more comfortable than it appeared. The quick and heavy raps of a worried Gemma, searching for Gabriella after not finding her in their shared apartment, had roused her to this new day. The more she thought about her relationship with Gemma, the more it resonated that the two of them defined an odd couple. While intellectually astute, Gemma seemed at odds with her mind and rational nature, resisting her intellect. Instead, she accentuated the stunning physical attributes that graced her. Many were quick to dismiss Gemma as beauty without brains, a superficiality of modern society that Gabriella fought against rather than exploiting. Gabriella was keenly aware that men and women considered her physical looks appealing. Still, it had always been her razor-sharp mind and intellect that she wanted to be known for, rather than her genetics.

Like Gabriella, Gemma had grown up in a family where at least one parent was a Christian, but both women abandoned the faith in their teenage years. However, Gemma had expressed a growing interest in discovering who God was in their lives, especially in light of whom their mutual boss potentially represented. Gabriella secretly hoped that Gemma would help her move from accepting God was real to—as Jackson said—having a relationship with God. The thought of seeking God and Jackson's intense passion for describing Draven Cross as the Antichrist led her to pick up and turn on her phone for the first time in weeks. She had two missed calls from Jackson.

She couldn't believe her eyes. Gabriella ran to the elevator as quickly as possible, hitting the ground floor and rushing out of the building. She glanced around to make sure no one was near her in the spacious but empty and useless headquarters parking lot before quickly pressing the call button on her display. The distinctive southern twang of Jackson's hello, caused tears to fill her hazel eyes, and emotions invaded her soul she thought had died.

Gabriella sniveled as she began a phone conversation that was only a dream moments ago. "Jackson, is this really you? I thought you were dead."

Jackson responded, "I thought you were dead."

Gabriella challenged, "You thought I was dead? Why didn't you call me?"

Jackson sighed. "We tried to call you but never got through. Plus, Christopher and I barely survived an avalanche in Alaska."

Gabriella said, "An avalanche? I guess that's a good excuse."

Jackson smarted off, "Yeah, Ms. Sassy, an avalanche. I'm more disappointed you didn't even call to confirm we were dead."

Gabriella said, "Whatever, Jackson, you need to get over it; I've missed your snarky attitude. Is Chris alive?"

Christopher jumped into the conversation now on speaker, "Yeah, I'm alive and trying to keep this crusty old man named Jackson alive despite his best efforts to die."

Jackson laughed. "Look who's talking? You should have seen him, Gabriella. He was a Popsicle."

Gabriella didn't try to hide her relief. "Hi, Chris, I cannot tell you how good your voices sound. Where are you guys?"

Both men answered, "Alaska."

"Still?"

Jackson asked Gabriella to repeat what she had said. "Hey, you're breaking up badly. I think we're losing you."

Gabriella agreed, "Yeah, I realize you're breaking up. The UE will have a fix soon."

Christopher asked, "How are things going working for Draven?"

Gabriella rolled her eyes. "Where do I start? Well, I slapped him."

Jackson howled with laughter. "I told you she's a firecracker. I would have paid a lot of money to have seen that."

Gabriella giggled. "I thought he killed you; it was the least I could do to him. He has decimated the world. President Rodgers's ill-fated rebellion against the UE is all but defeated. America took it on the chin; I'm afraid home will never be the same. Draven ordered multiple nukes against the US, and the final troops loyal to America are about to face a terrible bioweapon called Pyretos."

Both men asked, "What's Pyretos?"

Gabriella explained, "It's a tailor-made bioweapon that Draven designed at one of his laboratories years ago, for an unknown state actor, but never delivered. Draven plans to use the bioweapon weapon to end the rebellion, ensuring Draven's control of the world."

Jackson took control of the phone again. "We're heading out today to my homestead in Alabama to resupply and try to figure out where we can best be a thorn in Draven's side."

Gabriella wondered. "Alabama, huh? Well, I understand, and I think I can help direct you in being useful against Draven; more to follow. Be safe, guys, bye."

Gabriella nearly collapsed on the concrete into the small pool of tears that formed during the conversation. Knowing that Christopher and Jackson were alive gave her new energy; she had her purpose. A team started to develop that she could use to fight Draven.

ক

Jackson and Christopher high-fived each other after ending the call with Gabriella. Given the past few months of low points, the men were riding a wave of events worth celebrating, none perhaps bigger than Christopher's salvation, but hearing Gabriella's voice was a close second.

Jackson couldn't wipe the smile from his face. "Man, I knew that sassy Gabby was still alive. I could feel it in my bones, and she slapped the devil. That little lady is a firecracker."

Christopher remarked, "Sassy Gabby and little lady, huh? You know she would slap you into next week if she heard you."

Jackson laughed. "Ah, I would take a slap in the face to see that little firecracker. Let's get going. Based on Gabriella's description of what's happening down south, we need to get to my homestead in Alabama tonight."

Jimbo said, "Ranger Stinson, could you join us out here for a moment before you run us down to the helipad?"

As Ranger Stinson came out to the station's front porch, the men formed a circle holding hands. Each nodding to Jimbo to lead them in prayer, ahead of another trek into the unknown.

Jimbo prayed, "Dear heavenly Father, we come to You as humble servants in this time of tribulation. Thank You for watching over, Gabriella. Lord, we ask that You lead her in Your path, and You shield her from the attacks of the adversary. May she serve Your purpose and bring glory to the Kingdom of Jesus Christ in her position. Thank You for accepting Christopher into Your eternal family; give him the strength to lead us in the days ahead. Father, we thank You for our new Brother-in-Christ, James Stinson. Bless him and protect him in the dark days ahead. Lastly, Father, we seek Your provision, grace, and mercy as we embark on confronting Your enemy and protecting Your children."

As the men loaded into Ranger Stinson's vehicle to take them to the former government black-site helipad, Jackson prayed *2 Samuel 22:3-4* over the men from Rev's tabbed Bible, *"My God is my rock, in whom I take refuge, my shield and the horn of my salvation. He is my stronghold, my refuge, and my savior—from violent people, You save me. I called to the Lord, who is worthy of praise and have been saved from my enemies."*

Jimbo excitedly announced. "Amen, brother."

Jackson worried about the older James Stinson alone in the remote Alaskan wilderness. It seemed not enough to say thank you for all the man had done for them. "James, are you going to be okay out here by yourself? You could come with us."

Ranger Stinson laughed. "As much as I would've loved to be in the service like you young men when I was your age, my asthma stopped that dream; now I would be even less useful. I'll be fine out here. The park service always had a hard time filling this post. Takes a certain type to live out here, and I'm that type. You guys have given me a new lease on life, now knowing Christ Jesus. Other people need you and your unique talents."

Jackson, Jimbo, and Christopher all smiled and nodded at the strength of James Stinson.

Jackson turned to Jimbo as he watched him climb into the tracked snow vehicle with his one good arm. "Are you sure you're good to go? I mean, you only got one good tree branch or arm, as you call them. I can't take any more helicopter crashes."

Jimbo laughed. "No worries, man, I could fly with no arms."

Jackson replied, "Let's not try that."

Christopher encouraged the care for others Jackson always displayed. "Get in, Jackson. Oh, and know that Rev would be proud of his legacy living through you."

Jackson replied, "Thanks. It's time to start hunting bad guys again, but now, in service of God versus our country."

Christopher said, "I hope so."

~

Draven hadn't slept deeply since the disappearances over a year ago. He was powered by the thoughts that regularly filled his mind from the Prince of this World. His spiritual guide had always been a part of his life, providing advice during crucial business junctures or insight into a rival; the permeating presence of this powerful force helped him dominate in all aspects of life. So, he was not surprised to find himself working through the night for days on end, only to be given a new mission by his mysterious master.

"Bring your image-bearer before my sigil; I will empower you to give him the ability to perform wonders and signs before the world. He will draw many to me. You will use him to demonstrate my power before the world soon," came the clear message of the Prince of This World into Draven's thoughts.

Draven replied into the void before him, as if an entity were with him, "Yes, my lord. I live to serve you."

He dialed Evan's office suite. "Evan, on your feet and in my office in the next ten minutes. It's time to bring you and my plans for this world to the next level."

~

CHAPTER 6

AS JACKSON SAT up front in the technological marvel known as the SHADOW jet with Charlie Smith, a tightness rose in his legs up to his broad shoulders as he helped guide the final approach onto the dirt road landing strip that bounded his family homestead in Dallas County, Alabama. He was home, and of all the places in the world, this place pushed him all over the emotional map.

Charlie communicated into Jackson's radio headset, "I'm going to circle the strip a couple of times. I don't want to be caught off guard by any surprises that might be hiding." Charlie banked the jet low over the silty Alabama River, which served as the southeast border for Jackson's property. He scanned the hard-packed dirt landing strip from about a hundred feet off the ground, showing his skill as a pilot. The automated ground proximity warning was blaring a repeated message that imminent death was near, urging Charlie to pull up. "I don't see any trouble, but I can't be sure. I want you to be prepared to give me full reverse thrust when we touch down, pull back on"—Charlie tapped the two thrust controls in the sea of levers and buttons in the cockpit— "and I will keep her straight."

Now, fixated on the small cabin and barn that he knew like the back of his hand, Jackson didn't even respond to Charlie.

As Charlie pulled the SHADOW back above clouds to make sure he gave himself enough altitude and distance to make the approach just in case he missed something. Charlie told Jimbo and Christopher in the back to buckle up and hold tight.

Charlie quizzed the distracted Jackson. "You ready? Remember to pull on those thrust levers when I give you the word."

Jackson quipped, "About as ready as I am before a colon screening, but let's get down there."

Laughing, Charlie said, "Okay, be ready to adjust that thrust."

As the jet descended through the gray cloudbank again surrounding the homestead, the automated flight computer voice called out the altitude.

Jackson gripped the thruster tight as the wheels bounced off the Alabama clay waiting for Charlie's order.

Charlie yelled as the SHADOW lurched sideways, blowing dust down the road. "Hit it, Jackson."

Jackson slammed the thrust control into full reverse, and the pitch of the engines matched his actions.

As he gained more control of the jet and applied the brakes, Charlie ordered, "Okay, ease the thrust up."

Charlie shouted with beads of sweat lining his forehead, "where can I park this tough old bird?"

Jackson answered, "That big metal shed at the end of the strip will have to do."

Charlie added, "It looks like a five-star hotel to me."

Jackson felt the painful memories of his childhood rising within him as Charlie taxied the SHADOW near the place he had spent hours longing to escape. Now, this place of torment was an oasis in the storm facing him and his friends.

∽

The illumination pouring into John Barnes's room startled him out of restless sleep. As Barnes opened the blinds in an office that had been converted into his sleeping quarters, the sun played hide and seek amongst clouds over the DFW runways. The last ten days had been miserable, with rain and strong winds preventing the American rebels' final strike.

Barnes hoped he would get the call from General Ahuja that today would be the day to end the war. He started to get dressed to make his way to the warehouse, where the drones loaded with Pyretos were stored.

Barnes wanted to make sure everything was ready to go; if the mission failed, he did not want the blame.

So when Barnes finally reached the storage warehouse, he was disappointed to find the general already inspecting the drones.

General Ahuja chided, "I see you slept in today, Mr. Barnes. Why doesn't this surprise me? Frankly, I am more astonished that you did not find some manner of debauchery to undertake to pass the time."

Barnes shot back, "Sir, I think you underestimate my dedication to my work."

"Oh, I clearly understand your psychopathic tendencies and bloodthirst, but professionalism is not a part of your genetic makeup. In any case, the weather seems to be moving toward favorable conditions for our final strike. I see you and your goons managed not to damage the drones. I expect you to flight test them to ensure their readiness and be prepared for the order to strike the Americans to come at any moment. Frankly, I can't wait to leave this uncivilized land you called home," General Ahuja uttered as he left the warehouse with his aide.

Barnes swore and kicked a bucket full of rainwater, embarrassed and mad at being belittled. The bucket that had served the purpose of catching the torrents that had pelted the airfield for the past week, as water poured across the floor. He pulled out his phone and called his men. "Hey, get up and meet me in the warehouse. We need to start prepping the drones. It looks like today might be the day."

As Evan entered Draven's office, he was overcome by the same power that had invaded him on St. Peter's Basilica's cupola.

Standing between the sizeable wrought iron sculpture on his wall and his office door, Draven called Evan forward, "Come and kneel before the Sigil of the Light Bearer. It's time for me to empower you for the journey ahead. It's time for the world to marvel over me."

Evan exclaimed, "I remain committed to serving you."

Draven chanted, "You will serve me as I serve the Prince of This World. I give you the power to cause wonders and signs from the heavens.

You will have the ability to mystify people and draw them to me. You will proclaim my greatness until our master rules the universe."

Draven continued, "On your feet, old boy. Here's what we need to do in the next few hours. First, get that puppet of yours, Cardinal Conti, ready to hold his first 'mass' in St. Peter's Square. This will be the stage for your first global performance with your newfound power. I expect a wonder that makes the world forget those two old fools in Jerusalem. I plan to send Ahuja word to execute the Pyretos strike in both the United States and China tomorrow in conjunction with your St. Peter's affair. The Australian and European conspirator leaders' death penalties will also be carried out tomorrow, headlining the Interfaith mass. In the announcement, you will characterize the men as Christian terrorists, stuck in the past."

Evan gushed. "I understand, sir, and will make all you desire a reality."

Draven said, "Excellent, I am glad to see your new spirit is finally making you worthwhile. Now leave me."

❧

Apartment 5C in the UE housing complex was more like a townhouse than an apartment. Gabriella discovered that Gemma and her each had their own level of living area with the second level of the "apartment," serving as a communal area with a living room and kitchen. It was on a plush sectional that Gabriella found Gemma still up watching a British melodrama rerun.

Gabriella teased Gemma. "I see you've made yourself at home. You're even watching sappy British dramas in sweat pants. What, no ice cream?"

Gemma giggled. "Oh, shut it. I was glad to find that the telly worked, and I do have a bowl of crisps if you would fancy any."

Gabriella dug into the bowl of potato chips. "Yeah, I heard that the CubeSat launch was successful earlier today. Hence the reason your streaming service is working, among other technologies."

Gemma turned off the television. "Well, tomorrow will be a dark day, I'm afraid. We're going to need some ice cream or at least a good Chardonnay to take the edge off what's coming."

Gabriella jested. "What's on your mind, Gemma? Why is tomorrow going to be any worse than any other day so far? I mean, really, today was the worst day of my life only because yesterday is over and tomorrow is not here yet."

Gemma squeezed a pillow tightly while staring off into the fancy apartment, seemingly ignoring Gabriella's request for information.

Gabriella's intelligence training kicked in, realizing that the apartment, like her office, was likely wired to record sound at a minimum and likely video as well, as she stared at the blue LED-bezel of a nearby smart speaker.

Gabriella asked, "Do you want to take a walk? I need some fresh air. A walk will help you feel better."

"What?" A wide-eyed Gemma seemed to take a minute to interpret what Gabriella was offering. "I guess so."

Gemma and Gabriella stepped out into the cool evening breeze and were provided a rare treat, a star-filled sky. Rome had so few ambient light sources working at night that the light pollution didn't overwhelm the stars anymore, reminding both women of how beauty and sorrow were often side by side.

Gabriella started the conversation. "Gemma, we need to be careful about what we say in our apartments and offices. At the minimum, we should assume they're wired for sound—potentially video."

Gabriella pressed. "Now, please tell me what you know. Look, we're both going to go through tomorrow together, so out with it, okay."

Gemma said, "Draven ordered the conclusion of the war for tomorrow; he's using some sort of special weapon. I think that's code for he's going to drop more nuclear weapons on America and China."

Gabriella tensed. "It won't be nuclear weapons but a bioweapon named Pyretos. The attacks that Draven has done and is planning, like this bioweapon, are reasons I push to try to stop him. I know you care about me and please know I care about you. I want you to understand that I'm not finding people for Draven to slaughter, no matter what he says. In fact, I was able to help people through a resistance group in China. I plan to find others like them across the globe. Please tell me you understand what I'm doing?"

Gemma said, "I won't pretend I understand the feelings that are driving you to do what you're doing. That phone call where Draven ordered those men you captured to die was terrible. I lost sleep thinking about how you were changing and helping Draven be a monster. I believe you, but I still feel you're reckless. Draven will kill you when he finds out you're betraying him."

Gabriella couldn't argue with that. "He won't find out. You've said it yourself; he's a monster, and I won't sit back and help him kill innocent people. Also, understand, I did not capture those men. The main resistance group in China captured them to protect Christians. It's complicated, Gemma, but believe me, I am on the side of good."

Gemma said, "I trust you, but please be careful. It doesn't sound like you're dealing with the nicest people."

"Kerim is the leader in China, and while he is as tough as they come, he is a good man who I trust. Look, I need some rest. I'm heading out tomorrow for the States. I want to get a network set up there, if possible."

Gemma stopped walking. "Why so soon, Gabriella? You've only been back here a week. Plus, the attack will happen tomorrow. You could end up in the crossfire."

Gabriella walked back to Gemma. "This is for the best. I'm going to Seattle, hoping to find a resistance leader Kerim relayed to me. Based on what I know, Seattle's already in UE control, so I should be fine. I'll be careful, okay. I know what I am doing."

Gabriella could see, even in the low light of the UE housing complex, Gemma wasn't sure she did know what she was doing. Gabriella wasn't going to defend her actions further as she didn't want to fight with her friend.

As both women entered their shared townhome, they paused on the central staircase that led down to Gemma's level or up to Gabriella's.

Gemma said, "Thanks again for the walk; I'm sure it was a lifesaver."

Gabriella smiled. "No worries, have a good night. I think I'll try to reach a couple of friends now that the internet is more stable. I'll see you in the morning before I leave."

Gabriella wanted to send an encrypted message to Christopher and

Jackson because if anybody could slow down Draven's use of Pyretos, it would be them.

⸙

Now that the SHADOW was in the shed, Charlie inspected the jet to ensure the rough landing did not cause damage. At the same time, Christopher, Jackson, and Jimbo started to offload their gear.

Since Jackson's surroundings left him soaking in his tormented past, he left Christopher and the one-armed Jimbo doing the heavy lifting. The homestead was a place that Jackson did not visit often; it had become a storage area for supplies if things turned for the worst in the country. He laughed with the thought of how bad things had become in America, forcing him to use the homestead as a doomsday hideout. Jackson's phone vibrated, interrupting his thoughts.

Jackson tossed his communicator to Christopher. "Here catch; it's little miss trouble. I need a minute. I've already authenticated the message."

"Hey, you okay?" Christopher's question chased a non-responsive Jackson.

Christopher watched Jackson walk toward a well-worn trailhead that led down to the river. While worried about Jackson, Gabriella's message concerned him more.

> The message read, *"Hello, guys. I wanted to give you an update on what's going on around you, thanks to Draven. Tomorrow at some point, he's going to unleash a biological weapon named Pyretos that is lethal and contagious. Once the American and Chinese dissidents are eliminated, Draven will have complete control over the world. He plans to appoint ten regional ambassadors loyal to him and his plans. I recommend you get out of Alabama as fast as possible. We need to stop Draven's ability to use this bioweapon in the future. The lab with the source files and material is in Inverness, Scotland. You guys might want to plan a visit there and make sure it doesn't work as a lab in the future. Okay, it's late here, and tomorrow will be a day of days, I am sure. Be careful."*

Jimbo read Gabriella's message and came to the same conclusions as Christopher. Draven's biological program should be destroyed, and staying in Alabama would be shorter than planned.

Jimbo questioned. "Where will we go, considering America is quickly becoming dangerous?"

Christopher exclaimed, "I don't know for sure. Israel is the only safe haven that comes to mind that serves all our needs. General Havid has enough power to keep us undercover and resourced for our fight against Draven, at least for now. I'll call him."

Charlie said, joining the two other men. "Hey, guys, the plane's in good shape. We'll be able to get out of here whenever needed."

Christopher said, "That's good to know, Charlie, because we may need to leave as soon as tonight. I am going to go check on Jackson. We will meet you guys at the cabin soon."

Christopher found Jackson, skipping rocks like a little boy across the smooth flowing Alabama River. Two gravestones along the riverbank not far from Jackson read, "Thomas Jackson Williams III" and "Shelia Jean Williams."

Christopher prodded, hoping to get a snarky remark back. "What's on your mind, old man?"

Jackson kept skipping rocks, ignoring Christopher. Christopher could tell he had been crying as his face was wet and red.

Christopher remained silent, afraid to push his friend, and instead decided to join him in skipping rocks. Years had passed since Christopher skipped a stone, and his technique was off, causing him to create big splashes with each rock thrown.

Jackson chided, looking over at his battle buddy. "I should have known you skip rocks like a college boy. Let me guess. You played inside with your video games all day, didn't you?"

Christopher shot back. "Easy now, I need to warm up."

Throwing a handful of rocks into the river, Jackson said, "This was one of Sarah's favorite places. Can you imagine that? I remember bringing her back here to meet my mom. We sat here one night, and she was impressed as all get out by lightning bugs. God, I miss that woman."

"Lighting bugs, huh?"

Jackson turned to Christopher with a scowl. "Really, after I poured my heart out, you only focus on me saying lighting bugs?"

Patting Jackson on his back, Christopher said, "I'm joking, brother. I can only guess what this place does to you emotionally. I know you miss Sarah and your girls, your mom. Those folks would want you to remember the good times and not walk around miserable. Look, Jimbo, Charlie, and I are grateful that you opened up your childhood home for our safety. Know we all care about you."

Jackson turned and embraced his brother-in-combat. "Thanks, bro. I'm grateful you've got my back."

Christopher hugged him back. "I've got some bad news too; that message from Gabriella was trouble. We need to get to Israel and fast."

As the men walked in the fading sun toward the cabin, Jackson said, "Why I am I not surprised that Gabriella is sending trouble our way. But seriously, man, thanks for checking on me. This is a tough place to be right now. I think about my mama and the sorry cuss of a daddy I had, and all sorts of feelings are pushing up in me. Let's get up to the cabin and get started loading up some tools to fight that devil named Draven; if I stay down here, I might lose my mind."

Evan awaited the moment to send General Ahuja the approval to employ Pyretos ending the World War. His attention now shifted to his second major initiative for the day, the Interfaith conclave, which was off and running. Evan turned the television to ANN, propping his feet up on Cardinal Conti's office desk, or as Conti referred to himself the Pontiff of Interfaith, as the breaking news announcement rolled across the screen.

The Rome ANN desk anchor announced, "We apologize for interrupting the scheduled programming, but we have received word from UE headquarters that two of the masterminds behind the war former American President Rodgers started are about to be punished for their crimes against humanity. We have field reporters in both Sydney and Brussels. First, to Sydney and ANN reporter Maggie Waller. Can you tell us the mood there amongst the citizens as the former Prime Minister has been convicted and sentenced to death?"

Maggie Waller took over the broadcast. "Yes, we witnessed massive rallies here today. Thousands have taken to the streets, and there have been a few violent clashes between the supporters of the former Prime Minister and pro-UE groups. There are loud chants of praise for Secretary-General Cross and his message of universal peace. Police had to barricade off the Queen Victoria Building, and tear gas and rubber bullets were used to disperse protesters attempting to storm the building. The scene is relatively calm now as the execution will soon occur in front of the Queen Victoria Building, with thousands here and millions across Australia watching the event. Overall, the majority is pleased to see justice levied against those responsible for so much suffering in the world. It's a bit unusual to hold an execution in public and at night. However, those facts have not diminished the crowd."

The Rome ANN desk anchor volleyed the report to the next location. "Now over to Kris Peeters in Brussels."

Kris Peeters's smooth voice contrasted with chaos behind him. "Here in Brussels, the crowd continues to build in Grand-Place. Tear gas fills the air, and police sirens have been blaring all day across the capital city. The security forces have barricaded the gallows from the masses here. We will not speak the name of the NATO leaders who aided in starting this war, but let me bring in a young man to help give you an understanding of the atmospherics here.

"Sir, please tell me your thoughts on this historic moment."

The camera panned to a twenty-something man, speaking in a strong Flemish-Dutch accent. The man wore a Guy Fawkes mask and a black hoodie and yelled into the camera, "My name is Alexandre Janssens. Today these rich criminals will die; tomorrow should be the Two Witnesses in Jerusalem, so the world can have peace. Long-live Draven Cross!"

The Rome ANN desk anchor took over. "Well, there you have it from Kris Peeters in Brussels and Maggie Waller in Australia. We now return you to the live coverage of the first Interfaith conclave and mass at St. Peter's Square."

Evan turned the TV off, ready to woo the world for Draven.

In response to his late-night call to religious leaders worldwide, the early afternoon turnout left Evan impressed. Several leaders in the immediate region had flown overnight to be at St. Peter's Square by 2 p.m. Others joined countless numbers watching the event live via ANN. Draven demanded that no television coverage be given to the warzones or the Two Witnesses in Jerusalem during the event.

Pontiff Conti wore a purple papal miter adorned with a golden Interfaith insignia, an amalgamation of all the world's major religious symbols. His robe was purple, red, green, and trimmed in gold. As Evan watched the self-righteous man make his way along a security fence separating him from the tens of thousands gathered in the square, blessing people and kissing babies, it only confirmed Evan's view of the cardinal as a pompous peacock that would do whatever he was told, provided Conti's pride was boosted. He reached into his suit jacket and touched the speech Draven had directed for Cardinal Conti. Evan smiled with the thought the egotistical cardinal did not yet understand how little control he had in the situation.

Evan moved to the dais placed in front of St. Peter's column-lined facade, awaiting Conti to join him and several other religious and political leaders. Just as Conti arrived at the top of the stairs and moved toward the podium to speak, Evan stopped him. He pulled the prepared remarks from his suit and handed the document to a confused-looking Conti.

Conti asked, "What is this?"

"This is your introductory speech. Surely, you didn't think we would allow you to speak freely at such a critical moment. You will introduce me and then the Secretary-General. I have something special for the crowd."

Evan directed Conti to the microphone. "Ladies and Gentlemen, it is with great pleasure that I bring forward the Interfaith founder and a man endowed with the very essence of the supreme power of this universe, Mr. Evan Mallory."

Evan watched with joy as Conti seethed with anger reading the canned speech. Evan smiled as Conti was portrayed to the world as a master of ceremonies rather than an exalted religious leader.

As Evan moved to the podium, ten large copper cisterns were placed between the security gate holding back the masses and the platform with the world's newest leaders containing logs. Each cistern was filled with water until it overflowed and ran around St. Peter's Square. He chanted, and the sky grew dark with thick clouds. Lights emanated from them as he commanded the darkness that seemed to live in the blackened sky, "Oh you chief of princes, the angel of light, I command fire to consume this offering to you."

Ten fireballs fell from the clouds and consumed every ounce of water in or around the cisterns, leaving no trace of wood. Some in the square shrieked in horror, and panic rose from the throngs of people in attendance.

Evan stopped them in their tracks. "Silence! And do not be afraid. Blessed are you who have seen this event, but higher are those who did not see it today and will believe. Now, place your trust in the power that guides our leader, Draven Cross." With that, Evan grew weak, and two security guards rushed to help him into his seat as the sky returned near-instantaneously to brilliant blue.

Conti resumed his hosting duties as Evan was overcome by his spiritual spectacle. "We are fortunate to have witnessed the real power of this universe. Our future is bright in the hands of the Secretary-General and Deputy Secretary-General Mallory. Today is a great day for all of humanity. I am joined on the dais by leaders of all of the former major religions. Here at the center of one of those great religions, Christianity, we take the first of many steps of uniting the world's religions under one banner, led by Secretary-General Cross. In the days to come, you will see more initiatives from the Interfaith religion. It is my great pleasure to introduce the man of the hour: Secretary-General Cross."

The crowd erupted as Draven Cross joined the dais leaders, purposefully walking out of one of the cathedral's gated entrances to ensure his presence was the most prominent. Draven walked down the platform's steps toward the security gate, waving to the crowd as a conquering hero. Many in the crowd held signs aloft proclaiming Draven as the savior of the world and the man of peace. His image was magnified for the world on a live feed and large screen in St. Peter's Square.

Draven greeted the assembled leaders and flashed a brilliant white smile to the cameras before speaking, "Ladies and gentlemen of this united global community, I want to be the first to welcome you to the beginning of the new era of peace and prosperity for our world. As I promised at the start of this terrible war, brought on by the greed of the former American president, I would end this dreadful outbreak of violence. Today, I keep that promise after three months of worldwide death and destruction. I now direct your attention to the large screens around the square. Please watch the demise of two of the men behind this global tragedy."

With Draven's words, the entire world was allowed to witness two former global leaders' executions. As their bodies dangled between the gallows and the ground, gasps and brief screams came from a few in the crowd drowned out as the majority gave a loud cheer to the macabre scene.

The video monitors in St. Peter's Square returned to Draven's beaming face. "Now, with that unpleasant bit of business out of the way, we can celebrate. Today, here at the center of one of humanity's greatest religions, we bring together all the world's faiths. In the years to come, you will be able to tell your children and grandchildren that you witnessed the true spirit of religion which has lived within us since the dawn of time. Go in peace and be encouraged by all you have seen and heard today."

Draven approached Evan Mallory, who had recovered as he walked off the dais to an awaiting car. "Evan, send word to Ahuja to execute the final strike. I want this war done today."

John Barnes was anxious for his role in ending the war. He had gone over the plans for releasing the drones with both the element under his command at DFW and the remainder of the SAG team in China several times. Like yesterday, the new day's dawning looked promising as a sunny morning greeted Barnes's walk to the warehouse for mission preparation.

Barnes's men had the drones lined up and dispenser tanks filled with

Pyretos attached. He was thankful that his crew was as motivated to move from under General Ahuja's dictatorial thumb.

Barnes addressed his team, "Alright, we should get the order to launch at any moment. I want to run these things through one final dress rehearsal. It's the only way I will know if all systems are a go."

"Yes, sir," came the mechanical response from two SAG soldiers who moved to the drone flight control computer terminals under Barnes's watchful eyes.

The SAG team watched as fifty of the unmanned death machines went through their pre-flight checks. The *Shiva's* had an airframe the size of a child's battery-powered, ride-on toy popular in Barnes's youth when the machine's hinged wings folded. However, as the wheels deployed from each drone's airframe, the operators maneuvered the aircraft out onto the tarmac to achieve the craft's full wingspan.

As Barnes was about to give the order for a test flight, he noticed an approaching SUV, which signaled General Ahuja's arrival. He watched as the general and two aides got out of the vehicle and ardently strode toward the group.

General Ahuja said, "Gentlemen, the word to commence the final strike is expected at any moment. Barnes, are you ready to execute your duties?"

Barnes replied, "Yes, sir. The China team is ready and awaiting the order to strike, and we were planning a final flight run."

General Ahuja commented, "Well, get on with it. I want to make sure your failure does not reflect on my leadership."

Barnes ignored the slight and ordered the two drone operators to conduct the same practice program they had executed yesterday.

General Ahuja and the SAG soldiers watched as the drones, in two, twenty-five element flocks, rose all at once, in a vertical take-off configuration. Once they reached the designated flight altitude, the drones were visible against the blue sky only by their underbodies glowing different hues, like shimmering candy sprinkles against the endless blue sky. The two flocks hovered for a second, where the different shades of the fifty individual drones merged into two colors: red and blue. Then like a gaggle of geese migrating, the aircraft darted westward with the red flock in the lead and the blue flock following.

General Ahuja wondered aloud. "Impressive. These machines have replicated nature with such precision. They are moving like birds or locust riding the wind, it seems."

The *Shiva's* danced across the sky above DFW as if looking for a place to rest.

Barnes agreed, "Yes, sir. They are now synced to operate as two independent swarms. Each drone will update the others in the flock continuously over a target location, not only of where they are in respect to each other but also ruthlessly interrogating the environment to ensure all targeting metrics are achieved."

General Ahuja dismissed Barnes as his phone rang. "Yes, sir, it's my pleasure."

The general covered the phone call with Draven. "Mr. Barnes, provide those drones and your team in China the targeting data. We have been given the command to end this war."

General Havid sat in his home office on a bright, cloudless winter afternoon, deciding to work from home instead of his office, when his aide broke the solitude the general had been enjoying.

"Sir, you must listen to the Two Witnesses latest announcement," the aide said, as he grabbed a remote off the general's desk, turning on the wall-mounted television.

There was a rumble outside as if thunder approached. A shadow moved through the previously sunlight-drenched office.

Standing to see lightning flashing beyond his windows, General Havid asked, "What's going on?"

The aide pointed to the screen. "Here, sir."

General Havid demanded. "Turn it up."

The general was mesmerized, watching Reuel and Eliyahu standing side by side, proclaiming a message from God.

The Rome ANN desk anchor reported, "If you're just joining us, we are receiving reports from Jerusalem that the two self-proclaimed witnesses for God are calling for future attacks. We go live to the Wailing Wall in Jerusalem."

"*When the Lamb opened the fourth seal, I heard the voice of the fourth living creature say, 'Come!' I looked, and there before me was a pale horse! Its rider was named Death, and Hades was following close behind him. They were given power over a fourth of the Earth to kill by sword, famine, and plague, and the Earth's wild Beasts.*

The Two Witnesses said. "The Lamb of God, who came before you in truth and righteousness only to be mocked and rejected, has opened the fourth seal of judgment against this rebellious world. The war of the Beast you worship has brought about Death and the Grave. You will cry for bread and be ravished by pestilence. The animals of the field will hunt you, yet you will not cry out to God for mercy. Like your fathers before you, your hearts are hard and necks stiff. Repent of your sins, seek the salvation Christ Jesus offers and turn to the Living God of Heaven before it's too late."

Eliyahu proclaimed, "You marvel at the deceiver's powers, his ability to make signs in the heavens to bring fire from above. Yet, Israel, have you not witnessed the real power of Heaven. Were the prophets of Baal not defeated before your fathers, as God delivered fire from Heaven? Do not be deceived by the imitations of the adversary. Has the world not enjoyed the grace of God despite complete wickedness in your hearts? Now, you will experience the judgment of the King you've rejected. The pain in this land will cause you to cry out to the God of Abraham, Isaac, and Jacob."

As the ANN cameras panned through the crowd, panic arose.

The Rome ANN desk anchor broke into the live feed, "We're trying to get a field reporter to explain what is occurring. I don't want to speculate, but based on these terrorists' history, this may be an attack on the people gathered near the Wailing Wall. Wait, okay, we're going to Sam Morrow now."

Sam Morrow, ANN reporter covering the Two Witnesses, took over. "There is some type of illness developing in the crowd. The affected people's skin has scaled and turned a grayish-white color. They seem to be in great pain. Panic is rising as people are scattering; some people are being trampled. The Wailing Wall Plaza is turning into chaos. We're receiving police scanner reports across the city, where people are reporting the same symptoms across Jerusalem. Look, I'm sending the story back to you in the studio…"

The camera dropped, and the picture faded back to Rome's ANN studio, as Morrow yelled at her cameraman.

General Havid ordered his assistant to turn the television off.

The aide turned it off before noticing his left arm had begun scaling and turning white. The aide collapsed and screamed, scratching on the ground as the mysterious illness spread over his body.

"I don't understand, sir. What happened? What's going on?" asked the woeful aide.

General Havid held the aide in an attempt to comfort him. "God is responding to the actions of the evil one. The world is being turned over to its sin."

"You should not touch me, sir! You'll become ill!" screamed the aide.

General Havid didn't release the dying man. "I don't think I will, my friend."

As the general yelled for others in his household staff to help, he needed only to look at the thousand-yard stare of his aide to realize that God was separating friend from foe. While grateful that he was spared from the wrath of God directly, he feared the judgments to come and vengeance the world would demand against God's witnesses Reuel and Eliyahu.

"It's time for all of us to talk," General Havid said to the staffers filing into the room to help the unconscious man.

Gabriella was taking a significant risk in her latest attempt to thwart Draven. She had convinced the UE logistics office for a chartered flight, stating she had official business in the Unified North American States, city of Seattle. In reality, Kerim had sent her an email naming the leader of a potential resistance element gathering in Seattle as they fled the UE strongholds in the Eastern US.

Time was limited for her in Seattle. She had no leads beyond finding the resistance safe house in the downtown area. Adding to the pressure was Draven's plan to unleash Pyretos within the next twelve hours in Texas and China.

Gabriella had only been in Seattle, Washington, for a few minutes when the news from the Two Witnesses brought the SEATAC airport to a standstill. Seattle had become the de facto capital for America. Many of the nation's eastern urban centers had been destroyed in the war, and survivors fled west. However, Draven Cross's charisma reached here as many in the terminal shouted obscenities at God's ambassadors' proclamation.

A large middle-aged man summed up the mood in the former American city, "I am getting sick of these religious fanatics; I wish Mr. Cross would lock all these people up."

The roars of agreement and the heavy presence of UE soldiers told Gabriella that building resistance in America would be difficult. The shifting political culture in the former US brought Christopher and Jackson to mind in Alabama as the hostile environment placed them in the UE's crossfire.

Gabriella's stomach heaved, and head throbbed, thinking of the death yet again flowing from the mind of Draven. There were no signs of countering the UE here as there had been in China, and she began doubting Kerim's intelligence. Sounds of people fighting against the UE did not fill the air. As her rideshare raced away from the airport, the looks on the faces of people reflected acceptance that America was no more. UE soldiers exerted absolute control. Various military vehicles with the UE logo on their sides lined Interstate Five as Gabriella drove toward the city center. The iconic Space Needle no longer dominated the Seattle skyline. Instead, massive pillars of smoke rose from downtown Seattle.

Gabriella hoped her rideshare driver, Paul, could provide insight into people's willingness to resist the UE. "So, how bad have things been here in Seattle?"

Paul shrugged. "Lady, I don't know where you're from, but I can't describe a nightmare worse than my daily life. I never have enough to eat, and I lost my home in fires that broke out after the disappearances, forcing me to sleep in this car. However, I am a lucky person because I had no family when the disappearances and war started. Those with families have no shot. None are left intact; people have lost children, spouses, and everyone in between. Anyone with family members is only focused on survival, not fighting. It's hard to take care of yourself, much less other people. Suicides are rampant in the city; the world feels heartless now, and the UE ain't no friend to anybody. Does that answer your question, lady?"

Gabriella stared out the window. "Sadly, it does. Are there any resistance elements left in the city?"

Paul said, "When the war first started, there was some resistance against the UE, but not after Vancouver fell to the north and Los Angeles down south. The flood of outsiders coming here focused the UE's efforts against the city. We were overwhelmed by soldiers in a matter of months. You won't find many people here willing to resist if they're sane. Everybody focuses on living for the day."

Gabriella said, "It's hard to believe that everybody stopped fighting; there has to be a group willing to fight against the UE."

"I doubt it; look at this place. But where we're heading was once the heart of the resistance. You sure you want me to take you there? It's not safe for a woman."

Gabriella scoffed at his chauvinistic observation. "How safe is downtown for a man like yourself?"

Paul admitted, "It's not safe."

"Then it's a good thing you're going with a woman like me," Gabriella asserted.

It was Paul's turn to scoff. "If you say so, lady, a UE buck is a UE buck. I'll take you anywhere if the price is right. Cross has made Seattle the default American capital—or whatever country we are now. Most people depend on the UE to survive; you know, never bite the hand that feeds you. The UE keeps control of the people through food. The metro area is divided into three districts, with food distribution centers within each district. If you don't have a badge like mine, you will be detained if you try to leave your zone."

"After I check out this first location. Can you take me to one of these distribution centers?"

Paul pulled over to the side of the interstate, quickly slamming the car into park. "I only agreed to take you to this house because it's on the edge of the downtown district, and it's going to be a hefty fare. I'm not suicidal and not looking for trouble with the UE. So you need to get out now."

Gabriella reached for her UE credentials as Paul made his way toward the backseat to pull her from the vehicle.

Gabriella held up her papers like a shield. "Look, I'm a UE senior official! I can assure your safety and will pay double. I need to get to the house and a food distribution center. Please."

Paul looked over Gabriella's badge and the roll of money she held in her hand before swearing and getting back into the driver's seat.

"How can you be a UE official looking for resistance? You're setting me up, aren't you? I will take you, but…" Paul drifted off.

Gabriella assured him. "Trust me when I say I am a disgruntled UE employee. You will be fine. Now let's go; it's almost ten, which means we have time for me to finish my first meeting before noon when it should be busy at the food distribution sites."

The house address Kerim provided was located in a neighborhood that looked like a like scene from a dystopian movie. Houses were blown apart, covered in black soot from the fiery end they and their occupants faced. The few homes to include the one she was now parked in front of, had boarded and cracked windows. Then there was the rancid smell of burnt flesh and wood intermixed with aromas of sewage in the damp cold, northwest air; how far America had fallen.

Gabriella held up a photo she had taken on her phone of Paul's rideshare credentials. "This won't take long. If you try to leave me, I will report you to the local UE."

She watched Paul swear and bang his fist on his driving wheel as if his plan had been stopped before he could execute it. Gabriella made her way to the front door as a dog barked in the distance, causing her to pause on the porch and stare down the street toward the noise. As she turned to knock on the door, she stared down the barrel of a shotgun, with a scrawny, dirty blond-haired young woman at the opposite end flashing a smile missing several teeth.

"Whoa, ma'am! Look, I'm a friend of Jonah. Jonah Rider does live her, correct?"

The haggard woman continued to aim a shotgun at Gabriella. "Who's asking?"

Gabriella instinctively kept her hands in the air. "We have a mutual friend named Kerim, and my name is Gabriella. You think you could aim that shotgun away from me?"

The young woman began to shut the door on Gabriella. "Jonah's not here. So, go away before you get me killed."

Gabriella stuck a hand on the door. "Please, can you tell me where he is? I must find him."

The young woman yelled, "Look, lady, when the UE takes someone, there is only one place you go: the grave. Get lost!"

The door slammed on Gabriella, leaving her shocked by the encounter. Gabriella climbed back into the rideshare, heartbroken that the fight against Draven in China seemed impossible to replicate in her homeland. "Let's go to the distribution center."

Gabriella was lost in her thoughts from the former Seattle resistance leader's home. It was sad to see people turn from fighting to being satisfied with survival. She couldn't blame them, as Draven had accomplished what no other political figure was able to in little under two years: dominate the world.

Gabriella ignored the call from Jackson's phone as she had arrived at the UE downtown Seattle food distribution site. The UE funneled people through Pier 46 once a day to receive foodstuff. The place was surrounded by a mass of humanity lined up into three rows that wove out of the pier and onto Seattle's streets. The people in the lines looked like hollow shells. Their clothes were tattered, and faces were sullen and sunken.

Paul drove directly next to a guardhouse that blocked vehicles and streamed those on foot seeking aid into lines.

Gabriella listened as a UE soldier yelled at Paul, "You don't have the clearance to be here. Turn this piece of junk around."

As Paul argued with the gate guard, Gabriella watched what she assumed was his supervisor approach the vehicle.

"You need to exit your vehicle and wait in line for food like the others," a UE officer said.

Gabriella held up her UE badge. "I'm Director Gabriella Costa, so I will go wherever I choose."

The UE officer stared at the badge Gabriella held up, changing the tone he took with her.

"Ma'am, my apologies. What can I do for you today?"

"Nothing. I'm here to observe," Gabriella said.

The officer's face flushed after reading Gabriella's badge.

"My apologies, ma'am. I didn't expect any senior visitors today."

Gabriella waved the officer away as he shouted at another group to lift a barrier.

Paul whispered, "I guess you're the real deal."

As they drove the short distance along the pier front toward the rear of a massive warehouse where the lines terminated, Gabriella heard shouts and screams.

Gabriella ordered Paul, "Park near the warehouse and wait for me. I can't ensure your safety if you attempt to leave without me."

UE soldiers handed out prepackaged meals and bottles of water to individuals and families, with each person asking for more than they were given. Gabriella walked over to the massive warehouse filled from floor to ceiling with food and water to better understand the process. As she approached the warehouse, she heard the reason for the crowd's outcry when a UE officer repeated a bullhorn announcement that no more food would be distributed today.

She ran to the front of the warehouse in time to hear a UE soldier add an insensitive statement, "This is the last of the food. If you want it, then fight for it," before throwing several meal packages amongst the crowd, starting an instant brawl.

The scene of people fighting each other for food while UE soldiers laughed caused Gabriella to grind her teeth and her body tensed. She grabbed the pistol from the UE commanding officer's holster, firing several shots into the air, gaining the entire pier's attention. She followed up by snatching the bullhorn from the hands of the soldier that incited the violence. "Listen to me. Stop fighting. There is plenty of food for everyone. I need you to form back into your lines, and I promise you I will do everything I can to make sure everyone receives food and water."

Gabriella turned to the commanding officer's deputy, a wide-eyed, freckled-faced lieutenant. "I'm promoting you to be in charge of this distribution site effective immediately. I want you to arrest your commanding officers and each soldier involved with inciting the violence we witnessed. You are not leaving this site until every person waiting has the food and water they need, or you exhaust the resources here. If you fail, I assure you, I will have you executed. Do I make myself clear?"

The young lieutenant nodded in agreement.

The food distribution site commander swore at Gabriella as she strode back to her rideshare with two arms full of food packs.

Gabriella handed the food packs to Paul. "Please take me back to the airport."

Paul whistled. "Ma'am, this ride is free. I should be paying you for what you did."

"I only hope my actions lead to changes."

CHAPTER 7

GENERAL LAISSER HAD been ceding territory to the enemy for weeks. As he stood in the III CORPS headquarters at Fort Hood, Texas, watching from the command center, doubt ran through his mind on how long the remainder of the U.S. Army and Marine forces would hold the frontlines near Waco. If his units fell, the UE would complete a sweep across the country, and the republic named America would be no more.

Colonel Prescott said, "Sir, a report from the front."

The news only brought confusion to General Laisser. "I don't understand why the UE forces would be in full retreat. It doesn't make sense."

The colonel pressed. "Does it matter, sir? We should conduct a counter-offensive immediately."

Frantic shouts across the radios in the command center from the units fighting along the war front interrupted the general's thoughts on what to do next.

General Laisser snapped, "What's going on?"

A radio operator briefed, "Sir, our troops are being attacked by a swarm of drones. The drones apparently release a mist or spray from what I can gather from the radio traffic."

General Laisser's mind recalled in horror memory of his childhood that detailed what the UE was doing. He had been sprayed by a crop-dusting drone on his family farm. "It's a trap. The UE is using chemical or biological weapons. Put every unit into their personal protective gear right now."

A military policeman guarding the command center's entrance collapsed. Soon, others at computer terminals convulsed, drawing panicked screams across the command center.

Colonel Prescott stammered before collapsing, "Sir, what's going on?"

As General Laisser grasped a railing to keep himself from falling, he caught a glimpse of a security camera of the III CORPS headquarters, which showed drones whose movements resembled a large flock of geese circling the building before a wave of seizures overtook him.

Jackson had been tormented all night by the prospect of something terrible happening to his friends. He had gotten up early and watched the news in the living room on a dusty TV through an old HDTV antenna. The flashing report across the bottom read, "UE begins final assault."

Jackson yelled as he burst into the room that Jimbo and Christopher shared. "Hey, get up; you need to come to watch the news right now!"

Christopher growled. "What's going on? I mean, the world is already ending."

Jimbo remained sleeping until Jackson gave the twin bed the massive man poured out of a strong kick.

A startled Jimbo muttered, "What? What?"

Jackson left the room and yelled, "Guys, get up! Something bad happened in Texas and China!"

Jackson could hear Charlie grumbling his way toward the living room as he ran back to the TV.

Christopher and Jimbo stumbled out of the bedroom, trying to understand what had Jackson in such an uproar at eight in the morning, joining Charlie and him in the living room.

Christopher requested, "Can we get some coffee first?"

Jackson dismissed his question. "No, look at the news!"

Jackson turned the volume up on the small television.

"We want to welcome everyone to the ANN's war update. This morning at 6 a.m. U.S. Central Time, the UE conducted a massive assault against hostile forces in America and China. As you can see, our troops were in chemical and biological protective gear, as reports indicated that the rebels used a biological or chemical weapon to counter the UE troops' assault. We are also hearing that the agent used today against UE troops may have ties to the Two Witnesses and the Christian religious zealots. The good news is it looks like the war will soon be over, as UE forces are claiming victory in both America and China. Stay with ANN for more updates," the ANN anchor said as Jackson turned the television off.

Jackson waited for the reaction of the still half-asleep men. "That has to be the biological weapon Gabriella said was going to end the war."

Christopher advised, "I think we should make plans to leave here tonight. There is no need to linger as any US officials alive will be on the UE payroll this time tomorrow."

Charlie agreed, "Well, I know what I need to do; tell me where we're heading so I can get the plane and myself ready."

Christopher replied, "We're heading to Israel; it's our only shot of surviving. If somebody identified us as American soldiers, they would turn us over to the authorities, and we know what that would mean."

"I think we might be in trouble already. Come take a look at the storm heading our way." Jimbo pointed as he peered through the blinds of the front living room windows.

The other men raced to join him at the windows. They were greeted with the view of a large dust cloud swirling behind two law enforcement vehicles speeding along the dirt landing strip toward the cabin.

Jackson ordered, "Christopher, help me hide the weapon boxes. Charlie, I want you to sneak out the back right now and start making your way toward the plane. Jimbo, take a shotgun and move to the north side of the cabin. Once these guys are on the front porch and we determine their intentions, be prepared to get a jump on them."

As the vehicles pulled up in front of Jackson's family cabin, Jackson was relieved to see only two out of shape local sheriff deputies exit their respective cars.

Christopher watched the men draw their pistols. "Jackson, do you know these guys?"

Jackson nodded. "The fat one went to high school with me."

Christopher shot back, "They're both fat."

Jackson chuckled. "That's funny, even for you. Okay, listen; let me do all the talking. You hide in the back, ready to ambush these guys should the need arise."

Christopher's feelings were racing his mind for control. His instincts said rush the two men, but something deeper seemed to say that would be disastrous for both Jackson and him. Christopher's newfound relationship with God over trusting his abilities was facing its first test. He strained to hear the muted voices on the porch over his own labored breathing.

Get it together; you don't even know why the officers are here, Christopher thought.

Jackson's voice was louder than necessary, so Christopher and Jimbo could easily hear what was happening. "What can I do for you, gentlemen?"

The slightly larger sheriff deputy replied, "You're Jackson Williams, right? I think we went to high school together."

Jackson feigned ignorance of the man. "I think we did. Your Bill, right?"

Deputy Doyle replied, "No, it's Jeff Doyle, and this is Deputy Tom Shear; I'm not surprised you don't recognize me. You were a couple years ahead of me in school."

Jackson pressed for more information. "Yeah, it's your age throwing me off. Look, I know you guys didn't travel all this way to give me an invitation to the next reunion, so what can I do for you?"

As Deputy Shear began creeping around the side of the cabin toward Jimbo, Deputy Doyle said, "Right. Well, we got some reports this morning that a fancy plane landed here last night. We know your family doesn't live here anymore, so we wanted to check things out. I'm surprised to find you here."

Jackson announced, hoping to redirect the advance of Deputy Doyle. "Hey, why don't you guys come on in, and I can explain everything?"

"Sounds good. Come on, Tom, I think this will be a quick conversation. We might even make it back to town before the diner closes."

Deputy Doyle's jowls seemed to dance with the thought of eating soon, and both deputies holstered their pistols.

Jackson pulled his shirt over a pistol tucked into his back waistband as the two officers entered the dusty living room and sat on the lone, care-worn sofa.

Jackson stood over the two seated deputies. "I would offer you guys a drink, but I got in late last night, so I'm still cleaning up the place, as you can see."

Jackson's sense of humor wouldn't let him pass up the scene before him, where the two obese deputies consumed the sofa, blurring any distinction between the couch and themselves. He jested, "You guys comfortable? I don't want you to hurt that sofa."

Deputy Doyle attempted to ease forward. "We're fine. Look, are you still in the military, Jackson? Some folks say they saw a military plane land here. We're on orders to turn over any military folks to the UE representatives in Birmingham."

Jackson watched Deputy Shear reach for his sidearm but struggled to get enough clearance from the sofa and Deputy Doyle to pull his gun.

Jackson pulled his gun from his back holster. "I am in the military, but I don't think I'll be going to see anybody at the UE anytime soon. Stop moving, big boy and both of you raise your hands before you have an awful day. Hey, you guys, get in here!"

The two deputies were swearing at Jackson when Christopher came into the living room with Jimbo.

Jackson directed Jimbo as he pulled some rope from a junk pile. "Watch them while Christopher and I tie them up. Apparently, Mayberry's finest here was planning on selling us out to the UE."

"Get your hands off me, boy!" screamed Deputy Doyle as Christopher reached for the man.

Christopher connected a quick and vicious overhand right punch to Deputy Doyle's jelly-like jaw, knocking the man unconscious as he landed on the ground with a loud thud.

Jackson smarted off, winking at Christopher and Jimbo as Deputy Shear whimpered, "I guess I should have told you guys that major here don't take too kindly to people with bad manners."

Charlie entered the house after prepping the plane to find a scene of law enforcement officials being hogtied. "Hey, what in the world is going on here?"

Jackson smiled. "Oh, we had a good ole Southern disagreement. We need to get out of here before someone comes looking for these two idiots."

A wide-eyed Charlie mentioned, "The plane is ready to go. We need to stop for fuel before we can continue to our final destination."

A red-faced and squirming Deputy Shear attempted to shout profanities through his gag.

Jackson knelt down close to a rousing Deputy Doyle as he and Christopher moved the last weapons box to the plane.

Jackson gave the plump jowls of Deputy Doyle a smack before closing the door of his cabin on the angry men. "Jeff, your mama would be ashamed; you're selling your soul and country to the devil."

~

The cheers of elation by UE SAG operatives over the successful launch of Pyretos in Texas and China were drowned out by a tense exchange between General Ahuja and the SAG leader John Barnes.

The frantic shout of General Ahuja echoed as he questioned John Barnes on his post-mission operations. "You ordered the drones to do what?"

John Barnes answered, "Sir, I gave the order to have the drones dump any remaining Pyretos en route back to our bases in China and here. I didn't want to bring that stuff back for our folks to handle."

General Ahuja scoffed. "Why am I not surprised that you lack the mental aptitude to understand how bad of an idea that was, Mr. Barnes?"

General Ahuja ran over to the command terminal for the drones as Barnes quickly following him.

The general demanded, "Tell me the exact geographical areas where the release of the remaining Pyretos agent occurred."

Fast keyboard strokes were the only sounds to be heard as everyone in the hangar silently waited for answers.

A UE SAG operative responded, "Sir, over a large portion of Central

Texas, near Waco for the American drones and for the drones in China outside of Guangzhou and Xian, China."

General Ahuja swore at Barnes and threw his maroon UE beret at the man.

The irate general spat, "You idiot, I should shoot you where you stand. You've literally erased the strategic victory we gained with a mindless tactical error. Give me that phone."

General Ahuja dialed the UE command center in Rome, preparing himself for what would likely be his last update to Draven Cross before his untimely demise due to Barnes's blunder.

General Ahuja turned to Barnes. "Know that my death sentence is yours. I swear before I leave this Earth, I will ensure the last thing you see is my pistol on your forehead."

⁂

Draven sat in his office with Gemma and Evan, reveling in the news that Pyretos effectively ended the war by decimating the world's last military resistance forces.

Draven popped a bottle of champagne and sipped while propping his feet on his desk. "Evan, please have a drink with me as we toast the start to the new world and demise of the old. Gemma, I will even allow you to partake in the revelry tonight."

Evan gushed. "I raise a toast to your brilliance and the new era the world has entered."

"Evan, ensure the ten ambassadors are here tomorrow and plan for a media announcement highlighting the unification of the globe under the UE—" His phone ringing cut off Draven.

Draven commanded a surprised Gemma, who expected him to answer the nearby phone. "Well, answer it, Gemma."

Gemma stopped herself from rolling her eyes as she handed Draven the phone.

Draven was overwhelmed by the pace of General Ahuja's words. "Sir, my deepest apologies. I have failed you. Pyretos was released in unauthorized areas—"

Draven cut the general off. "Vivaan, first calm yourself. I cannot understand you in such an emotional state. I do not see this as a problem, the spread of Pyretos will only help me destroy those two fanatics in Jerusalem and these Christian zealots."

General Ahuja didn't seem comforted. "I'm unsure as to how this blunder helps you, but I trust what you're saying."

Draven continued, "I commend you and look forward to your arrival in Rome; your efforts will be rewarded. One last thing, Vivaan, make sure those drones are destroyed; the last thing I need is someone attributing today's attack to the UE."

General Ahuja responded, "I will not fail you again. Your command will be executed flawlessly."

Draven concluded the phone call, "Excellent, General, cheers."

Draven suspended the phone receiver in the air for Gemma to take and hang it up. "It seems that the jackal named John Barnes has blundered into something that benefits me. Barnes ordered the release of the remaining Pyretos over populated areas."

Evan queried, "Sir, I do not understand why this would make you happy; there will be consequences that we will have to deal with."

Gemma stunned the two world leaders. "It makes him happy, Evan because it will create an unprecedented pandemic. Millions will die, thus lessening the strain on the UE. Plus, I'm sure the boss has a cure, further driving the world to love him, as Mr. Cross will yet again have the answer to the unsolvable."

Draven laughed. "My, my Gemma, I underestimated you. That assessment was spot on. Evan, take notes; Gemma may take your job yet."

Glaring at Gemma, Evan did not appreciate the assessment as much as Draven.

Draven ignored his right-hand man's anger. "Yes, as Gemma stated, I have the anti-viral at the Inverness lab. We have on hand over 500 hundred million vials of a tailor-made anti-viral that eliminates the virus in the infected and vaccinates those yet not sick. That's enough for almost two billion people; of course, after this pandemic has run its course, we will have a surplus."

As Charlie began his descent into Bangor, Maine, in the last rays of the setting sun to refuel before continuing the journey to Israel, Christopher marveled at the beauty of the rugged landscape. Bangor had seen its share of devastation from the Rapture but was mostly spared from the war that destroyed the rest of the nation. The snow-covered scene Christopher looked upon from his window almost hid the horrors of the last year. However, airplanes' twisted and charred frames on a remote end of the runaway told the story that the Rapture was real.

Charlie provided instructions as he taxied toward a row of fuel trucks. "Listen up, guys, I want you to lay low during refueling. I'm not sure my government purchase card will work or if it will bring some unwanted attention. Worst case, we make a quick departure, so stay buckled up."

Charlie's warning brought Christopher into the present. The realization that due to all four men being former American government employees, their lives were now in danger within America was surreal.

Christopher turned to his men. "Jackson, throw me the phone; I want to give Gabriella a call to let her know where we're going."

Jackson tossed his phone to Christopher as Charlie made another announcement.

Charlie told the group, "Alright, boys, get ready; the welcoming party is coming out to greet us."

"Well, as long as they don't ask me to step outside in the cold, they won't have a problem with me," Jackson said.

Jimbo and Christopher rolled their eyes at each other as Christopher waited on an answer from Gabriella's ringing phone.

CHAPTER 8

THE SPECIAL OPERATIVES found themselves in Israel searching for a new place to find themselves and a sense of purpose in the wake of the war that destroyed the U.S. Christopher was grateful General Havid offered up his home for Jackson, Jimbo, and Charlie, but he was leery of the general's desire to reform Omega Group as a Christian special operations force targeting Draven Cross.

Christopher watched as Jackson, ever a people person, endeared himself to General Havid. In mid-chuckle, Jackson explained what a "snipe hunt" was to the general when his quantum phone announced an incoming call. Jackson held up his hand to signal silence.

Jackson said, "Hello, what's up? You're where? Hey, General Havid, could you have your driver turn down the radio. Okay, now what is that son of the Devil doing?"

Gabriella answered, "Jackson calling him that is not helpful. Can you focus and tell me where you're at in the world?"

"I understand that Gabriella, but the man is pure evil. We arrived in Israel about forty-five minutes ago."

Gabriella seemed pleased with his response. "Israel. So, that means you're staying with General Havid. I think you guys should work with the general and make plans to destroy the Cross Industries National Lab in Inverness, Scotland. The source files for Pyretos are located there. Destroying those files will prevent future use of this weapon."

Jackson said, "Okay, I got it, Inverness, Scotland. I'll talk with the guys and get back to you. Be careful, goodbye."

Christopher asked, "What's up?"

Jackson updated Christopher and everyone else. "Gabriella is on her way back to Rome from Seattle. She wants us to destroy the Cross Industries National Lab in Inverness, Scotland."

Jimbo questioned, "Destroy the lab? I think it's a little too late for that to matter. Don't you guys?"

General Havid added his experience to the conversation. "No, our young friend at the UE is correct; you gentlemen must destroy that lab, as it will at least slow down future use of the weapon. This mission will also serve as a test run for the previously discussed use of our unique military skills in service of the Kingdom of Jesus Christ against his archenemy."

Christopher said, "I'm not so sure this mission will be straightforward. First, we are short-handed and a little banged up. Jimbo's arm still needs a few more weeks, and Jackson's leg, while better, could stand more time to fully heal."

General Havid pushed back on Christopher. "Yes, there are many challenges your team faces, but don't let them become excuses to serve. There are problems, and then there are fears; you must know the difference, as the leader of this group. Jimbo can support the mission. You've found a pilot in Charlie. And, Jackson, how does your leg feel?"

Jackson hesitated as he gave Christopher a pleading look. "Uh, it's good to go, sir."

As General Havid leaped from the vehicle now at his home, he left Christopher, Jackson, Jimbo, and Charlie pondering the next steps. "You see, Jackson is ready, and before you complain, I have resources here in Israel at your disposal; you've already met Gilana Edri. So, let us start planning to become a thorn in Draven's side. For you, Christopher, you need to learn that trusting God over yourself is a continuous choice."

᯽

After a long flight, Gabriella arrived back in Rome in the early morning hours after the Pyretos attack. Gabriella had let Gemma know of her arrival and told her they could catch up later in the day. Gabriella was confused and dazed when she awoke to Gemma's frantic shouts and violent shaking.

Gabriella moaned. "What is going on? Why are you shaking me!"

Gemma explained as she rummaged through Gabriella's closet for clothes, "I have been calling you for the last half hour. Draven wants you in his office now!"

Gabriella smarted off, "Let me guess, the world is falling apart."

Gemma threw a dress and shoes at Gabriella. "Not funny, dear. The release of Pyretos I briefed you on during your flight back here yesterday has spread a mysterious, almost supernatural disease worldwide. Droves of people are dying."

Gabriella turned to Gemma. "I'm sorry, but what did you say about people dying?"

Gemma hovered over Gabriella like a mom trying to get a teenager out the door for school. "The Pyretos bioweapon has morphed into a pandemic. The spread of disease was first reported early this morning in a few cities in America and China, making sense. What's odd, especially considering international flights are limited to UE personnel amidst the war, is that new reports of outbreaks are coming in across the globe over the last few hours. It's like the disease decided to be everywhere all at once. Draven plans to address the world before announcing the regional ambassadors later today."

Gabriella, now coherent, frantically searched for her phone amongst the scattered clothes and luggage that decorated her room. "I need to get up to headquarters. Where's my phone?"

Gemma chimed in, bewildered by the flurry of activity by Gabriella. "It's on the pedestal in your loo."

Gabriella nearly fell as she tripped over a pile of clothes and a suitcase as she grabbed her phone from the bathroom sink. She needed to update Christopher and Jackson but had to lose Gemma first.

"Gemma, thanks for getting me up. I'm going to get cleaned up and will be at HQ in thirty minutes."

Gemma winked. "You better make it twenty. I'll let Draven know you were tracking down some leads on this illness."

Gabriella sighed in relief. "You're the best. I will see you in a few minutes." She closed the bathroom door turning on the shower to indicate her eagerness to get ready. Gabriella then hit send to call Jackson's phone.

ↄ

The fact that Jackson's phone had gone straight to the voice messaging system worried Gabriella. However, she didn't have much time to reflect on the matter as she entered the executive suite conference room. Draven was lecturing the staff, particularly Evan Mallory and Michael Verd, the UE communications director. She crept to her seat, hoping not to draw the ire of Draven as his emerald eyes flashed with fury.

Hovering over the beleaguered communications director, Draven shouted, "I do not want to hear one more excuse! This public health crisis cannot be viewed as the UE's fault but should be placed squarely on those two fools' shoulders in Jerusalem and these Christian zealots around the world. Why is this so hard for you to portray, Michael?"

Verd's nerves started to fray. "People all over the world are demanding that we do something. I continue to promise the UE is working quickly to address the crisis. I can only do so much; we need some action here at the headquarters to change things!"

Draven chided. "It's an action you desire, Michael. Security, escort Mr. Verd off the premises; he is no longer employed at the UE. How's that for action?"

Michael Verd shouted as two burly UE security officers shoved him out of the conference room. "You're a joke, Cross, and the world is going to know it!"

Draven displayed an eerie sense of calm considering the debate he was in moments ago. "Evan, I'm sure you know what must be done regarding the messaging in this matter and ensure Mr. Verd receives the proper action he desired."

Evan nodded. "I do, sir, and will send out a press announcement immediately through ANN. I also will oversee Mr. Verd's termination… from the campus."

Draven smiled. "Great. Now that the unpleasantries are complete, we can focus on two quick items ahead of the regional ambassadors' announcement. First, Gabriella, I heard you created quite a stir in Seattle yesterday."

Gabriella prepared to defend her brazenness as it seemed yet again her penchant for letting her anger drive her was going to bring the ire of a superior.

Draven surprised her. "I'm glad you said something. While your actions seem counterintuitive, I'm giving you the benefit of the doubt having UE officials arrested and berating other employees was born out of the ill-manner the officers were conducting themselves. However, we will discuss the matter more fully a bit later. Second, we will only attain lasting global peace if each of you remains committed to promoting a vision that the UE stands for peace above all other factions. Now go. I will see you at the ambassador event."

Gabriella stood and watched as the UE senior staff departed, leaving her with Draven to take their places at the stage built on the global gardens patio where Draven would announce his organization of the world into ten regions controlled by the UE, or better said by Draven.

Draven addressed her, "Gabriella, Pyretos has performed better than I could have expected. However, the effect it has had on animals, given the reports of widespread animal attacks in contagion zones, is strange. I digress. I want you to track down the leaders of this Christian zealot movement and target them for elimination. As part of the Sentinel program, I expect to have the ability to track and monitor anyone on the planet within the next eight months. Eliminating these final radical elements will prove essential to establishing lasting peace."

Gabriella challenged. "Sir, I'm struggling to understand how the countless deaths and targeting of individuals expressing their universal right to dissent equates to your pro-peace persona and vision."

Draven pressed, looking intently at Gabriella. "Gabriella, don't be so naïve. These zealots are not peacefully resisting the change that I'm fostering, a change the world has demanded for years. These groups plot my demise and all that the UE stands for every day. Look at the hate that these radical groups and their growing number of followers spew. You think I am deaf. I know they call me the Son of the Devil, the Antichrist. Do you believe that's who I am?"

Gabriella dared not respond but simply shook her head, affirming what Draven expected.

"Good, then I expect you to brief me tomorrow on where I can send Barnes and his team to rid the world of the Christian radicals."

Gabriella said, "Sir, that's a big assumption on your part in what you are asking of me."

Draven demanded. "Enlighten me."

Gabriella elaborated, "We have identified 144,000 Jewish men to be precise that are creating rallies all over the world. This is not a counter-terrorism threat where we can target the core leaders and watch the organization eat itself from within. I recommend we use cyber and psychological operations to discredit these groups' messaging."

Draven stood over Gabriella before departing for the Regional Ambassador event. "I give you credit for identifying the exact number of miscreants. If I cannot kill the 'core leaders,' as you've described, then I will kill enough to scare the rest. One final thing, I understand your sympathies for the former United States. I should have killed you for slapping me on the plane; yet, here you are pushing the boundaries of my mercy. It's as if when I look at you, I'm compelled by some greater force not to enact vengeance upon you. However, don't rely on your guardian angel always being there for you. If you ever again undermine me as you did yesterday in Seattle, you will rue the day we met. America is paying the price for starting a war it could never win, a fight with Draven Cross. Don't forget who you work for. You have your orders; now get out of my sight and execute them."

As Gabriella left the conference room trying to compose herself after Draven's not so veiled threat on her life. She felt a tug on her mind and spirit that she could not explain, as if she was meant to challenge Draven. While the stunt in Seattle was risky, ensuring suffering people had food was worth Draven's threat. Maybe, it was God looking after her and staying the hand of Draven; perhaps she had garnered some favor with God for trying to stop his efforts to kill millions.

It was hard for Gabriella to understand why Draven's tone and policies with the Christians seemed personal. He sought to exterminate all Christian symbols and vestiges from the world for a reason Gabriella chose not to comprehend. The words of the mysterious Samuel she met back in New York, the lone leader of the Christian evangelist movement she knew of, a man who represented a priority for her to hunt down, rang in her head, "Before the end of this time of tribulation, you will serve the Kingdom of God greatly."

General Havid continued being a great host to Christopher's new "team," providing a meager meal for the men and the ruggedly beautiful and dangerous intelligence operative Gilana Edri. The group settled into General Havid's study to discuss the mission of destroying Draven's bioweapons lab in Scotland.

Seated behind his study desk, General Havid remarked, "I hope all are satisfied with the meal. I apologize for the lack of variety and meager portions, but food supplies continue to decline since the Rapture. Can I offer anyone dates, fruit, or coffee?"

Jackson patted his full stomach. "Sir, that meal was fine."

"Yes, sir, thanks for the hospitality." Christopher turned his attention to Gilana. "Do you know the religious relationship between the general and my team?"

The abrupt transition to a serious matter caught everyone in the room off guard, minus Gilana, who held her stare with Christopher.

Gilana said, "Yes, I know you're all Christian zealots. I admit that General Havid's discussion of his conversion and description of Jesus has me confused on many levels. Still, I have not, as you say, 'accepted Jesus' salvation offer.' However, I present no security risk, if that's what your question was seeking to answer. So, let's finish planning our attack on the coward named Draven."

General Havid said, "Well, Christopher. I think Gilana completes the team you need."

Christopher agreed, "Sir, I've given the mission some thought. I think we will need to conduct an air insertion, in particular, a high-altitude-low-opening, what we call a HALO jump."

Jimbo asked, "Why such a risky move?"

Jackson added, "Yeah, please explain this move, especially considering it's been a few years since I've done a HALO jump."

Christopher answered, "It's simple, guys. The information that General Havid was able to provide"—he nods to the General who hands Charlie, Jimbo, Gilana, and Jackson a manila folder with imagery and intelligence reports on the Inverness National Lab—"indicates there is only one road leading into the lab with at least two checkpoints. Furthermore, the lab, which occupies a complex on the grounds of the ancient Urquhart Castle, is bounded on its west and north side by Loch Ness, leaving two tactical insert options."

Jackson smarted off. "Maybe we could get the Loch Ness monster to destroy the lab."

Christopher flipped to an image in the folder. "Anyways, jumping in provides us the element of surprise and stealth."

Gilana matter-of-factly stated, "Yes, there is only one choice, we jump out of a plane and land within the soft inner security cordon."

Jimbo challenged the plan. "Okay, so, beyond the river monster, why can't we take the river?"

Jackson rolled his eyes at Jimbo's comment but was cut off by Gilana before he could smart off.

"Read the first intelligence report in the executive summary."

Christopher watched as the other men read the report as Gilana had directed. Everyone let out a collective sigh after a moment of reading.

Jackson spoke first. "So, there is a double-layered, ten-foot-high, 15,000-volt continuously electrified fence protecting the lab and, for good measure, a steep cliff face from the river up to the lab. Got it."

Charlie asked, "Why did you say continuously electrified fence?"

Jimbo answered, "Most electric fences use quick pulses to repel animals or people, meaning you'll get a nasty shock but can live to tell the story. If you find a continuous electrified fence, you are ensuring that anything that makes contact with that fence will be dead, not deterred."

Charlie tilted his head. "Wow. So, what about a plane and the logistics of getting to Scotland?"

Jackson chimed in. "I can already see the pain train heading my way.

So before I get on board, can we break for some of that strong coffee I know the general has; I can see tonight is going to be a long one."

General Havid waved a servant over. "Jackson, my friend, you have an interesting way with your native language, but coffee will be good for our spirits."

Gabriella enjoyed the mood the UE global gardens provided her every day but today. The gardens made for a near-perfect backdrop for Draven's announcement of a one-world government under his leadership. The *Palazzo Caelum* bound the Roman-style garden with lush and well-manicured hedges on three sides. The Tiber River created a natural southern boundary for the garden that extended to its banks. It was a social media influencer's dream video location.

As Gabriella observed Draven's directing the final touches, it was easy to see that the view before the man was as he envisioned the moment, the point of his life where he became the unquestioned ruler of the entire world. Gabriella enjoyed the smoke rising from Rome across the Tiber, ruining the social media post-worthy view, as it added the truth to an event full of lies. She knew Draven would force the communications staff to edit the stain of war from future publications of the moment. Gabriella's attention shifted as she watched Gemma give Draven the nod indicating that the regional ambassadors and, more importantly, the ANN cameras were ready.

Gabriella nearly found it amusing to see Draven genuinely filled with nervous pride as he moved to a microphone-stuffed podium flanked on each side by the soon-to-be regional ambassadors. But she knew Draven's mannerisms were an act to fuel his evil ego. He took one final opportunity to bask in the pride of his accomplishments before speaking. There was no doubt in Gabriella's mind that Draven savored the thought of the world proclaiming him as the greatest man to ever live, the leader the world had been asking for since the dawn of time.

"Good afternoon. I am humbled to be standing before the amazing United Earth staff, who tirelessly work each day to achieve lasting peace for all humanity. Thanks to the UE's outstanding efforts, billions are watching this event around the world today across a space-based communications network. Let's all take a moment to applaud these heroes," Draven said, moving from the podium, pointing to UE staff, who were as raucous as a concert crowd.

The scene and mood amongst the relatively young UE staff reminded Gabriella of clips she had watched from Silicon Valley technology giants and the seeming worship that their CEOs commanded from their employees.

Draven continued after the UE self-praise died down. "I must address a bit of unpleasant news. As you all know, our brave UE security forces recently won a decisive victory in the war. Sadly, the resistance forces, aided by Christian extremists in populated areas, released a biological weapon with the hope of denying the world its freedom. The result of that choice is a pandemic of historic levels. The good news is that the UE stands ready again to serve the needs of humanity. An esteemed panel of scientists that will oversee the anti-viral' s distribution within a matter of weeks briefed me.

The UE staff erupted again, and Gabriella held the bile rising in her throat down as she watched staffers wiping tears from their eyes and praising Draven Cross.

Draven was enjoying his moment. "Now, without further delay, let's celebrate the joy of this special day. Today, the entire world is unified under one government, for the first time in history. Each of the world's nations has made a choice represented here today to move from the struggles for national power and interest toward a collective future of prosperity. Former enemies stand together now hand and hand as friends. The devastation of the disappearances produced the fruits of unity and harmony. Today, I stand at the head of a government-organized for one purpose, to ensure that humanity lives in peace."

Draven soaked in the applause from the UE staff and dignitaries before concluding the ceremony. "I will now call forward the men that will represent the vision of the UE across the globe."

One by one, each of the designated regional ambassadors came forward and kneeled before Draven as he placed a gold diadem on each man's head. The diadem's each contained a distinctive rare gemstone above a symbol that integrated the globe and the eye of providence. Draven placed the final crown beset by the other regional gems, with a large diamond in the center on his head as the ruler over the others.

Draven again waited for the applause from the crowd to culminate before he finished speaking.

Flashing his dazzling white teeth, Draven said, "I want to leave a stark warning for the enemies of unified global peace. The world will not tolerate those that wish to sow discord and cause strife through intimidation. The cost will become unbearably expensive for those that seek conflict. Thank you, and may peace reign on Earth."

Gabriella felt hollow after witnessing Draven complete his domination of the world. She knew he had lied and started the war that killed millions. Gabriella could not shake from her mind Draven's orders that created the pandemic ravishing the world. If she allowed herself to focus on the thought before defeating it with logic, every ounce of her knew Draven was the Biblical Antichrist. He was not some improved dictator that achieved what other megalomaniacs only dreamed. The truth was he was evil incarnate and had to be stopped.

Gabriella left the dais of self-congratulating officials and staff, focused on thwarting Draven Cross no matter the cost—first step contact Christopher Barrett.

❧

The assembled group of covert warriors remained silent as General Havid clicked the television off in his study. The group reflected on Draven Cross's celebration of creating a one-world government, their words lost in emotions.

Breaking the silence, Jackson exclaimed, "I see Saint Cross is now the ruler over all he sees. There can be little doubt that he is the Bible's Antichrist."

General Havid remarked, "I'm afraid you're right, Jackson. While he has yet to take on the full power given to him by his dark master Satan, there is little evidence pointing away from Draven Cross being the Antichrist."

Trying to reframe the dark discussion surrounding Draven Cross,

Christopher said, "I think it makes what we're working on all the more important. Let's run over this plan one last time. I think we've gotten the kinks worked out."

Jimbo said, "Go for it."

"Charlie will fly us out of Ben-Gurion to Sofia, Bulgaria, in the SHADOW. Once there, we will link up with his contact and a cargo plane that will enable Gilana, Jackson, and myself to conduct a HALO jump into the Inverness Lab. Jimbo and Charlie will stage the SHADOW at the Inverness Airport, awaiting to extract us after the mission is complete. The only thing we need to determine is when the anti-viral is shipped for distribution, the last thing we want to do is destroy the lab before Draven produces a cure for the world."

Jackson questioned the plan, "Charlie, can we trust this contact of yours? How likely is it that he sells us out to the UE?"

Charlie assured him. "If we give him the right price, about a 50 percent chance. We don't meet his price 100 percent chance."

"Oh yeah, I like where this mission's going. Heaven, here I come," Jackson responded.

Gilana challenged Jackson on his cavalier approach to the mission. "Nothing is sure. You've seen what this man accomplished in a short amount of time. We must do what we can to slow him down. Think about your family and homeland."

The thought of his family and the loss of America stung deeper than Jackson wanted to acknowledge, and he simply nodded to Gilana and the group his acceptance of the risk.

General Havid slapped the table. "It is settled. I will work to get the final plans and intelligence on the lab and the HALO equipment you will need. I will also ensure that Charlie's contact is compensated well for his efforts. Christopher, I need you to ensure we find out what we can from Gabriella without compromising her. The mission will proceed only after the anti-viral is complete."

Jackson's phone rang as he departed the study. He tossed the communicator to Christopher.

"You alright?" Christopher's words chased his departing friend.

Jackson kept walking. "I will be once Draven Cross is suffering for eternity in Hell."

As Jackson's footsteps echoed down the hallway, Jimbo offered, "I'll talk to him."

Christopher countered as he hit the accept button to speak with Gabriella, "Give him a minute."

ର

Gabriella had paused the call with Christopher as she rushed back to her office to determine the schedule for moving the anti-viral from the Inverness Lab to the regional capitals using her personal laptop to hack through the UE database. It was a risk to speak in her office but needed given the circumstances. Gabriella placed her secure communicator on speaker mode, resuming the call with Christopher. Christopher's voice always provided Gabriella hope and warmth, though she dared not express her feelings to him. She started the phone call with a broad smile while continuing furious keystrokes on her laptop.

"Yes, it's good to hear your voice too. If you thought watching the ceremony was bad, it was worse being there. I don't have much time. The Pyretos weapon has caused a pandemic to emerge. During the speech, Draven lied to the world to allow, get this, more deaths to ensure his glory when the anti-viral is delivered. It will be moved from Inverness late tomorrow night; however, Barnes and his goons will be guarding the lab at least until the anti-viral departs. I'm not sure if Barnes will leave personnel there; let's hope not. I recommend a strike the day after tomorrow. We must take the Inverness lab offline. Yes, I'll be careful. You guys, please be careful, okay, bye," Gabriella concluded the call just in time as Gemma entered her office.

Gemma said, "Hello, love, we have a meeting with guess who to discuss the next big step in world domination. I'm sure meetings at the headquarters are mundane compared to your field operations."

"Did Draven really say world domination?"

Gemma laughed. "No, I've begun playing this game in my head where I translate what is being said into the truth."

Gabriella said, "Well, it wouldn't have surprised me if he had said world domination. And yes, being back here in the headquarters is dull, but I know it's a necessary part of this game. Okay, let's go and get this meeting over with."

~

Reuel and Eliyahu rose early in the Jerusalem morning, a day after Draven's declaration of controlling the world, to provide Heaven's response. Their ministry and the Earth were reaching a transition period after nearly two years of ministering God's word. The first four seals opened by The Lamb of God only set the conditions for trials to come with millions of people already losing their lives and likely their souls.

Yet, many were turning to the salvation offered by Christ Jesus, even in this midnight hour. The 144,000 witnesses had created an evangelism movement never seen before across the Earth, with a countless sea of people coming to the LORD in these final days of human history.

The two men of God prepared to deliver another opportunity for the world to turn to God. Sleepy camera crews awoke as a strong wind moved over the Temple Mount with the new day's dawning. Their eyes opened to the Two Witnesses standing atop the Temple Mount, having moved from their spot in front of the Wailing Wall.

Sam Morrow, the ANN field reporter assigned to the Two Witnesses, yelled at her cameraman as Reuel and Eliyahu stood with the rebuilt Jewish Temple behind them as the sun rose. "Hey, get up! Those two nuts are at it again."

Reuel was the first to break the morning's stillness with a voice so loud it seemed as if he was yelling into every Israelite's ear. "The world has anointed a man of war as King of the Earth and called him the Prince of Peace. Oh, Israel, why do you reject the truth before you? How much suffering will be required to bring repentance from your mouths? Jesus Christ, the true Prince of Peace, stands waiting for you to return. Yet, you continue to play the role of a harlot with the Beast and his false prophet. The world will suffer as the Beast begins persecuting those precious to God."

Eliyahu stretched his hands toward the sky. *"When he opened the fifth seal, I saw under the altar, the souls of those who had been slain because of the word of God and the testimony they had maintained. They called out in a loud voice, 'How long, Sovereign Lord, holy and true, until you judge the inhabitants of the Earth and avenge our blood?' Then each of them was given a white robe, and they were told to wait a little longer, until the full number of their fellow servants, their brothers and sisters, were killed just as they had been."*

Eliyahu's voice boomed like thunderclaps. The piercing sound of his voice forced the gathering crowd to cover their ears. "The LORD of Heaven will not forsake those that have chosen to serve Him, even in this season of tribulation. He will separate the chaff from the wheat, and a countless number will worship him at the cost of their lives. The God of Abraham, Isaac, and Jacob, the GREAT I AM, will wage war on the Beast who sits in Rome and his followers. The world must choose its side, for you will either be for the LORD or against Him, as He will spew out the lukewarm from His mouth, and His wrath will fill the Earth."

After Eliyahu stopped speaking, a bright light flooded the Temple Mount, causing the ANN cameras to turn off and people to fall to their faces.

❧

Draven's anger was visible as Gabriella joined the rest of the UE security staff already in his office. He was fixated on the now replaying ANN broadcast of the Two Witnesses' latest announcement.

"Sir, I can—" Evan was cut off.

Draven berated the group. "I don't want to hear excuses or what you think will fix the situation with these two. I am baffled as to why the Prince of This World holds my hand back from destroying these terrorists where they stand. I relish the day when their time comes."

Draven continued, "The reason for this meeting is to begin striking back against these religious terrorists at their heart, the Christian evangelical groups being led by these Jewish men all over the world. It seems that these two idiots want a fight with me, and I will not back down nor be bullied by anyone. Gabriella, please provide a brief update on the next mass rally being held by these misguided Jewish men."

Gabriella hesitated to speak after scanning the room. She made eye contact with a woman in the back row amongst the senior staff executive assistants that caused her to pause. Gabriella swore it was the mysterious woman she encountered when first arriving in Rome. But it couldn't be the woman, right? Gabriella froze and starred in the woman's direction for a few moments too long as Draven shouted her back into reality.

Draven ordered, "Get on with it, Gabriella. I don't have all day."

Gabriella took one more glance toward the strange but comforting woman to only find her gone. Gabriella smiled as she began the brief, unsure if God or her mind were sending her the vision.

Gabriella said, "My apologies, sir. The next major gathering for the Christian evangelicals is scheduled to occur in Jakarta, Indonesia, next week. Reporting indicates that over 100,000 people are expected at the rally."

Draven nodded. "Excellent. I want to provide a unique greeting for all in attendance at the rally and blame the tensions between the legacy Islamic fundamentalist and burgeoning Christian influence in Indonesia. Now, drink the contents of the cup in front of you."

Gabriella and the others in the room hesitated, looking at the clear effervescent liquid in the cups at the conference table.

Draven smirked. "Trust me; I need all of you for the moment. The anti-viral to the pandemic ravishing the world is in those cups, so it's to your health to drink up."

Gabriella was the last to drink, watching as she held the cup to her lips to determine if Draven's words were valid on the safety of the liquid.

Draven smiled. "Good, the last thing I needed was for the disease to strike my senior staff. Additionally, I want Mr. Barnes to find and eliminate the rally's Jewish leaders. The time has come, as you Americans were fond of saying during the war on terrorism, to 'cut the head off the snake.'"

John Barnes, who was attending the meeting via telecast from the Inverness Lab, agreed to head to Jakarta and begin surveillance after ensuring one shipment of the anti-viral arrived in Beijing, the new capital of the Unified Asian Nations region.

"Lastly, Evan. Effective today the world will move to a single currency, the UE dollar. This policy will also aid the UE in tracking dissidents once we enable the Sentinel tracking program. Are there any—"

Draven's attention shifted as Gemma burst into his office, screaming at Pontiff Conti of the Interfaith Religion.

"I demand to speak with you, Mr. Cross," Pontiff Conti exclaimed.

"I'm sorry, sir, he would not listen to me," Gemma plaintively tried to explain.

Draven clenched his teeth. "It's okay, my dear. Apparently, the Pontiff's agenda is more pressing than mine. Everyone, leave."

Evan tried to intercede, "Sir, I think I should handle this." Draven dismissed him with a hand.

Gabriella was glad that the Cardinal or Pontiff, or whatever he was called today, broke up the meeting. There was much to relay to her own team.

❧

Draven's demeanor exuded calm as he moved back to his desk. However, like white-hot magma coursing through an underground lava tube before an eruption, Draven's temple veins engorged with blood as his face reddened.

Pontiff Conti exclaimed, "Secretary-General, I will not be made out to be a puppet. I sat through the ambassador ceremony, never acknowledged, and was treated as a mere master of ceremonies for my first global Interfaith event. I have a value that you sought out, and I demand to be given the proper respect for my office. I am, in fact, the leader of millions and should be treated accordingly."

Draven traced the outline of his handgun secured under his desk, unseen by the pompous Conti, as he contemplated killing the man where he stood for such disrespect. However, his instincts led him to see a use for the man that would ultimately serve him well.

Draven gestured toward a plush chair in front of his desk. "You're right, Pontiff Conti, please sit."

Pontiff Conti's eyes widened, and he glanced over his shoulders as if Draven were speaking to another person as he sheepishly took the seat. "I am surprised you've taken such blunt criticism so well."

Draven stated, "Your statement proves how I am mistaken. I am, above all things, a man of peace. All I ask in the future, Pontiff, is if you have an issue, please provide me the respect and honor of fixing the matter before deriding me in front of my staff."

Conti looked abashed. "Yes, I was wrong in my manners. I only wish to serve the world and bring many to understand the divine light within themselves."

Draven rose to walk near the seated Conti. "I understand. I will ensure you receive the treatment and accolades coming to you in the future. Now that we have that unpleasant business behind us, I want you to take it upon yourself to be more vocal in confronting those fanatics in Jerusalem."

Conti was disarmed with the task of engaging the Two Witnesses and unfolded his arms. "Gladly, Secretary-General. Those men are spreading hatred against the vision of peace you've outlined."

Draven could tell by Conti's body language that he could tell him anything at his point, and the pompous man would believe it. "I meant to include you in the ambassador ceremony. A slight to be corrected here and now. I'm officially conceding the title of the 10th regional ambassador to the Unified Arabian States and appointing you today, the new regional ambassador, besides being the Interfaith religion's Pontiff. I hope this honor assures you of the value I hold for you."

Pontiff Conti's pride swelled. "I had no idea you desired me to be a regional ambassador in addition to my duties as Supreme Pontiff of Interfaith. Thank you for your time and understanding. I will not fail you or the faithful followers of the Interfaith religion."

Draven ushered Conti to the door of his office to meet his aide Giuseppe at Gemma's desk. "Now, if you don't have anything else for me. I think we both have a better understanding of ourselves and this relationship."

Conti said, "No, sir, thank you for your time."

Draven ordered, "Gemma, have Evan meet me in the press room immediately."

ꟹ

Evan attempted to take notes as Draven made his way into the UE pressroom for a televised briefing on the global economy and challenges facing the world.

Draven expressed his frustration as he opened the pressroom door. "Evan, if you have to take notes on everything I say, then perhaps you're too incompetent for the lofty position of being my image-bearer. It's simple; Pontiff Conti is an arrogant peacock that desires to be a celebrity. In giving him the ambassadorship, I will allow him to build his own noose. I will allow him to live, for now, so he distracts the masses from the carnage of the war and disappearances with his contemptible yet undeniable charisma. Simply monitor him to ensure he is not plotting a coup d'état. I hope you can remember something so basic."

Evan explained, "Yes, sir. My notes ensure I don't miss a detail of your visions and plans."

Draven walked into the UE Press Room. "If you want to impress me. Get the loyalty identification system up and running for the Sentinel program. It will be good to have the ability to track anyone I choose at any time and place."

CHAPTER 9

CHRISTOPHER HAD BEEN praying for the past hour as the SHADOW made the trip from Tel Aviv to Sofia, Bulgaria, his first military mission, not in the United States' service. While his prayers had been mainly for mission success, Christopher also prayed for Jackson. Jimbo mentioned that Jackson blew up at him when he tried to talk to him back at General Havid's house. It was out of character for Jackson to lose his cool so quickly. Christopher tried to shrug off Jackson's attitude as stress. There was no denying there was a dark edge emerging with Jackson.

As Charlie announced the final approach into Sofia, Christopher admired the city's ancient landmarks as they came into view. Each monument detailed a 2,000-year history of Roman, Greek, Ottoman, and Soviet occupation. The town was social media post-gold—the setting sun behind the Vitosha Mountains provided an idyllic backdrop for the historic city. The War of Rebellion, as the UE propaganda described the present global conflict, left scars across Sofia. A large tent city had risen outside of Sofia International Airport after the Unified European Nations forces crushed the Sofia resistance, ushering in yet another occupation in the city's long history. Now there were tens of thousands of dead, and quarters of the city smoldered. The sight of widespread death and destruction was something Christopher hoped he never got comfortable with seeing.

As Charlie completed taxing the jet into a private hanger, Christopher set the tone for the next phase of the mission—picking up the cargo plane. "We're about to face our first test. These are UE loyal troops and personnel operating here. General Havid established a front company and backstories for us all. We work for a private security firm named Trinity only if asked. Our job in Sofia is to protect a medical aid group dealing with the pandemic. Gilana, please pass out our identification docs."

Gilana passed out passports and identification badges that affiliated everyone as employees of a fictional security firm. Charlie and Jimbo joined the group from the cockpit.

Charlie said, "Okay, I spoke with Vasil on the phone; he's heading our way now and will take us to the cargo plane. When he gets here, let me lead the conversation. I believe we can trust him, but I've never placed my life in his hands."

Jackson added, "Well, we all have at this point."

Christopher attempted to reassure everyone but fought his own doubts and trust issues, praying his newfound faith would hold. "Everyone, keep your weapons concealed. We only show them if we need to use them."

Everyone nodded except Jackson, who merely stood and pulled his ball cap lower on his furrowed brow.

Charlie reported, "Vasil is here."

"He's not the only one," Jackson pointed out as he stared at fifteen armed UE soldiers walking with Vasil.

"Lord, help us," Christopher exclaimed as he walked down the airplane door ramp.

Gabriella felt her heart was about to explode when John Barnes briefed that his departure from Inverness National Lab was delayed an hour due to weather. She knew that Christopher and his new team of operatives were drawing closer to Inverness at that very moment; how close she was unsure. Gabriella wanted to run from the meeting to call Christopher to warn him. She was trapped and felt helpless to warn her friends of the danger they faced.

The voices in the room began to fall away as she started silently asking God for help, unsure of what she was doing. She resisted the urge to dismiss the act of reaching out to God. Gabriella begged, "God, I don't have the right to ask anything of you, but please delay my friends on their mission for You."

While doubting her request was heard, she was glad the meeting was wrapping up. She gathered her laptop and headed for her favorite place to discuss things—the UE garden—to call Christopher and his team to warn them.

&

Christopher was glad Charlie didn't get stage fright. His friend and pilot went right into character, embracing the six-foot-four Vasil, with a group of UE soldiers staring down Christopher and his team.

Charlie jumped into character. "Vasil, my old friend, it is good to see you. The last time we met, I was still working for the Agency, and you were just getting started in your current business. I'm about to make you a richer man."

Vasil returned Charlie's embrace but immediately questioned the presence of Christopher and his team in a heavy accent. "Why does it look like you're transporting military soldiers?"

Charlie dragged Christopher by the arm in front of Vasil. "No, soldiers, only private security contractors. If it makes you feel better, check their credentials."

Christopher and Vasil starred at each other with intent gazes as if they both understood the game being played. Vasil looked at Christopher's badge and nodded in silent agreement that Christopher and his team were who Charlie said.

Charlie spoke Vasil's language as Gilana handed him a duffel bag of Euros. "Here's the money promised for your services. Now, can we get moving to the hangar with the cargo plane I paid for, and what's with your armed bodyguards?"

Vasil's face softened as he thumbed stacks of Euros. He waved over one of the UE soldiers and handed him the bag.

The middle-aged Vasil waved Charlie and the others to follow him. "These men are my insurance policy; Sofia is rougher than times past. I cannot afford a lapse in security in my line of work. You realize I'm giving you a discount. The UE dollar is now the only currency in the world. The conversion rate is horrible. Follow me."

Charlie quipped. "That's interesting to hear about the UE dollar, but I've never been a person to turn down a discount."

Christopher hinted. "One second, Charlie, we need to grab the gear we left on the plane. Remember?"

Charlie picked up Christopher's suggestion. He watched Gilana, Christopher, and Jackson board the plane, remerging with portable security boxes filled with weapons and ammo. "Right, we'll wait for you guys."

Christopher gave Charlie and the others a pensive look as they moved from the hangar with the SHADOW onto the airport tarmac. It was an unnerving experience walking between the armed UE soldiers and the morally questionable Vasil. Christopher fought the urge rising within him to take the lead from Charlie. Placing his trust in someone besides himself was still a new emotion. So, when Jackson's communicator rang, the unexpected sound nearly caused him to draw his pistol on the nearest UE soldier.

Jackson threw the phone to Christopher after authenticating the call from Gabriella.

Christopher said, "Hey, Charlie, hold up. I need to take this call; it's the office."

Charlie kept his eyes on his contact. "Meet us in that big hangar in front of us."

Jackson said, "I will stay with him."

Charlie, Gilana, and Jimbo proceeded with starring at the two men.

Two of their UE babysitters stood by, but thankfully out of hearing distance for the phone call.

Christopher took the call. "Hello."

Gabriella said. "Hi. Are you preparing to depart for Scotland?

Christopher responded. "Yes, we were about to start loading out for Inverness."

Gabriella continued. "Barnes and his team are still at Inverness. There was a weather delay."

Christopher said. "What? I'm glad you called; meeting that maniac could have been a bad situation to jump into tonight. How long will Barnes and his gang be there?"

Gabriella answered. "I think if you can delay an hour, it will provide enough distance between the two groups. Be careful."

Christopher acknowledged the reality of the request. "An hour delay, well, I think we will be fine considering the gear needs to be loaded on the plane. Plus, Charlie will need to prep. Call me back if something changes."

Jackson questioned. "What's the problem?"

Christopher whispered as he started walking with Jackson and their UE chaperones toward the large airplane hangar. "It seems that Barnes and his group of mercs are in a weather delay at Inverness. Gabriella thought we would need to hold here for at least an hour to make sure Barnes and his men were gone before we made the jump. I told her that we needed at least an hour to get prepped, much less flying out."

Jackson's sentiment came out with such coldness that Christopher stopped walking, confusing the UE handlers as one kept up with Jackson and one stopped with him. "I wish Barnes would be there when we get there. I have some unfinished business with that killer."

Christopher and his shadow resumed walking to catch up. "Are you okay, Jackson? You seem angry."

Jackson entered the hangar with another chilling statement. "I *am* angry for being left behind in this nightmare, but more than anything, I am angry with Draven Cross and all the death he's brought to this world. Think about back home; we can never go back to America, and it's his fault. I hope I get the chance to kill that man."

Christopher did not know how to respond as he walked into the hangar. Jackson was changing, seemingly for the worst. While Christopher's instinct to pray versus demanding control since leaving Tel Aviv signaled a change within himself. A change he did not fully understand. All these changes were converging to create a disaster at Inverness. For the first time in years, Christopher accepted he was in a situation that was beyond his control. As a seed of doubt grew in his mind, Christopher was unsure if his trust in Jesus would end well for those he was charged to lead.

❧

Gabriella sat typing dubious intelligence collection requirements to complicate finding the Christian evangelist movement leaders while near-continuously glancing up at her office clock and her personal laptop. The time was a reminder that her friends once lost were heading into harm's way to save future lives. Simultaneously, her computer reminded her of the network of rebels in China also saving lives. Gabriella felt a sense of duty to prevent Draven's henchmen from slaughtering innocent people. She was grateful for her former Agency laptop's security technology enabled her to accomplish this mission through Kerim. Though they were infrequent, Kerim's email updates about rescuing Christians and helping people survive against the UE brought hope. The thoughts of people starving back in America and being attacked like Li Wei by Draven pushed her to stay focused on her task.

Gabriella glanced at the time again after reflecting on two groups she cared about, both in harm's way, but time seemingly had stopped. She had sent word to Gemma asking for notification when Barnes and the Pyretos anti-viral shipments departed Inverness. Gabriella's nerves were on edge now that hours had passed with nothing from Gemma. She considered calling Christopher to make sure he hadn't taken off. Yet, she couldn't risk compromising his mission.

Gabriella jested. "I need answers!" she exclaimed, ironically right before a knock on her door. "God, I hope this is your answer. Come in."

"Hi, Gemma. It's good to see you. Any news on Barnes's team; I hope they were able to get the anti-viral on its way to those in need."

Slumping on Gabriella's sofa and removing her heels, Gemma said, "Barnes left about two hours ago, love. I am sorry for the delay, but I was caught up with preparing for Draven's upcoming press conference."

Knowing that her enthusiasm resided in knowing that Christopher and Barnes would not meet at Inverness National Lab, Gabriella said, "That's good news; I'm glad that the anti-viral is on the way to help those in need."

Gemma nodded. "I agree. It's sad to see how many people have died. I think the world is in such a mess despite what Draven says."

"Our current estimate is over 15 million dead and climbing from the pandemic alone. I'm guessing that many more will die before the anti-viral gains an upper hand over the disease," Gabriella murmured.

Gemma said, "I'm off to the salt mine. If I'm gone for too long, Draven will lose his top. I'll see you later tonight, okay."

"Yes, I will see you later." Gabriella's mind turned to Christopher and Jackson as she stared intently at the clock in her office. Hopefully, the mission will run smoothly.

ᖰ

Christopher wondered how trustworthy Vasil was, but he had delivered all the team needed. Vasil also had enough cunning not to ask too many questions. Christopher assumed Vasil realized that his team was more than mere private security contractors. Vasil just hadn't determined a way to profit from the knowledge yet. Christopher relied on Vasil's love of money and fear of a premature death preventing him from asking the details. At this point, they were delayed almost two hours, and Christopher hoped to get into the air and away from Vasil and his UE soldiers before his desire to help switched to wanting to harm.

Interestingly enough, Vasil's curiosity was more potent than Christopher's efforts to minimize communicating with the man. Vasil approached him and shared his past with Christopher, providing a bridge between his history with Charlie and his ability to procure high-end military equipment.

Vasil whispered to Christopher. "I was *Spetznaz* when I was in the Russian military. I know what you need with the equipment Charlie requested."

Christopher turned to face the man, fearing he would speak with UE soldiers on the true nature of the efforts underway.

"Look, you better—"

Vasil cut Christopher's threat short. "I don't care who you are or where you're going as long as you don't interfere with my business, and you pay me."

Christopher said, "Good, let's keep our business to ourselves."

Vasil declared, "No worries, my friend. I got you the best gear for a HALO jump. I'm providing you high-cut special operations ballistic helmets with high-altitude oxygen demand regulator masks. Thermal reinforced wind suits, backlit automated altimeters, you name it. Best of all, you have American MC-6 parachutes, meaning you will land softer than a baby placed on his mother's chest."

Jackson chimed in, "I'm glad to hear that; I hate the feeling of smacking the ground like a sack of dropped potatoes."

Christopher reached to connect with distant Jackson. "I'm glad to see you still have your sense of humor."

Jackson responded as he picked up a duffle bag with the gear needed for the jump, "Charlie sent me to tell you that he and Jimbo are ready to take off when we are."

Christopher turned to their contact. "Vasil, thanks for getting us this stuff, and I hope our paths don't cross in the future."

Vasil turned from Christopher, ordering his UE entourage in Bulgarian. "Yes, the cost may be much steeper if we see each other again."

Christopher stared at the useful but treacherous Vasil, picking up the veiled threat the man levied.

Gilana shouted over the start of the cargo plane's engines roaring to life. "Christopher, let's go!"

~

Christopher was sweating despite being in a non-pressurized airplane cargo hold miles above the Earth. He'd been praying for safety the last forty-five minutes while inhaling pure oxygen that worked to drive the nitrogen from his blood, a critical preparation for descending rapidly from 30,000 feet. The red light that filled the cavernous cargo hold was good at protecting the team's night vision but did little to ease his unsettled stomach.

Jackson and Gilana were also purging their bodies of nitrogen. Still, both looked calmer than what Christopher felt. Jackson, on schedule, seemed to be in a deep sleep given his head position.

Jimbo previously assisted Charlie with flying. Now, with less than twenty minutes left before the jump, he helped Christopher, Jackson, and Gilana with their final preparations in the cargo hold.

Jimbo keyed the radio built into his oxygenated helmet like those of others. "I wish I were going with you guys."

Christopher enjoyed the dialogue for a moment as it seemed to bring out Jackson's typical protective nature, as he had done numerous times before in high-stress missions, lowering the tension with humor.

Jackson smarted off, causing everyone but Gilana to laugh. "Well, if that oak trunk you call an arm was a little longer out of a cast, you could have taken my place."

The men watched as the lone female operative moved toward the cargo doors, seemingly oblivious to the humor.

Charlie announced across the radio, "Ten minutes to the jump point. Get ready."

Christopher and Jackson joined Gilana near the cargo doors as they opened. The night sky's void at 30,000 feet over the Scottish Highlands exposed the peril of the mission. The distant flashes of lightning provided brief cracks in the black wall in front of Christopher.

Christopher went over final preparation as a jolt of turbulence made his voice crack across the radio. "Listen up, everyone. I want to cover the exfiltration and non-permissive environment plan one last time. Primary exfiltration will be via air, as we link back up with this plane at the Inverness airport after the mission, skirting Loch Ness back to Inverness. However, if things go bad, we will execute our personal escape and evasion plans with link-up back in Tel Aviv within three days. Gilana, you will use a hybrid water-ground exfiltration route along Loch Ness to Edinburgh before flying to Tel Aviv. Jackson, you will use ground transportation to Glasgow before flying to Tel Aviv. While I will make my way back to the aircraft and fly back to Sofia and then on to Tel Aviv with Charlie and Jimbo. Any questions?"

Jackson sassed, "No questions, but if you scream as we descend, I'm going to make fun of you."

Jackson's last comment caused the stoic Gilana to snicker.

Charlie called, "Two minutes, jumpers get ready."

Christopher stepped in front of the others near the edge of the cargo ramp and starred at the faint twinkle of lights piercing the black curtain of the night sky. A brief glance at the southwest showed the target area built upon the ancient ruins of Urquhart Castle. He gave a thumbs-up to Jackson, Gilana, and Jimbo that was returned and prayed one last time that he and the others would live through the hours ahead.

Jimbo yelled. "Go, go, go!"

Christopher stumbled more than jumped and could hear Jackson start to laugh as the rush of the wind pushed him head down as his feet began to rotate over him. He caught a brief glance of the red light filled cargo hold and Jimbo before the plane was consumed in darkness. Christopher's challenge was getting his body under control. He was tumbling end over end and felt he was going to pass out. His electronic altimeter was calling out the ever-approaching ground, and the immediate death it represented if Christopher did not gain enough control to deploy his parachute.

The robotic soulless female voice of the altimeter called out, "20,000 feet."

Christopher knew he had to arch and gain control as he struggled to remain conscious. He calmed his mind to retrieve previous HALO training from the archives of his memory.

The altimeter called out, "15,000 feet."

Christopher was at terminal velocity and fighting to maintain the hard-earned yet tenuous stability he currently enjoyed. He had to hold it together long enough to deploy at the 1,000 feet mark the team set before the mission. If Christopher hit his parachute too soon, he'd be blown off course; too late, and it would be a short mission. Christopher heard a beeping sound, meaning his primary oxygen system had failed; he was now on his bailout bottle. "God, please let me make it."

The altimeter called out, "10,000 feet."

In a stable freefall, Christopher tried to scan the sky for Gilana and Jackson. He did not see them as he fought to keep the correct posture for the remainder of his descent.

"5,000 feet, warning."

Then "1,000 feet, warning."

Christopher felt as if his spine and stomach launched out of the top of his head as his parachute jerked him out of the terminal velocity freefall. However, he only momentarily slowed as his rapid descent resumed.

His primary chute had tangled. Christopher fought the wave of panic that flushed over him as the altimeter called out, "500 feet, warning."

Christopher jerked once again after cutting away his primary chute and deploying his reserve, as the altimeter called out, "200 feet, warning."

He flared the parachute as much as possible as the semi-illuminated Inverness Lab came into full sight, and the low fog bank melted away. He hoped he could slow enough not to break anything. Christopher watched as the lab grounds, covered with more trees than he expected, raced up at him. Christopher steered his chute toward a break in the trees near a small building, and at 25 feet, he dropped his assault pack and braced for landing.

As Christopher hit the ground, his chute dragged him perilously close to the electrified outer fence protecting the Inverness compound. The jarring landing stunned him. Christopher swiped at his quick harness release but kept missing as the fence grew larger in his vision. He felt an intense pressure on him as Jackson tackled him and hit his parachute release moments before the chute began to sizzle in the nearby fence.

Jackson keyed the radio headset. "You like tempting fate, I see."

Gilana shouted as she moved over to the two men. "Get up, and let's go!"

Christopher took a moment to find his stomach after the riskiest airborne operation he'd ever experienced. He gained his composure and shed his protective wind suit while retrieving his weapons and assault pack.

Christopher keyed his radio. "I'm okay; let's go."

Gabriella's nerves agitated her. She had spent the past few months globetrotting the world attempting to undermine Draven Cross, believing she was the only one alive to do it. Now that she knew that some of the most influential people in the world regarding slowing Draven were in harm's way, the thoughts coursing through her mind were overwhelming.

Christopher and Jackson were at the forefront of her mind. Thankfully, she had access to the one place in the world that could ease her worries, the UE Intelligence Operations Center. As the Director of Intelligence for the UE, Gabriella oversaw information that would have made the heads of her former Langley boss's swim. There was no leader on Earth that the UE did not have access to their personal email accounts, banking information. In addition, cameras wired for sound were placed into their private offices and residences. This intensive intrusion was a part of Draven's Sentinel effort and a way to evaluate the senior UE officials' loyalty within the regional governments' structure.

Gabriella made her way to the Unified European Nations regional desk. She asked the officer to pull up any activity at UE facilities within the European region in front of a bank of monitors. Gabriella did not want to draw immediate attention to Inverness. She covered her intentions by asking the officer to give her a brief rundown of the procedures used to collect intelligence in the region.

As the UE officer began her speech, she paused with the flash across a monitor labeled U.K.

The UE intelligence officer typed at a keyboard to push the data to a large screen. "Ma'am, there seems to be something happening at a facility named Inverness Lab in Scotland. I also have a report that six Inverness private security guards and six UE SAG operatives are at the lab."

Waves of anxiety rushed over Gabriella as sweat gathered at her armpits. *Am I about to witness the demise of my friends*? She thought.

As Christopher adjusted his night-vision goggles, he heard the unmistakable crack of air signaling gunfire trained at Jackson, Gilana, and him from a large building at the center of the complex. Wafts of cordite filled the air, followed by the loud bang of Gilana's M4 rifle. Christopher was impressed by the former Mossad officer's aggressive response to the UE's attack. Christopher and Jackson joined Gilana in returning gunfire as the team moved to the nearby unlit utility building and the protection the darkness offered.

Christopher spoke into his radio mic as Gilana continue returning gunfire. "Okay, Jackson, we'll provide you cover fire as you place the explosive charges on the critical buildings."

Gilana responded, "Great plan, now keep shooting."

In between gunshots to keep the UE from advancing, Christopher watched Jackson preparing the bundle of C4 explosives. Christopher knew from the mission prep that the lab formed a triangle with the main building located within the center. He realized that the small building protecting the team sat at the top point of the triangle. The bottom points were a security facility on the southwestern point and living quarters on the southeastern end, explaining the guard's direction.

Jackson keyed his radio. He laid three small circular wads of C4 in a triangle near an exhaust port of a generator beyond the wall. "Let me get these folks' attention. This building houses the main power generator."

Christopher directed, "Alright, lay down some cover fire and move toward that runoff ditch across the road in the direction of the center building."

The trio simultaneously opened fire on a group of guards advancing toward them from the southwest as they ran across the road to the safety of the ditch.

Christopher ordered, "Now, Jackson."

The remote detonation of the C4 created a thunderous crack in the cold Scottish night as the secondary explosion of the generator raced across the complex, causing darkness to engulf the entire lab. Christopher quickly wiped the sweat from around his night-vision goggles. He peered out of the ditch to see the guards had broken into two different groups in an attempt to surround them.

Christopher commanded, "We need to get moving. Gilana, you take the group on your right; I will take the group on my left. Jackson, get ready to run to the main building."

Jackson nodded to Gilana. "Okay, let's go."

Christopher stood and opened fire on the four men advancing toward him while lobbing a hand grenade. Gilana joined him, firing on the group, moving toward the right of the ditch. Jackson ran an endless 100 meters with Christopher and Gilana protecting his back by drawing attention to the ditch.

As Christopher's attention returned to Jackson, his heart sank, watching in horror as an emergency floodlight illuminated Jackson wrestling with a guard. The two men rolled on the ground with what looked like Jackson's assault pack flying off his back.

Christopher grabbed two hand grenades and watched Gilana do the same. "We need to get up to Jackson, throw the grenades, and run toward the center of the complex."

The two groups of guards both slowed their advance and took shelter from Christopher and Gilana's attack behind a large cargo truck on Christopher's side and a half-constructed building near Gilana. The hand grenade explosions brought a lull to the fighting as Gilana and Christopher ran toward Jackson, now lying on his back near a central lab wall, as the gunfire returned.

Christopher asked for an update from Jackson after seeing the lab guard lying next to a bloodied combat knife. "Are you hurt?"

Jackson responded after refitting his assault pack and M4, "Nah, only a small cut on my arm. The guy got the jump on me, so it could have been worse."

Christopher took in the deteriorating situation. As all three teammates lay on the cold, wet ground near a cluster of Alder trees. The mossy smell of the damp Earth flashed a memory of being wet and miserable during Robin Sage at Fort Bragg years ago; the lesson in the memory was he needed to make a decision. Thankfully, they were near the primary lab as the gunfire started seeking them from three different directions.

Gilana's announcement over the radio amongst her gunshots shocked Christopher beating him to a decision. "We need to split up; there are too many guards and not enough of us. We put everyone at risk if we try to fight our way back to the plane."

Christopher yelled no in his radio mic in between a few shots.

Jackson keyed his radio as he stacked C4 against the nearby wall and around the building's backside. "Gilana is right. No time to argue. You guys hold these clowns off for a few moments while I load this building up with some C4."

Christopher knew that ammo was dangerously low for everyone, as the team bounded to the lab's rear, joining Jackson. He fought the idea of splitting up despite the odds being against them. Christopher watched as a group of six guards slowly advanced toward them amongst the Alder tree cluttered central building area.

Jackson shot two guards attempting to come around the back of the central lab before keying his radio. "If we stay here much longer, we're going to run out of ammo. There looks like a trail by the security shack that might lead down to the river. Let's move across the road and blow this building and hope for the best."

Christopher approved the lab's destruction, still wavering on the decision that followed how to survive the assault together as a team as they ran across the road. "Okay, do it."

The explosion was muted compared to the generator explosion. Silence filled the night air for a few moments as Christopher, Gilana, and Jackson ran down the trail past the guards' smokers shack only to find a padlocked gate.

Gilana drew her pistol and placed two close-range shots into the padlock holding the now unelectrified security gate.

Christopher faced a decision he dreaded for the last few moments. Doubt raised in him, and Heaven was silent as he yelled in his radio mic. "Look, we can get back to the plane together; there is no need to split up!"

Jackson had also decided to key his radio one final time as he began executing his escape and evasion plan. He was heading off into the night along the Loch toward the A82 highway. "Trouble is heading our way; we all have plenty of money to get to Tel Aviv. I'll see you in a few days."

Gilana joined Jackson's decision and keyed her radio one more time. She moved down the riverbank toward the black Loch Ness. "We will be fine, Christopher, now go. I hear guards approaching."

Christopher fired off a few shots toward the rattled but determined remaining guards, hoping they would chase him over the others. He ran toward an Alder forest surrounding the now destroyed Inverness National Lab, in the direction of Inverness airport. Christopher knew the twenty-five miles would take him another eight hours to navigate, mainly due to using evasion techniques and the terrain. Christopher prayed they all lived to see each other again in Tel Aviv as the forest consumed his figure.

CHAPTER 10

GABRIELLA WONDERED WHAT was occurring in Scotland. However, her attention was diverted as an unmatched manipulative power over people spewed from Draven Cross's lips. The unsuspecting global audience would have the impression that the world was in capable hands. The briefing's secret was each question asked was scripted and controlled by the UE. In truth, the world lay decimated and in chaos, and Draven's control came at the cost of countless lives lost.

Cities worldwide had long abandoned, attempting to identify or bury the numerous dead bodies that littered vacant or destroyed businesses, homes, and cars. Mass graves or incineration were used to reduce the strain on overwhelmed city morgues. Reliable essential services were a constant challenge as electricity and access to clean water were scarce.

What food was available, UE soldiers distributed. There were daily reports of the soldiers being overrun and attacked due to desperation. Diseases, long-since eliminated in the Western world, ran rampant multiplied by the lack of doctors and nurses and amplified with the Pyretos epidemic. Draven skillfully led the world to believe all the chaos and suffering were an aftereffect of the late President Rodgers's followers' rebellious actions. Gabriella feared that the truth would never get out to the world on who Draven really was, and she doubted that if the reality reached the public, many would not believe the news.

Gabriella wondered how Draven would react to losing his bioweapons lab as she watched Evan wait for the "perfect" moment to deliver the news that Christopher and his team had destroyed the Inverness

National Lab. A smile crossed her face as she thought of the attack as a measure of American revenge against Draven.

Evan's darting in and out of the press room door finally caused enough of a distraction in the room that Draven realized that something other than him was drawing attention.

Gabriella saw the disappointment rise in Draven's face as he noticed an overly zealous Evan, waving him down as if he were attempting to hail a cab in midtown New York. He tried to maintain his composure walking over to Evan. Gabriella enjoyed the panicked conversation that Christopher and his team had wrought amongst the UE senior members.

Draven asked, "What do you want, and why can't you handle it?"

"Sir, the Inverness National Lab, the location of the—"

Evan was cut off by Draven. "I know what's at Inverness, Scotland, Evan. Get to the point."

Evan exclaimed, "The lab was destroyed by an attack; several men are dead or wounded. We are attempting to determine who it was now."

Gabriella was bewildered as she watched Draven's reaction.

Draven smiled before returning to the podium. "Perfect. I will make this work."

Draven feigned distress at his announcement. "Ladies and gentlemen, please excuse the interruption. I was informed that the lab that produced the anti-viral to the biological weapon that the former American president's surrogates released on all of us was destroyed."

The UE press pool instinctively reacted to Draven's now off-script proclamation, which delighted him.

Draven answered a UE press pool question. "Yes, I have a response to this cowardly and heinous attack. We will track down and ensure that justice is brought to those who seek to use violence to intimidate the UE from reaching its peaceful aspirations."

Draven. "I believe the attack emanated at the hands of religious fanatics. An attack born from the hate spewed at these mass Christian rallies around the world."

The enthusiasm Draven had in hearing that the Inverness Lab was destroyed became apparent. He used the event to justify to the world his plan to target Christians. Gemma approached the pressroom, briefly joining Evan and her.

Gemma had been coordinating senior UE officials' questions regarding Inverness and was late to the ongoing press conference, where she served as Draven's deflector. As another question was asked regarding the evidence pointing to the Christian rallies, Gemma emerged at Draven's side. "The Secretary-General would take no further questions."

Walking out of the press room to a hail of reporters' questions, Draven whispered, "Good timing, Gemma."

Evan and Gabriella met Draven and Gemma outside the press room as they emerged.

Draven ordered Gemma, "Get Barnes on the phone and let me see the footage from the lab attack."

Gabriella hoped that Christopher and his team were safely on their way back to Israel because the wrath of Draven would soon turn to find the perpetrators of the lab attack.

⁂

With the mid-morning sun perched over Loch Ness, Christopher's legs were burning and tight, while his back throbbed after the past eight hours of playing a dangerous game of cat and mouse. The local law enforcement agencies and only God knew who else searched for Christopher's team since the lab's attack in the early morning hours. He was, according to his map and compass, a few short miles from the Inverness airport. Christopher hoped that Gilana and Jackson's journey to their exfiltration points was less exciting than his adventure.

Christopher took the silence of the snow-covered Loch Ness lowlands, where he had not heard dogs or sirens for the past hour and a half, to mean that he had finally put enough distance and terrain between himself and his pursuers to ditch his assault gear. He pulled a smaller black backpack out of his assault pack, which contained a pair of jeans, a light jacket, a flannel shirt, and a local Aberdeen Football Club ballcap to complete his look of a homely tourist.

Christopher took an apprehensive look at his assault pack that now contained his M4 rifle, pistol, and combat clothing used in the mission before filling the bag with rocks. He watched the assault pack sink in the frigid River Ness. Christopher's wits and God's provision were the only things available for his protection now; Christopher tried to suppress the doubt rising within him that God wouldn't come through. As Christopher made the walk toward a petrol station and a cab filling up, he prayed his faith in God over himself would prove the right choice for his team and himself.

Gilana's hybrid exfiltration route provided a scenic but cold and wet view of the lower Loch Ness. She was surprised no one seemed interested in pursuing her. While grateful for the relatively smooth journey, she wondered if Jackson and Christopher had the same luck. A few hundred Euros, which thankfully were still welcomed, secured a ride with a Scottish highland beef distributor bound for Edinburgh. Gilana approached the driver, and his assistant at a truck stop near Fort Augustus on the A82 highway after leaving the Loch Ness shoreline. Gilana was no longer surprised, as she once was as a new Mossad agent, at how enough money made most people do what you asked with few questions. The satisfaction of getting a measure of *naqam* against the UE who took the life of her beloved Uri brought a smile to Gilana's face as the meat truck neared Edinburgh Airport.

Jackson had been breaking brush through the dense Alder forest for what felt like an eternity. He was scratched up and felt twenty years older as he emerged along a highway named A82 near Lewiston. Jackson was grateful for the young Glasgow University student, Gavin Brown, picking him up despite the poor post-mission clothing options Jackson had selected for himself. Jackson's mind had not been focused on the potential that he would have to exfiltrate or the need for clothing that would aid in commercial travel. The result was a mix-match between his assault gear and civilian clothing. Jackson had only packed a long-sleeved cotton thermal shirt. He was sure he looked like a clown at best and more likely like a deranged criminal escapee, dressed in a brown, long-sleeve shirt, black tactical pants, and black boots, but here he was warm inside Gavin Brown's car.

Jackson could see Gavin building the courage to ask him how he landed in a Scottish highland forest. Gavin finally asked in a thick Scottish accent, "Did you get yourself lost?"

Jackson replied, attempting to provide a backstory that matched his looks, "You could say I did. I was on an adventure tour and separated from my group last night. The name is Bruce Smith."

Gavin stated, "Yanks are chancers, aren't you?"

Jackson could hear Christopher's laughter at the exchange between a Scot and himself, considering Jackson was a Ph.D. in American-South slang. For the first time in his life, he understood what others went through when he used Southern slang, as the Scotsman's reference was lost on him.

Jackson's thought made him laugh. "I am sorry you lost me with what you said."

Gavin clarified, "You've been pushing your luck. Late winter in the highlands has killed many men. You're lucky I'm heading back to university, or you've been dead by nightfall."

Jackson responded, "You have no idea, Gavin."

As the two men made small talk along A82, a wave of panic arose in Jackson as they made their way back toward Urquhart Castle, where black pillars of smoke billowed. Law enforcement officials had blocked the road and were questioning traffic as it passed through.

Jackson's tone shifted, matching the threat facing him at the roadblock. "Listen, Gavin, we don't have much time to discuss this. You see that smoke coming from the castle, my friends and I did that. If you play your part in getting me past this roadblock, then you will be fine. If you try to be a hero, my friends will find you, and nothing good will come from that experience. Understand? I need you to trust me. I will make it worth your while when we get to Glasgow. I am your uncle, and we're on our way back to Glasgow after visiting family…where are you from again?"

"I am from Lewiston, but I don't want to get involved."

Jackson turned in his seat to stare intently at the young man. "I don't want to hurt you, Gavin, but trust me when I say I'm not going with these folks either."

Gavin exclaimed, "Okay, you're my uncle. Let me talk because your yank accent will give you away!"

Gavin brought his small compact car to a stop at the roadblock while Jackson donned a ski jacket from the backseat to mask the mud-stained shirt he was wearing.

A police officer asked Gavin, "Where you coming from, and where are you headed?"

Gavin's voice cracked, drawing a smoldering stare from Jackson. "My uncle and I are coming from Lewiston going back to Glasgow after a visit with family."

The police officer turned his attention to Jackson. "Ah sir, what's your name?"

Jackson smacked Gavin on the arm while Jackson pointed to his mouth and acting out sign language.

Gavin winced. "Ouch. I'm sorry my uncle cannot speak; his name is William."

The officer gave the two men a long look. Thankfully, traffic began to build behind them, and the officer waved them through the checkpoint without further scrutiny. After a few miles of silence, Jackson opened up.

Jackson glanced behind the vehicle expecting someone to be following them. "You kept your cool back there, Gavin. I cannot say thank you enough."

Gavin exhaled as if he had been holding his breath. "That was the second most exciting thing that's ever happened in my life. The day of the disappearances was the most exciting, but it's a bad way to describe such a horrible day. Are you some kind of criminal?"

Jackson laughed. "No, I'm trying to stop a criminal. And the disappearances are the reason for needing to stop this monster."

Gavin questioned Jackson, "What do the disappearances have to do with you stopping a criminal in Scotland?"

Jackson laughed again, as he hoped Gavin would take the bait to hear about Jesus Christ. "It's a long story, but since we have two hours until we reach Glasgow, I'm willing to share if you want."

Gavin perked up. "Yeah, I would love to hear the story. My mates at the university accounting club will not believe me when I tell them about meeting you."

Jackson chuckled. "You're in the accounting club, never would have guessed. Trust me; my friends won't believe me when I tell them this story either."

~

Gabriella sat at her desk, manipulating an intelligence report from the Inverness lab attack, attempting to "support" the continuous loop of propaganda pushed by ANN regarding the event. She only had a few hours to finish the report before flying to Jakarta to link up with John Barnes. Gabriella made Draven allow her to be "on the ground" to provide intelligence support to Barnes's thugs. Gabriella knew that she owed it to Kerim and other believers to mitigate any harm Draven meant for the Christians in Jakarta.

The UE had a press release to link the lab attack and the Christian evangelist movement. This was all a pretext for Draven increasing his persecution of those challenging him, namely Christians.

While Christopher and associates had destroyed the source of Pyretos, Draven had allocated Barnes' SAG operatives to handle a small but lethal tactical assignment. The problem lies in not knowing how to stop any future Pyretos release. Gabriella wanted to bargain her acceptance of God's salvation in her life for yet another concrete example that He was really listening to her. She needed God to show her how to stop Draven's efforts in Jakarta.

Gabriella answered a knock at her door. "Come in."

"Hello, love. I figured you were hiding in your office. I wanted to let you know a bit of good news. I will be joining you in Jakarta," the ever-enthused Gemma announced.

Gabriella picked up Gemma's message between rattles on her keyboard. "What? Why, Gemma? You know this could be dangerous."

Gemma's frustration with Gabriella's attitude to fighting Draven broke the surface. "I figured you would try to stop me. If you're putting yourself in harm's way, then I would rather die with you than live next—"

Gabriella cut off Gemma and moved to embrace her friend as both women cried.

"I love you, Gemma. Let's take a walk as this is not the place to have this conversation." The women remained silent until reaching the UE gardens, where days ago Draven consolidated his hold on world power.

Gabriella broke the silence. "Honestly, when I am out trying to get some level of revenge against Draven, I don't care if I live. I only want him to suffer as I have, but I'm glad you want to be with me; maybe it will keep me from doing anything crazy."

Gemma shrugged. "I wish I could understand your feelings, but you have a lot to live for, my friend. Maybe you will even join me at the Christian rally. I feel compelled to hear these men speak in person; it's fascinating that they are willing to give their life for a belief that's so new to them. Remember before you say no, I am your best friend in the world, and it would break my heart. I need to get back to my desk, but I will see you on the flight to Jakarta."

Gabriella remembered why she had no girlfriends. She never got excited to hang out and talk mindlessly about relationships and other things she labeled critical for women like Gemma. Yet, for some reason, she loved being in Gemma's company; there was a warmth about her that Gabriella had never experienced on a significant level with a woman outside her mother. Perhaps attending the rally would cause Draven to reconsider using the weapon. The thought made her laugh. *Draven would kill me for the irony alone*, she thought. *God, I need your help*. Gabriella walked back toward her office to prepare for Jakarta.

&

As Draven sat in his office, his pride swelled. He was the absolute ruler of the entire world with no challengers in sight. Draven would have been happy if his day ended with thoughts of domination by his one-world government. Yet, Gemma's intercom message announcing

Evan had a pressing matter seemed destined to derail his moment of self-appreciation.

A frown rose on Draven's face as Evan began while he was still in stride to inform him that Pontiff Conti was developing into a more substantial headache than anticipated.

Draven challenged, "Explain to me again, Evan, how Conti is undermining my work. I was thinking of more pleasant thoughts as you were droning on."

Evan protested, "Conti is taking his role as the Unified Arabian Nations ambassador and Interfaith leader too far."

Draven laughed. "It has been only a few days, and you have Conti taking over the world. It seems to me that there is a bit of jealously in your complaint, Evan. Conti is taking your beloved Interfaith to levels you could not."

Draven enjoyed the sting his words brought to Evan, knowing the man loved his created religion dearly.

Evan shot back, "It is not jealously, but concern for the greater vision you have produced."

Draven challenged, "Give me an example of how Conti is now my biggest concern. It's to my benefit to have this pope in new clothes delude the masses with a religious platform. It helps me keep the world subdued. You should know this. Plus, those two fools in Jerusalem and the growing rabble who believe their message and these 144,000 Jesus-following converted Jewish men are bigger headaches."

Evan made a few clicks on his laptop keyboard before spinning the computer around on Draven's desk to show Conti's recent interview in Amman, Jordan.

Draven watched and listened to Conti in Amman's Hashemite Square, a video highlighted by a massive crowd chanting his name.

"Good afternoon, everyone. I am Susan Gregory of ANN, speaking with Interfaith Pontiff Conti. What brings you to Amman, Pontiff?"

Conti clarified, "I prefer being referred to as Eminence in my current duties here in Jordan. I am also one of the ten regional ambassadors within the Unified Earth Government, in addition to my role as the leader of the UE state religion, Interfaith."

Susan Gregory corrected, "My apologies, your Eminence."

"I am here not only to demonstrate the benefits of embracing a religion where the canon centers not on making people feel bad about their lifestyles and choices, but I am also here to alleviate suffering," Conti explained.

Susan Gregory dug deeper for clarification. "Could you elaborate on how you're alleviating suffering?"

"This is the first stop of a world tour where I will hold Interfaith rallies, where the message of our great religion can be taught in contrast to the hatred being spewed by these two crazed 'witnesses,' in Jerusalem and their thousands of blind followers around the world holding these archaic Christian rallies."

Susan Gregory shifted on her feet. "I want to challenge you on what you've said, Eminence. You're telling the listening audience that your charitable efforts are above what Secretary-General Cross has done and continues to do in terms of alleviating suffering."

Conti pointed away from the camera to the city behind him. "Look at the crowd. These people came seeking a hopeful spiritual message in such trying times, but are also walking away with food, water, and other essential items all provided through the Interfaith religious network."

Draven felt a wave of heat rise across his face as the video showed the camera panning across Hashemite square to show UE soldiers handing out goods to the crowd.

Conti gushed. "You see, for the first time in human history, religion is not working against the advancements of humanity but working to solve the problems facing all of us. I am working in areas where the Secretary-General cannot operate. I am both a spiritual and political leader, the perfect combination, in my opinion. Thus, I am solving issues Mr. Cross cannot."

Susan Gregory concluded, "That is a bold statement, but if your work here in Amman is any indication of what is to come, Interfaith and your leadership are welcomed changes to the world."

Draven slammed Evan's laptop shut, rubbing his hands across his face.

Evan said, "Now you see what I was telling you."

Draven practically growled. "His ego is bigger than expected. Yes, I see that Conti is yearning for more. I should have killed the fool for disrespecting me last week. No matter, I must give him credit for doing something you have struggled to do, which is counter the hatred directed at me by those Two Witnesses."

Evan stated, "I've defended you and the UE at every turn. But I can see the usefulness in taking his ego and using it for our purposes. I will keep an eye on him to ensure his ambition doesn't turn to treachery."

Draven agreed. "Keep an eye on Conti; while he's saying all the right things publicly, he could be plotting my demise secretly. Also, I want you to direct him to make sure he remembers who enables his success, me."

Evan continued, "I understand and will make sure I keep him on a short leash. No matter what he tries, I will ensure it works to glorify you and the Prince of This World."

Draven stated, "Make sure you do, Evan; I don't trust Conti. I can tell when a man has ambitions greater than his current station, and Conti wants the world."

As the sun rose over the seven hills surrounding Jerusalem, Christopher enjoyed the blend of aromas from fragrant juniper trees and the black Arabian coffee he nursed sitting in General Havid's garden. Today was the second morning he had been back since the Inverness lab mission, and Jackson was still missing. Gilana arrived late yesterday with no issues. General Havid mentioned while the UE was upset, there were no leads on who conducted the attack, meaning Jackson had not been caught. So, where was Jackson?

Christopher's worry for him was interrupted by the commanding presence of General Havid, who took a seat next to him on a small garden bench overlooking Jerusalem. The general broke the silence with questions; only a man with similar experiences to Christopher could have asked.

General Havid questioned, "You're wondering if you did something wrong, yes? You think that Jackson's failure to arrive yet is your fault?"

Christopher responded, "I have been going over the mission and the decision for everyone to split apart at the lab. I am afraid my decision may have cost Jackson his life. We could have stayed together."

General Havid did not immediately respond as if he wanted Christopher to think about what he had said. The general reminded him of Colonel Delmar, the former Omega Group leader. Both men would pose a question, so you thought about a situation from a different perspective.

Christopher said, "You believe I am struggling with my faith. That I am thinking God's influence was not to be trusted in how I thought about the lab mission."

General Havid again questioned Christopher, "You remember what I told you when you last visited my home, and I suggested creating this piecemeal covert unit for attacking Draven Cross?"

The learning method employed by General Havid caused Christopher to chuckle, as the technique reminded him of Colonel Delmar, the former Omega leader.

Christopher answered, hoping to get to the heart of the conversation. "No, I don't, sir."

General Havid rose to leave Christopher with some final thoughts. "I told you two things that should provide you solace if Jackson does not return and allow you to not lose your faith. Remember, we must continue to fight against the evil of Draven Cross no matter the cost. First, we must give all we have, even our lives, for Christ Jesus, who died to provide us with eternal life. Secondly, your obsession with holding on to the past is poisonous. The mission is complete, but here you are, still worrying and living out an event you can do nothing to alter. If Jackson is gone, he is in a better place than us. However, I feel we will see our strange-speaking friend soon."

Christopher starred out at the city of Jerusalem, soaking in General Havid's words. He watched as the seasoned warrior returned to his home, grateful that God again provided a leader and mentor to help him through trying times.

Christopher called after him, "Sir, thank you!"

General Havid remarked, entering his home, "You're more than welcome, my friend. There are dark days ahead of us that will test our faith and commitment to God. I will need you at some point."

Christopher prayed that Jackson would return soon. No matter what, Christopher prayed for the strength to serve God with all his heart until Jesus returned.

CHAPTER 11

A WAVE OF FEAR gripped John Barnes as the thought of Christopher Barrett being alive and stalking him from the evening shadows growing around the Gelora Bung Karno football stadium. He needed to focus on the task, placing a final Pyretos dispersant canister near the stage for the Christian rally. Shivering and shaking his head, Barnes imagined Draven's reaction if discovering the Omega Group survived the Alaska attack. Despite the destruction he orchestrated in Alaska, the Inverness lab attack's precision told him that it was not local religious fanatics. His gut told him Christopher Barrett was alive.

Barnes couldn't focus too long on solving the Inverness mystery. The job of identifying the leader of the pending Christian rally and extracting information on the operations of this network of Christian missionaries remained vital. News reports claimed millions of people followed these men and were actively proclaiming Christianity over the UE Interfaith religion. Barnes cared little about people's religious choices and only saw the Christian rallies as a threat to eliminate. He listened as the SAG operatives reported completing emplacing their canisters around the stadium.

Barnes keyed his radio. "Okay, meet me at the main stadium entrance." Barnes watched as ten of his SAG operatives and an additional fifteen men from the most prominent local violent extremist organization joined him. Unbeknownst to the extremist was Barnes's plan to scapegoat them after the attack, as their fingerprints were the only ones that would be found on the dispersant canisters.

Barnes addressed his men, "Listen up, guys. This was only part of the job. We have a day to find the Christian leader here in Jakarta. Ahmad, this is your city; where would these Christians stay before the rally?"

Everyone's attention turned to a slender man with an oily complexion, speaking with a mouthful of voids where teeth should've been—the leader of the *Jundallah* or 'Soldiers of Allah' violent extremist organization in Jakarta.

In heavy-accented English, Ahmad answered, "The Christians moved from Kelapa Gading as the sea rose; many are in South Jakarta. I make some calls."

Barnes replied, "Good, we don't have much time. You should expect a call from me tomorrow after I meet with my intelligence officer. Hopefully, we can make a plan to grab the Christian leader before the rally."

The *Jundallah* followed Ahmad toward the entrance of the *Ratangga,* the colloquial name for Jakarta's mass transit system. While Barnes and his operatives got back into their SUV's to return to the hotel.

As he watched Ahmad wave before disappearing into the transit station, Barnes remarked, "It's amazing how desperation and the promise of money make people naïve."

~

Evan was not surprised, based on the recent performances of Pontiff Conti, with his insistence on a more lavish mode of transportation. The Interfaith version of a papal plane would never be mistaken for modesty, exposing an ego in Conti that surprised Evan. The seat covers in the recently acquired luxury business jet were dark purple silk with the gold-stitched Interfaith symbol in the center. Conti had an opulent bedroom and office in the front of the plane. There were twenty lie-flat business class seats for the press pool and senior staff, a lounge area comprised of a few sofas and an island bar, and a full-service galley.

Evan quipped, "I'm glad to see you take a humble approach when it comes to your personal transportation."

Conti tensed. "Evan, I am not deaf to your sarcasm. The comfort I surround my staff and myself with allows me to better serve the legions of people looking to me for hope."

Evan said, "I believe you misspoke; the world looks to the

Secretary-General for hope. You would be wise to stick to that message when addressing the masses."

Conti dismissed his warning. "Evan, you have seen the effect I am having on the world. I remain in service to the Secretary-General, but I am endowed with the same spirit that guides Draven and you. I must not deprive the public of my gifts. It would be wise for Draven to support my efforts. Now excuse me, I must prepare for my mass before we arrive."

Evan trembled and grew warm with the thoughts coursing through his mind. Conti was right in saying that his influence was growing through these Interfaith rallies, where food, medicine, and clothing were given to those attending. Conti was becoming a rival to Draven's grip on the world, and Evan knew that Draven would kill Conti rather than have his own fame diminish. The question was how to leverage Conti's ambitions and eventual death to his benefit.

It was late evening as the Omega team awaited Jackson's arrival at headquarters, better known as General Havid's home. The laughter and conversation created an atmosphere of optimism—the joy of fellowship amongst the new team members echoed across the general's residence. The potent smell of coffee perfumed the house as the general's aides prepared for a late evening of reflection among the occupants.

Jackson's return kept a buzz flowing through the team since their notification from him earlier in the day. Jackson had taken a full three days to report in from the Inverness mission. Considering he did not need to evade the authorities and took a commercial airliner from Glasgow to Tel Aviv, Jackson's delay piqued Christopher's mind even more.

As they heard the front door opening, Christopher had to force himself not to run over and scream, "*Where have you been*?" like a worried parent awaiting the arrival of a curfew-late new teenage driver.

Gilana took a stern look as Jackson entered the house. "What took you so long? I thought you died or something."

Christopher and everyone else were somewhat shocked by Gilana's pointed approach. However, gratitude was also written on all the faces in the room by the remark.

Jackson chuckled, hearing the steely Gilana voice concern for his overdue return. "Who knew that woodpecker lips were soft sometimes?"

The puzzled looks on everyone's face made Christopher laugh and move to embrace the man who was like a brother to him.

Christopher joked. "Glad to see you still know how to escape and evade."

"This old dog still knows a few tricks. Look, I know you folks have been worried, but do you mind if I get a hot shower before we dive into this story?"

Everyone shouted in unison, "Yes, we mind!"

Jackson laughed in a way Christopher hadn't seen in a while. "In that case, I'm going to need some of that strong coffee I smell brewing."

Jimbo offered to serve Jackson. "I got you covered."

The rest of the team moved to General Havid's study.

Jackson told the Omega team a similar evasion story to the others, with the exception of his delayed arrival. The similar traits amongst each operatives' recounting of the attack spoke to the training of the group. The meeting with Gavin and the long ride back to Glasgow was the distinguishing mark for Jackson's tale.

Jackson was more tired than he had expressed but could tell everyone had been worried about him. He was grateful to see Jimbo return with a steaming cup of Arabian coffee. "Thanks, brother."

Jackson continued, "So, once we got past the local law enforcement checkpoints, I took the rest of the ride to share my story with Gavin. Telling him, I never knew anything about Jesus beyond a surface level growing up, about the disappearances and my family. Most importantly, I told him how I found Jesus Christ. How that decision allowed me to live and face death, knowing my destiny is secure in Jesus's hands."

While impressed by Jackson helping others with faith while evading the UE, Christopher still had questions. "That is amazing, but it doesn't explain why it took you another two days to get back here."

Jackson proclaimed, "That's the best part of the story. Gavin invited me to speak to his accounting club friends, and I led five of them to salvation in Christ."

Everyone in the room clapped at this news but Gilana. He assumed she was still wrestling with coming to accept Jesus as the Jewish messiah.

Above the din of laughter and revelry for Jackson's return and story, Gilana interrupted, "Any word on our next mission against Draven?"

Christopher's smile faded. "I'm waiting to hear from Gabriella. My guess is we will be on the move again soon."

Gilana added, "Good. Making the Beast's life painful is all that matters. I will be at home when you need me."

Christopher looked at General Havid, who merely shook his head as the men watched the lethal and troubled operative leave for her apartment. Christopher hoped that Gilana could find peace, but he understood the struggle to trust and accept God more than most in the room. He knew that accepting Jesus as your personal savior was a feeling that he wanted Gilana and others like her to experience before it was too late.

Gabriella was mentally unprepared for this trip outside of the new global capital of Rome. While she had traveled to China and the US since the disappearances and understood the world was in ruin. The scene before Gabriella was heartbreaking. From her UE caravan, Gabriella watched brown sludge tides from the Java Sea crash against beaches of garbage and rotting animals as the procession drove from Soekarno-Hatta International Airport to the city.

The landscape along the highway leading into Jakarta was a massive shantytown made of tin and driftwood shacks. The squatters were sprawled along the garbage seacoast, leaving the shantytown as the only visible marker of Jakarta's former northern sector. The gaunt faces of the destitute people moved along the overcrowded garbage-filled streets. Their skeletal frames seemed to be empty shells of former people covered with tattered clothes. Jakarta's most vulnerable seemed oblivious to the pomp of Gabriella's police-escorted UE caravan as it sped by the shantytown.

This was far from the world that Draven painted in Rome. With control over the internet and the media outlets and travel limited to UE approved persons, the UE was able to manipulate the narrative that the world's recovery was going well.

As the vehicles came to a stop at the hotel, Gabriella was accosted by the overpowering death scent as her door opened. She donned her facemask, not for fear of the still rampant Pyretos virus, but more out of hope to mitigate the stench. The nearby sea of garbage mixed with the Javan winter's balmy air created a thick haze of putrid air. She thought about the long days ahead as she entered the hotel lobby.

Gemma exclaimed, "That was a horrid drive. Did you see the look on those poor people's faces and the smell of the city? I thought the entire world was doing at least as well as Rome."

Gabriella added, "This is the worst I've seen during my time away from headquarters, but I would have been more surprised to find recovery efforts underway."

Gemma shifted to a pressing need. "It's 8 p.m., and I didn't eat anything on the flight here. Let's get settled into our rooms and find a bite to eat. I'm starving."

Gabriella laughed. "It's really not fair that you literally eat whatever you want and have a figure that could cut through steel."

Laughing, Gemma replied, "Thank you. Now, let's get settled and find some *Satay*."

Gabriella raised her eyebrows. "Find what?"

Laughing, Gemma said, "It's a chicken dish."

"In that case, let's eat."

Gabriella's enjoyment from the meal and conversation with Gemma at the hotel restaurant was short-lived, as John Barnes yelled at her across the lobby before she could board the elevator to her shared room with Gemma. She didn't hide the revulsion flowing across her face as Barnes made his way across the lobby, leaving his group of hired killers at the check-in counter.

Gabriella rolled her eyes. "I will catch up with you later, Gemma."

Gemma chuckled. "Gladly."

As his eyes wandered across Gabriella's body, Barnes said, "I knew it was you from across the room."

Gabriella asserted, "I could do without your harassment, and your manners are disgusting; Look, I'm tired; what do you want?"

Barnes laughed at Gabriella's response. "There are a lot of things I want and will get one day. For now, I want to know where the Christian rally leaders are located. I have a local source tracking them down, but I figured you would have better intelligence."

Gabriella said, "I know they're here and likely staying in the old Christian neighborhoods in the Kelapa Gading district. Once I find out more, I will tell you."

"You're wrong—" Barnes was cut off by his phone ringing. "What do you want? Well, keep a few of your men watching the place. I'll take care of the problem tomorrow."

Gabriella chided. "Let me guess you found a brothel."

"You think so little of me. I'm going to surprise you one day with who I really am. Plus, I did your job for you."

Gabriella asked, "What do you mean you did my job?"

"Tomorrow evening, my team is going to eliminate the Christian rally leader, which will be accomplished without intelligence provided by you. Plus, we have a nice surprise awaiting all those religious nuts at the stadium, so they won't be disappointed."

Gabriella hoped Barnes's stupidity would allow her to save thousands of lives. "Barnes, where is the Christian leader? I can't support you if I don't know."

Barnes answered, "He's at a western-style house in South Jakarta, near the *Pondok Indah Grand Mosque,* and we've placed Pyretos-bombs across the stadium. By this time tomorrow, I will tell the Secretary-General that this Christian movement is all but dead. Sweet dreams, make sure you think about me."

Gabriella winced, not only at Barnes's remark but also with the thought of what needed to be done. *I hope there's enough time for all the pieces to fall into place*, she thought, pulling out her communicator to call Christopher Barrett.

Draven's anger rose as he sat in his office watching the latest Interfaith Rally in Paris. Pontiff Conti was lauded as a "rising new leader in the world." ANN coverage praised him as his motorcade traveled from *Charles De Gaul Airport* to the *Esplanade du Trocadero* in the shadow of the *Eiffel Tower* for the rally. It was assessed during the telecast that the Interfaith religion would eventually surpass the Secretary-General in popularity. While this shouldn't have bothered the man in control of the Interfaith religion, Draven's pride caused him to throw the television remote across the room, screaming incoherently into the void of his office. It was in this moment of rage that he felt the invasion of his mind and body, a prelude of a visit from his unseen master.

In the next moment, Draven was standing at the peak of a tall mountain, looking across a vast plain filled with cities as far as he could see.

"Tell me what you see," ordered a loud authoritative voice behind him.

Draven turned to look at the speaker but found himself alone and surprisingly cold. The steam coming from his mouth and the brisk wind stinging his ears told him this experience was as real as him sitting in his office moments ago.

The voice shouted, "Answer me!"

Draven dropped to his knees at the top of the snow-covered mountain, stammering, lost for words. He babbled an answer covering his head in fear of the response. "It's a country, I think."

A voice that echoed like thunder in Draven's ears answered, "It is more than a country. It is all that I have given you. Each of the cities you see represents a nation, and this mountain is the world, with you at its peak. The false religion your image-bearer created will serve its purpose *in my time.* It is time to see the potential in using the false religion for your benefit. Stand and worship me, for I am the Prince of this World. Now go before the people and demand their respect!"

"Thank you, my lord. I won't let—" Draven's words were cut off as he was thrown off the mountain, falling toward the ground below.

Draven screamed for help as he tumbled toward an endlessly dark chasm growing deeper in the ground with each second; he rushed toward the pit. As his screams for the Prince of This World to help went without an answer. Draven braced for what he assumed was an imminent death as the rim of the pit consumed him, only to flop into his plush office chair, sweating.

The Prince of This World let a sinister laugh fill the air. "Never forget that I alone control your life."

Draven's mind was racing. He composed himself and pushed the intercom, drawing a junior assistant's cheerful voice, filling in for the absent Gemma.

The assistant answered, "Yes, Secretary-General, how can I assist you?"

Draven ordered, "Get my plane ready to depart for Jerusalem first thing tomorrow morning and get Evan Mallory on the phone."

"Yes, sir."

Draven thought as he prepared to depart for Jerusalem. *It is time for me to benefit from this growing interest in the Interfaith religion.*

ᘏ

The adrenaline of awaiting Jackson's return and the successful conclusion to the revived Omega team's first mission against Draven Cross was subsiding, leaving thoughts of what was to come. General Havid started laughing as he watched Jimbo, Jackson, and Charlie depart for bed, leaving Christopher and himself on his plush office couch.

Christopher questioned, "What's so funny?"

General Havid's voice thickened. "I thought about the conversation my wife and I had when deciding on the size of this home. In particular, how many bedrooms we needed. She thought I was ridiculous in wanting to have a guest wing built, with four bedroom suites in addition to the three in this part of the home. I told her I could see a future use, perhaps adopting many children."

The general continued, "My sweet Abagail would have made a wonderful mother, but it was not meant for us to experience the joy of parenthood. However, the bedrooms did prove wise, did they not? I was finally on the right side of a disagreement with her."

Christopher expressed his appreciation, "We're all grateful that we have a safe place to stay. I did have a question, or better said, a confession."

"My home is your home, now please tell me what's on your mind," General Havid said, sitting again next to Christopher.

Christopher continued, "I have my doubts about trusting God. The recent mission and the delay with Jackson brought back a flood of doubt. I struggled to trust God was watching over me, I mean us. I guess I'm wondering if my belief in Him was real."

General Havid said, "I am no expert and have only been committed to Christ Jesus a little while longer than you, but here are my thoughts. If honest, I think we all have doubts and fears about the faithfulness of God in our lives. The world we live in is terrifying and growing worse by the day. Think about the great King David, a man the Bible declares was after God's own heart. In *Psalm 13:1*, we see David's darkest hour, his fear and doubt in God's faithfulness. David says, *'How long, Lord? Will you forget me forever? How long will you hide your face from me?'* Christopher, we all doubt God at times, even King David. The key is not allowing your doubt to produce fear. The emotion of fear separates you from trusting that God will see you through every situation. Even in the face of death, you must know that God is with you."

Christopher did not get a chance to respond to the general when the team's communicator, as Jackson referred to his quantum phone, rang. General Havid's cell phone also rang simultaneously, causing the men to give each other puzzled looks. Christopher accepted the incoming call from Gabriella moving away from the couch and the general.

"Hey, Gabriella, what's up?

"Hi, Chris. I don't have much time. Look, Barnes is planning to kill the Christian leader of the big rally planned here in Jakarta. Worst of all, he plans to release Pyretos here."

Christopher asked, "Are you sure?"

"Yes, I'm positive. I wanted to let you know I was hoping you could stop Barnes's plans. I'm not sure my operative friend in China can respond quickly."

Christopher's resolved to help. "I look forward to meeting this other team working against Draven someday. Okay, I will get the team heading your way as soon as possible. If we leave by 2300 my time, we should land in Jakarta around 0430. It's a good thing the rally won't start until 1900, which will give us plenty of time to finalize a plan."

Gabriella sounded relieved on the other end. "Great, I have to go warn the Christian leaders. See you when you get here."

Christopher said, "No, wait; you're going to do what? No, Gabriella, wait for us to get there. Listen to me! Hello…Hello…." Gabriella had hung up on Christopher.

General Havid questioned, "I take it there is another crisis requiring the team's services?"

Christopher relayed the brief conversation he had with Gabriella.

General Havid remarked, "I agree Gabriella is placing herself in great danger if she is discovered aiding our efforts. I worry more about John Barnes and his operatives being in the same location as your team. You will be outnumbered and beyond any help if a conflict with Barnes erupts. I will begin collecting any intelligence and ensure you have vehicles waiting for you when you land. I, too, will be required to act my part tomorrow. It seems Mr. Cross is making an unannounced trip here, likely coinciding with the Interfaith rally in the afternoon. I need to ensure security is tight, hence the late-night call from the Prime Minister."

Christopher remarked, "This can't be good if Cross is coming to town. I'm sure the Two Witnesses will have much to say tomorrow. I hate that I will miss the show."

General Havid said, "I will have front row seats, so I will fill you in later. Go get your team ready to depart for the plane. You need to leave for Jakarta as soon as possible; I will call Gilana and have her meet you at the airport with a gift to aid your safety. Now go; time is not on our side."

"Thanks, we will figure it out. I will be in touch," Christopher said.

Christopher ran to wake up Jimbo, Charlie, and Jackson, praying that he could get to Jakarta before thousands of lives were lost, including Gabriella.

Evan stood outside the royal suite of Pontiff Conti. He debated spilling the news, despite being told not to inform anyone that Draven would be attending the rally in person tomorrow. He liked watching Conti squirm with jealousy. Draven's decision to join the unannounced final stop on Conti's global tour had Evan torn. Conti sought a showdown between the Two Witnesses and himself, and Israel was to be his battleground. He told Evan that his ground swelling of public support ensured his success against the most hated two men in the world. Evan didn't have Conti's confidence in defeating the Two Witnesses. The best-case scenario for Evan was the event would deflate the support of the arrogant Pontiff.

"Evan—"

A startled and then angry Evan cut off Pontiff Conti. "Let's get this relationship straight once and for all. You will not refer to me by my first name as if we are old schoolmates. You will address me as Deputy Secretary-General or Sir for short. You have forgotten your place; I picked you for your current role with as much thought and concern as I pick my undergarments each day. I can replace you at will."

Evan, now moving back to his seat as the nearing airport illuminated through the windows of the plane, finished his rant, "We all work for and support the Secretary-General and his interest, not your own self-serving visions of grandeur. My last bit of advice don't make a fool out of yourself tomorrow. You will live to regret it."

Conti crossed his arms. "So be it."

Pontiff Conti trembled with rage as the scene had caused staffers to leer and Giuseppe, Conti's loyal aid and guard, to move quickly toward the sounds of aggression. Conti returned humiliated to his nearby suite, trailed by Giuseppe.

As the door on the two men, Conti said, "I long for the day when I can shake free of Draven Cross and his dog Evan Mallory's yoke and assume my destined place as leader of the world."

"*Fate attenzione*," Giuseppe pleaded with his boss in their native Italian.

Conti began buckling into his oversized chair. "I will be careful, my dear friend. A tyrant cannot rule the world, and I am not the only leader that feels this way. The time will come to rid ourselves of Draven Cross, and I will be prepared to lead the world in his wake. Tomorrow begins the end of his rule."

Gabriella burst into her shared room with Gemma like a hurricane, frantically disrobing and putting on a pair of jeans and a Princeton alumni T-shirt from her disheveled travel bag.

Gemma sat up in bed watching ANN's reporting of Pontiff Conti's rally in Paris earlier in the day, expecting a call demanding something from Draven at any moment when Gabriella stormed into the room.

Gemma questioned, "What's going on? Why are you getting dressed as if heading out to view the tourist attractions?"

Gabriella was searching for her sneakers. "I don't have time to explain. If anyone asks, I told you I was working for a while in the hotel business center."

As Gabriella jammed on sneakers, she watched Gemma start to change clothes.

Gemma got up to put on her jeans and a T-shirt. "I don't think so, ma'am. I'm coming with you. It sounds like you're going to need some help."

Gabriella pleaded, "No, Gemma, this is not a safe thing to do; stay here."

Gemma refused. "Not safe, then why are you going? Now, I know I'm needed."

Gabriella was exasperated. "Look, I need to get to the Christian leaders for this rally; I don't want to see innocent people die because of their beliefs. I also don't need the guilt trip if something happens to you, so head to bed, and I will be back before sunrise."

Gemma stated, "You are not my mum, so pass me those trainers near the door. I am coming with you. You know I had considered joining MI6 right after university. I can be as sneaky as anyone. Stop trying to save everyone by yourself. I'm here with you, and I feel that this little excursion is why I came on this trip. Now, accept my help and tough love, and let's get going."

Gabriella thought over Gemma's challenge and laughed as she picked up Gemma's sneakers.

Gabriella relented, realizing at the minimum that two sets of eyes were better than one. "Okay, fine agent OO. Listen, you will do what I say when I tell you. This is serious business, Gemma, do you understand?"

Gemma squealed. "Yes, fine. You are in charge. This is so exciting."
Gabriella shook her head. "This is a bad idea, but let's go."

❧

Jackson broke the silence that filled the SUV. As he watched the neon glow of nightclubs and men's clubs along Israel's Highway 1 illuminating the four Omega men. They were again on their way into the unknown to thwart the Antichrist as they made their way from Jerusalem to Ben Gurion International Airport. The clubs looked busy despite the economic crisis, the Pyretos pandemic, and general chaos that was now daily life. The call to be carnal was too strong, it seemed for many.

Jackson observed. "I've traveled more now than I ever did as a soldier. It's too bad there's no reward plan for all these frequent flyer miles."

Jimbo, who was driving, responded, "There is. We have to get to heaven before we can claim the reward."

Jackson looked out the window. "I'm looking forward to getting there."

Christopher made eye contact with Jimbo in the rearview mirror and shook his head. He glanced at Charlie, engrossed in working a flight plan for the mission on his laptop and then at the half-illuminated face of Jackson. Christopher wondered if getting to Heaven would happen sooner than they all thought. Doubt started rising in him regarding the LORD, and he closed his eyes, attempting to slow the feelings filling his mind and soul.

Christopher repeated a prayer as they drew near the airport. "God, help me trust You. Please forgive my doubts, fears, and belief in me over You. I want to serve You; please help me."

Jackson smacked Christopher's shoulder. "Wake up, college boy, it's time to do what the good LORD put us on this Earth to do."

Christopher was not sure what the LORD had placed him in this world to do, but he was going to do his best to save those around him in the hours ahead.

❧

CHAPTER 12

IN JAKARTA AT two in the morning, a city bustling with chaotic energy was revealed, despite the Rapture's scars and the war of rebellion against Draven Cross. Gabriella and Gemma had avoided the raucous UE SAG operatives who found entertainment in the bottles of the hotel bar and the drinking girls that frequent Western traveler-dominated hotels across the city. Now, as they sped for seemingly no-good reason through the streets in the back of the musty and dingy cab, Gabriella questioned the sanity of the excursion.

Gabriella pleaded through her facemask. "Sir, we're really not in a hurry to get to the mosque. You can slow down."

The maskless and haggard face of the driver looked back at her with a crooked smile while speaking in broken English, "Okay."

Yet, the pace of the drive did not wane. Gabriella's stomach churned, a sensation apparently shared with Gemma, who had rolled down her window, allowing the thick-swampy night air to flow through the car.

Twenty gut-turning minutes' later and 50 UE dollars fewer, Gabriella and Gemma found themselves in front of the pyramid-shaped *Pondok Indah Grand Mosque.* The mosque was a famed attraction in Jakarta, given its unique shape. Now, Gabriella needed to find an equally impressive building in Jakarta, a western-style home.

Gemma first noticed something out of place in the neighborhood. She knew what to be looking for as Gabriella provided the details of the late-night adventure as the friends waited for their cab. Now at the mosque, she spotted what looked like an odd-looking privacy fence. "Gabriella, look at that fence. Seems out of place, does it not?"

Gabriella confirmed the neighborhood oddity as the women moved toward the fence 100 meters south of the mosque within a residential neighborhood. "Good job, Gemma. That's an American-style fence if I ever saw one." The fence was four-feet tall and made of white pickets; it was quintessentially American. Beyond the fence, Gabriella could see the gabled-roof typical in most suburban American neighborhoods. There was no doubt this was the correct house.

Gemma stopped walking with Gabriella as they drew within twenty meters of the fence.

Gabriella's senses piqued with Gemma's sudden stop. "What's wrong? Why are you stopping? We're almost there."

Gemma said, "Look at that car parked next to the fence facing away from us. Two men are smoking in the vehicle. I don't think we should walk directly to the house."

Gabriella looked at the vehicle as a man tossed a cigarette butt onto the sidewalk, where it joined a growing pile, indicating the men had been there for a while. "Those two are either guards for the Christian leaders or the guys Barnes have watching the place. Give me a minute to think about this."

Gabriella was lost; there was no back alley to get to the house, nor a way to get there without drawing the wrong type of attention to themselves. She let out an empty, "God help," as she dejectedly joined Gemma leaning against a more typical Jakarta sheet-metal security fence gate.

As soon as Gabriella admitted defeat in solving her problem, two police officers approached the vehicle out of the poorly lit street's darkness. The officers started yelling at the men in what she guessed was Indonesian. The vehicle's occupants opened their respective car doors, followed by the undeniable clink of glass bottles rolling along the ground. The men's tone and officers' responses told Gabriella that they were arguing over the bottles' contents.

She grew excited to see the officers placing the men under arrest as they sat on the ground with their hands behind their backs. One of the police officers left, returning in a patrol car, loading the angry and likely drunk men into the vehicle's back seat. The second officer walked toward Gabriella and Gemma. Gabriella swore the officer looked familiar.

Despite the urge to run and Gemma saying they should get out of there, Gabriella could not move as the officer drew within a few feet of the two women. It was then under the faint light of a nearby streetlight that Gabriella recognized the woman's face from the conference room and the bathroom back at the UE HQ.

Gabriella said, "I've seen you before, but how are you here? I must be dreaming,"

Gemma grew nervous and attempted to salvage the situation. "Officer, we were just taking a late-night walk, as we couldn't sleep."

The officer stated, "Gemma, you have nothing to fear. Gabriella asked for help, and considering the importance of her task tonight, I was sent to help you."

Gemma's face blanched. "How do you know me?"

Gabriella ignored her friend. She had to solve this mystery once and for all. "You're an angel, aren't you? I mean, I can't believe that left my mouth, but it would explain a lot."

The officer tilted her head. "I am a messenger and servant of the God of Abraham, Isaac, and Jacob. More importantly, know that you're not alone here tonight. Neither are you, Gemma."

Gabriella questioned, "How does the other officer not realize you're not Indonesian? You don't look like either Gemma or me, but you definitely don't look like you're from Indonesia."

The angel smiled. "Is there anything too hard for the LORD? Gabriella, you are too analytical for your own good. I told you that once before. Now, go and finish what you started. This night is more about Gemma and you than you can contemplate right now."

As heaven's messenger finished speaking with the two women, the first officer yelled in Indonesian. The angel replied in the same tongue and turned to walk toward the patrol car.

Gabriella begged. "Please wait. I have so many questions."

The angel called over her shoulder, "Gabby, you have all the answers you need. Place your trust and life with the LORD, and accept Jesus's salvation. He will never leave you or forsake you. Look at how faithful

God has been in answering your mother's prayers, watching over you all these years, even here tonight."

Gabriella crumbled into a sob of tears on the ground at the words of the angel.

Gemma was confused and concerned with the supernatural situation. "Gabriella, are you okay? Talk to me. How did you know that woman, how did she know my name, and why did you say she was an angel?"

Gabriella waved her off. "I can't explain what happened."

Gemma began to weep. The two friends sat for a moment on the cold concrete consoling each other, both overwhelmed with the experience.

Gabriella wiped the tears from her cheeks and put on her business face. "Let's finish this, okay?" She helped Gemma up from the ground. "For the record, I'm glad you came agent OO. You've been a great help tonight."

Gemma squeezed Gabriella as the two walked arm and arm through the white picket fence. "I'm glad I came too. Now, let's see if we can save some lives, shall we?"

It was 4:30 a.m. as Gabriella and Gemma knocked on a heavy wooden door. Gabriella found herself lost on what to do next. Why would whoever answered the door trust her? She would not trust someone showing up in the middle of the night, saying her life was in danger. As she started overanalyzing the situation, the door cracked, revealing a dark void.

Gabriella hoped the people she wanted to speak with understood English. "Hello?"

Gabriella and Gemma thought about their next move under a now illuminated porch as the door closed. As Gabriella attempted to knock again, the door reopened to a tall, slender-looking man, who asked what they wanted.

Gabriella became briefly distracted with thoughts of America by what seemed to be a New York City accent. "Sir, I know this is strange to hear, but I need to let the leaders of the Christian rally know their lives are in danger. We both work for the UE and do not want innocent people to get hurt."

The tall man questioned, "Is it only you two? No one else."

Gabriella nodded. "Yes, sir, it's only us. I promise you we mean no harm."

The man looked around again and then beckoned Gabriella and Gemma into the home. The man pointed to a shoe rack for the women to place their footwear. The cold tile floor that extended to the modestly furnished living room tingled Gabriella's feet. Gemma chose a pair of house slippers offered to her and joined Gabriella on a well-worn love seat.

"My name is Jacob, and this"—he pointed to a lanky man entering the living room from the back of the house—"is Michael."

"Hello, Jacob and Michael. This is Gemma, and I'm Gabriella."

Jacob said, "I am guessing you're the visitors promised to visit us a couple days ago. Who knew the LORD would send you at such a late hour?"

Gabriella puzzled. "You were expecting us?"

Jacob hesitated. "Before I answer, please forgive my manners. Can I offer you tea or water?"

Gabriella responded, "Water is fine for me."

Gemma nodded. "Yes, I will take some water as well."

Michael left the living room to get the water, while Jacob took a moment to grab a small, folding, wooden chair.

Gemma whispered to Gabriella, "Are these guys' angels too? How did they know we were going to come here?"

Gabriella overanalyzed the situation. "I'm sure they're not angels. I think Jacob is associating a desire for help to our arrival."

Gabriella continued a plea to Jacob for his and Michael's safety, "I know what I said about you both being in harm's way sounds crazy, but you must listen. The UE will attack the rally tomorrow with a biological weapon, the same one behind the pandemic that raced across the world after the war. I am asking you to call off the rally and leave Jakarta."

Michael had returned with the drinks as Gabriella finished explaining the reason for her late-night visit to Jacob. Michael and Jacob held a stare, and then smiles broke across each man's face.

Gabriella and Gemma didn't understand the humor of the situation. Gemma challenged. "I am failing to see what could be humorous in what Gabriella said." Gabriella added, "Yes, please tell me what could make you smile out of what I told you."

Jacob said, "Please take no offense at our reactions. The faithfulness of God and His providence brings a joy I hope you find one day. Michael and I were leading an evening prayer service here for a few believers a couple nights ago. The meeting closed with several people telling us that God was sending help. The message was clear the rally must go on. That's why I said God sent you here."

Gabriella argued, "I'm listening for the reason that makes sense for holding a gathering where thousands of lives are at risk, including both of yours."

Jacob asserted. "No, you're not listening, Gabriella, and that's your problem. You are attempting to analyze God with your finite mind. This is despite your soul wanting you to listen, and Gemma is not far behind you."

Gemma and Gabriella fidgeted on the sofa at the personal direction the conversation took.

Jacob asked, "Did you not meet a messenger from the LORD tonight? An angel that cleared the path for you to reach us?"

"Yes, but—"

Jacob cut off Gabriella. "This rally will occur, and God will be glorified in the end. The Holy Spirit has told us not to fear tomorrow but to remain focused on sharing the gospel with all that will listen. We understand that many who hear us will lose their lives in the months and years to come. These lives are not lost in vain. They will gain eternal life at the cost of their temporal physical lives. This is not a plan that any of us can understand, as it belongs to God, Gabriella. It is the circumstances we find ourselves living, and our trust must remain on God who knows the ending to these trying days."

Gemma crossed her arms. "How can you say it is worth losing my life? I mean, people losing their lives for the hope of something after death? You are going to hold an event knowing that people might die. I cannot see God being a part of that."

Jacob questioned, "Gemma if I told you right now that I could give you something that was priceless, more valuable than anything you could imagine. The gift I offer would bring you peace in bad times and hope when all seemed lost. Your eternal destiny is secured by accepting this gift. The only price for this gift is you would lose your life at some unknowable point; perhaps seconds after you receive the gift would you take it?"

Gemma wrung her hands. "I'm not sure. It sounds too good to be true."

Michael stood moving away from the quaint living room. "Ladies, follow Jacob and me; there is something you need to see. It will help you be sure in answering the question."

Gabriella and Gemma sat for a moment, unsure of their next move, before following Jacob toward a large glass window in the house's formal dining room.

ൾ

Gabriella was unsure what she was looking for as she focused her attention out to the pre-dawn darkened main street, where earlier God presented her with more evidence of his presence.

Michael questioned. "You don't see them, do you?"

Gabriella said, "I feel a bit silly as I don't see anything but cars along the street."

Gemma questioned, "I'm with Gabriella. What should we see?"

Jacob joined Michael in praying that the LORD open Gabriella and Gemma's eyes.

As the men finished their request to God, Gabriella yelled in excitement. "I see her. It's the woman or angel from earlier. She's sitting in a car with someone."

Gemma said, "Yes, I see her too. Look, there are several other people, or angels, correct?"

Jacob laughed. "These Heavenly emissaries are providing not only for us believers worldwide but for you two as well. God faithfully provides, protects, and guides us forward in our assignment. Even this house we were guided to was built by Christian missionaries who departed during the Rapture. No matter what we face in life, even death, God assures His followers that He is with them. The gift of salvation offered by Jesus Christ has no comparison."

"I was going to ask about this house. What about—"

Gemma cut off Gabriella. "How do I have God watch over me?"

"It's simple, Gemma; all you need to do is pray with me and ask to receive Jesus as your savior. God will do the rest and provide you with the best helper, the Holy Spirit, to bring repentance and lasting change to your life.

Gabriella's senses were competing with her analytic mind. She couldn't stop looking at the angel protecting the house. She thought, *how is this real.* Now, Gemma was being caught up in the emotion of the night while Gabriella struggled to process everything. What she couldn't do was deny the comfort she felt with these strange men and supernatural beings all around her. Gabriella was overwhelmed and kept her eyes on the angels as Gemma trusted her life with Jesus.

Jacob grabbed Gemma's trembling hand. "Pray with me. Heavenly Father, I know that I am a sinner, and I know that You sent Your Son, Jesus Christ, to die on the cross for my sins. I understand that through Jesus's sacrifice and accepting Him to be my LORD and savior that I am redeemed as one of Your children. Father, I accept Jesus Christ as my savior today. I believe He died on the cross and rose again and lives today. In Jesus's name, I pray to You. Amen."

Gemma hadn't felt any spiritual connection on a personal level since her childhood when her mother would read her Bible stories before bed. God was real again in her life. The fear of the last two years and anxiety for living to the next day at this moment seemed distant and like a bad dream. Gemma embraced Gabriella, burying her head in her shoulder as waves of sobs rolled over her.

Gabriella thought. *Why can't I accept God?* She knew her mind was losing the battle to what she had experienced since the Rapture. God had answered Gabriella's challenge to provide her not only a purpose, but also all she needed to accept His offer through Jesus Christ for salvation.

She responded to her own heart as she thought about the faith of her mother. Gabriella never moved past, viewing her mother's faith as delusional. After all, she died anyway. How can God be real if good people die instead of the bad? If I pray to accept Him in my life, the suffering of the world by Draven won't stop.

This makes no sense; Gabriella challenged herself pushing to affirm Gemma's decision. "Gemma, I am so happy for you. I hope this decision brings you peace," Gabriella said.

Gemma said, "It's hard to explain, but I feel good. I mean, I have a feeling of surety that I've never experienced. I'm not sure what the future will hold for me, but I am okay with that for the first time."

Jacob smiled. "Amen. I'm glad that you've given your life into the hands of the only one that can sustain us all, Jesus Christ."

Michael added, "Yes, welcome to God's eternal family, Gemma."

Jacob attempted to seize on the moment. "Gabriella, would you like to pray with me? I feel God has answered all your demands. The analytic road that's guided your life leads to only one possible conclusion: God exists."

Gabriella grew anxious, turning on her phone. "We need to go. If you want to have your rally, then know you've been advised against it. Gemma, let's get going; it's almost six in the morning."

Gemma grasped Michael's hand. "Thank you for everything."

Jacob ran into the dining room. "Gemma, wait for a second."

He returned with a Bible for Gemma and one for Gabriella. "Ladies, I pray that God stays close to you."

"Thank you for the Bible. Please take no offense to my tone; I'm worried about all of you. I know what Draven is capable of, and it scares me.

Gabriella glanced at her illuminating phone as it came alive with the display highlighting a missed call from Christopher.

She grabbed Gemma. "We need to go."

~

Christopher's worry escalated before the team departed Israel due to Gabriella's voicemail recording picking up instead of her. She last told him that she was going to find the Christian leaders, ignoring the danger. He knew Gabriella was placing her own life at risk but could not stop his headstrong friend. Christopher prayed that he would get the chance to see Gabriella again as it had been a while since they last talked face to face.

Jackson interrupted his thoughts, "Sorry to bother you, but I wanted to know if you reached Gabriella before we went wheels up."

Christopher shook his head. "I've not been able to reach Gabriella. In any case, let's get everyone together to figure out our game plan."

Christopher stood from his seat at the front of the SHADOW and tapped on the cockpit door to tell Charlie and Jimbo to set the autopilot. Jackson moved to the back of the plane to wake Gilana. She had been impatiently waiting on the team at the airport and slept since their departure.

Christopher started to lay out the situation. "Okay. Here's what we know. Gabriella passed a message that Draven is planning on killing the Christian leaders at their rally in Jakarta tomorrow night—"

Jackson interrupted him in an attempt to lighten the mood. "You mean later today; we've crossed the dateline."

Christopher gave his snarky friend a stare, which made everyone laugh. "Excuse me, later today. The rally leaders are somewhere in the city, and Gabriella, I'm afraid, is trying to contact them. There is also the bad news that the UE has its special activities group, led by John Barnes, executing the attack. These are former special ops operatives from around the globe, so we have a potentially tough fight ahead."

Gilana sat up upon hearing that the UE SAG operatives would be in play during the mission.

Christopher noticed Gilana's attention surge at the mention of the UE SAG. He had been with her on a fateful night shortly after the Rapture when SAG operatives took the love of her life, Uri, outside of Babylon, Iraq. He aimed to keep the temperamental Gilana focused on saving lives, not enacting revenge.

Christopher ordered, "Gilana, this seems like a good time for you to help us better understand the unknowns with the gifts General Havid sent with you."

Gilana pulled several items out of the overhead bin. "The general provided us access into the Israeli intelligence network via this quantum laptop. We were also provided an anti-viral to the Pyretos bioweapon from the recent Israeli supply. The anti-viral will allow us the freedom to intermix in the rally without worry."

Gilana continued, "The primary threat beyond the UE will be the lingering Islamic fundamentalist extremist groups, none larger or more deadly than *Jundallah.* We should expect these terrorists will be drawn like a moth to a flame to the stadium filled with Christians."

Jackson suggested, "Let's take that anti-viral now; I want to make sure it has some time to work before messing around with that Pyretos-stuff."

Gilana handed each person an auto-injector syringe. As she put the anti-viral-carrier back into an overhead bin. She noticed the men staring at her holding their needles.

Gilana teased. "Men are such babies." Without hesitation, Gilana rolled up her blouse's left sleeve and placed the anti-viral auto-injector to her arm, applying pressure to release the dose. Gilana then convulsed and flopped into a nearby empty seat as she heard panicked screams from the men on the team.

Jackson yelled as Christopher, Charlie, and Jimbo rushed to Gilana. "I knew this stuff was poison!"

Gilana erupted into guttural laughs. She laughed in a way that none of the men had ever seen. "You should see the looks on your faces; you guys are such babies. Take the anti-viral, and let's get on with business."

Christopher allowed a nervous smile to rise on his face. "You got us, Gilana."

Christopher applied the auto-injector to his left arm, with the other men following.

Christopher continued, "Okay, with the fun out of the way, here is what I think we need to do. Gilana, can you pull up a map of Jakarta on the laptop?"

Gilana was wiping tears of laughter away from her face as she made a few keystrokes that allowed her to access the plane's Wi-Fi hotspot. A high-resolution map of Jakarta appeared a few moments later.

Christopher pointed to their destination. "We need to approach this mission simultaneously. The primary goal will be to get as many people as possible away from the Gelora Bung Karno football stadium. I suggest a distraction or disturbance that will get folks out of the stadium. Any thoughts?"

Charlie suggested. "We could call into the local authorities to tell them there will be a bombing at the stadium."

Jimbo offered, "Or we could set off a small explosion at the stadium as soon as we arrive, that will force a delay to the rally tonight."

As the team debated on how to save the rally-goers lives, doubt began to rise in Christopher. His struggle of trusting others was pushing him to make a decision. In this moment of building pressure, Christopher felt the quiet whisper of the Holy Spirit invade his mind. "*Trust in the LORD. The rally must go on.*"

Christopher announced, "Guys, the rally must happen. We should not stop it. It's the LORD's will."

The din of the plane's engines was all that could be heard after Christopher's announcement. Each of his teammates faced the same doubt he had moments before reaching this decision.

Christopher broke the tension. "You need to trust me. It's hard for me to understand, but this thought is flooding my mind. The LORD will take care of the believers no matter what."

Charlie, Jimbo, and Jackson sat back in their respective chairs and looked at each other.

Jimbo questioned, "Are you sure this is the LORD's direction?"

Gilana protested, "Are you crazy? God told you that we should let innocent people die. So, I am the only one on this team that has common sense. What about the people that do not believe? Like me, do our lives not matter to you people?"

Christopher said, "Yes, I'm sure this is the Lord's guidance, and Gilana, your life matters, but I think God has something big planned, and we cannot stand in his way. Perhaps, it would be best if you stayed on the plane."

Gilana swore at Christopher. "I will not sit this mission out; I owe it to Uri to avenge his death. I'm going if not to the stadium then to rescue the Christian leaders." Gilana swore again, punching a seat on her way to the rear of the plane.

Christopher felt bad. "I know my decision—I mean God's decision—is difficult for any of us to accept or understand. Our best effort in this mission will be to guard the Christian leaders and get them to safety. We will need to find Gabriella and go from there."

The rest of the men resigned themselves to the plan. The group trusted Christopher's judgment that God's will would take precedent in the mission. Jackson moved to the rear of the plane to console Gilana while Charlie and Jimbo headed back to the cockpit. Christopher felt a wave of nausea rising within him as he prayed that his trust would not lead to countless deaths in a few hours. He recalled the wisdom of General Havid to trust God despite his doubt; Christopher hoped the general was right.

Evan grew excited on the prepared platform facing Reuel and Eliyahu, the UE's greatest enemies, knowing Draven's motorcade was on its way to Jerusalem. This would be the Secretary-General's stage to reassure the world that he alone was the architect of the global recovery efforts. Draven planned a dramatic entrance at the Wailing Wall rally to show the world who was in charge.

It had been a couple of hours, and Evan had yet to receive an update on arrival from Draven on his assistants. *He has to be here*, Evan thought. He made his way to greet Israeli Defense Minister General Havid as the dais began to fill with Israeli national and civic leaders.

Evan said, "General Havid, it is a pleasure to meet you. I'm sure we won't have any trouble from these two fools today. Evan gestured toward Reuel and Eliyahu.

General Havid took exception to Evan's description of God's ambassador's but kept a neutral face before taking his seat with other Israeli leaders. "If violence erupts, those men will not start it. Have a good day, Deputy Mallory."

Evan was unsure what to make of the general's remarks, but it felt in line with the tension-filled atmosphere. However, he had other concerns.

He grew worried and tried to call Draven to no avail. A growing crowd gathered near the Western Wall Plaza, anticipating the start of the rally. Thankfully the UE installed monitors and speakers around the area. There was an expectation of a large crowd pouring into the plaza to participate in the rally. UE soldiers handed out water and food to people as Conti prepared to approach the podium to confront the Two Witnesses.

The two stoic men had remained silent and unmoving as the barricades and camera crews invaded the plaza around them. The barrier to prevent the foolhardy from attacking the men was all that remained between the dais and the men of God.

Conti's executive secretary concluded, "Ladies and Gentlemen, the aid will pause until after the rally. Pontiff Conti wants you to know there is plenty for everyone. Please make your way near a monitor, and the ceremony will begin in a few moments. Thank you."

Evan looked at his watch and phone, neither easing the worry swelling in his mind. As Evan stood to go and attempt to find Draven, he retook his seat with Conti's arrival to the speaker's podium on the dais. He took a moment to reinforce the threat he issued on the plane to Conti. "Don't forget you're not the Secretary-General; tread lightly today."

The crowd cheered as Conti waved to the present masses and those watching around the world via television. The Interfaith Pontiff and the Unified Arabian Nations Ambassador nodded to the sign language and automated translator operators to prepare.

Conti glanced at Evan before speaking. "We will begin today's ceremony with a prayer. We call upon the light within all of us to shine today. I gratefully invoke the supreme deity of the universe, the Morningstar, and Prince of This World to bless everyone here and to remove the enemies of peace from amongst us."

Conti said to such loud cheers that he paused his speech. "These are trying times the world faces. We have lost billions of people to war, disease, and the disappearance of those that sought to undermine the advance of humanity. Interfaith has taken the lead during this unprecedented global crisis to alleviate suffering."

Evan gave Conti a death stare as the two men's eyes met during the uproar at Pontiff's remarks. It was clear to Evan that Conti would not willingly yield to the hand that was feeding him.

Continuing, Conti said, "Here sitting before us are two charlatans. They have convinced some that Interfaith and the UE are evil and that they alone represent a loving deity. Yet, how many have died at their hands and their God. Death and destruction are rampant due to their God. Therefore, I ask everyone under my voice, can their God be good, or have I provided you access to the goodness within everyone? I represent the real God. Today, I brought you food and water, while these men and their supporters bring you horrors through terrorism. The witnesses tell you every day that each of us is sinners. Israel, good news today. I will bring you..." Conti stopped speaking as a murmur rose through the people near the plaza, and Reuel and Eliyahu stood for the first time in days.

The monitors panned from the Two Witnesses to a motorcade with the UE flags emblazoned on the doors. The Western Wall Plaza reverberated with the shouts of joy when Draven Cross emerged from his limo. He wore a tailored, charcoal-gray suit and flashed his radiant white teeth on the high-definition monitors for all to see. As Draven made his way through the throngs of people toward the platform, the cheers grew into a single shout of praise. The crescendo of the enthusiasm came as Draven greeted the dais leaders, waving to the adoring crowd.

Draven moved to the podium as a bewildered Pontiff Conti scrambled away, trying to remain graceful despite the apparent embarrassment of being upstaged at his own event.

Evan stood and smiled at Conti as Draven approached the lectern to speak. "I want to thank the Pontiff for inviting me to take part in the celebration of my efforts to provide for the people of this world. I hope you have enjoyed the food and supplies I provided the Interfaith organization. The Pontiff has done a tremendous job leading this UE outreach effort. Let's give the Pontiff a round of applause for such a good job supporting my efforts on the frontlines."

Draven smiled at Evan as Conti looked ill and depressed. Conti's face was like that of a child who dropped their ice cream cone in a mud puddle.

Evan hoped that Draven would publicly embarrass the Pontiff on the global stage. He felt the Prince of This World tell him; *Conti will make the world worship my chosen one. Today will set him on that path.* Draven turned to Evan on the stage, nodding as if he had heard the same message.

Draven forced Conti to confront Reuel and Eliyahu. "Pontiff, I hear that the people of Israel have been without rain for too long. How about you demonstrate the power of a real God?"

Evan watched as Conti called on the Prince of This World for rain.

Reuel drowned out cheers from the crowd as Evan, Draven, and Conti cowered. "The spirit that abides within you, Draven Cross, makes your heart hard like the ancient Pharaoh this same spirit once controlled. Woe to you, Man of Sin. Draven, you are like a whitewashed tomb, which outwardly appears beautiful, but within is full of dead people's bones and all uncleanness. You lead the world to its destruction on a path covered with blood. The jester of your False Prophet, Pontiff Conti, dares to defy the God of Heaven by calling for rain. Pontiff, you have no power over God's creation.

"Your False Prophet, Evan Mallory, and his religion pushes the world to forget the continued mercies of God and to worship, you Son of Perdition, the Beast long predicted to rise before this day. Israel will see you betray her, for you're the Beast. You dare compare your dark master, the source of your power, to *El-Elyon* and *El Shaddai.* Cardinal Conti, your blasphemy of the Great I AM will not go unpunished."

At Reuel's words, Conti grasped his throat and collapsed, struggling to breathe. His purple and gold papal miter rolled off the platform as he collapsed. Panic erupted across the Wailing Wall Plaza.

General Havid refused to leave the VIP platform despite the pleas of his security team. The general was the only dignitary beyond Evan and Draven that remained. He felt compelled to watch the confrontation between the enemies of Israel and the God of Israel. General Havid watched Evan rise quickly to the podium, attempting to calm the fleeing crowd as security and medical teams worked to get the writhing Pontiff

Conti to an awaiting ambulance. General Havid stood to gain a better vantage point of the Two Witnesses. The two men of God both stood, eyeing Draven and Evan.

Evan joined Draven at the front edge of the platform, returning their stare. "Silence. Don't fear these evil men and their supposed God. Prince of This World, demonstrate your power to the unbelieving. Let it rain."

The general watched the sky across Jerusalem grow dark with clouds producing thunder and lightning, shifting the late winter day atmosphere from serene to ominous. The winter winds swirled around the plaza bringing a sharp edge and a growing smell of sulfur that forced all but the foolhardy or brave to seek shelter.

General Havid was unsure which group he fit within, as he instinctively moved farther away from Evan and Draven but remained on the platform. The clouds over the Temple Mount appeared to pulsate with life, like a child kicking within its mother's womb. Evan pointed to the Two Witnesses staring at them.

Reuel provided God's answer. "The rain your false prophet commands will not come as you ask. For the LORD of Hosts has shut the sky until the due time. The blood on the hands of the Beast will be returned to him for the next three days."

Draven moved to speak, but the voice of Eliyahu overpowered him. "Have you not ears, Israel, and will you not listen to the words of God's prophet? I already spoke as God commanded, and as the God of Israel lives, it will not rain until the due time has passed. The Beast and his false prophet tempt you as a prostitute lures the weak and simple. God is a consuming fire, and He will overthrow His enemies with His burning wrath, consuming them as stubble."

Draven shouted, "Evan, I have heard enough of this!"

At Draven's words, General Havid and the world via ANN watched as the sky burst with baseball-sized pieces of black-streaked rancid smelling hail, causing shrieks and cries of pain to mix with the battering of metal and shattering of glass. Even for the battle-hardened general, the piercing sounds of terror around him induced sweating and shaking.

The general's security team lead gave a frantic shout, "Sir, we must go, *now*!"

General Havid relented. "Yes, let's go."

The general could not resist a longing look at the Two Witnesses. They stood with arms outstretched and their heads toward Heaven, untouched by God's answer to Draven. He prayed to have their faith and boldness in the face of enemies as he fled the torrent of God's judgment.

Evan attempted to make himself as small and unattractive a target of Draven's wrath as possible, as the only other occupant within the UE Secretary-General's luxury Presidential Suite. He watched as Draven laced the air with expletives and launched a chair across the room, creating a loud crack as the chair exploded on the marble floor.

Draven screamed, "Why is it that these two dolts thwart my efforts every time I set foot in this cursed nation?"

An aide interrupted Draven's tirade, temporarily lowering Evan's heart rate.

Draven scolded, "What do you want?"

"Sir, Pontiff Conti is in stable condition. The doctors believe he will make a full recovery as his symptoms are similar to what happened to you when—"

Draven cut off the aide. "I don't want to hear one more word from your disgusting mouth. Get out of my sight before I have you shot. I could care less if that pompous impostor lives or dies."

Draven paced the floor, cursing and disheveling his clothes with every frantic movement. His always regal appearance was replaced in a moment with an air of commonality.

Draven commanded into the void of the room. "Answer me, Prince of This World, why can I not kill those two men? They have made me look like a fool too often. Answer me now."

Flung out of his hiding-corner, Evan landed on the cold floor next to Draven, who had begun to whimper. Neither could move nor speak as nightmarish sounds filled the room.

The Prince of This World responded from the haunting animalistic noises filling the room. "You dare challenge me. I allow you both to live for my service and worship. Everything that is happening in this world is within my control. These events will serve the purpose of bringing me glory in the end. My enemy's two representatives will die at your hands, Draven, at the appointed time, which is drawing near. Focus your energy in making the enemy's followers suffer, until the due time of the witnesses."

Evan dared not move as he watched Draven slowly rise to his feet. The piercing voice of their mutual spiritual guide resounding in his ears.

Draven nervously regained his composure. "Get up, Evan. There's work to do. I will have my vengeance on those two fools at the Wailing Wall. While not as soon as I would like, I will savor their deaths when they come. Get my plane ready to depart for Rome as soon as possible. We will see how many people follow these idiots once the bodies start lining the streets."

CHAPTER 13

AS CHARLIE COMPLETED taxiing the SHADOW into a private hangar at Soekarno-Hatta International Airport outside Jakarta, the pre-dawn light changed the dark night sky into a warm pink hue. Christopher noticed two black SUVs parked in the hanger, likely courtesy of the Israeli Embassy in Jakarta. He laughed as he looked at Jackson, sleeping per the norm before any mission.

Christopher shook him. "Hey, wake up, Jackson. We're here."

Jackson squirmed slightly. "Yeah, sure, let me know what you need me to do."

Gilana asked, "So, what *are* we doing? Have you heard from Gabriella?"

Christopher shook his head. "No, but let me call her again. We cannot do anything until we make contact with her."

Christopher pulled out his quantum phone and placed the call to Gabriella only to reach her voicemail. The irritations of nervous energy filled his stomach as he listened for the voicemail's beep, allowing him to leave a message. "Hey, Gabriella. We are here and waiting for you. Call me as soon as you get this. I hope you haven't gotten into trouble." Christopher knew that if she did not answer that message within the next fifteen minutes, her phone would automatically clear the message history. He had no choice but to wait and pray.

It took only a moment for Christopher's prayer to be answered as Gabriella returned his call.

"Hi. Yes, we arrived a few minutes ago. Where are you?"

Gabriella said, "I found the Christian leaders. It's a long story. Are you at the airport?"

Christopher answered, "Yes, we're at the far western tarmac in the first large hanger. I'm sure if you flash your UE badge, you will be allowed through the security checkpoints."

Gabriella agreed. "Okay, I'll see you soon."

Christopher kicked Jackson's foot as Charlie and Jimbo poked their heads into the cabin from the cockpit. "Gabriella is on her way. We should move our gear to the SUVs."

Jackson snapped, "You remind me of my wife. Always pushing me to go, and then you're not even ready."

Everyone laughed, even Gilana, as Jackson's quip led to the resumption of his snoring. Gilana dropped a duffel bag on Jackson as she deplaned, causing him to yelp as he fell out of his seat.

Jackson yelled, "Hey, what gives? Can't a man have a little cat nap around here!"

Gilana responded, "It's time to work."

Christopher and Jimbo laughed as Jackson staggered behind them.

Jackson sassed, "I can already see that this day is going to be about as fun as getting a new driver's license."

&

With the SUVs loaded, Jackson—along with everyone else this time—took a power nap.

As Christopher began to drift off, the phone rang. "Hello."

General Havid was on the other line. "Christopher, it's good to hear from you. I've had the most amazing experience with God. Draven and his goons were humiliated. You must watch the replay on television."

Christopher said, "Yes, sir, I will find a television as soon as possible. Gabriella has made contact with us and is on her way here now. I will update you a little later."

General Havid said, "Excellent news. I'm sure you've discovered the SUVs I had the embassy deliver. I will be praying for your team's success and protection."

"Thanks, sir. Goodbye." Christopher ended the call, overcome with excitement. "OH, man! You guys need to wake up!" Christopher yelled.

Charlie and Jimbo groaned awake in the front seats, while Gilana sat up in the back of a nearby SUV. Jackson had selected a bed of three wooden cargo boxes and did not flinch with the scream to wake up. Christopher laughed as he strode over to his sleeping brother and gave the boxes a quick kick.

Jackson scowled. "Hey, what's your problem?"

The tired but awake rest of the Omega Team joined Christopher and Jackson as Christopher explained what had him so excited.

Jackson said, "Let me guess, you heard from Ms. Sassy Pants, and she's sending trouble to find us."

Christopher said, "Yes, I did hear from Gabriella, and she is on her way. That's not exciting news. General Havid called and said Draven and the Two Witnesses had a showdown for the ages now running on a televised loop."

Jimbo perked up. "We need to find a TV."

The Omega Team explored the previously unremarkable airplane hangar spacious enough to accommodate a 787 with room to spare. Gilana spotted what promised to be an office and perhaps a way to satisfy their curiosity about what happened in Jerusalem.

As the team made its way to the office, they discovered it looked less like a work office and more like a waiting room at a car dealer's service department. The good news was there was an operational television for their use. Jimbo did a quick search to find a channel covering the event. It didn't take long because every channel was reporting on the same thing.

Jimbo stopped on the ANN channel, where a news anchor provided an update.

"If you're joining us expecting to watch the Interfaith Rally in Jerusalem, we apologize as a breaking news event is ongoing. An hour ago, the Two Witnesses attempted to assassinate UE Secretary-General Draven Cross and several other dignitaries. Initial reports indicate that the Secretary-General is unharmed. However, the Interfaith leader, Pontiff Conti, was injured attempting to protect the Secretary-General. We have no further reports at this time on his condition. The following is a previously recorded video of the attack. I must warn viewers the footage is graphic."

Christopher and the Omega team watched in awe as the power of God flowed from the lips of God's servants for the world to hear. Reuel and Eliyahu's display of power left little doubt of who was in control of the world. Christopher's focus returned to the broadcast as the ANN anchor announced going to Sam Morrow, a field reporter in Jerusalem, for a live update.

A frazzled and scratched up Sam Morrow began her report. "Good evening from Jerusalem. My crew and I are fine. We are bruised but alive, huddled in a small café near the Wailing Wall with a few others. I cannot say the same for all that were at the Interfaith rally today. Numerous bodies are lining the road, and several car accidents have occurred due to the hailstones' size falling right now. The café owner tells me that hailstones are falling all over Israel, causing widespread damage and panic.

"It is interesting to note that a black sulfur-smelling substance with a consistency of tar covers each baseball-sized hailstone. As you can see, as we pan out to the front of the cafe, the melting hail flows through the drainage ditches and streets like rivers of molasses. From Jerusalem, I'm Sam Morrow back to you in Rome."

Jimbo clicked the television off as silence invaded the small space the covert warriors of Omega occupied.

Gilana was trembling, sitting on a cracked, faux leather couch. "Why does Yahweh attack my homeland?"

Jackson answered Gilana's rhetorical question, "I wouldn't say God is attacking Israel. He's stopped restraining the natural consequence of sin, which is death. God is going after for sure that devil named Draven, and the Good LORD is only getting started with him. Today's events in Israel will seal the decisions for millions of people. One group will accept the Two Witnesses' messages and 144,000 preachings worldwide. They will accept Jesus as their personal savior securing their souls but at a cost, likely their lives. While countless others will reject God for all of eternity."

Jackson continued, "I think God is beginning to carve two clear eternal paths for the world to follow; either the path of salvation and acceptance of his offer of redemption through Christ Jesus. Or, the path of following Draven toward destruction and an eternity separated from God's presence."

Gilana burst into tears and ran from the office. The men of Omega looked at each other in shock. Jimbo decided to go after her.

Jackson looked out of the office as Jimbo chased after Gilana. "I didn't mean to hurt her feelings."

Christopher responded, "I don't think you did. I can sympathize with the struggle Gilana is facing in trying to accept God and what He is doing amid this upside-down world. I mean, each of us in this room did not want to have anything to do with God when the world was normal. Accepting Jesus Christ as the messiah needed in their lives is not an easy decision for many people. I pray that Gilana settles her war against God and His son Jesus before it's too late."

Before anyone could respond to Christopher, the three men heard the shouts of "hello," in the distance, announcing Gabriella's arrival. The real reason why they were in Jakarta quickly came back into focus.

Jackson ran and picked up Gabriella, twirling her around like a father picking up his daughter after a long day at work.

Gabriella laughed. "Put me down, goofball. I missed you so much. It's so good to see you."

The two friends embraced deeply, evidence of how they had become like family in such a short amount of time.

Gemma was with her. "Good to see you again, Christopher."

Christopher said, "It's nice seeing you too, Gemma. I can only imagine the stories you have working for Cross."

Gemma stated, "I like the way you phrased your last statement. Draven is showing sides of himself I never expected."

Gabriella held a stare with Christopher's brown eyes longer than both felt comfortable. "Give me a hug, Chris. I thought I had lost you forever."

Christopher teased. "It will take more than a post-apocalyptic, Raptured world, World War III, and an avalanche to get rid of me."

Christopher and Gabriella both laughed as they held their embrace.

Jackson snickered as he watched Christopher and Gabriella awkwardly move apart from each other as Gabriella continued introductions of Gemma and herself to Charlie. He watched Gabriella introduce Gemma and herself to Gilana and Jimbo as they returned, completing the Omega Team reunion.

Christopher asked, "What's so funny?"

Jackson chuckled. "You two have more chemistry between you than a fast-food burger and fries."

"You're crazy."

Jackson shrugged. "Crazy like a fox."

As the introductions and smiles waned, Christopher used the opportunity to push away from the topic of his feelings for Gabriella to the information she had for the mission. "So, what's up with the mission to save these Christian leaders?" Christopher blurted, causing the entire group to stare at him, given the abrupt shift in topics.

Gabriella said, "I see your zeal for work is still strong."

Before Christopher could respond, Gabriella continued, "This mission is short and sweet. The two Christian leaders for the rally, named Jacob and Michael, don't want our protection and say God wants the rally to happen."

The Omega Team all looked at Christopher with Gabriella's announcement that the rally would proceed. Her statement was a confirmation of Christopher's similar view on the plane.

"Why are you guys starring at Chris?" Gabriella said.

"I told the team on the way here that I believe God didn't want us attempting to stop the rally," Christopher said.

Gabriella sighed loudly, running her hands through black locks. "Does anyone associated with this rally care about saving lives? So, let me guess, you guys are going to attend the rally now."

Gilana interrupted, "Should we be discussing such matters with Gemma present? She is Cross's little secretary."

Gabriella arched her eyes and pointed to Gilana, offended at her bluntness and assertion that Gemma was a spy.

Christopher could see Gilana's lack of trust for Gabriella and

Gemma, coming to a confrontation between the strong-willed women. "I think—"

Gabriella cut off Christopher. "Gilana, I realize you've known Gemma and me for a whole ten minutes, but you can trust me when I say that neither Gemma nor I are fans of Draven Cross. Gemma is a believer in Jesus, like most in this hangar. She loses her life if Draven finds out. Plus, if I wanted to sell you out, that could have been accomplished weeks ago in Scotland. So, let's drop the Mossad-tough-girl routine and play nicely with others."

Gilana laughed a seemingly risky choice of emotion to everyone watching. "I like this one; she could have been Mossad, possibly. I trust Gemma and you, but only as far as I can throw either of you, and I am not a believer in Jesus. I believe in justice against the Beast named Draven." Gilana bowed as if she submitted to Gabriella.

Jackson laughed. "You two are feistier than two cats thrown into a bucket of water."

Gabriella snapped, "Jackson, you're out of line right now."

Christopher attempted to restore order. "Calm down, everyone. We all want the same things: to take care of the vulnerable and undermine Draven Cross. Gilana, I would trust Gabriella with my life, and everyone here has already done the same with the Inverness mission. If she says Gemma is a trusted agent, then that's good enough for me. Gabriella, Gilana means well in her direct manner, and I trust her. Let's go over what we can do *together* to ensure that we support God's plan."

The dawning of a new day in Israel did not look promising for Draven as he stared across the surreal landscape carved by an unprecedented hailstorm. Worst of all, the hailstorm continued, preventing his departure for Rome despite the stones' sizes reducing from baseball to quarter. As far as Draven could see from his wall to floor windows, a white and black licorice-striped blanket canvased Jerusalem and the Judean Hills. The stripes were rivers of bitumen, called "black blood," according to panicked locals and his staff. In truth, the black blood was a foul-smelling substance that UE scientists concluded was a mix of sulfur and brimstone that contains an unknown biological agent with properties similar to algae.

The lone spot of contrast against the white and black backdrop was the Wailing Wall, where Reuel and Eliyahu sat defiantly. Though he could not see them from his hotel room, Draven seethed. The sight of the Wailing Wall plaza's brown-hued stones compared to the hail covered surrounding area caused him to grow warm. The mental image of his greatest enemies caused him to yell for his aide to summon Evan.

Evan anticipated why he'd been summoned. "Sir, I know you want to get back to Rome, but the pilots say we will be killed if we take off in a storm like this."

"That's not what I called you for, Evan. I want to plan my vengeance on these Christian terrorists around the world. The two fools here in Jerusalem spur the Christian rebellion. I need to take the wind out of the witnesses' sails, do you understand?"

Evan did. "I do understand, sir. When you called, I was attempting to finalize an initiative I spent last night working on to end the archaic fascination in Christianity over following you."

Draven demanded, "Well, impress me."

Evan sat next to Draven at a small, gold-rimmed coffee table, producing a slide presentation on his laptop.

Draven was insulted by the presentation. "Really, Evan. Slides? Tell me the plan; I'm more than capable of remembering the details."

Evan turned his laptop off. "My plan is straightforward. First, we limit Conti's public appearances and promote the Interfaith religion in a more corporate matter. Your face versus Conti's will highlight promotional videos and advert materials, thus blurring the line between worshipping Interfaith and you. This step ensures that everyone associates the messages of peace and the goodwill efforts of Interfaith rightly with you."

Draven added, "You're off to a good start, continue."

Evan was buoyed by Draven's praise. "Next, I have word from our technology applications division that the personal tracking system is ready to begin implementation. I estimate it will take almost a year to emplace the tracking chips in the entire world population, willingly or unwillingly. I plan to send guidance and the initial trackers to the ten regional ambassadors today with your approval. Soon you will have the ability to separate those loyal to your message and anarchists. The UE will gain complete control over society through this tracking system, as all financial transactions will require having our tracking chips to buy or sell anything."

Draven stood and began pacing. "Evan, without a doubt, this plan is your best effort to date, but still far from perfect. There are expectedly glaring flaws. You did not account for resistance in your timeline. The resistance to authority is an innate human attribute. We will build political prisoner camps to eliminate those rebelling. These prison camps will also be the testbed for the implementation of the trackers. Publicly these prisons will be named Interfaith Educational Centers and spread across every UE region.

"The world should believe that we are providing rehabilitation for those struggling to adapt to my vision for peace. In truth, these prisons will hold violent radicals unwilling to align with my vision until they can be eliminated. The manner of their demise should be public. I have always been fond of the impact hangings have on society; the mere mention of hanging a person invokes terror."

Draven concluded his vision of persecution. "Lastly, ensure we have a way to execute a hanging at any site where the trackers are being applied. Every IEC prisoner will be given a simple choice that leads to two end states, life or death. They will declare absolute loyalty to me and accept my mark, thereby commuting their death sentences to life in hard labor. Alternately, they reject my loyalty chip and will be executed immediately. The described methodology for implementing the loyalty marks will be replicated in the global population as soon as possible.

We will inspire loyalty with the presence of death for disloyalty. I want to test how much faith these zealots have in the face of death. My instincts tell me that most people will renounce their religion rather than die."

Evan said, "I will make all the required arrangements."

Draven commanded, "Don't disappoint me."

Draven returned to the windows of the suite and the dismal scene that lay beyond. The Prince of This World had inspired him that Reuel and Eliyahu would meet their demise at his hands. Small comfort for the indignities he faced in Israel. He was willing to do whatever it took to win control over the world and its destiny, including killing anyone that stood in the way.

Chapter 14

AS THE OMEGA Team prepared to attend the Christian rally, Christopher took a moment to speak with Gabriella during a walk along the tarmac near the hangar, as the two soaked in a hazy view of downtown Jakarta in the distance. "Listen, Gabriella. I think you should come back to Israel with the rest of us, bring Gemma if it makes you feel better."

"Chris, I appreciate your concern. We both know that if I don't go back to the UE, then the cost will be steep in terms of lives lost. I have seen the suffering flowing from Draven's mind first hand."

Christopher pushed back. "What about your life? How long do you think you can play this game with Draven?"

Gabriella considered her response. "I think we should both ask those questions. It is only a matter of time before Draven realizes that the Omega team survived Alaska. He will hunt you with ruthless zeal. I feel like I have a purpose now. I have been working to develop a resistance network. If we work against Draven together, me from the inside and you out here, we can slow him down and, who knows, maybe even kill him. There is no better use of my time and life right now."

Christopher disagreed, "You're mistaken, Gabriella. If Draven is who I believe he is, then no one on Earth can kill him. We can only slow him down."

"Then we slow him down. I'm going to fight him until it kills me."

Christopher confessed, "I accepted Jesus as my personal savior, and honestly, it feels good not to be angry anymore about my relationship with God."

Gabriella stopped and looked at Christopher. "Wow, I knew Jackson had accepted Jesus, and I assumed everyone had on the team, but for some reason, it's hard to picture you as Christian."

Christopher was puzzled. "Why? I couldn't deny everything He had done for me in my life. When I was buried under that avalanche, I thought about how I would die still at war with God. So, living through that and reminded by my wife Erin's faith before she Raptured, here I am as a Christian. What's holding you up?"

Gabriella struggled to find a creditable answer to that question. From Gemma to Christopher, she found herself increasingly alone as the non-believer. "I really can't give you an answer besides saying I feel like I'm going to lose myself."

The two old friends continued their walk in silence for a few moments, both unsure of what to say or do next.

"Chris, I want you to know how I feel about us. I wish things—"

Christopher cut Gabriella off. "There are some things that need to be left unsaid, especially in the world we live in. I do not like your decision to continue working for Draven, but I respect it. I wish you would accept Jesus, but again it's something I can't force on you. Omega, including Gilana, is indebted to you. All I ask is you call me if things get too risky; don't be stubborn."

Gabriella's vision blurred with tears as she buried herself into the strong embrace of Christopher.

Jackson yelled out from the hangar, "We need to get going, you two!"

Gabriella lifted her head from Christopher's chest. "Gemma and I need to get back to our hotel before someone starts looking for us. Chris, I do not know the next time I will see you. I know you want to leave some things unsaid, but I need you to know you mean a lot to me. Be careful, and try not to worry about me."

Christopher and Gabriella held their embrace until the sound of SUV tires drew close behind them. Gabriella grabbed Gemma's hand as she jumped from the lead SUV. Gabriella blew a kiss to Jackson and began walking toward a pedestrian path to the main terminal. Christopher donned his sunglasses as wet trails raced down his cheeks. As he looked back at the women, Christopher doubted he would ever see Gabriella alive again and prayed at least to see her in Heaven.

Jackson thought about his two friends and their complicated relationship as he drove toward an airfield exit and into the unknown of Jakarta. "You alright, brother."

Christopher mumbled, "With God's help, I will be."

General Havid had spent the last two days in his home office reflecting on what God was doing across Israel and in his heart. The display of God's power by Reuel and Eliyahu against Draven made the point clear for the seasoned combat-veteran; Omega could not back down in attacking the UE. The general realized, looking across his lawn that looked more like a tar-tinged ski-slope than a well-manicured suburban landscape, that his time to serve the nation of Israel grew short. He knew enough about the Bible to understand the unholy alliance between Draven and Israel would end within the next eighteen months. The general wondered if the breaking of the treaty between Draven and Israel would also end his decades of service.

As the general returned to his study desk, placing his hands behind his head, the next practical step came to mind. He would build a stockpile at a location where the Omega Team could survive until Christ's return, a little over four years from now. *If Draven wants a fight, then I will ensure we have the tools to wage war,* the general thought, as he began typing the survival plan for Omega.

Last night, John Barnes went to bed worried that the rally's Christian leaders would slip by Ahmad's men. His concern was warranted, given the early morning call from Ahmad that the two men assigned to watch the Christian leaders were arrested. Given what happened in Jerusalem overnight, Barnes knew that failing to strike a blow against the Christian insurgency would draw Draven Cross's ire. He needed to grab these men and end the Christian rally for his own safety. More than anything, he could not shake what Ahmad told him the men saw at the Christians' house, two women that fit a description of Gemma and Gabriella. It did not make sense, but his gut told him to follow up.

Picking up his phone, he dialed the SAG deputy. "Hey, get the guys up and ready to roll to pick up these Christians within the hour. Ahmad has proven to be as worthless as he looks. I also need you to track down Gabriella and Gemma; I'll explain later."

John Barnes had also tried to locate Gabriella and Gemma after his knocks on their hotel room door had gone unanswered for the past few minutes. He'd tried each woman's cell phones, to no avail. His operatives said that neither woman was in the hotel, increasing his suspicions that Ahmad's men may have correctly identified the women at the rally leaders' home. Barnes could not wait all morning to determine where the women were. The *Jundallah* and his UE SAG operatives were waiting outside the hotel to detain the Christian rally leaders at home.

As Barnes joined his team in the nondescript SUVs and made their way to South Jakarta, he wondered if Gabriella was working against him. Barnes returned his focus on the mission at hand, as the convoy made its way onto the rally leaders' street, only to find the roadblocked by local police. He watched as a female officer, who seemed different and out of place amongst the other police officers, approached his vehicle, tapping on his window.

Barnes questioned, "Good morning, officer. Can you understand me?"

The officer said, "I speak English if that's what you're asking. The better question is, how can I help you, gentlemen."

Barnes handed the officer a memo he drafted to bypass any local legal obstacles. "We are a UE security unit looking for two suspected high-value transnational security threats. I am under the direct authority of Secretary-General Cross. So, move your vehicles and let me continue my mission."

The officer asserted, "Mr. Barnes, my authority supersedes Secretary-General Cross, and you will not be allowed to continue your mission.

The Christian leaders were detained by the local police overnight. Your team will return to your hotel until your master calls you."

Barnes's urge to respond to the officer was met with confusion. He struggled to understand what was going on. The words of the officer rattled his mind as he pushed the microphone on his radio. "Listen up, everyone, we're returning to the hotel. The mission is accomplished. We have the information needed to report higher."

A part of Barnes struggled with the answer he had been given. He couldn't overcome the overwhelming sense to obey the police officer. "Thanks, officer, for the information, and make sure you keep a close watch on the men detained."

❧

The angel smiled as the convoy of mercenaries departed. She then approached the two men of God, climbing into an awaiting police vehicle heading for the rally.

Jacob asked, "How did you stop those men from attacking us?"

The angel responded, "You should know the answer best as part of the 144,000 chosen by God. Is it not written, 'M*ay those who want to take my life be put to shame and confusion; may all who desire my ruin be turned back in disgrace.*'"

Michael nodded. "Psalm 70:2. God's merciful hands never stop moving."

The angel agreed, "Yes, now go. Your work for our God has only begun today."

❧

Christopher did not understand the scene before him as the two Omega SUVs arrived at the Gelora Bung Karno stadium. Tens of thousands of people were filing into the venue for the rally.

Jackson said, "This makes no sense. Why are people going into the stadium so early? Gabriella told us the rally didn't start until 7 p.m."

Christopher said, "I am not sure, Jackson, but let's park and find out."

Jimbo and Gilana in the trailing SUV had already parked and were talking with a group of locals. Gilana broke away from Jimbo and the locals and approached the SUV with Jackson and Christopher.

Gilana provided an update. "The rally was pushed up to 1 p.m. in an attempt to throw off those wanting to stop it. The bigger problem is the two-armed groups patrolling. One group of armed men are providing protection for the Christians. The other armed group is the local police. We have landed in a pit of sleeping lions, and once the UE figures out the time switch, it will be feeding time."

The piercing sounds of cars honking and a police siren chirp behind Christopher and Jackson's SUV interrupted the ad hoc meeting in the street as Jackson pulled into a nearby parking area.

The Omega Team watched as the crowd erupted into cheers as two middle-aged men emerged from a police squad car and were escorted through the crowds of people.

Christopher assumed on the fanfare for the men that these were the Christian leaders for the rally.

Jimbo wondered. "Now what? The plan to search the stadium before the crowds arrived is shot."

Christopher began providing radios and handsets to his team. "Divide and conquer. Jimbo and Jackson try to find the Pyretos bombs. Gilana and I will try to get a few moments with those two men. I am guessing they are the rally leaders, based on their reception. I hope we can convince them to keep the event short and sweet. Use these for comms during the rally."

Jackson reminded the team as Jimbo, and he mixed into the crowd heading into the stadium. "Keep your heads on a swivel. There are a lot of armed people here."

❧

Evan stopped the virtual staff meeting between himself and the UE HQ. The announcement from an ANN anchor of a massive Christian rally in Jakarta caught his attention. "Does anyone know where John Barnes is at this moment?"

General Ahuja answered, "He remains in Jakarta on the mission of stopping this very rally from happening."

"That's what I thought." Shouts from Draven interrupted Evan as he watched the door burst open.

Draven demanded, "Why am I the only person in this organization capable of getting anything done satisfactorily? Someone track down John Barnes and Gabriella and determine why the news is describing an event that was not scheduled to occur!"

"Yes, sir, we were working—"

Draven cut Evan off. "Stop talking and end this rally. I'm tired of my enemies having the upper hand."

General Ahuja. "Sir, I'm directing a nearby contingent of UE forces to Jakarta now. We will detain the leaders and anyone else attending the rally."

Draven did not respond to the general or anyone else as he stormed out of the room, leaving Evan and the UE staff scrambling.

⁂

Gabriella and Gemma's absence seemed to go unnoticed as they had made it back to the hotel and changed without anyone questioning them. Gemma chose to get some sleep after an eventful evening while Gabriella got to work walking into the hotel's conference room, now converted to support the mission of finding the Christian leaders.

Gabriella hoped for a peaceful event as the closed-circuit camera feeds around the *Gelora Bung Karno* stadium complex filled with people. Her cell phone ringing with Evan's number in the display cast a shadow on her hopes. She walked out of the conference room to the hallway. "Hello, Evan."

Evan asked, "Where is John Barnes, and do you realize that the Christians are about to begin their rally?"

Gabriella exclaimed, "No, I do not know where Barnes is, and yes, I can see that we did not detain the Christian leaders. Have you tried to call Barnes?"

Evan sounded furious. "No, I assume you two were working in proximity."

Gabriella knew her next move. "Well, start with that, Evan. I can direct him to the rally, but I am not a soldier. Goodbye."

She walked back into the conference room, locating the intelligence support officer. "Commander Jones, I need to step out for a moment. I'll be right out front, so grab me if something significant occurs."

Commander Jones acknowledged her orders. "Yes, ma'am."

Gabriella moved outside the hotel conference room to warn Christopher of the approaching storm. "Chris, listen, I don't have much time. Barnes's team and likely others are going to be heading to the rally soon."

Over the phone, Christopher said, "Thanks for the heads up. I figured it would only be a matter of time before the UE figured out the time change for the rally."

"The time change did catch the UE off guard. It was a good move by Jacob and Michael; those are the rally leaders' names. In any case, I am glad they moved the rally up. Be careful, bye."

Gabriella jumped as she turned to go back into the conference room as John Barnes was standing in her path.

"John, you startled me. Can I help you with something?"

"Where have you been, Gabriella? I came by your room this morning around 6 a.m., and you didn't answer."

Gabriella said, "It's not your concern to worry where I've been."

John Barnes's eyes narrowed. "It is my concern as the lead for security while we're here."

Gabriella rolled her eyes. "Gemma and I couldn't sleep, so we went out for a walk and then ended up getting coffee nearby. Is that okay with you, John?"

"Gemma said the same thing, but…." Barnes's phone rang.

Gabriella knew it was Evan—or worse Draven—calling. Barnes's face grew sullen as he was likely being chewed out because of the rally and his failure. Gabriella enjoyed the fact that their evil plans were at least delayed and possibly thwarted.

Barnes ran off to grab his henchmen. "I've got to go, Gabriella, but you have some explaining to do. Don't think I'm taking all the blame."

Christopher prepared his team for trouble heading their way based on the heads up from Gabriella. The good news, he told everyone, is no one is looking for us. Christopher did not want to confront John Barnes or the UE unless it was necessary. As Gilana and he attempted to get to the rear of the stage set up for the rally, a counter indicated the rally would start in five minutes. The team had not identified anything that looked like it could be a makeshift explosive. A sense of nausea rose in Christopher. *All these people and I cannot help them,* he thought.

Christopher did what previously was counter-intuitive in these situations; he prayed. Considering he would not get the chance to speak with the rally leaders or find the Pyretos bombs before the event started, prayer was the only option. *God protect those in harm's way and guide me to where I can be useful.*

As the rally began, over 70,000 voices joined in unison to sing praises to the name of Jesus Christ and the living God of Heaven. Though he could not understand the words, the electric charge of the atmosphere told him precisely what was happening as the tears flowed from Christopher.

Jackson keyed his radio mic to speak, "This is amazing. God is good."

Christopher wondered. "Where are you two?"

Jackson responded, "We're near the rear of the stage. It was as close as we could get."

Christopher resigned that the team was in the best positions possible. "Okay, stay there. Gilana and I are near the front of the stage. If something happens, move toward the rally leaders, and then we'll make our way toward the vehicles."

A tall man took the stage with a presence that commanded authority and reverence as a stillness settled in over the stadium. Written translation in several languages scrolled across the jumbo screen with the speaker's first words.

"Good evening, my name is Jacob. Welcome, everyone listening to my voice either here or around the world via radio and the internet. I will be as brief as the Holy Spirit will allow me, as there are evil men led by the Beast who aim to end this rally. However, God will sustain us."

Shouts of defiance and optimism rose from the crowd with Jacob's declaration of God's provision.

Jacob quieted the crowd and continued, "Lift your Bibles and your heads toward God and pray with me. God, we gather here for many to discover who You are and who Jesus is. Let hearts open to receive You. Father, give everyone listening strength for the days ahead. I pray all of us boldly proclaim Your gospel to the world until Jesus returns or You call us home to You. Amen.

"So, the fundamental question that draws all of us here today is who Jesus Christ is? Until the disappearances, I would have told you that Jesus was not the Messiah of Israel and Savior of all humanity. That the name of Jesus had brought nothing but pain and suffering to my people and that I had no desire to know anything about him.

"Some have said that Jesus never existed. A common objection to Jesus's existence is the belief that Jesus's life and his message are patchworks from stories of other ancient traditions. Others argue that his most significant claim of being the Christ, the Son of God, demonstrates that Jesus, while potentially a historical figure, most likely was deranged, as there is no God. Was he a philosopher, a prophet, or an ordinary man? What matters at this moment is who do you say Jesus is, and are you willing to call him your Savior?

"Jesus was and is the Christ, the Son of the living God. In this simple but profound statement, we find the hope of life, sustainer of life, and an eternal redeemer that died so that you can live. *Colossians 1:15-20* provides us clear reasons why Jesus reigns supreme over all things. Jesus made the invisible God visible, serving as God's living image on Earth. Jesus is the sustainer of all things in both the spirit and physical worlds; and, all things bring glory to him as their creator. Jesus was the first to rise and never to fall again to death and the grave.

"Jesus is the only one to be born into this world with the fullness of God; he was the living God and embodied God in human flesh. Jesus reconciles through his bloodshed on the cross, all who believe in him back to fellowship. No other prophet or person who has lived can make these claims. I do not have the words or the time to tell you how amazing

Jesus is today. Receive him now at this moment before it's too late and allow him to change your life forever."

Jacob continued, "I will conclude by bringing my fellow teacher, Michael, to provide an invitation for all attending to receive Jesus as their personal savior."

Michael implored. "I beg you not to put off this decision for death is ever-present in times which we live. Come toward the stage if you will. If you do not feel comfortable coming forward, stay in your seats, and repeat the following."

Christopher watched as thousands of people tried to make their way toward the stage, and many more stood with arms outstretched and tears flowing.

Michael began the prayer of salvation, saying, "Lord Jesus, I know that I am a sinner, and I ask for Your forgiveness. I believe You died for my sins and rose from the dead. Help me turn away from my sins; I invite You to come into my heart to change me into a new person. I want to trust You with my life and follow You as my Lord and Savior. Jesus, in your name, I pray. Amen."

A gunshot shattered the rally's peace as the sign language translator next to Michael dropped to the stage. Screams and panic invaded the stadium.

~

Christopher froze for a moment as additional gunshots intermixed with the terrorized voices of thousands. As a stinging sensation grew in his ears, Christopher felt weightless slamming to the ground, attempting to understand what had occurred, as he found himself lying around bodies. Gilana's shouts in his face made him realize that he survived a near miss from a Pyretos bomb.

Gilana helped Christopher to his feet. "We need to move."

Christopher's head swam as he unslung the assault rifle from his back, covered by an oversized tactical shirt, and moved toward the stage with Gilana where a firefight was occurring.

Jackson updated the team across the radio. "We need some help here. The Christian guards and UE have us pinned down between their firefight."

Christopher watched as two UE soldiers and four other men advanced on the Christian guards protecting the fleeing rally leaders. Gilana took aim, dropping the lead UE soldiers. The other four soldiers sought cover amongst the overturned sound and music equipment on the stage. Gilana's shots also brought the sharp crack of air from return fire from five other men and an operative that looked like John Barnes fifty meters away.

Christopher felt a sense of relief watching the Christian guards disappear behind the stage with the rally leaders, leaving his team and the UE in a standoff.

Christopher directed Gilana. "Our best bet is to fight our way to the rear of the stage to link up with Jackson and Jimbo."

"I agree," Gilana said, ducking and returning fire amongst the stadium's seats.

Christopher keyed his radio coordinating team. "Jackson lay down covering fire to your three o'clock on the word go. We're coming your way."

Jackson said, "Got ya."

Christopher keyed the radio. "Three, two, one, go!"

Jackson and Jimbo emerged from behind a steel container to open fire on the UE forces drawing their attention as Christopher and Gilana made a dash across the stage and behind the rear of the platform.

Jackson screamed as Christopher and Gilana gathered themselves now on the backside of the stage. "Man down, man down!"

Christopher peered up to see Jackson receiving incoming gunfire as he knelt again behind the steel storage container. The massive body of Jimbo lay unmoving on top of a growing pool of blood across the stage several feet away.

Gilana shouted and ran toward Jackson, firing wildly at the UE, who sought protection from her fury. Christopher joined her and Jackson to assess how they could get to Jimbo and not lose their lives.

Jackson repeated, "He's gone, man; Jimbo's gone."

Gilana yelled into the team's radios. "We need to go; they will flank us at any moment."

The cold and harsh reality of the situation tore at Christopher's heart as he stared at the lifeless body of Jimbo. "Gilana's right. We can't get to him and live."

Jackson said nothing but returned fire toward three advancing UE operatives. He led the way from the stage toward an exit tunnel leading out of the stadium. The team tried to hide amid the fleeing crowd. However, the UE operatives and soldiers gave pursuit, firing indiscriminately on the group.

Christopher heard Gilana shriek and tumble from a gunshot, spilling people around her onto the ground like spaghetti falling out of a bag.

Jackson demanded as he returned fire toward the stage with Christopher eliminating the gunman, "Get up, missy, I'm not losing anybody else today."

Gilana grimaced. "I will be fine. The bullet hit my shoulder."

The trio exited the tunnel with gunshots and screams of dying people echoing as the UE chased.

Christopher discarded his radio handset yelling. "Where are the vehicles?"

Jackson threw his radio on the ground as he supported Gilana across the street to the vehicles while Christopher provided a rear guard.

Christopher's team was now taking gunshots from the local Jakarta police. He hesitated for a moment before pulling his trigger as he stared at the nervous police officer. Christopher knew the officer in his gun sights was only doing his job. However, fate was against him. Christopher thought no one else on his team was going to die today. If it came down to anyone on his team or himself giving their lives, then this officer's life had to end today. The officer fell out of Christopher's sight picture with the squeeze of the trigger.

Jackson helped Gilana into the second row of the SUV as Christopher took more well-aimed shots at their aggressors.

Jackson shouted, "Get in the truck!"

Jackson's blood ran cold as he made eye contact with John Barnes. He watched as Barnes took aim and heard the ping of bullets off the SUV as the vehicle careened its way through hordes of people and cars toward the hope of safety at the airport.

Police cars blocked three of the routes leading to the Outer Ring highway from the stadium. Jackson prayed the last option was open as he rounded the final turn before the exit. Why this specific departure was available became apparent as the narrow thoroughfare led to a gated checkpoint crawling with police officers.

Jackson paused too long for the comfort of Gilana and Christopher, both screamed, "What are you doing?"

The powerful up-armored SUV lurched forward, providing Jackson's response as he entered a high-stakes game of chicken with an oncoming Jakarta police vehicle. Police sirens behind him left only one hope. The oncoming officers valued their lives more than detaining Jackson and his associates. Moments before the impact and thirty meters ahead of the checkpoint, the police vehicle swerved into a grassy median. Jackson saw the break he needed. "Thank you, Jesus."

Seconds later, the thin-wrought iron front gate of the Al-Bina Mosque exploded. The Jakarta police had left the mosque vehicle traffic bypass unblocked. They now fired their weapons in an attempt to stop the runaway SUV.

Jackson yelled. "Keep your heads down!" He smashed wooden benches on his way across the mosque entrance to the screams of attendees and through a makeshift security gate separating the mosque and the *Jl Pintu Satu Senayan* highway. Jackson did not slow down for the heavy traffic, slamming a small sedan with such force that he knocked it sideways.

The ensuing traffic jam rendered the pursuit by the immediate police threat over, as Jackson caught sight of a sign that indicated the Outer Ring road was ahead. He weaved the SUV over the median and around traffic, mentally sighing but still driving aggressively in an attempt to get to the airport.

Jackson asked, "Gilana, are you okay?"

Gilana said, "I will be okay for now. The bullet went through, and I'm keeping pressure on the wound."

Jackson knew they would not make it back to the plane without bringing most of the city's police and UE. They needed to hide and get Gilana taken care of at the same time.

They needed a distraction. "Christopher, pull out your phone and call Gabriella. We need a distraction."

Christopher agreed, "Great idea, keep driving. I've got this." Christopher dialed Gabriella. "Listen—"

Gabriella interrupted him. "Are you guys, okay?"

"I don't have time to explain. We need you to call a nearby hospital and tell them UE special operatives are heading in with a wounded member. We are on *Satu Senayan* highway heading north."

Christopher could hear frantic concern by Gabriella attempting to open the map app on her phone.

Gabriella directed. "Head to Pelni hospital off *Jl KS Tubun*. I will call them now."

Christopher nodded, even though Gabriella couldn't see him. "Sounds good." Christopher's head snapped to the side as the vehicle suddenly spun, ending the call.

Jackson fought to regain control of the SUV as it skidded through the *Satu Senayan* highway intersection leading to the stadium complex's third entrance. He looked in the rearview mirror to see John Barnes and his thugs had clipped them. He floored the vehicle despite being in the wrong lane as bullet pings indicated Barnes's pursuit.

Jackson noticed a second SUV pursuing him from the correct lane of traffic, attempting to draw close with armed men hanging out the windows. Jackson intuitively ducked his head with the shattering of the rear window. Gilana proceeded to spray Barnes's SUV with gunfire. The wild spray of bullets caused Barnes's SUV to swerve into a family van, flipping the van over the median and slowing Barnes's pursuit.

Jackson watched Christopher take aim at the second SUV as the *Satu Senayan* highway merged onto the Asia Afrika road. Christopher's gunfire forced the second UE vehicle to stay on the wrong side of the Asia Afrika road, buying Jackson time to plot his next move. He noticed city police weaving through traffic. Jackson took a quick scan of the vehicle's GPS, which displayed a golf course on his left. He sprang into action, praying that the massive SUV could withstand what he hoped was a thin brick wall.

Dodging a barrage of honking cars, Jackson jerked the SUV left across the sidewalk and through the Senayan National Golf Club's outer wall. A flash of light and a firm smack on his face signaled the deployment of the airbag. Jackson, stunned for a moment, tried to get his bearing through a dust cloud enveloping the SUV.

Jackson yelled, "Y'all, alright!"

Gilana moaned. "Yes, but let's not do that again."

Jackson hit the gas pedal, ripping up the lush 17th fairway, driving along a cart path leading toward the clubhouse, drawing screams and curses from shocked patrons. He glanced out the broken rear window to see one of the SUVs pursuing him through the elite golf club.

The Omega Team exited the golf club at the fifth hole. They made their way onto *Patal Senayan Simprug*, a narrow residential street lined with cars 300 meters from the *Tentara Pelajar* freeway. Jackson realized the constrictive road was his last chance to lose Barnes and the police.

Jackson stopped the SUV and opened the trunk to the screams of Christopher and Gilana.

Christopher demanded, "Jackson, get in the SUV. What are you doing? They are right behind us."

Jackson dug through one of the team's weapons boxes, looking to find the tool of their salvation, grenades. "I hope they keep coming. We got 'em."

Christopher and Gilana watched Jackson quickly throw four grenades under a vehicle parked along the tight street. Jackson jumped in the SUV as Barnes's vehicle prepared to cross from the golf course onto *Senayan Simprug* Street, as the grenades detonated. The explosion pushed the two small cars and debris into the street in such a way that made further pursuit a time-consuming event.

Gilana swore and fired a few pop shots at Barnes's SUV as Jackson merged onto the northbound freeway and toward the Pelni Hospital.

❧

Gabriella wanted to scream, "They got away," at the top of her lungs after Barnes's curse-filled report to the Intel OPS center saying Omega had escaped him. She fought back the urge, given her location. Gabriella had not been this nervous since the Omega mission in Afghanistan a year and a half ago. Gabriella had struggled for composure listening to Barnes's radio updates and the police scanners during the hair-raising chase of her close friends. Now would come the wrath of Draven, given the spectacular failure of the UE in Jakarta.

A UE intelligence officer said, "Ma'am, the Jakarta police are reporting they have the body of one of the attackers on the rally. They are saying he was American military."

Gabriella's heart sank, trying to guess who from Omega died. She wished it were one of Barnes's goons.

Gabriella pressed for information. "What else do we have on this dead American? Why do they think he's American military?"

"The Jakarta police department identified the deceased with the westerners fleeing the stadium. I think Mr. Barnes will be able to provide us better details, considering he pursued the suspects."

"Thanks, and keep listening to the police scanner. Let me know if they find those other suspects."

Gabriella felt lost. She had moved from elation to desperation in a matter of minutes. Barnes was on his way back after losing the Omega Team. Knowing that Barnes saw them, there would be no place safe for Omega now. Draven would search the world for the one set of persons outside the Two Witnesses that could hinder his plans.

❧

CHAPTER 15

AS CHRISTOPHER SAT with Jackson in the empty Pelni Hospital emergency waiting room waiting for word on Gilana, the mission's adrenaline subsided. His left leg would not stop bouncing as he watched the ANN's coverage of an event that nearly cost him his life. The lifeless body of Jimbo laid out on the stage flashed in his mind. The UE propaganda machine labeled Omega as an unknown terror group. It was only a matter of time before the unknown became clear with Jackson's pictures and himself likely posted worldwide. He found it strange to be on the opposite side of the global most wanted terrorist list. The hunters now became the hunted, reducing the odds of surviving to Christ's return.

He closed his eyes, questioning the decision to allow the rally to happen. Jimbo's asking his surety on God, saying the rally should continue now haunted him. Christopher had always struggled to trust God, and now his faith was being tested in the wake of Jimbo's death after his decision. Christopher felt an overwhelming sense of calm, similar to his feeling on the plane right before his fateful announcement on the rally.

He knew the feeling to be the Holy Spirit. Christopher calmed his mind anticipating hearing God's message, as God's words began flooding his mind, "*Christopher, this was not your decision. It was the Lord's and His alone. Remember God's words in the book of Isaiah: 'For my thoughts are not your thoughts, neither are your ways my ways, declares the Lord. As the heavens are higher than the earth, so are my ways higher than your ways and my thoughts than your thoughts.' You're serving the God of Heaven and*

Earth, and all answers will not be provided to you. Take comfort in knowing that Jimbo is at home with the Lord, and many came to accept the Father's offer of salvation because of your efforts of protection for God's servants. Do not lose faith in this time of trial and tribulation. God will not leave you or forsake you."

Tears streamed from Christopher's face. He felt like he was in the very presence of God at how loved and comforted he felt after receiving the Holy Spirit's message.

Jackson grew worried about Christopher. "Are you beating yourself up for Jimbo's death?"

"I am trying not to go there as I did after Rev's death if that's what you're asking."

Jackson stood and stretched. "What I told you then remains true now; our line of work is a rough business. You're not at fault for Jimbo's death. The big man is in a better place than we are right now. All I want is revenge. We need to hit Draven someplace; it will hurt."

Christopher responded, "I know he is for sure." As he finished, a doctor approached them.

The doctor asked, "You are the friends of Sofia, correct?"

It took Christopher a second to remember that they had admitted Gilana under a false name. "Yes, we are her friends. Is she doing okay, doc?"

"She will be fine. It was a minor procedure, but I had to sedate her to ensure the wound was clear of shrapnel and sew it closed. However, Sofia will need to say overnight for observation and is in a recovery room. I will allow her to see you after you complete the debrief with your UE superiors."

Christopher's mind raced. His hope that it would take the UE longer to canvas hospitals in the city in an attempt to determine if the terrorist had been wounded was quicker than expected. "What debrief with my superiors? I didn't get a call."

"I'm sorry. I don't have the details. The charge nurse told me as I inquired about the whereabouts of Sofia's companions. The nurse may have more information."

The doctor pointed to a now-empty nurses' station. "The nurse is likely outside smoking. Check with her when she comes back. Have a good day, gentleman."

Christopher and Jackson scanned the hallways for an enemy they knew would arrive at any moment. The ANN breaking news update made the doctor's announcement worse.

The ANN anchor said, "We are breaking from the scheduled programming to provide an update on the terror attack earlier today in Jakarta, Indonesia. The pictures you are seeing are those of the masterminds behind today's attack. The terror group leaders are the former U.S. Army Major Christopher Barrett and his accomplice, the former U.S. Army Sergeant Major Jackson Williams. These men are considered armed and extremely dangerous. If seen, report their location to the local authorities immediately. We now return you to your scheduled programming."

Christopher whispered, "We need to grab Gilana and get out of here. Now."

Jackson agreed, "No rest for the weary."

❧

General Havid's worst fears removed his attention from planning Omega's evasion and survival plan for the coming years after an ANN breaking news broadcast of unrest in Jakarta. The general turned the television in his study up.

The ANN anchor stated, "Hours ago, a group of terrorists unleashed a biological weapon on a Christian rally in Jakarta. The assailants armed with automatic weapons killed and wounded several Jakarta City police officers and UE security forces during their escape from the *Gelora Bung Karno* Stadium. One terrorist was killed fleeing. There are no further details on the affiliation of the terror group at this time. The whereabouts and number of terrorists still at large remains the priority for the Jakarta City police. No group has come forward to claim responsibility for the attack at the moment.

The civilian death toll is anticipated to climb following today's attack. First responders are attempting to treat causalities at the stadium, reporting victims displaying symptoms similar to those relating to the recent pandemic."

General Havid turned the television off as an aide entered with his lunch. His heart sank as he weighed the unknowns and the possibility that an Omega member had fallen.

The general mumbled, "God help us," before answering his phone.

Gabriella had barely finished her call with General Havid informing him of Omega's status when John Barnes burst into the hotel conference room, demanding to speak with her.

"We need to talk now."

Gabriella wanted to push Barnes away, given her concerns for her Omega friends. "Is this important or another pathetic attempt to flirt with me?"

Barnes said, panic in his voice. "Gabriella, we are in trouble. The last thing I am thinking about is flirting."

Gabriella conceded, given Barnes's pacing and sweating, as he awaited her response. His theatrics provided enough credibility. "Okay. Where do you want to talk?"

Barnes said, "Follow me."

Gabriella followed him to a round table with two empty, high-back chairs in a secluded corner adjacent to the conference room. She forced Barnes to reveal his hand as she sat with folded arms. "You said we needed to talk, Barnes, so talk. I don't have all day."

"Ease up, okay. I'm trying to save both our lives here."

Gabriella said, "Spare me the lies and drama; get on with what you need to say."

"Okay, I got a call from Evan Mallory a few minutes ago. He wants me to call Draven in an hour and explain what went wrong here in Jakarta. I think Draven is looking for someone to blame, and I don't see this as entirely my fault. I mean, how did Christopher and Jackson even get to Jakarta, and why didn't you know their whereabouts?"

Gabriella scoffed. "Here's a pro tip for you; do not lead off with the

Secretary-General's first name. It's the kind of thing that will lead to early retirement for you."

Barnes shouted, causing a hotel staffer to peer around a corner at the odd couple, "Would you listen!"

Gabriella leaned toward him. "Calm down. I don't have answers for you on how or why Barrett and Williams were at the rally. That is what you need to tell the Secretary-General. As far as blaming me for not knowing they were here, I think you are the person that reported the Omega group's demise in Alaska last year. I had no intelligence that indicated they were alive. I need to go and get ready for our flight back to Rome later tonight. Pull yourself together, Barnes, and admit that you failed and will do better next time."

Barnes's eyes narrowed. "I think you mean we failed. You said it best; there was no intelligence of value provided for this entire mission. You better believe I'm telling the Secretary-General that fact."

Gabriella's phone rang, displaying a call from Christopher. The incoming call stopped her from responding where her emotions were leading her. "Do what makes you feel better."

☙

Draven was transfixed all day by the news from Jakarta. Even now, as his senior staff virtually briefed the plans to end the Christian movement, minus Evan and Gabriella, Draven could not stop watching clips of the carnage. The videos and interviews of Christians clinging to their faith and blaming the UE for the attack incensed him. He had pushed the UE staff and Evan to pinpoint who was at that rally helping the Christians. Facial recognition analysis from cameras at the event, coupled with John Barnes's report, identified the attackers as leaders of the former U.S. Military Omega Team. He wanted answers to why former Omega operatives that were reported dead helped protect the Christian leaders. Draven believed that the American rogues must have had assistance from within the UE. He would not rest until eliminating this threat. Draven's propaganda machine was hard at work, ensuring Major Barrett and his compatriots were labeled terrorists.

Evan leaned over to Draven next to him. "Sir, do you have any questions on the staff's updated plan?"

"The plan is lacking the most critical element: fear. You have failed to understand the purpose behind the IECs to support another bureaucratic acronym within this organization. You describe these facilities as places for rehabilitation. The reason for stamping out this religious rebellion is societal control. These Christians are growing in numbers that challenge my ability to control the world. I want five maximum security, nightmare-producing prisons built in the most hostile possible environments. These facilities are meant to punish those foolish enough to rebel against me. The IECs are prisons and must be isolated and inhospitable in every way possible."

Draven continued, "I want the Christians and anyone else daring to challenge my vision or me to suffer. These Christians and anyone else plotting insurrection should be afraid to meet together. Everyone must fear even speaking against the UE. Do you understand the objective now?"

Evan nodded. "Yes, sir, we do."

Draven abruptly ended the meeting by closing the laptop before him and standing over a still seated Evan Mallory. "Evan, there is more to the fiasco in Jakarta. The fact that we know that former American Omega operatives were involved leads to troubling questions. Get Barnes on the phone; I want to hear his accounting of the events. I suspect we have a traitor within our ranks. Give the task of tracking down and eliminating everyone associated with these Americans to that sycophant General Ahuja. I don't trust Barnes or Gabriella with this matter."

"I understand and will have Barnes on the phone shortly."

Draven's focus shifted as an assistant ushered two scantily clothed women into his suite. "Don't rush back."

Christopher watched as Jackson rushed ahead of him and out of the hospital toward the nurses' smoking area. At the same time, he placed a call to Gabriella. By the time Christopher made it to the door leading to the smoking area, Jackson had pulled a reluctant nurse back through the door into the hospital.

Jackson gave Christopher a head nod to follow him. "I'm going to have her take us to Sofia so we can get out of here," Jackson said.

Christopher nodded in agreement waiting on Gabriella to answer the phone. "Hey, the UE is sending some folks here to 'debrief' us; you know anything about that."

Gabriella said, "No."

Christopher rolled his eyes. "I was afraid you'd say that. We are going to grab our injured friend. We need to get to the airport. You think you can create some space for us?"

Gabriella seemed optimistic. "Yeah, I'll head back into the support center and say I got information that you guys were spotted in East Jakarta. The opposite side of the city from the airport. Be careful."

"That sounds like the perfect distraction; I'll call you once we reach the plane."

Christopher followed Jackson, who walked the nurse through the hospital toward signage that said "Recovery Ward" in Indonesian and English.

The nurse begged in a thick accent, "Please don't kill me."

Jackson assured her, "Ma'am, if you cooperate, you will be fine. I need you to take us to our friend Sofia."

The nurse hesitated. Jackson pushed two fingers into the small of her back to simulate a gun.

The nurse panicked. "Okay, don't kill me!"

Christopher watched Jackson wink at him, pleased with his fake gun rouse despite having an actual pistol in a back holster. "Get moving, and don't make a scene if you want to keep living."

The trio entered the main corridor. Christopher noticed Gilana's doctor talking with two UE uniformed men at the nurses' station. Jackson pulled the nurse down an adjacent hall and walked through a double set of doors that led to several recovery rooms. She raised a shaking hand, pointing at the third room on the left of the hallway.

Christopher ordered Jackson, "I'll stay with the nurse; you grab Sofia."

Before Christopher could respond, two other nurses came around a corner, starring at Christopher and the distraught nurse in his grasp. The nurse slammed her hands into Christopher's face, pushing away, screaming in Indonesian.

Christopher nearly fell from the bruising blow to his face. He recovered to find all three nurses had fled, and a piercing alarm was blaring in the hospital.

As Christopher attempted to make his way to Gilana's room from the hallway, he was slammed against a wall with his left arm pinned to his lower back. The warm blood of his crumpled nose flowed into his mouth, creating a metallic taste and waves of pain in his mind. He instinctively spun to meet his assailant leading with his right elbow. Christopher's elbow sunk into the UE operatives jaw, causing air and a tooth to expel from the man as he fell unconscious. Before Christopher composed himself, the unconscious man's partner landed a solid right cross to his face, nearly knocking him out. Christopher fell to the ground with his back against the wall, now covered with his blood. Dazed, he watched the second officer level a pistol on him as he began to accept his final moments.

He expected the flash of the gun muzzle aimed at him. Instead, he heard a piercing whistle drawing the man's attention, followed by a flying chair striking the officer. Jackson followed quickly behind the chair with his dirty boot collapsing into the officer's temple ending the fight.

Jackson extended his hand. "Let's go. I can't be the only one saving people here today."

Christopher rubbed his jaw and wiped his nose, trying to remove the smell of blood from his mind. He stood overwhelmed for a second grateful to be alive. "I had it under control, wise guy, but thanks."

Christopher accepted a fist bump from Jackson as he heard hospital staff coming toward the sounds of the fight. "We need a new way out."

Christopher followed Jackson, who grabbed the chair he'd used to save Christopher's life and ran back into Gilana's room. Jackson broke out the sizeable single pane back window. Christopher was thankful that the recovery ward was on the hospital's first floor as Jackson climbed through the opening.

Jackson cleared the remaining shards of glass. "Pick up Gilana and hand her to me."

Christopher grabbed the unconscious Gilana and handed her to Jackson's waiting arms, who placed her in a firefighter's carry. After climbing out the window, Christopher took the lead, pulling his pistol from a leg holster to provide protection during their escape.

The challenge of getting to the SUV escalated quickly as two UE Operatives advanced toward the group along a landscaped path. The operatives were moving as if they were unsure where Christopher's group might be amongst thick vegetation. Christopher waved Jackson to hide behind a large cooling unit while he crouched behind two rainbow eucalyptus trees.

As the UE men passed Christopher, he shot the men in the legs, causing both to writhe in pain. The men cursed Christopher as he threw their pistols into a nearby Koi pond.

Jackson, with Gilana on his back, joined him at the pond. "You should have killed them."

Christopher kept walking. "We should only kill when required. The parking lot should be around the corner; let's go."

Christopher moved to the hospital's corner, peering around to find the parking lot empty of threats. He led the group to their SUV, providing cover for Jackson as he loaded Gilana into the back of the vehicle. As Christopher ran around the passenger seat and began to leave, two other UE operatives emerged from the hospital's front entrance firing on the SUV.

Christopher ordered, "Jackson, go to the airport. Gabriella is sending out a report of our location on the opposite side of the city, which should buy us time to get away."

Jackson said, "Gladly, this has been one long day."

◆

Gabriella sat fidgeting in her seat next to Gemma, hoping that her friends made it safely to the airport. A sense of dread settled over her as a flight attendant announced the main cabin door's closing and the requirement to power off her cell phone. Gabriella had not gotten a call as promised by Christopher, and her flight was moments from departing for the UE headquarters in Rome. As she began turning off her phone, it chirped with an incoming text notification.

Her eyes filled with tears spilling onto her phone screen as she read:

"Gabriella. We are loading up now and will be back in Israel tomorrow evening. We lost Jimbo today. Expect a call soon; we will not let Jimbo's death be in vain. Take care."

Gabriella sobbed as she turned her phone off, causing Gemma to grab her and ask, "Are you okay?"

Gabriella held her hand up and looked out her window, unable to speak with the runway lights speeding by as the UE charter flight started its journey back to Rome. As the plane banked to the northeast over the Indian Ocean, Gabriella gathered herself to speak.

"Gemma, I had been so scared for Christopher and the team today. Chris told me it was Jimbo who died. Realizing that Jimbo died, not a terrorist, not a faceless Christian convert standing up for their beliefs, but someone I knew made the news so real that it's hard to breathe."

"He seemed nice, and I'm sorry that he's gone, but I believe he's in a better place than us. Christopher and Omega did a great thing today, ensuring John Barnes did not get the chance to kill Jacob and Michael at the rally. You were a big reason for that, love. Keep your head up. I love you, and I am here for you."

Gabriella buried her head in Gemma's embrace, crying uncontrollably. As the cabin lights dimmed, she whispered, "I love you too."

As the SHADOW taxied during the last of the evening light into the now-familiar private hangar at Ben-Gurion International Airport, Christopher spotted General Havid. After previous missions, the general never greeted the team; Christopher hoped his presence did not signal an unwanted surprise.

Christopher rushed off the plane, addressing the general to ease his concern for the breach of protocol. "General, I'm surprised to see you here, sir. Is everything okay?"

General Havid said, "I wish I were meeting you on happier terms. In truth, I am waiting to receive Jimbo's body. After learning of Jimbo's fate, I devised a ploy to ensure we honored him not only as a warrior but also as a servant of God. He deserves a proper burial and a moment for us to grieve. I arranged through the Israeli Embassy in Jakarta for the nation of Israel to claim Jimbo's body. I told the Embassy that he was the son of a citizen that wished to bury him in Israel. He will be buried at Mount Herzl in a private ceremony. Herzl is fitting, as Jimbo sacrificed his life serving the true king of Israel, Jesus Christ."

Christopher broke down in tears as the other Omega members joined the two men. The general repeated his announcement for the others, and the tears flowed anew.

General Havid took a deep breath. "The plane carrying Jimbo is scheduled to arrive in an hour, which provides enough time for me to discuss the plan for the way forward with everyone. Gilana, you seem tired. Are you sure you do not want to lie down? Christopher can bring you up to speed later."

Gilana insisted she was okay. "I slept the entire flight home. I need to know how we pay back the UE."

General Havid's response started with walking over to a portable tower heater stored against a wall, dragging it to the middle of the hangar, and lighting it before beckoning the Omega team to join him. Christopher and his team pulled up chairs and boxes next to him.

The battle-hardened military officer and now devout Christian's face furrowed, and he paced, clasping his hands before speaking. "Over the last three days, God has displayed His power for all to see. I witnessed Draven Cross, the most powerful political leader in the world, cower before the God of Israel. The streets were covered with hail and flowed like rivers of tar as the hail melted. Despite these marvels before the eyes of the entire world, my beloved Israel, as a whole, refuses to acknowledge that Jesus Christ was our messiah. I fear there are forces and circumstances yet seen that will hinder the chances of all of us surviving until Jesus's return. The retaliation from Draven will be fierce and will provide a bridge for ushering in the final three and a half years of tribulation."

The general continued, "With these feelings in mind, I have begun moving supplies, weapons, and all I think we will need to a large underground facility in the Negev desert. The facility, which previously served as a storage and testing site for weapons, was mothballed after Israel's leaders signed the peace accord with Draven. The underground base is ideal for our purposes as it has a landing strip and limited road access. You cannot return to my home at this moment; Draven has declared Christopher and Jackson enemies of the global state. The chessboard between the friends and the foes of God is being set. I will communicate with you near-daily via the radios and phones at the base. I expect to join you there, God willing, at some point within the next eighteen months."

General Havid concluded, "My allegiances to God and my role as Defense Minister of Israel will become irreconcilable once Draven reveals his true intentions, which I anticipate will begin soon. The Two Witnesses announced weeks ago the opening of the fifth seal, which is the martyrdom of the saints of God. The remaining judgments of God will push all of us to our breaking points to survive."

The Omega team rose with the roaring approach of a cargo airplane.

General Havid continued, "I need you to hide in the hangar office until the military honor guard brings Jimbo's body off the plane. You will have a few moments to mourn him before the honor guard returns. The military believes his family wanted a private moment."

Christopher, Charlie, Jackson, and Gilana made their way to an office above the main floor to observe the ramp ceremony. Eight Israeli soldiers carried Jimbo's casket draped in the Israeli flag off the ramp of the plane, with an additional soldier at the casket's head and feet. An Israeli Defense Force Rabbi led the solemn procession directly to a bier in front of a saluting General Havid. The honor guard soldiers left the general alone and departed the hangar, signaling the Omega team to join him.

General Havid prompted, "We do not have much time. Would anyone like to say anything?"

Christopher stepped forward, placing his hand on the closed casket. "Jimbo, you were a great warrior, friend, and brother in Christ. I will miss your calming presence and remain grateful you helped save my life in Alaska. I look forward to seeing you in a few years."

Charlie waved off, speaking as tears rolled down his careworn face.

Gilana stood before Jimbo's coffin next. "I knew you a short time but had much respect for you. Your death will be avenged, my brother."

Jackson was the last team member to honor the fallen member of Omega, "Jimbo, I can see you now in Heaven flapping those big tree trunks you called arms while you praise the LORD. I will miss you, brother."

The Omega team chuckled with Jackson's typical disarming use of humor.

General Havid closed the memorial. "Dear heavenly Father, we thank You that we had the opportunity to know such a man like Your servant Jimbo. We ask that You guide us to serve You faithfully in the days ahead against Your enemies. In Jesus's name, we pray. Amen."

The Omega Team hid in the office until the honor guard departed with Jimbo's body and then returned for a final time to speak with General Havid that evening.

The general described the next steps, "Tomorrow will be the interment at Mount Herzl. I knew that you could not be there, so I am glad we had this moment together to salute a warrior and friend. Charlie, here are the coordinates to the airstrip, and Christopher, here is the entry code to the main facility doors. I will coordinate with you before further shipments of arms and supplies arrive. You will be more than comfortable, but do not expect to spend much time at the base. I will send you on your revenge mission, if you will, against Draven within the week. I leave you with this blessing, '*The Lord bless you and keep you; the Lord make his face shine on you and be gracious to you; the Lord turn his face toward you and give you peace.*'"

As General Havid's sedan faded from sight across the tarmac and the engines of SHADOW came to life, Christopher hoped this was not the last time he saw the general on this side of eternity.

ঌ

As Draven's convoy made its way from Leonardo da Vinci International Airport to the *Palazzo Caelum* through the battered and impoverished streets of Rome, his mind raced. John Barnes's explanation for what had occurred in Jakarta was inadequate. Draven's suspicions of Barnes and Gabriella were rising, given their previous ties to the Omega group. Draven hurried from his limo, conveying his concerns to Evan.

"I want the first group of prisoners inserted with the loyalty program trackers by the end of the week. I do not believe it is a mere coincidence that a former American military unit's leader remains alive. I expect the first IEC built by the end of the month. If you fail me, it will cost you dearly."

Evan assured him. "I will not fail."

Draven strode silently into an elevator allowing the doors to close in Evan's face, leaving his deputy and image-bearer to bring the dark plans given to him into reality.

CHAPTER 16

AS GABRIELLA SAT alone outside on the UE cafeteria deck starring at the distant Tiber River, she reflected on the increasing peril hunting her over the last year. The recent death of Jimbo and conversion to Christianity by Gemma made Gabriella question her mortality. She felt an obligation to protect unnamed faces and her closest friends in Omega from Draven's schemes despite the pressure of trying to stay alive.

A lingering streamer from an underwhelming UE New Year celebration three months ago glistened on the deck railing. The streamer's festive tone reminded Gabriella that a megalomaniac employed her, at best, but, more likely, the Bible's Antichrist. The irony of celebrating new beginnings amid a ravished and destroyed world had been lost on Draven. The typical optimistic feelings about starting a new year were replaced with the desire only to live to the next day.

As Gabriella reflected on the past few months since Jakarta, she was proud of the support she provided Kerim and his resistance efforts to subvert the UE. The most significant success in her mind had a name and face for Gabriella, Li Wei. Kerim told her that Li Wei had gone from a helpless victim to saving Christians and becoming a follower of Jesus.

Being a Christian weighed heavily on Gabriella. She often thought, *Why can't I commit to God.* Her mental anguish was the constant questioning of the relationship between God and herself. Gabriella's soul was in jeopardy, as Gemma daily reminded her. While stopping Draven Cross consumed Gabriella, it seemed God was determined to pursue her.

Gabriella hardly slept through the night anymore; the dread of having to implement Draven's next order and attempting to find salvation in Jesus was too much for her. Gabriella had earned a reputation in the CIA for finding the obscure informants and coming up with solutions to challenging intelligence problems. However, now all her talents felt wasted; it seemed that Draven and his evil were unstoppable. Millions would lose their lives in the years to come, and no one would be able to stop it.

Gabriella noticed Gemma slowly approaching as if attempting not to startle her. It was the small things like this that Gabriella loved about her.

Gemma said, "I believed I would find you here. This seems to be your favorite place since Jakarta."

Gabriella admired the rare view of a boat drifting along the Tiber River. "Yes, I like the view. It helps me think of how bad I want to stop the evil that surrounds us that destroyed Rome and the world."

Gemma was mindful of their surroundings. "Speaking of the evil, it's focusing a lot of energy in finding those tied to the Jakarta event. The evil believes they are the only ones who will hinder future operations."

Gabriella stood and waved Gemma to join her as they made their way to the UE gardens, where they could speak freely.

Now in the seclusion of the gardens, Gabriella said, "Draven's attempts to find Omega and other groups to ensure his projects stay on track is nothing new, Gemma. Thankfully, between the two of us, we have been able to keep ahead of him and create problems."

Gemma asked, "Have you heard the stories about these IECs? They are horrible. The 'lucky' individuals accepting the loyalty mark regret not requesting an immediate death. As the reprieve from the gallows means an extended stay in an IEC. Prisoners are worked for twenty hours a day and are fed minimally. They are housed in squalid, disease-generating conditions, isolated from all others unless the prisoners are working. Confessions of plots against Draven and the UE are tortured out of people. It seems commonplace during update meetings with Evan and Draven to learn of IEC staff raping women prisoners. Draven laughs and says horrible things when he hears these reports; I dare not repeat his words to you."

"Yes, I can imagine how bad the IECs are. I know Draven had the ANN hire actors to be depicted as prisoners for an ongoing propaganda campaign. The 'prisoners' renounce their crimes and beg to get an opportunity to pledge their lives to the UE vision of peace. Things will only get worse once Draven starts forcing everyone's loyalty."

Gemma said, "I'm growing afraid, Gabriella. I will not take the loyalty mark, no matter the cost. My Bible-studying sessions have taught me that taking this mark will forever separate someone from God. You need—".

Gabriella cut her off. "I know, Gemma, I need to accept Jesus Christ. I have heard this daily from you for a few months now. I heard the same from Jackson, Christopher, and even an angel and my mom for many years. I know on the surface, it makes sense to accept Jesus's offer for salvation. It's hard for me because I feel like I will lose my most prized position, my intellect; my very identity must be surrendered to God. Sorry, but this is so hard for me, but thanks for pushing me. Look, let's continue to focus on slowing down Draven. When the time comes, we will plan our exit from here before taking the mark. Deal?"

Gabriella changed the subject. "I need to get back to the office so I can monitor how Omega's attempt to save some Christians from the horrors of the fifth IEC in China is going. I'm linking them up with Kerim and his group finally. You coming?"

Gemma shook her head. "No. I needed a break as much as you. I will see you later."

Gabriella said, "Okay, bye."

Gemma pursed her lips as she still hadn't figured out how to break through her beloved friend's cavalier attitude toward salvation. She had stopped trying to convince Gabriella to remain a background player. As Gemma waved good-bye and prayed for Gabriella and the other Omega members, a wish for Gabriella to accept the impact of her efforts, rose in her mind. Countless lives were spared, and souls were saved through the resistance networks Gabriella supported.

Gemma thought. *God save my friend.*

∽

The City of Turpan, China, an ancient Silk Road oasis town, was the latest stop for Christopher and the Omega Team in the battle against Draven and the revenge mission for Jimbo. Thanks to Gabriella's efforts, the four-member Omega Team spent the months since Jakarta freeing Christians from UE control and establishing resistance contacts worldwide. Christopher hoped that Gabriella's "friend" would be a valuable ally in the war against the UE. Despite Gabriella not saying much about the Jiātíng Jiàohuì, their reputation proceeded them. Abdulkerim Hoshur, the leader of the Jiàohuì, were known as fierce opponents to all things Draven Cross and the UE within the underground resistance community.

Christopher hoped Abdulkerim, or Kerim as Gabriella knew him, would accept his invitation to meet in the busy city market atmosphere. The Jiàohuì had developed a network of logistics nodes, assembled skilled laborers, and acquired weapons. Thanks to the Jiàohuì and Gabriella's efforts, a network of similar groups formed worldwide, using shortwave radio, dark web internet, and even couriered documents sent from Gabriella detailing UE movements or the Gospel of the Bible. Daily the hope of God and resisting Draven Cross in these final days was reaching millions.

Survival was all that mattered in life now, and it seemed everyone's actions reflected this realization. As twilight lingered across Turpan, survival was the only thought etched on every face Christopher watched from his seat at the most famous kabob street vendor in town. People haggled and argued over every UE dollar or item to be bartered. Christopher could see the suspicion and mistrust over resources hardened looks on people's faces as they walked by each other. The fact that everyone was forced to live in such a primal sense of self-preservation from day to day inspired him and Omega's efforts even more.

The New Year had changed the dynamic of gracious tolerance preached by Draven. Countless numbers of people had died since the Jakarta mission for their beliefs in Jesus Christ. Draven's increasingly open persecution of Christians dwarfed anything any government ever dared to call religious persecution. The reality of every day was most people were scared they would not live to see the next moment; Draven's utopia of a peaceful and unified planet was less a concern. The persecution intensified with the building of the IECs, as Gabriella called them. Most of the IECs were filled with Christians, and every IEC prisoner had a date at the gallows. The tolerant UE before the Jakarta mission was gone.

As the other Omega members approached Christopher's table with a large man, Christopher felt his soul's exhaustion. How long before he was on the gallows? How many Christians had they failed to protect? Who on the team would die next? The questions in Christopher's mind pushed his trust in God to the brink of breaking every day. Omega had been playing a dangerous cat and mouse game with the UE since Jakarta, with Gabriella tipping and queuing them away from the snares of Draven. Christopher prayed daily that the personal war between Draven and the followers of the God of Heaven would not be paid in the blood of anyone on his team.

Gilana made introductions as she, Charlie, and Jackson took seats next to Christopher. "Christopher, meet Abdulkerim Hoshur."

The look of formality on Abdulkerim's face led Christopher to avoid going with the name Gabriella had given him. "Nice to meet you, Abdulkerim."

Abdulkerim Hoshur reminded Christopher of Jimbo as the man was a towering presence not only in his height but massive build.

Abdulkerim gave a pensive look at his watch. "We don't have time for civilities. There are believers in danger. I was told by Gabriella that you will help,"

Christopher said, "Abdulkerim, I can appreciate your haste to help those in need, but I am sure you can understand the importance of knowing a little about who you're working with. I would think you'd want to know more about me, rather than trusting the word of Gabriella."

Abdulkerim disagreed, "I would trust Gabriella with my life. Perhaps I have been watching you while you sat here in the market, and it is you who doesn't know who they are dealing with."

Abdulkerim ran a tan hand across his jet black hair, causing six armed men to emerge from the market crowd encircling the table.

Abdulkerim gestured to them. "Christopher, I understand completely the business we operate within. So, if you can help my cause, I am grateful, and Gabriella was correct about who you are; but, if you're wasting my time or mean to harm us, you will not leave Turpan alive."

Christopher attempted to keep the situation from escalating. "You can relax. We are on the same side fighting a common enemy in Draven Cross. I think we can agree that no one likes secrets amongst armed groups."

Abdulkerim ignored Christopher's response. "I need your team to provide a lethal distraction while my operatives rescue the detained believers. Your pilot, Charlie, will ferry my rescue team and the believers on an aircraft we have waiting to Ürümqi. I will ground convoy with you, Gilana, and Jackson, to link up with your aircraft in Ürümqi. Now let's go."

Before Christopher could stop him, Jackson grabbed Abdulkerim's arm, causing the man to twist awkwardly. The secretive Jiàohuì operatives quickly raised their weapons on the Omega members. Abdulkerim waved to them to lower their guns.

Christopher yelled, "Jackson, calm down!"

Jackson ignored Christopher. "I don't know who you think you are, but we don't take orders from a stranger, even if you know Gabriella. You need to give us something that says we can trust you."

Abdulkerim laughed and then spoke in what Jackson assumed was his native Uyghur to his operatives, causing them to laugh. "You arrived in Ürümqi yesterday evening. Your plane is in a secure hangar at the airport, and you drove here in a large vehicle parked three blocks east of here. I've been watching your team from the moment you arrived, and you still are alive. Trust is best earned in battle, not sipping Chi in a market. Does my answer suffice for you, Jackson?"

Jackson looked at Christopher for an answer.

Christopher wondered, *Why does God always test my trusting Him?* "We will support you, Abdulkerim. You need to understand me; if anything happens to any of my people, I will kill you and any that stand in my way."

Abdulkerim nodded. "I respect your response. Call me, Kerim. By this time tomorrow, we will be brothers in arms. Now, let's go."

Pontiff Conti paced his office at the Vatican as he watched on television yet another Interfaith event without him—led by Draven Cross. He had felt isolated and ashamed since the incident in Jerusalem with the Two Witnesses months ago. "Giuseppe, how long should I tolerate such insult? The people of the world require spiritual guidance, not a dictator using Interfaith to hide his atrocities. During the past few months, I have been limited to an occasional mass and attending UE events as nothing more than *il fantoccio*. I know other leaders feel as I do that Draven's leadership has been inadequate."

Giuseppe said, *"Fate attenzione, Pontiff.* You are playing a game with our lives. How can we plot against the monster leading the UE? We need more than religious men, *eminenza*."

Conti's frustration bubbled over. "I am confined from my destiny. I am rotting away in nothing less than house arrest, and you are worried about proceeding carefully. I have ambition Giuseppe and a vision for the world. I will not waste away while Draven destroys my legacy. A higher power than Draven Cross sought me, and I will have my revenge. I need you to call the Grand Ayatollah that attended the World Religious Conference last year. The Ayatollah will want to hear how Draven has killed many of those who held his beliefs."

While effective at masking Christopher and Jackson's location, the lightweight desert camouflage netting failed to diminish the sun's intensity. Christopher's polarized-sunglasses did little for the sweat running into his eyes as he rubbed them for the millionth time, trying to focus on the target below him after the searing sting of perspiration blurred his vision. He was suppressing urges to express critiques of a mission he was not commanding. Christopher questioned the sanity of executing the rescue mission during the heat of the early spring day, given the area is known as one of the hottest places in the world. He accepted Kerim's rationale for a daytime mission; as Kerim explained, the UE only moved prisoners during the daytime to mitigate attacks due to the heat. However, having this knowledge did little to ease the suffering.

Christopher keyed his radio mic. "Jackson, I know why they call this place the Flaming Mountains; I swear this guard in my scope caught on fire when he stepped out of the guard shack down there."

Jackson commented, "Yeah, it's hotter than the Devil's toenails. I hope the prisoner convoy comes soon."

Christopher laughed, losing his focus through the spotter scope he was using to support Jackson. The latter held a rocket launcher provided for the lethal distraction. The rocket launcher was overkill in Christopher's mind, as the 120mm rockets would destroy, not distract any of the UE forces destined for the IEC. His gut told him killing and not scaring the UE was utmost in Kerim's mind.

Kerim announced across the radio headsets of the men, "Get ready; the prisoner convoy is approaching the ambush point."

Jackson moved from under the camouflaged shelter, standing and arming the rocket launcher awaiting the order to fire. A steady tone emanated from the LED display on the rocket launcher, signaling the laser designator had locked onto the first vehicle in the oncoming convoy 850 meters away.

Christopher observed the lead vehicle, and as it rounded a bend, he ordered Jackson to fire.

Jackson said, "This is for Jimbo."

Christopher winched as the heatwave of the backblast passed his face. Looking through the spotter scope, he watched the rocket streak toward its unsuspecting target. The impact caused ripples to race across the up-armored vehicle before being engulfed in flames and light. As Christopher scanned to the rear of the convoy, the last truck was in the midst of a similar experience provided by Gilana. The L-shaped ambush had been textbook as the prisoner vehicles were now trapped between two burning craters of debris. The trap was sprung over half a mile away from the IEC in a curved section of the valley road to slow response forces from the prison. Nevertheless, the sounds of destruction could not be hidden. Sirens of alarm were blaring from the nearby UE stronghold.

Kerim's operatives swept onto the ambush site freeing the Christian prisoners from the open-aired caged transport vehicles.

Christopher watched as a wounded UE driver was dragged from his vehicle and executed on the side of the road; it was a brutal act to watch. However, he felt a moment of conflicted-endorsement from the act of revenge against a servant of Draven, considering the suffering Christians endured.

Kerim ordered, "Move to the rally points."

Christopher and Jackson ran down a footpath that led away from their ambush point to two ATVs, which would provide their escape to the link-up point with Kerim and Gilana. A mile later, they arrived to see Kerim and Gilana waiting on them in a non-descript truck.

Kerim yelled, "Hurry. We are not out of danger yet!"

Christopher asked, "Did Charlie and the Christians take off yet?"

Kerim answered, "Yes, we will meet Charlie and my team in Ürümqi, about three hours from here."

Jackson nodded. "Good. The road trip will give us a chance to catch up with each other, you know, build trust."

Kerim laughed. "I told you we would be friends by the end of this mission."

❧

Gabriella watched a computer's monitor shattered into countless pieces in Rome's UE operations center as Draven's temper exploded with reports flooding in regarding the Turpan IEC attack.

Draven shouted, causing junior staffers and analysts to scurry out of the operations center. "Everyone not named Evan or Gabriella, get out of my sight!"

Draven continued, "How long should I tolerate the incompetence and betrayal on this staff? There have been multiple attacks against me, including now every IEC. Do the two of you expect me to believe that these Christian terrorists have more capabilities than the greatest government ever formed: mine?"

Gabriella dared not speak first. Over the past few months, she felt Draven was growing weary of her "inability" to locate Omega and the other Christian terror groups, as Draven referred to the believers of God resisting his reign. She knew her adventures building a resistance network were drawing to a close. Thankfully, Evan was always seeking to please his master, sparring Gabriella.

Evan said, "Sir, we need to make an example of the sympathizers and hidden protectors surrounding these Christian terrorists; executing prisoners has little effect. Perhaps, the approach has been too cautious."

Gabriella winced at the fury flashing in Draven's eyes as he took exception at the hint that he might be wrong.

Draven cut off Evan. "If any policy approach has failed in this organization, it is due to your timidity and ignorance in the execution. I would line these Christians up in the street and shoot them all if I had my way, especially those Two Witnesses in Jerusalem. The only thing preventing that is my concern of a global revolt from the masses, which could be solved if I had a staff that could produce the loyalty trackers faster. Gabriella, do you have anything of value to add to the conversation?"

Gabriella, now on the hot seat, took a different approach to Draven. "There is not much I can say, sir. I have failed in providing actionable intelligence to mitigate these attacks against you. Unlike Evan, I will say that speeding up the application of loyalty trackers beyond the imprisoned population may create more issues."

Draven challenged. "How?"

Gabriella hoped to appeal to Draven's logic. "You may force people underground who see the tracking chips as an attack on their freedom. I say we proceed with a slow rollout of the loyalty marks. Your use of public executions for those prisoners refusing the marks also hurts your cause, in my opinion."

Draven scowled. "Gabriella, you exude weakness like Evan. You speak the truth in saying your failure in providing relevant intelligence is adding to this problem. You are wrong in assuming that people will not respond to the pressure of submitting to my will or lose their life. People will give anything to save their lives, including providing unquestioned loyalty."

Gemma interrupted the meeting with a message. "Sir, you have an urgent call from John Barnes. He wants to ensure you got the email he sent you. You can take the call on line one."

Draven stared at Evan and Gabriella before snatching a nearby phone handset. "What do you want, Barnes."

"Sir, you were correct to suspect Omega is involved in attacking the IECs. I saw Christopher Barrett and Jackson Williams link up with two others yesterday in Turpan. I'd gotten a tip-off that some American's arrived in the city the day before the attack. So, I had the source follow them."

Draven said, "You have my attention."

Barnes continued, "I sent you in the email a photo of an unknown woman that I believe is working with Barrett and Williams. I lost the group in the market crowd. However, I did identify the man they were speaking with as the leader of a terror group operating across China. I suspect Omega and these other groups are aided by an insider, maybe even Gabriella."

Draven looked at Gabriella continuing his call with Barnes. "Well done. I agree with your assessment of the threat. I will review your email and get back to you if needed."

Draven ended the call hanging up the phone in a better mood than when he picked it up, which concerned Gabriella.

Glaring at Evan and Gabriella, Draven said, "Well, it seems that at least one person under my charge has succeeded today. Gabriella and Gemma, you are dismissed. Evan, follow me to my office. There is a loyalty problem I wish to discuss with you."

❧

Draven paced his office as Evan read the note on his phone from John Barnes.

"Well, Evan, have you finished reading? It seems you read as slow as you think."

"I have finished, sir; I'm puzzled as to why Barnes thinks someone on the staff, especially Gabriella, is aiding the rogue Americans."

"It makes perfect sense. I underestimated the gesture by President Rodgers, offering up Gabriella's services as my intelligence officer. She is a former CIA operative and has done little to find these men since the Jakarta attack. Gabriella has the perfect background to be a spy in our midst."

Evan inquired, "How should we handle this?"

Draven fumed. "Over the next 24 hours, I want every region to hold public executions of anyone being detained, especially Christians. I want the message of fear to penetrate these terrorists' hearts the next time they think about attacking me. Ensure Barnes knows to tie the executions to the people supporting the terrorists in Xinjiang province. We need to deny a safe haven for these fanatics to operate. Regarding my suspicion of Gabriella, we need to craft a plan that leads her and these Omega pests into a trap."

Evan declared, "I have a plan, sir. We tell Gabriella of a new facility under construction to torture Christians. If she is the spy on the staff, she will lead her friends to their death. Barnes's men and some UE soldiers will be at the destination of our choosing springing an ambush on Omega, thus killing two birds with one stone."

"Finally, Evan, you present a solid idea. Now go make the necessary arrangements."

Chapter 17

PONTIFF CONTI'S LATE afternoon arrival in Qom, Iran, to meet with the Grand Ayatollah of the *Qom Hawza* was less inviting than expected. Three armed men in military attire and one in a business suit stood near a decrepit, bullet-hole-riddled van awaiting Giuseppe and the Pontiff as they exited the train station.

Conti protested, "This is unacceptable. I am the most important dignitary in the entire Unified Middle Eastern States and the Interfaith religion leader. I will not depart this location without a proper vehicle nor without Kamran Farshid greeting me."

The man dressed in a black business suit approached the Pontiff, causing Giuseppe to stop his approach.

The man half-smiled at Giuseppe's attempt to protect Conti. "Good afternoon, my name is Dariush Farshid. Ayatollah al-Farshid is the proper way to acknowledge such a revered leader, not by his given name. Qom is a holy place. You would be wise to understand our customs and traditions, Pontiff Conti. His holiness is prepared to receive you at his home."

Conti's pride left him unable to acknowledge his fault. "This vehicle remains unacceptable to transport a leader of my stature."

Dariush Farshid addressed the ignorance of the Ayatollah's guest. "Pontiff, your eyes view the world like so many other westerners. You place value on an object by the way it looks. This vehicle's status is higher than any luxury vehicle in all of Iran. Ayatollah al-Farshid drove this van years ago to protect a former supreme leader from assassination, thus preserving our revolution. We only use this vehicle to transport the most respected dignitaries or the most sacred deceased in our society. So, please, enter the van. I do not wish to keep Ayatollah al-Farshid waiting."

Giuseppe's eyes pleaded with the Conti to get in the van before insulting the Ayatollah's men further and escalating the situation.

Conti relented. "Fine. In the future, spare me of such an honor."

The noble van of the revolution carried Pontiff Conti through the twilight lit *kuchehs* of Qom. These narrow high adobe and brick-lined passageways shaped the urban landscape of the ancient section of the city. The vehicle pulled into a circular driveway at the end of one of the narrow streets to a beautiful sandstone-colored home. Conti pulled himself from his smartphone, reading the internal staff memo sent by Evan announcing Draven's demand for public executions. The home's design in front of him created a sense of awe as the fading sunlight glistened off the golden and turquoise-colored mosaic covering the *Iwan*-structured entrance.

Conti had enough experience in Iranian culture to understand what would come next as he entered Ayatollah al-Farshid's home. The Pontiff would have to navigate the ritualistic foundation of Persian etiquette, *Taarof*, a complex cultural construct if he hoped to gain the Ayatollah's support. Conti and Giuseppe's escorts brought them into a well-decorated sitting room adjacent to the doorway, where Al-Farshid waited to greet them.

Al-Farshid provided a warm welcome. "*As-salaamu Alaikum*, Pontiff Conti. Welcome to my home."

Pontiff Conti began his charm offensive. "*Wa-Alaikum-Salaam*, Ayatollah Farshid. I am grateful for your hospitality and for welcoming us into your home.

Al-Farshid took Conti by the hand and led him through a winding passageway ending in a courtyard that held a small pool surrounded by a garden with trees of figs and pomegranates. A large table filled with colorful dishes of lamb, rice, and vegetables were arrayed before the Interfaith leader. The Ayatollah led Pontiff Conti to the table's head, asking him to take his place as the honored guest.

Conti understood that under *Taarof,* he had to make an elaborate expression of refusing hospitality. "I cannot accept such an honor. I insist you sit at the head of the table, Great Ayatollah."

After a few more refusals, Conti accepted his seat at the table, and the meal commenced. It didn't require long to finish the small portions offered, evidence of the lack of food since the disappearances even in the wealthiest households. Conti seized the moment when the attendants began removing dishes to launch into the purpose of his visit. "Ayatollah al-Farshid, how do you feel about the Secretary-General, Draven Cross,"

Al-Farshid held his hand up to Conti as he spoke in Farsi to Dariush. Dariush then spoke loudly to all the servants leaving the Ayatollah alone with Conti and Giuseppe and himself.

Al-Farshid proceeded once his servants were gone. "Pontiff, what exactly are you asking of me?"

"How many followers of Islam have died at the hands of Draven? He speaks like a man of peace but seeks only power. The Interfaith religion, which you boldly proclaimed could unite all humanity, is now used as a prop to boost a vile man's ego. I am asking you to help me bring him down."

Al-Farshid stood from the table and moved to a mural of a Persian warrior standing atop a castle wall before speaking in his accented English. "Pontiff, do you know what this mural represents?"

"I don't, Ayatollah."

Al-Farshid explained, "This is a depiction of Alamut Castle, the ancient headquarters of a group dedicated to ensuring that enemies of the Islamic faith were eliminated. I am a descendant of this sect called *Ḥashashiyan* or The Assassins. When I agreed to support the abomination you call religion, my support would have bought a safe haven for Muslims against the West's oppression. I was wrong, and Draven Cross has all but destroyed the people of my faith."

Conti seized the moment. "Then help me destroy Cross. He does not deserve to lead the world, using religion as a pretense for his bloodlust."

Al-Farshid turned to Conti. "I will right the wrong of my decision to align the Holy faith with infidels, thus avenging the *šahīd*, those martyrs that have paid the price for my mistake under Draven."

As Conti stood to shake hands on the alliance to end the reign of Draven, he stumbled into the small pool as the ground convulsed beneath his feet. The sounds of screaming servants running into the courtyard drowned his pleas for help as Al-Farshid's home collapsed.

~

Christopher and his Omega teammates had only gathered minor details of Kerim's background between Gabriella and thus far in the drive to Ürümqi. Christopher decided the conversation needed a blunter tone. The sky was starting to turn orange and red, indicating nightfall was approaching—a road sign for Wulabo Reservoir placed the odd group minutes away from Ürümqi.

"Kerim, you need to give us some details on who you are beyond you're a believer and what your organization has been doing since the disappearances."

Kerim grew frustrated. "What more do you need to trust me? We have a mutual friend. I worship the same God you do and hunt and kill the same enemy."

Christopher defined trust for Kerim. "Trust in this shadowy, paramilitary world we both operate in means knowing something that leaves you vulnerable to me and me to you. How do we not know you are a double agent for the UE? You are a man of contradictions, a Christian amongst a population of people that predominately are Muslims. Special ops trained in the PLA military that crushed peace protest, but at the same time fighting to save Christians. Why do you speak English so well? Should I keep going?"

Kerim jerked the vehicle quickly off the road in a whirl of dust. "You want to know me, here you go. Due to my height and size, I was placed in a special operations program. Yes, we were taught to track down people that were a threat to the communist party, to harm people expressing their own ideas, but it was through brutal example."

Kerim raised his shirt to show Christopher and the others in the vehicle burn marks and scars of his torture.

Kerim leaned his head back on his headrest and starred out the driver's side window. "As far as my English-speaking skills, I was taught English and Russian at Beijing University. The Chinese government sent me on cultural immersion training at embassies located in Western nations to improve my English. The Rapture happened before I left the Chinese army, but I used the chaos afterward to escape and have fought the UE every day since then. I got involved with the house church in honor of my parents, and soon after that, I accepted Jesus Christ as my savior. So, is that enough transparency for you, Christopher?"

Christopher felt sick to his stomach. His old nature of not trusting anyone reared its head. The thoughts of jealously for not leading the rescue mission in Turpan faded away in the shame of his distrust of Kerim. "Kerim, I owe you an apology. I did not trust you until moments ago. I took for granted the struggle you have been on, and for my mistrust, I ask you to forgive me."

Jackson pleaded, "Forgive me too, brother."

Gilana boldly proclaimed, "I knew you were telling the truth in your desire to fight the UE. I could see the fight was personal in your eyes. Please forgive me for planning to kill you in case Christopher and Jackson were right."

Christopher and Jackson raised their eyebrows at Gilana while Kerim erupted in laughter.

Kerim acknowledged the shift in the mood. "Gilana is tougher and more honest than any of us. Now that we are friends, I pray we can have many more successful missions for the Kingdom of God."

The joy of a new friendship quickly faded as traffic increased at a flash UE checkpoint.

"Let me talk. If asked, you're western construction workers coming back from Turpan. Do not do anything hasty, trust me."

Trusting others, the ever-recurring theme for Christopher and his constant struggle. God was going to get him to trust other people, even if it killed him, or so it seemed as he watched UE soldiers pulling people out of the cars ahead of them and ransacking their vehicles.

ఴ

Kerim spoke with a UE soldier in his native Uyghur in a rushed and terse tone. Christopher's finger traced his pistol as he silently prayed for resolve to see Kerim's plan through and not do something that got everyone killed.

Kerim directed, "Christopher grab the white envelope in the glovebox. There is enough money in there to hopefully make us a less searchable vehicle."

Jackson noticed. "Two more soldiers are heading our way. We should hit the gas and get out of here, run them over if need be."

"No," Kerim said.

The UE soldier started shouting at Kerim as Christopher rustled through the litter-filled glovebox for the white envelope. However, one of the two guards approaching the vehicle yelled and waved at the angry soldier at the truck. The three UE soldiers huddled around a handheld radio and then waved to Kerim to drive.

Christopher asked, "Kerim, what's going on?"

"The UE received an order to support a mass execution in the city center. I fear that some of my people have been detained."

Gilana questioned, "Why do you say that?"

"They mentioned Christians."

Kerim pulled out his satellite phone and dialed the operatives who were supposed to meet them at the safe house, along with Charlie. The immediate voicemail pickup was not reassuring, considering the UE mentioning they had detained Christians.

Kerim's silence and face told a story of concern. "I was not able to reach the team that traveled with Charlie. I think they may be in trouble. I believe our team and the Christians have been captured by the UE. I recommend we head toward this UE rally and prepare to rescue them."

Christopher challenged Kerim. "We are walking into the unknown, for we don't know how many UE forces are here or dispersed in this crowd. We could all end up detained or dead if we don't play this right."

Jackson questioned, "If we were willing to risk it all to get these folks out of that prison, what's stopping us from doing the same thing here?"

Gilana added, "I am with Jackson. We have a mission to stop the UE at all costs."

Christopher felt outnumbered and being pushed down a path that was going to lead to disaster. He tried to gather his thoughts before causing further division on the team. Christopher watched as Kerim followed UE vehicles and crowds toward a UE rally. The function checks of pistols and rifles filled the truck. When they arrived, Kerim parked near a gathering crowd at Nanhu Lake. Kerim attempted to contact his team lead that had flown ahead with Charlie and the Christians, to figure out what was going on.

Jackson asked, "So, what's the plan, Christopher?"

Christopher was growing frustrated to be pushed for a vital decision without enough information. "Relax, Jackson. Let's see what Kerim has and then figure this thing out together."

Kerim shook his head that he had not made contact with his men. He seemed uninterested in debating between saving those he cared about or his own life, walking to join the execution's gathering spectators. Jackson and Gilana, both consumed with attacking the UE, quickly gave chase to Kerim. Christopher was left with feelings of doubt about what was the correct move. He was not sure about trusting Kerim's casual approach to the volatile situation. Christopher's pride and anger rose. He refused to submit to another blind plan of Kerim's with the stakes so high and leaned back against the car with his arms folded.

Jackson turned and got in Christopher's face. "Are you serious right now? You're going to sit here and pout while lives are on the line, maybe even Charlie's, all because we're not following your plan?"

Christopher leaned forward from the truck. "Jackson, you're not thinking, and neither are you, Gilana. Have you both forgotten Jakarta? I can still see Jimbo's body in that pool of blood. We walked into a hornet's nest in Jakarta, and you two are willing to walk into the same trap. Why? I think it's because both of you are consumed with revenge against an enemy that only God can defeat. Wake up and take a second to think before acting. Kerim, you are reacting off emotion, not tactical expertise. We all know we do not have the right equipment or personnel to rescue anyone we find on the gallows. If we die here tonight, how many others that might be saved will die?"

Kerim and Gilana stopped and walked back to the truck.

Jackson pointed to the lights shining on the large wooden platform. "This is all I have left; protecting people caught in Draven's path while wondering when my time to pay the ultimate price will come. All I worry about is dying; all I see everywhere is death. But dying to save people is always worth it. You use to believe that, bro. You are always worried about trusting people and living for the next fight. Man, some of us don't see living here worth the fight. Some of us have lost everything. So, don't stand there and tell me I am not thinking!"

Gilana and Kerim came between the friends as Jackson's shouts drew stares from those walking nearby.

Gilana held the two fierce warriors apart with her strong arms. "Enough both of you. We are family or as close to family as any of us have right now. Christopher, I understand your concern, and Jackson, I understand your desire to protect those in harm's way. We are here, and we need to ask ourselves what we can do together. Kerim, I understand we barely know each other. Still, Christopher was right in saying how many people will die later if we rush foolishly into danger. Your men, like all of us here, accepted our fates when we chose to fight against that animal named Draven."

Christopher tried to find a compromise. "How about we do a search around the rally? If we see our friends, then we find a way to save them. Recon first before action. How about that?"

As the team started to respond, people ran away from the gallows, and chaotic screams overtook the Nanhu Lake plaza. Christopher felt the ground ripple beneath him as the distance lights flooding the plaza toppled. A large chasm opened through the lake toward the gallows, and as he watched the lake and countless numbers of people, but mainly the UE soldiers setting up the gallows, disappear into the void.

Kerim shouted, "What's going on?"

"I think God is providing a response to Draven's persecution of his people," Jackson said.

CHAPTER 18

AN HOUR AFTER Draven's proclamation to mass execute Christians, God's Two Witnesses provided a response by unleashing devastation across the globe. Darkness had fallen across Israel as Reuel and Eliyahu stood in front of the ancient temple wall. Their sudden movements caused a stir amongst the news crews assigned to report on the most hated men in the world.

Viewing the men through a high-definition display, ANN reporter Sam Morrow said, "Looks like we are about to hear more doom and gloom. I wonder why they look so solemn."

Eliyahu was the first to speak, "*I watched as he opened the sixth seal. There was a great earthquake. The sun turned black like sackcloth made of goat hair, the whole moon turned blood red, and the stars in the sky fell to Earth, as figs drop from a fig tree when shaken by a strong wind. The heavens receded like a scroll being rolled up, and every mountain and island was removed from its place.*"

Reuel spoke next, "*Then the kings of the Earth, the princes, the generals, the rich, the mighty, and everyone else, both slave and free, hid in caves and among the rocks of the mountains. They called to the mountains and the rocks, 'Fall on us and hide us from the face of him who sits on the throne and from the wrath of the Lamb! For the great day of their wrath has come, and who can withstand it?'*"

Reuel continued, "The entire world has fallen under the deception and charm of the Beast. Israel, why do you seek the embrace of the evil one led by a spirit that drives the suffering and destruction of God's people. The world has been turned over to its sins, as God has used the Beast to give life to humanity's evil desires. You blame God for your suffering at the hands of the Beast; however, mankind's suffering was forged in centuries of immorality. Why are you unwilling to accept the atonement for sin paid by Jesus Christ on the cross? Soon you will face the Wrath of the Lamb."

Eliyahu spoke again, "The calamity that will follow my voice is the start to sorrows unseen before and never will befall the Earth again. The opportunity to move from enemy to friend with God is drawing to a close. Jehovah, Your will be done."

As soon as the Eliyahu Witness finished talking, panicked shouts rose from the reporters camped around the Wailing Wall plaza as the ground rolled like waves crashing at the beach. Car alarms and emergency response sirens across Jerusalem became a single piercing wail. The night sky filled with bright streaks of burnished bronze light racing toward the ground, as if the stars of the heavens were all falling. Nature was reacting to the God of the Earth, taking His creation and shaking it like a snow globe. People scrambled to find refuge from the Wrath of God.

Gabriella and Gemma sat outside on their shared apartment's stoop, going over her laptop and quantum phone's security protocols.

Gemma grew worried. "Are you sure about this, Gabriella? Why do I need to learn how to take over for you?"

"This is an insurance policy. My gut is telling me that I'm on borrowed time working for the UE. Always remember to find an outdoor location when speaking specifics."

Gabriella set up an alternate authentication process, which would enable Gemma to communicate with Christopher and Jackson.

Handing Gemma the phone, Gabriella said, "Text messages and voicemails will not be saved. If you miss a call, you will see a notification, but no phone number will be listed. There are only two other people in the world that can call this phone, so missing a call is not a problem. You know who to call back."

Gemma nodded as Gabriella picked up her personal laptop, a modern marvel of spying technology, and began explaining how to use the tool. "If you ever need to research something, then use the partition file tool, which allows a secure search and storage application."

Gemma's head was hurting, and her stomach was growling. "Can we take a break; I need a bite to eat."

Gabriella was sympathetic to the pressure she was putting on Gemma. "Yes, we have covered all the important items. We can relax for the rest of the evening."

As the two friends moved inside to the second level, the television fell off its stand, plates and dishes flew out of cabinets. The women screamed as their apartment swayed as if it were a tree caught in a gust of wind during a summer storm. A bright flash followed by an explosion of the living room wall was the last thing Gemma and Gabriella saw before falling as rubble toppled on them.

ꟹ

The loud noises of construction equipment and someone screaming were the instruments that pulled Gabriella into consciousness. Intense pain raced across her back and legs. The streaks of sunlight dancing off the suspended dust particles in her would-be tomb provided her a sense of time. The memory of falling from the second level of her shared townhome with Gemma brought a wave of panic over her as Gabriella screamed, "Gemma! Gemma, where are you?"

"I'm right next to you, love. Thank God we landed between this beam, or we'd likely be dead. I've been screaming for help for what feels like hours. I screamed for you but…" Gemma trailed off

Gabriella realized that Gemma had thought she was dead and that she was alone facing certain death. "I am still with you. It will take more than a fall to take me out. Though I think I broke something in my back, and my legs feel numb."

"Hello, is there anybody in here?" A rescuer shouted, followed by the barks of a dog.

The two friends screamed in unison, "We're here; help us!"

An hour later, both Gemma and Gabriella were being prepped for surgery in what used to be the UE convention and visitor center adjacent to the main UE complex. Draven had the facility converted into a hospital to tend the wounded at the UE and across Rome. Gemma had a fractured left arm and more bruises and aches than she could count. While Gabriella took the worst of the fall, suffering a dislocated right shoulder, breaking two ribs, and a fractured right ankle.

Gabriella tried to focus on harried nurses' and doctors' faces as she was wheeled into a "surgery room" comprised of two sets of partitions, providing a sense of privacy. The medical personnel was so few that nurses stood between the operating rooms at large trays designated for patients handing items to the surgeons. The sight of this brought on waves of panic and fears of infection for Gabriella. However, the nurse prepping her provided a familiar face and voice, quieting her worries.

The nurse said, "You will be fine. Place your trust in God."

Gabriella recognized the nurse, now placing the anesthesia mask on her, as the Angel she had encountered previously. Gabriella faded off as anesthesia overtook her. "You're my Angel. I want God in my life."

❧

Draven cried out as the top floor of the *Palazzo Caelum* buckled as God shook the foundations of the Earth. He entered a flurry of keystrokes on his laptop, bringing up the UE command center's main screen and a video stream of ANN. They were broadcasting the global devastation brought on by an unprecedented earthquake. As a distant explosion blew out the windows of his office, Draven scrambled to hide under his desk. It was only with Evan's panicked voice along with a few UE security personnel that Draven dared emerge. The rolling of the building was starting to subside after nearly fifteen minutes of sustained shaking.

"I'm relieved, sir, to find you alive. It seems we have experienced an earthquake and countless meteor strikes according to the command center," Evan said.

Draven gingerly emerged from under his desk. He attempted to physically wipe the fear from his face. The earthquake had shaken him to his core, similar to his first encounter with the Two Witnesses. He brushed the ceiling dust and rubble bits from his suit, attempting to hold a poised appearance.

"Of course, I'm fine. I quickly found shelter as the ceiling began crumbling and coming down during the earthquake. Now, give me a status update."

"I do not have pleasant news, sir. The earthquake was not limited to this region. This event was a global catastrophe; no area in the world has gone unharmed. Several volcanos erupted, and large meteors rained down, leveling several cities. The UE HQ withstood the earthquake, a bit of luck, I would say."

Draven boasted. "There was nothing lucky about the HQ's structural integrity, Evan. I oversaw the engineering improvements for this building years ago. My insight and knowledge saved countless lives here tonight."

"Yes, sir. However, we did experience some loss of life when the rock ceiling in the cafeteria collapsed. In all, the UE HQ lost 100 staffers, and the number likely will climb after we clear the residential dorms on campus. A twenty-five-meter in diameter meteorite impacted outside of Rome, causing blast damage across the city and here at UE HQ campus.

Draven asked, "Is that all, Evan? The population reduction will speed the recovery process."

Evan was briefly shocked by Draven's coldness but quickly fell in line with his boss's emotions. "Yes, sir, we should be able to recover quickly. The worst news is it seems the Two Witnesses predicted this disaster; they are calling it—"

But Draven cut off Evan before he could finish speaking. "I don't care what those two say. The time is soon coming when I will deal with the witnesses. In the meantime, this current crisis only delays my order, not revokes. The Christians that follow those fools in Jerusalem will pay dearly. I want you to double your efforts to get all the loyalty marks emplaced. You have your orders."

ര

Kerim had wisely kept the Omega team from fleeing Nanhu Lake plaza into the rubble-strewn streets of Ürümqi. The scene before Christopher reminded him of the immediate aftermath of the Rapture. People were screaming everywhere. Bodies were lying in unnatural positions in wide fissures in the ground or amongst the rubble of collapsed buildings and cars.

Gilana looked toward the site of the UE rally. "We should search where the gallows stood; we might find the Christians or Charlie."

Christopher's first inclination was to rebuff the idea. "Look around, Gilana." Christopher had a change of heart as he heard the wails of those in pain or afraid and thought of Charlie perhaps needing help. "We're lucky to be alive. But let's get as close as we can and see if we find any of Kerim's men or Charlie."

Christopher led the group of Jackson, Gilana, and Kerim through the battlefield of carnage. They navigated a series of fissures that led toward the site where the gallows should've stood. Instead, there was a deep dark chasm that filled with water. There were no screams for help in the large cracks in the ground and no signs of life. Christopher turned to the group and raised his hands in desperation, knowing they could do nothing.

Christopher watched Jackson move toward Gilana, where, even in the low light provided by a nearby emergency source, he could see Gilana's hands trembling. Christopher feared Gilana was going into shock.

Kerim conceded that his friends were likely gone. "You're right, Christopher. We need to take shelter. There is nothing we can do right now. I know of a place not far from here. I hope an old Jiàohuì safe house is still standing. Do you think you guys can keep up?"

Jackson and Gilana nodded as they joined Christopher and Kerim, making their way from the park plaza toward the unknown horrors of a destroyed city.

Conti could hear Giuseppe's screams and others looking for him and Al-Farshid through the rubble of the Ayatollah's home in the aftermath of the unknown event.

Conti tried to push a pile of rubble lying across him to draw attention to himself as he heard Giuseppe's voice near him in the small courtyard pool.

Giuseppe called, "*Tua eccellenza*, can you hear me?"

Conti pushed the rubble pile again and then saw a flashlight darting around him. He was wet, indicating that he had fallen luckily face up in the courtyard pool.

Giuseppe used his smartphone flashlight to look Conti over for wounds. Conti pointed out a large bleeding bruise on his head, but he was otherwise fine. "Yes, Giuseppe, I'm fine. What happened? Where is the Ayatollah?"

Conti was pulled to his feet by Giuseppe. He scanned the courtyard by the light of Giuseppe's smartphone, surveying the now destroyed home of Ayatollah Al-Farshid. Several of Al-Farshid's servants were frantically moving rubble from on top of what looked like the buried thobe of the Ayatollah about ten feet from where Conti was lying. A wail of excitement or mourning rose from the men as smartphone flashlights darted like fireflies, and the Ayatollah was lifted from a deep crack in the ground. The raised hand of Ayatollah Al-Farshid confirmed he was alive. Al-Farshid slowly made his way toward Conti.

Conti wanted to solidify Al-Farshid's desire to destroy Draven Cross by lying about the event's origin. "Giuseppe, follow my lead. I have a plan to make this disaster work in our favor."

"My friend *Ar-Raheem* has smiled upon us tonight," Al-Farshid stopped speaking briefly with Pontiff Conti to yell at his servants in Farsi. The result was several smartphone lights aiming at the men to provide illumination of their faces.

Al-Farshid continued, "Sorry, it would be rude to speak and not see your face clearly. I see you have a wound that requires care."

Conti waved him off. "Thank you for your concern, Ayatollah. I will be fine, and I am grateful that you survived the attack tonight."

Al-Farshid seemed lost on what Conti meant by an attack. "Who attacked us, my friend?"

Conti applied the hook of his lie deeper. "This was no mere disaster. It seems that our mutual adversary at the UE had pre-planned this attack on our gathering this evening. My aide Giuseppe was informed moments before the earthquake began by a trusted agent killed for sharing this information that a bomb was planted at your home. I think most of the damage you can see was caused by the explosion. The goal was to kill you and me to solidify the UE's hold on religion and the world."

Giuseppe's eyes though faintly seen, widened with Conti's announcement. The Ayatollah threw his tattered Turban to the ground and spoke for a few moments in Farsi. Al-Farshid reached and took Conti's hands into his, while his eyes danced with fury.

"The *Ḥashashiyan* will bring revenge for both of us to the house of Draven Cross; I swear it."

☙

Christopher kept hearing Kerim say they were getting closer to the safe house. The problem in believing his statement was the dangers of the chasm and crater-filled landscape of the Ürümqi streets never relinquished. The sounds of desperation from the wounded slowed the team. Christopher saw the hearts of his companions, what made them tick, after stopping several times to help people out of gashes in the Earth or wrecked vehicles. It was impossible to ask those who had dedicated their lives to serving their nations, silently protecting millions who never knew their names, to pass over someone in distress.

Shortly after Kerim's latest announcement of getting closer to the safe house, the newest rescue effort demanded the four operatives form a human chain to reach an elderly man and his wife trapped in a crater left by a nearby SUV-sized meteorite. It was tough for Christopher to process the heartache that immersed him as Kerim pleaded with the man in his native Uyghur to let go of his wife. The tactical lights on their rifles showed the man clinging to his wife's arm. The woman's arm was the only visible part of her body as their vehicle's passenger side was buried under rocks and dirt. Kerim pulled the inconsolable man out of the hole and leaned him against a building as if he were placing a carton of eggs on the ground.

Jackson asked, "What's he saying?"

Kerim paused before saying, "He keeps asking me to kill him. He wants to die because his beloved has left him alone."

Gilana was overcome with the man's heartache of losing his soulmate, a feeling she could relate to after losing Uri last year. "We cannot leave him here. We must take him; I will take him to the safe house."

Christopher, Jackson, and Kerim nodded in agreement.

Jackson asked, "How much farther is almost there, Kerim? And don't you dare tell me it's close, or I'm going to lose it like a toddler on a road trip."

Christopher could see even in the faint light provided by emergency street lights that Kerim was lost to what Jackson was saying.

Kerim asked, "What is he talking about?"

Christopher answered, "How close are we?"

"There," Kerim said. Christopher followed the light from Kerim's rife mounted tactical light as the beam cut through the darkness leading his vision to a street littered with building debris and people scurrying amongst the ruins looking for loved ones, items for survival, or something of value to loot.

The group of rugged rescuers moved at a deliberate pace as Gilana was all but carrying the old man. As they approached a former three-story building, Kerim held up a fist signaling everyone to stop. Instinctively, Christopher, Jackson, and Gilana—with her guest in tow—moved behind crumbled concrete and overturned cars to find cover.

Christopher whispered. "What do you see?"

Kerim did not respond. It was the first time Christopher wished he had the stomach-turning green glow of night-vision goggles. Kerim began what could best be described as a bird call. A few moments later, Christopher heard another "bird" and watched four men approach the group, two from the destroyed safe house and two others from behind them.

As he intuitively knew that his Omega associates had trained their rifle sights on the dark shadows moving closer to the group, Kerim ordered, "These are my men; put your rifles down."

Kerim spoke to the men in Uyghur as Jackson joined Christopher.

Jackson questioned, "Is everything okay? Why are we not going inside the safe house?"

Christopher kept his guard up. "I don't know, Jackson. We need to sit tight and follow Kerim's lead; stay ready if we have trouble."

Interrupting Christopher and Jackson, Kerim said, "There will be no trouble. Follow me."

Christopher followed Kerim and his operatives toward the safehouse as Jackson helped Gilana bring the old man, whose sobs and wails had given way to a stone face. They passed another SUV-sized meteorite immediately outside the building and another in what looked like a café or coffee shop's lobby, following discreetly placed chemical lights providing a path. They walked through the shop's kitchen where the lingering smell of grease still hung in the air, only to have the flashlights on their rifles illuminate a stainless-steel meat locker door. One of Kerim's men used the butt of his rifle to bang on the door only to have it crack, and murmurs in Uyghur fill the kitchen. Moments later, the door swung wide, and the group went down a flight of stairs into a large underground space filled with cutout rooms, lit by kerosene fuel lanterns and packed with what Christopher assumed were a hundred people.

Christopher and Jackson began looking around the makeshift shelter, hoping to find Charlie amongst the mentally and physically broken people. At the same time, Gilana cared for the catatonic elderly man. As they rounded a corner of hospital beds, they noticed what seemed like Charlie's form.

Jackson yelled, running over to the section of hospital beds. "Look, it's Charlie!"

Charlie looked dead to Christopher as he approached his bedside, and he prayed that he had not lost another friend.

Christopher was glad Charlie was not dead, but he looked halfway there. He had a bloodied T-shirt wrapped around his head, and his left leg was broken, given the unnatural way it was bent on the table. Thankfully for Charlie, he was unconscious.

Christopher stood with Jackson observing a middle-aged Chinese man with a wild unkempt black wisp of hair speaking with Kerim near

Charlie. Christopher knew, even at a distance, the man was a chain smoker as the heavy scent of cigarettes radiated from his clothes.

Kerim provided an update on Charlie. "Christopher, the doctor says that Charlie will be okay but will need to have his leg set. He stitched up the wound on his head earlier before putting him out."

Jackson joked, "What did he put him out with? A hammer?"

"No, with this. It's called Baijiu or white alcohol," Kerim said, throwing Jackson a bottle filled with a clear liquid.

Jackson nodded at the clear liquid. "Oh, moonshine. We had this back home. Charlie won't fill a thing for a few days. I can help the doctor set Charlie's leg."

Kerim gave Christopher and Gilana a puzzled looked.

Christopher explained, "Jackson is an 18D, also known as a U.S. Army Special Forces Medical Sergeant. 18D are some of the finest first response and trauma medical technicians in the world. He can help the doctor with the wounded. And for the real question, your face is asking, moonshine is an American high alcohol by volume drink like your Baijiu."

"Thank you, Jackson," Kerim said before translating everything to the doctor.

A smile rose across Christopher's face as he watched Jackson put a strong arm across the back of the doctor. The scene brought him to the past. A time where he and Jackson helped indigenous populations while serving together in the 5th Special Forces Group. The smile faded as quickly as it came with the realization that the world of his memories was forever gone, and the wails and moans around him were the post-Rapture reality.

Kerim and one of the operatives that had brought them into the safe house approached Gilana and Christopher. "It seems that the reason I couldn't reach my men was that they had been captured once they touched down in Ürümqi. He told me that the men spoke on the phone with a man named Barnes. Does that mean anything to you?"

Christopher and Gilana looked at each other and nodded.

Kerim continued, "Well, it seems Barnes observed our rescue mission from the prison and called ahead to his men. Barnes's men were on the gallows, including Charlie and my team when the earthquake began. My operatives saved Charlie and a few others, but some were lost to the chasm."

"Is Barnes dead?" Gilana asked.

Kerim asked his operative, giving an answer while they spoke, shaking his head no.

Christopher said, "So, Barnes watched the operation and then set a trap for what he likely hoped was all of us."

Christopher was interrupted by a loud announcement from a nearby TV broadcasting ANN. He watched the cameras from the Temple Mount zoom in on God's ambassadors. "We want to bring you the latest proclamation from the Two Witnesses. This was prerecorded half an hour ago. The Two Witnesses both stood together saying in unison, '"*When he opened the seventh seal, there was silence in heaven for about half an hour. And I saw the seven angels who stand before God, and seven trumpets were given to them.*" This is the calm before the storm. God even now grants you mercy. Turn from your evil ways and accept Jesus Christ as your Lord and Savior before it's too late for the dawn of the Great Day of God's Wrath approaches.'"

CHAPTER 19

GENERAL HAVID WORKED from his home as the Israeli Ministry of Defense had collapsed during the earthquake from the sixth seal opening a little over a month ago. He felt that the calm of the storm, as Reuel and Eliyahu had called this brief period of a lull between Heaven's judgment of the world, was nearing an end. The general found himself under increasing scrutiny. He knew in his heart from the moment he accepted Jesus Christ as his savior that he would be forced to leave his beloved Israel. General Havid had received questions from the Knesset members and the Prime Minister regarding Mossad agents working with a religious terrorist group. The UE claimed to have photographic evidence from the raid on Turpan prison in China's Xinjiang Province of a female Mossad agent named Gilana Edri. Since then, General Havid's loyalty to the peace treaty between Israel and the UE was questioned continuously.

Of course, General Havid knew the intimate details behind the destruction of the UE prison in China. The trio executing the bold attack against Draven's regime comprised the most wanted people in the world. He would never surrender Gilana, Christopher, or Jackson to the enemy of God, even if it cost him his life. It had been a significant risk, but worth it, to dispatch a government business jet to pick up his soldiers in China, as he had come to think of Christopher, Jackson, Gilana, and Charlie. An aide interrupted his reflection on the challenges rising around him by announcing a video call from the Prime Minister's office.

The general removed the cover over his video-capable desk phone, dreading the conversation he was about to have. "Good morning, Prime Minister. How may I help you today?"

Israeli Prime Minister said, "Hello, my friend. I hope you're doing well in these difficult days."

The general had never been fond of the sly tongues of politicians or fake sentiments. He regretted almost as soon as the words left his mouth, forcing the conversation to progress to its point. "Prime Minister, I am sure you didn't call me to ask about my day. I know you're busy, so what do you want?"

The Israeli Prime Minister's face contorted for a second at the abrupt and blunt tone General Havid had taken. "I have known you for years, Benjamin, and I have only believed you to be the epitome of a patriot to the nation of Israel. However, your lack of insight into Gilana Edri's presence at the UE facility's attack is troubling. There are calls within the government for me to remove you from your ministry position. How do you think I should handle this matter?"

General Havid shrugged. "I think you should do what you believe is best for the nation. I continue to stand by my words that I do not believe Gilana is the threat to the nation that many have labeled her. Israel has placed too much trust into the hands of Draven Cross."

Israeli Prime Minister grew angry. "How can I defend such language? Mr. Cross has done what no other world leader ever did for us. He has brought us a sense of lasting peace."

General Havid said, "Daniel, I am not asking you to defend me. I stand by everything I have said today and in the past. Israel is foolish to trust one person and organization for its security. Gilana is not a terrorist."

Israeli Prime Minister announced, "General Havid, effective today, you are suspended from your duties as the Minister of Defense. Given your distinguished years of service to the nation of Israel, I will not make this decision public or final if I receive a public denouncement of Gilana Edri as a traitor to the state."

"Then your decision should be final, Daniel, as I will not say Gilana is a traitor to our beloved Israel. So my suspension is an absolute, old friend. This is my last call as an official of the State of Israel. I resign effective immediately. Goodbye."

General Havid hung up and sat back in his office chair, staring out across his lawn toward the Old City of Jerusalem. He felt the calm of the Holy Spirit invade him, filling the void that the hardest decision he ever made had created. The general was grateful to have a hand in undermining Israel's most significant threat Draven Cross, through the Omega Team. His spirit was buoyed the last month since the team had made it back to his home, where Charlie was recovering.

"How bad are things, General?" Christopher asked, having caught the last part of the conversation.

General Havid said, "I'm sorry you heard that, but things are dire, my friend."

⁂

Gabriella noticed Draven had a broad smile on his face as he was in the midst of a phone call with someone as she hobbled into his office, where Evan and Gemma were already seated. The air cast was cumbersome and heavy; thankfully, Gabriella only had a few more weeks to wear the burden. She almost laughed, staring at the bandaged and wounded UE senior staff at the meeting as she thought back on a joke an old associate at the Agency would say when management tried to enforce workforce happiness, "The beatings will continue until everyone is happy." Yet, her battered psyche could not find humor in the faces of the injured. The presence of Draven's office seemed to settle on Gabriella whenever she was in the room and today felt oppressive.

"Ladies and gentlemen, the Prime Minister of Israel called me to grovel for mercy. He is preparing to publicly disavow his Defense Minister, pledging that he had nothing to do with Ms. Edri's assistance to our American friends' attack on the Turpan IEC."

Gabriella's interest was piqued, knowing that General Havid was going to be ousted. *What's going to happen to Christopher and the Omega Team*? she pondered.

Evan exclaimed, "That's great news, sir. I am glad Israel remembers who provided the peace these past two years they have enjoyed."

Draven said, "I'm not sure they do, Evan. I have twice been attacked by those two fanatics in Israel, yet they continue to breathe and spread lies about me each day. The Jewish Rabbis are not committed to the Interfaith religion; they only care about their daily supplies for sacrificing to their God in the Temple I provided them. No, Israel is an impudent child and needs to be reminded of the proper order in this world."

Gabriella asked, "What do you have in mind?"

Draven smirked. "My dear, I have the same fate in mind for the rebellious nation of Israel that I have for your American friends."

Gabriella attempted to play the game that Draven had laid before her. "I'm not sure how I can convince you, sir, that the former Omega operatives are not my friends."

Draven remarked, "You will have your chance sooner than you expect to prove your loyalty. Evan, bring up the large screen."

Gabriella and Gemma held a glance after Draven's chilly declaration for Gabriella to prove her loyalty.

Draven began briefing, "Evan, you can be seated now. I've got this. As you see on this chart, before the global earthquake, we had finished our projects to gain societal control over the world. The IECs were built and operational in every region. Thanks to Gabriella's associates, we will need to rebuild the Unified Asian States IEC in Turpan.

Gabriella resisted shouting at everyone to quit staring at her as random staffers glanced her way after Draven's comment.

Draven continued, "The loyalty marks will allow us to isolate those seeking to operate outside of our economic structure. Life and death will be held in the choice to take a symbol of loyalty to me. No one will be able to buy or sell anything without my mark of allegiance. The best benefit of the loyalty marks is forcing out into the open those undesirable elements lingering in the world. These terrorists and traitors will have to rise from their sewers where we can eliminate them once and for all. Evan will begin immediately holding rallies around the globe tied to Interfaith and pledging fidelity to me. It will be public confirmation for citizens to either support the UE or die for their beliefs."

Gabriella realized that her best efforts would be relaying this information to the Omega team. "Sir, I'm not sure you needed my intelligence staff and me here for an economic meeting."

Smiling at Evan before continuing, Draven said, "Gabriella, your inability to see the big picture is surprising for a trained CIA operative. Intelligence will ensure those refusing to receive the loyalty mark will be hunted down and ruthlessly dispatched. There is one other matter I want your team to accomplish. I am building a more adequate IEC in the Australian outback focused on punishment. This facility will be exclusively used to execute Christians. The facility will be operational within two months, on the second anniversary of the disappearances. I thought it a fitting date for those claiming God took millions to Heaven. If you want to prove your faithfulness to this organization and me, your job is to find and help John Barnes's team kill your Omega friends. Gabriella, have I made my expectations clear enough? Failure to achieve all I desire could prove to be a fatal blow… to your career. Meeting adjourned."

Gabriella's fear, the same paralyzing terror she felt on the UE plane a year ago, gripped her hobbled body. She knew the warning that needed to reach Christopher to stop the suffering Draven had planned. Time was not on her side, but Gabriella had a plan forming as the UE executive floor elevator doors closed. As the doors opened to the UE HQ ground floor, Gabriella made her way past the UE cafeteria arriving in the gardens. The UE Gardens had become Gabriella's own private classified workspace. She dialed the Omega phone.

Gabriella said, "Hi, Chris. I will be brief. Draven knows about General Havid. He is also planning to build an IEC for the sole purpose of torturing Christians in Australia."

Christopher paused then said, "I'm guessing you're calling so we can destroy the site?"

"You guess correctly. This will also be the mission where I ask you guys to bring me in with you. Draven suspects me."

Christopher's voice rose an octave, "Barnes likely set you up. He spotted us in China at Turpan. Look, you should leave now."

Gabriella disagreed, "I can't leave now as I'm being watched. We can plan a link-up location in Australia for my pick up after the mission.

Okay, I need to go. I will leave my communicator with Gemma as she will be our eyes and ears now."

Christopher added his own fears, "I'm worried about this plan, but I promise you, I will get you out of Australia."

Gabriella smiled. "I know you will. I'll see you soon."

Pontiff Conti's face seemed to flush, and he grew warm watching Evan Mallory hold Interfaith rallies across the globe, proclaiming that Draven Cross was worthy of worship as the definitive epitome of inner peace and harmony. As he stood to turn off the television, his cell phone chirped, announcing an incoming text message—the message from an unknown number providing a video of the *Ḥashashiyan* shooting head-shaped targets at various ranges. The last target indicated a distance of 1,000 meters. The message for the video read, "The plan remains to have our man infiltrate Draven's bodyguards, with your assistance. Shooting the Beast will be our plan of last resort. We will be ready."

Conti responded, "I am pleased with what I have seen. I see no issue in placing the *Ḥashashiyan* into Draven's bodyguards when the timing is right. Continue the training until the appointed date for our vengeance."

The Pontiff smiled as he looked across St. Peter's Square and watched the sun dip below the Apennine Mountains in the distance. The thought of crafting the demise of Draven Cross made the scene before him all the better.

The Omega team, including Gilana, Jackson, Christopher, and Charlie, joined General Havid in his office, wondering what the future held now that their powerful ally was jobless. Christopher had brought the team up to speed on the General's decision and Gabriella's mission request.

Jackson wisecracked, "Sir, let me get this straight. You quit your job. Gabriella wants us to destroy another prison and then save her from the hands of Draven. Nothing like jumping from the frying pan into a boiling pot."

Christopher wanted to laugh at Jackson's description of the situation

Omega faced. However, Jackson's complaint rang true on too many points to be funny. "I get it, brother, but this is the hand dealt. The best thing we can do is find a way to make it work. We need to develop a plan to take down this torture camp Draven is building. Any ideas?"

General Havid suggested, "Yes, you need to bring in our new ally, Kerim and his associates. He has more personnel, and based on what you have told me, he is more than capable as a soldier."

Christopher nodded. "I agree, General. Do you think you can get our hardware out of the base? I realize it was being dug out, but if we could at least get our weapons crates transferred to the airport, we will be better equipped for future missions."

General Havid agreed, "I expect any influence I held within the government will fade quickly. Let me make a few calls. I will try to ensure you have not only weapons but a new plane."

General Havid departed his study for his gardens to call in some final favors.

Jackson smarted off, "Let's cut to the chase; things are tougher for us than passing a kidney stone while riding a bull blindfolded."

Christopher and Charlie laughed while Gilana and Jackson starred at each other.

Jackson said, "I take it, you found what I said funny or something."

"Why do you speak like this? You sound like a madman." Gilana's question caused Christopher and Charlie to laugh much harder.

General Havid walked back into his study to find the mindset of the team in the wrong place. "What is wrong with all of you? You're laughing and cavorting like school children. You realize the stakes of the task before us. Gabriella could die, or worse, be tortured by that monster Draven Cross. The plan we develop may tilt the balance between life and death for anyone in this room. Get your mind on the task ahead. Do I make myself clear?"

Christopher and the rest of the team nodded their heads in silent agreement after being rebuked for the lapse in professionalism.

"Now, here's the first thing I want you to do. Get Kerim on the phone. He needs to be intimately familiar with the rest of the plan."

Gilana gestured for Christopher's phone. "I have this covered."

Christopher unlocked it, enabling Gilana to make a secure call to Kerim.

Gilana said, "I have Kerim on speaker, General."

General Havid briefed the foreign operative. "Now, Kerim, here is the situation. I am no longer the Minister of Defense here in Israel. My assistance to Omega will be limited going forward. I know you have some assets, and we need to work together to undermine Draven."

Kerim said, "I understand, sir, and am willing to aid you where I can. I've lost several men over the past few months; however, thanks to Gabriella, I have connections throughout the UE regions."

General Havid continued, "Thank you, Kerim. The plan I envision is twofold. I want you to work to get reconnaissance on the new facility that the UE is building in Australia. From the detentions of those unwilling to accept Draven's mark at the past two Interfaith rallies, I expect this Christian prison to be full soon."

Kerim agreed, "No problem, I will get in touch with a group of believers in Australia to determine the pattern of life."

General Havid displayed the years of military planning experience he commanded. "Here's how we will attack this specific IEC. We take the same plan from Turpan, with slight modifications. It would be suicide to attempt to breach the prison and rescue anyone, inside. The best we can do is hope to destroy most of the facility, which will allow the prisoners the opportunity to escape. I want to focus our limited firepower and effort on disrupting any prisoner movements before reaching the IEC. Christopher, your team will destroy the IEC. At the same time, Kerim and our Australian allies will rescue any Christians and deliver your unit to Sydney for exfiltration."

Christopher nodded in agreement with the plan. "I like it, sir. I mean, there are some logistics to work out. However, I think it will accomplish the mission of destroying another one of Draven's torture prisons and save Gabriella."

Kerim added, "I am ready."

General Havid concluded the meeting. "Excellent, I must lunch a long-time colleague; he wants me to reconsider my resignation and possibly provide the team support going forward. The weapons are secure, along with a new plane at the same hangar we received Jimbo's body. We will discuss any gaps at dinner tonight."

Christopher grew concerned for the safety of the general. "Hey, be careful. You're operating in a non-permissive environment now."

General Havid turned to Christopher with a smile. "Israel will never be a hostile environment for me. I will be fine. I'll see you tonight."

∽

John Barnes relished the cool evening sea breeze, enjoying a view of the Sydney Harbor Bridge from his hotel's balcony. As Barnes looked across Sydney Harbor, he thought about his last mission at the nearby Point Piper home of Martin Sorenson. The former head of the All-News-Network met his demise at Barnes's hands. Here he was again planning to end someone's life. This time, it was his rival's.

Draven had been clear that the Omega team was not to leave Australia alive. Barnes felt confident that his plan to kill the Omega team was foolproof. He returned to his suite to watch the Interfaith rally's conclusion led by Evan Mallory in Buenos Aires. It was his favorite scene in the rallies. He turned up the television to ensure he did not miss anything.

Barnes watched Evan make an appeal to the crowd. "Ladies and gentlemen, it is time to make a decision. You have witnessed today my power, the same light that guides our great leader Draven Cross also performed wonders of healing the sick and providing for your needs. If you want to live in a world of peace and unimaginable prosperity, accept the mark of loyalty to the UE. If you refuse, you will not be able to buy or sell in the coming months, costing the lives of your family or you. Make a choice to live."

Barnes watched UE guards emerge near the stadium's exits to detain anyone attempting to refuse the loyal mark. The beating and dragging of the first few fools took the fight out of the crowds. Barnes knew the fate awaiting those being sent for rehabilitation, a torturous path to the gallows of an IEC, which brought a smile to his face. Despite the Omega Team's efforts to liberate as many Christians as possible. He was proud to be a part of the process of bringing lasting peace to the world.

A call from his deputy brought Barnes out of his daydream and into the reality of his trip to Australia. "Tell me you got his family. That is great news. Did you have them call him yet? Excellent work. I am sure he will be calling me at any moment. Take them to the safe house and await my instructions."

Barnes switched calls as his phone beeped. "I take it this is Noah Brown, the Christian Resistance of Australia leader. It does not matter who I am; all that should matter to you is that I have your family. If you ever hope to see them alive again, you will do as I say. I'm glad I have your attention, Mr. Brown. You will likely receive a call from a woman soon asking for your organization's assistance to attack a UE facility. You will help them and report their plans back to me.

"Additionally, you will send a group of men to detain this same woman and traitor to the UE. I anticipate her arrival within two days. You think you can handle this simple task, Mr. Brown. Remember, I have your family. Answer your phone when I call."

If Omega reached out for help, it would spell their doom and Gabriella's. Like a hunter in a blind, all Barnes needed to do was wait for his prey to come to him.

CHAPTER 20

GEMMA FELT MANIC as she waited with Gabriella outside of their townhome for a taxi to take her to the airport and on to Australia. She could not shake the feeling that this time the trip was doomed for her dear friend.

Gemma starred down the road hoping not to see a taxi approaching. "Explain to me again, why is it that you need to go on this trip?"

Gabriella squeezed Gemma's hand. "If I stay here, I believe Draven will kill me as soon as the Ayers Rock IEC is attacked. He seems convinced now, rightly, that I have been working against him. Though he doesn't have proof—or at least I don't believe he has proof—of my deception. The termination phase is a part of spycraft that is often the hardest to know when to execute. When do you end the relationship with a source before it gets you compromised and potentially killed? Gemma, this is the time to terminate my efforts of being the UE source for Omega and other groups before I get killed, or worse, something happens to you."

Handing her quantum phone to Gemma, Gabriella said, "I have made contact with Noah Brown, a resistance leader in Australia, and he's working with Kerim to ensure they have the right equipment to bring down this IEC before Christians are harmed. I'm glad you held onto my quantum phone during our fall; it's your only way to get hold of people that can get you out of this nightmare when the time comes. It's too bad, my laptop was destroyed."

Gemma was crying, and though she wanted to say something, she could not find the words. Gabriella approached her, and the two friends held a close embrace.

Gabriella needed her friend to help her on another essential journey. "Gemma, there is one last thing I want to do with you before I go."

Gemma wiped her face. "Anything, you name it."

Gabriella's mind and heart had reconciled, and she was ready to accept the truth about God. "Will you pray with me to receive Jesus as my Lord and savior?"

Gemma squeezed Gabriella tightly, and both friends wept for a few moments before Gemma said, "I would be honored to pray with you. Repeat the following after me, heavenly Father; I come to You as a sinner. I have lived my life without You, denying You exist. I am grateful that You never gave up on me. I believe that You loved me so much that You sent Your son Jesus Christ to die on the cross for my sins. I believe that Jesus rose again on the third day and now sits at Your right hand. Please forgive me for my sins, as I accept Your son and now my savior Jesus Christ into my life now and forever. In Jesus's name, I pray to You, Father. Amen."

Gabriella didn't know how to describe how she felt beyond relief. She felt a sense of welcoming and peace with what, deep down, she knew was right. That God existed. "I have to go now. You know where I'm staying in Sydney, and once I link up with Christopher, I'll give you a call. Remember, I'm only a phone call away. I love you, Gemma."

Gemma fought to keep her composure. "I love you too. I will be praying for all of you. I will keep the team informed on what the Beast is up to, I promise."

Gabriella nodded, leaving Gemma waving outside their shared temporary room, entering the UE sedan awaiting to take her to the airport.

Night had fallen over Jerusalem. General Havid had yet to return to his home, even missing dinner. Christopher grew worried with each passing minute. The harrowed approach of the general's aide invited a sense of doom.

General Havid's aide ran into the general's study. "Mr. Christopher, please help. I received this message on my phone."

The text read, *"The traitor to the peace of Israel will be turned over to the UE. The peace of our nation is greater than one man."*

Christopher's worries were confirmed. "Go get the rest of my people, quickly."

The aide ran from the study. "Yes, I will get them."

Jackson, Charlie, and Gilana joined Christopher in the general's study and read the aide's message.

Gilana demanded, "We need to find him."

Jackson ran his hands through his auburn hair. "We don't even know where to start. Besides, the message said the general was being turned over to the UE, which means we cannot trust anyone in the Israeli government."

Christopher hoped Gabriella could help. "I'm going to give Gabriella a call. She'll be able to tell us where he's being taken."

Christopher dialed Gabriella. "Hello, Gemma, is that you? Why are you answering Gabriella's communicator?"

Gemma said, "I can't talk for long right now. She's already on her way to Australia. I'll call you back."

Gilana was near frantic with concern over General Havid and couldn't stop pacing the room. "What's going on?"

Christopher updated everyone. "Gabriella departed for the mission in Australia, and she turned over her communicator to Gemma. I'm guessing she gave Gemma the equipment, so we still had someone close to Draven. Gemma couldn't talk but said she would call me back as soon as she could."

Charlie added, "I think we should start making our way to Australia. It could be a long trip depending on the type of plane the general was able to secure."

Jackson nodded. "I agree with Charlie."

Gilana was near a breaking point. "What about the general? We need to save him. I refuse to leave Israel without knowing he's safe."

Christopher paced for a few moments. "First, we need to move to a more secure location. If someone was bold enough to grab the general, we need to assume they might be looking for us here. The best option is, as Charlie said, we leave Israel. Gilana, I know the general was like a father to you, but we cannot help him until we know where he is, and we cannot help him if the UE takes us to an IEC or worse kills us where we stand now. The general is a great soldier; think as he would right now."

Gilana nodded as she trembled in Jackson's comforting embrace. The group watched the general's aide reenter the room with tears streaming down his face, as apparently, he had been within earshot of the ongoing discussion in the study.

The general's aide approached Christopher. "Mr. Christopher, please take the general's SUV. He would want me to help you. I pray, God watches over you."

General Havid had orchestrated the very situation he found himself in several times. The general had been conversing at an outdoor café with a long-time friend, the Israeli Minister of the Interior, who had allocated a business jet for the Omega team before Mossad agents snatched him from his seat and into a van. The hooding material surrounding his head had a familiar scent and texture, as he had used it on his own missions numerous times. The quick zip ties rendering him immobile had been approved for purchase by him. The techniques used to take his freedom had been briefed and rehearsed in front of the general countless times. The irony of the moment was not lost on him to fall victim to a nation he had devoted his life to. The general also knew what was to come and steeled his mind for the pain.

Draven buzzed Gemma in as he finished a conference call with John Barnes and Evan. "Gemma, things are looking up for me, my dear. I'm on the verge of eliminating several enemies in one fell swoop."

Gemma played coy, knowing that she was being trusted to provide vital information to the Omega team. "I'm not sure I understand what you mean, sir."

"I will dispatch several thorns in my side in Australia, and the Israeli government handed over a senior defense official that aided the Turpan IEC attack."

Gemma wanted to cheer as this was a part of the information needed. "That is a significant update. How can I assist you, sir?"

Draven said, "I need you to schedule two press conferences. The first will occur later today. I plan to announce the detainment of the Israeli general. The second press conference should take place two days from now on, the second remembrance of the disappearances."

Gemma now had a tentative timeline for the UE plans. *Gabriella would be proud,* she thought. "Is there anything else, sir?"

Draven handwaved Gemma. "No, you can leave now."

Gemma was always happy to leave Draven's presence but now was even more critical. She grabbed Gabriella's phone and headed for the UE gardens to let Christopher know that General Havid was in trouble.

Hiding amongst some shrubs and shadows of the lights along the tarmac with Charlie, Christopher watched the runway leading back to Ben Gurion International Airport's central area. Gilana and Jackson cleared the hangar for any potential surprises that the Israeli government might have prepared.

Christopher asked Charlie, "You sure you can fly with that air cast on?"

Charlie half-turned to the partly illuminated Christopher, wanting to smack him on the head for underestimating his flying skills. "I could fly anything with one leg and an arm. Now keep your eyes focused on the horizon. The last thing we need is a situation where I have to run."

Christopher laughed at Charlie's fighting spirit as Jackson signaled the hangar was clear using his rifle's tactical light. The team was glad that they would not be required to fight their way out of Israel, but time was not on their side. Kerim had texted to report his link up with the Christian resistance group in Australia led by Noah Brown. Brown's group assured Kerim that he would provide the vehicles, a helicopter for exfil, and ammo for the attack. All that was left was for Omega to load their weapons on the business jet General Havid had provided.

Christopher had set the attack date for two days from now. Charlie calculated the trip would take over 18 hours in this jet compared to the destroyed SHADOW, meaning that Omega would have less than a day to prepare once they arrived in Australia. Christopher knew that less planning time was risky, but they had no other option.

Jackson could see the concern on Christopher's face. "What are you thinking about?"

As Christopher began to respond, his phone rang, displaying a call from Gemma. "Gemma, what's going on?"

Gemma breathed as she'd been running. "Oh my, there is much to say. Draven plans to attack your team in Australia. I'm not sure how but when you go to IEC, you should be on guard."

Christopher interrupted the nervous rant of Gemma, "Okay, but slow down, I can barely understand you. Do you know where the general is right now?"

"No, I only determined that the general is being turned over to the UE at some point. Are you on your way to Australia?"

Christopher said, "Yes, we're heading to Australia. Well, try to find out more about the general and be careful. I will call Gabriella when we get to Sydney."

Gemma said, "Yes, I will do all I can to determine his location. Goodbye."

Christopher replied, "Goodbye."

Gilana joined Christopher and Jackson as he finished the frantic call with Gemma. "So, does Gemma know where the general is located?"

Christopher replied, "No, she doesn't. I told her to try to find out, but Gemma is risking her life helping us. Draven is hunting his enemies now, especially us, so we need to be careful. We risk our lives by pushing Gemma, who is not trained on spycraft, to collect information against Draven. We will find the general in time; I believe that. Right now, we need to focus on saving who we can from Draven's newest torture camp and getting Gabriella to safety."

Gilana and Jackson nodded as Charlie started the engines to the jet.

Christopher silently prayed as he climbed the jet ramp and closed the cabin door, "God, keep Your servants safe."

ᨒ

The warm air invading the business jet as Christopher lowered the door ramp at Alice Springs Airport in the Northern Territory told him that there would be no reprieve from the Australian summer. He could only laugh at the exchange between Jackson and Gilana as the odd couple consistently bantered over Jackson's English use.

Jackson felt snarky as the warm air overtook him. "We are on a roll lately for traveling to the hottest places in the world. We left Jack Frost's front porch in Israel and traded it for Satan's kitchen during lunch; this is going to be a long couple of days."

Gilana remarked, "I will never understand the way you speak, Jackson. Yes, it's hot, but don't you Christians believe it is hotter where we will send the UE soldiers to wait for Draven."

Jackson laughed. "Draven and his henchmen getting what's coming to them puts a smile on my face. Thank you for the motivation, Gilana."

Once the jet's engines stopped running, Christopher dialed the hotel where Gemma messaged Gabriella was staying. He needed to finalize the plan with her before Kerim and Noah Brown arrived. After several rings, the familiar voice of his dear friend greeted him.

Christopher didn't try to hide the relief in his voice, "I was wondering if you had decided to take in the sights after it took so long for you to answer the phone."

Gabriella said, "I needed to shower if that's okay."

Christopher smiled. "Yes, showering is acceptable and welcomed."

Gabriella sighed. "Listen, I always take time to care for myself. What can I do for you?"

Christopher said, "I'm joking with you. So, listen. We are meeting up with the local Christian resistance leader you provided, Noah Brown. Brown's team will pick you up late tomorrow evening and then drop you off at our exfil point outside of Sydney. Stay lowkey, and don't do anything that will make Barnes want to follow you."

Gabriella said, "Keeping Barnes distracted is your job. At this point, I'm awaiting rescue from my Prince Charming, but you'll do in a pinch."

Christopher laughed. "I'll always be the Prince Charming you need.

In any case, I plan to end Barnes as a nuisance tomorrow with any luck. Take care, bye."

Christopher ended the call with Gabriella as Kerim and Noah Brown entered the Omega operatives' hangar, driving a Hilux.

Christopher extended his hand to Kerim. "A good choice for a non-descript vehicle. If you've seen one Hilux in Australia, you've seen a hundred."

Kerim deflected attention to the man helping in the operation. "I wish I could take the credit for being so smart, but Noah here is the owner of the vehicle and a former 2nd Commando Regiment, Special Air Service veteran who will help us save some fellow Christian brothers and sisters tomorrow evening."

Noah Brown said, "It's a pleasure to meet you all; the name is Noah Brown, CRA leader."

Christopher questioned, "CRA?"

Noah Brown replied, "The Christian Resistance of Australia."

Christopher followed up on Kerim's intro of Noah to provided details to his team. "Let me formally introduce my team and our backgrounds. I'm the leader of this team, and former Omega Group, Jackson Williams, former U.S. Omega Group; the lady is Gilana Edri, former Israeli Mossad. Our great pilot is Charlie Smith, former CIA."

Noah nodded. "Right, you have all the skills needed for the task ahead. I'm glad you're here."

Gilana took a typical blunt tone. "Great, we're now friends. Shall we finish the plan for tomorrow?"

Noah picked up on the direct nature of Gilana. "Cheeky one we have here. Okay, so I have two teams of former Australian SAS operatives supporting the mission. One group will extract your friend Gabriella from her hotel and ensure she makes it to the exfiltration location outside Sydney in one piece. The other team, which I will lead, is providing overwatch of the Ayers Rock IEC. They have been reporting Christian's flowing into the prison in midday and evening waves over the last couple of days. I recommend we strike during the evening.

"Charlie, I have a thirty-passenger transport helo scheduled to land here at 1700 tomorrow with a pilot to assist you. You will stage approximately three kilometers from the prison and await my signal to come in for the exfil. The ground assault team comprises fifteen of Kerim's folks, ten of my team, and Christopher and Jackson, I assume.

Jackson chose the moment to attempt humor. "You assume right, mate."

Everyone stared at Jackson after his lousy attempt for an Australian accent.

Noah responded, "I like a guy with a sense of humor. I hope we're all laughing tomorrow night. Okay, that's it, folks. You'll find a couple of crates with ammo and grenades in the back of my truck. Any questions?"

Christopher was worried about the threat facing the team. "Yeah, how many UE folks are at the IEC?"

"We have counted approximately forty UE personnel. Nothing special from what I've seen; the UE soldiers at the IEC look like a gaggle of conscripts. We should be able to make light work of them. Anything else for me?"

Jackson also picked up on some deficiencies in Noah's plans. "How are we getting to the fight? I didn't hear you mention any transport for us."

"Sorry, mate, you will be traveling with Charlie and my pilot and then rucking into an overwatch position tied into the Eastern flank of Kerim's team. It's 268 kilometers from Alice Springs to the IEC prison, so expect about an hour and a half helo flight, after which your three-kilometer ruck march will ensure you arrive at Ayers Rock after sunset. The evening Christian transport will not arrive until 2100. After the cleanup against the UE, you'll caravan with my unit back to Alice Springs, then fly back to Sydney and home. Easy, right?"

Christopher noticed that Noah kept looking at his watch and seemed eager to go. "I think we're good. We'll see you tomorrow, Noah."

Christopher watched as his team pulled the ammo crates from Noah's Hilux, and Kerim pulled a sleeping bag from the cab of the truck. He couldn't shake the feeling that for such a highly regarded SAS veteran, Noah's mannerism indicated he was a very nervous man. "Everyone, make sure you carry a double combat load for tomorrow and get some sleep. We need to be ready for anything."

As Christopher looked out the back ramp of a military transport helicopter at the Australian outback's vast Martian-looking landscape, which stretched forever, it sunk in that the Rapture took place two years ago today. Two years later, without a country to call home and now fighting in support of God, Christopher found himself starting another mission to save Christians from the hands of Draven Cross. Christopher's new reality was stranger than any fiction novel he had ever read.

Charlie's familiar voice ended Christopher's thoughts of the past, "Two minutes to touchdown."

As Christopher, Jackson, Gilana, and Kerim departed the military transport in a whirl of dust. The world faded from a rust-brown hue to shades of gray and black in the fading sunlight. Soon Christopher would need the dreaded green-glow of his night-vision goggles in a pattern that brought him back to the beginning, back to a few days before the Rapture. Christopher prayed that this mission's outcome differed from the fateful night that cost him, Rev.

John Barnes had moved from his Sydney hotel to the Ayers Rock IEC, preparing for the attack. Barnes sat atop the Ayers Rock IEC outer wall ruminating on the mission to come. He soaked in the scene of a rising red moon over Uluru, the famous Australian landmark's indigenous name. The site posed as a dramatic backdrop for the fake IEC. An IEC built for one purpose, ending the lives of the Omega Group. His cell phone rang, ending his reflection on the future. "Noah, you better have good news.

Noah said, "Your Omega friends are here. I've done my part, so let my family go."

Barnes replied. "All of my friends are here now; that is good news."

Noah pressed about the whereabouts of his family. "Let me talk to my family. I want to see them; I need to know they're alive.

Barnes chastised. "Look, I told you, Noah. Finish the job, and then you will get the chance to be with your family. This time tomorrow, all of you will be together, I promise. Good night."

Barnes dialed his deputy. "Noah confirmed Barrett and his crew are here. Kill Brown's family before picking up Gabriella at the hotel. I will take care of Noah after the firefight here. I want no loose ends."

~

Gabriella grew warm, and her face flushed as she revisited the cold-hearted words of John Barnes when he confronted her in the lobby. She prayed, "God, please protect my friends and me." Gabriella had been at her new UE laptop for what seemed like hours sending phony intelligence reports back to Draven in Rome. She had painted the picture that Omega was en route to the Ayers Rock IEC from Israel. Gabriella knew the truth was Omega was already nearing the IEC. And with any luck, she would be on her way to safety with them in a few short hours.

A loud knock at her door startled her, considering it seemed too soon to be picked up by Noah Brown's team. She took a peek out of the door's peephole finding two men dressed in military gear. There stood a large, red-haired man and a muscled, black-haired man with a full sleeve tattoo on his right arm. Thankfully, she did not see any weapons.

Gabriella answered the knock, "Who's there?"

The burly, red-haired man responded, "Ma'am, we work with Noah Brown and are here to get you to safety. We need to go now. The UE is on to us."

Gabriella questioned while watching the men in the peephole to observe if there was hesitance in answering, "If you work for Brown, where are we going from here?"

"We're taking you to an exfil point outside of Sydney. Please, ma'am, we need to be on our way. The UE could be here at any moment."

Gabriella was uneasy but relented, not having any reason to resist further. She left her laptop and grabbed a small backpack of essential items before closing the door on her UE existence. Something felt strange as she boarded the elevator with the red-haired man and the black-haired man. Right after the elevator doors closed, Gabriella noticed the black-haired man fidgeting with a syringe. She wasted no time grabbing the needle and slamming the auto-injector tip into his leg.

The red-haired man slapped Gabriella against the elevator doors causing her to hit the stop button. The elevator's sudden stop sent the red-haired man into his woozy compatriot and onto the elevator floor. Gabriella's face seared with pain, but she hit the elevator button, hoping to stop on the next floor. While the black-haired operative was knocked out, the red-haired man resumed the fight. He lunged at Gabriella, grabbing her by the throat. She felt herself growing faint and swung her right leg with all her strength into the man's groin. The giant man collapsed to his knees, holding Gabriella's left leg as the elevator door opened on the next floor. Gabriella swung her backpack at the man's head, knocking him to the ground as the elevator doors closed behind her.

Gabriella made her way to the staircase at the end of the floor, racing down the two stories it would take to reach the ground floor and hopefully the street. As she exited the stairwell at the lobby, Gabriella attempted to portray a calm and non-attention-getting demeanor as her salvation at the front exit drew near. The cool evening breeze of the street wafted through the revolving door as she made her exit to the road.

She had made it and now needed to find a ride away from the hotel. No sooner than this thought crossed her mind did she notice two men in military gear walking toward her. As Gabriella turned to run back to the hotel, she felt a sharp wave of pain race across her face, and she began to fall. She looked up to see the red-haired man standing over her.

The man pulled Gabriella up to his face by her sweatshirt before saying, "John Barnes sends his regards."

The world faded away as a solid punch rendered Gabriella unconscious.

The relatively short walk to the target site was appreciated by the looks on the team's faces. However, Christopher knew that each of them had to carry heavier loads further distances during their careers. Kerim's second in charge ran to embrace his leader and friend, and joyful optimism broke out amongst the warriors for God. Noah Brown's insistence for rushing had not changed, which failed to reassure Christopher of his resolve. Noah ran along the prominent protrusion on Uluru's southeast side, which overlooked the IEC 300 meters to the northeast, barking instructions to his team. Uluru's crevices and fissures allowed the operatives a place to observe, hide, and rest while waiting to attack the UE.

Noah pulled Kerim and Christopher aside to dictate the final attack. "Kerim and I will take our men down to the last bend in the trail before the prisoner convoy reaches the IEC. We will ambush the convoy and protect the Christians until the helio arrives, which should take less than five minutes. Christopher, I need you to hold off the UE from the IEC or distract them for five minutes. Once we have the convoy Christians loaded onto the bird, we can regroup and clear the IEC, hopefully saving more people. One last thing, here are a few handheld radios so we can communicate; obviously, stay off the net until the shooting starts."

Kerim gave Christopher a shoulder shrug, but Christopher's spirit did not have a sense of peace with the plan. The distant but nearing dust cloud from the prisoner convoy left no time for debate. Kerim and Noah raced down to their positions while Christopher explained the goal to his team.

While unsure of Noah Brown, Jackson was confident in his team, Kerim, and their equipment. "I'm glad to know we brought rocket launchers."

Christopher provided final guidance. "When this thing kicks off, we light up the IEC with the rocket launchers, aim for that front entrance to keep whatever vehicles that are there inside."

A frantic shout across the radios from what seemed like Kerim sent chills through Christopher. "Shots fired. He's attacking us. Come help."

Christopher yelled, "Take down the IEC, and then let's help Kerim!"

Seconds later, three AT-4 rocket launchers with 84-mm high explosive warheads raced toward the Ayers Rock IEC, slamming into the wrought iron and concrete fortification, creating a bright flash of light in Christopher's night vision goggles and a thunderous roar across the Uluru plains. The destruction of the IEC entrance and front wall was better than hoped for as Christopher observed the damage through a starlight spotter scope.

Gilana was the first to run down the trail to reach Kerim's team. Jackson grabbed a second AT-4, and Christopher followed suit.

Christopher heard Gilana shout over the radio as she raced in front of Jackson and himself. "Kerim, where are you? We're coming to your location from the ridgeline!"

Kerim's radio response allowed the rapid gunfire in the distance to echo in Christopher's and the others' ears. "We're pinned down behind the third vehicle; Brown ambushed us."

Christopher's heart sank with Kerim's report. He thought betrayal was a dish being served too often lately.

Christopher shouted, "Gilana, hold up. Jackson, let's light up the first vehicle. Charlie, if you're monitoring the radio traffic, start heading our way!"

Jackson and Christopher quickly took aim on the lead vehicle, about 100 meters from Kerim's position. The explosion sent several men and vehicle parts flying through the cold Australian night air.

Kerim yelled on the radio, "Thanks. Now, get down here."

Christopher called on the radio, "Thermals on."

Gilana, Christopher, and Jackson began picking off the shocked troops of Noah Brown from their flank, while Kerim advanced on the front. A few grenades later, and the firing had stopped. The mournful last gasp from the dying filled the night along with the whirl of an approaching helicopter.

Christopher relayed his element's position. "Kerim, we're approaching from the southeast; hold your fire."

Christopher keyed the radio again for confirmation. "Kerim, did you hear me?"

Kerim responded, "Yes, we are behind the third truck."

As Christopher and his team approached the third truck, the distinct tones of Uyghur pierced the stillness.

Kerim swore and spat on a bleeding Noah Brown.

Kerim yelled while trying to hold back some of his men, "There were no Christians in those trucks; they were empty. He sold us out!"

Christopher watched as one of Kerim's men shot Noah in his right knee, causing the man to wail in pain.

Jackson shouted, "Enough, Kerim. We need to know why he did this."

Noah begged for mercy from the betrayed men. "Please, listen. I had to do it. Barnes has my family. If I refused, my wife and mother would be dead."

Christopher's thoughts turned to Gabriella, who had been in contact with Brown ahead of the mission. "I don't care about your gutless excuse. Where is Gabriella?"

Noah pleaded, "I am sorry. I gave Gabriella to the UE."

Christopher shot Noah Brown twice, once in the head and once in the chest with his rifle, ending the heated debate on what had happened.

Jackson radioed, "Charlie, where are you? We need you here now."

Christopher and the other men on the radio heard a frantic struggle that matched the helicopter's first sighting. In horror, the team watched a helicopter buzz low overhead, flying in an erratic motion heading in the IEC direction.

As Christopher and everyone raced after the helicopter, Charlie's voice over the radio brought the group to a halt. He was fighting for control with Brown's pilot. Two gunshots brought everyone to a standstill as the helicopter began a rapid descent directly toward the IEC.

Charlie spoke in a completely calm voice, "I won the fight but lost the war. Brown's guy took out the controls before I shot him."

A brief scream from Charlie followed by an explosion of the helicopter brought to a close the betrayal on Christopher's immediate team wrought by Noah Brown and John Barnes.

There was no movement or sound for what seemed liked forever as the Omega team came to grips with all they had lost in the last forty-eight hours. While grateful to have Kerim as a trusted ally, his Jiàohuì had lost many members since they first met Gabriella almost a year ago. The group of warriors made the slow walk around the final trail bend to witness what they all knew, or better said, wanted to believe as they watched fire engulf the former Ayers Rock IEC; Charlie had saved them by destroying any remaining UE; hopefully including John Barnes.

Christopher, Jackson, and Gilana, and Kerim, plus four of his men, walked toward the IEC and a group of weapons that had survived the onslaught.

Christopher knew getting back to Alice Springs and then on to Sydney was their only hope of finding Gabriella. "Let's try to get a couple of these vehicles up and running and head back to Alice Springs. I'm going to call Gemma and let her know we're alive and see if she has any resources she can get for us to get out of Australia."

Christopher watched the operatives now bonded by their faith and through multiple conflicts to get the vehicles started, as he called Gemma. The numerous rings without her picking up worried him.

Jackson called out, "Let's roll; we got three trucks, hotwired."

As Christopher rode away from the Ayers Rock IEC with what was left of his team and ally, he wondered how far Brown's betrayal had spread. He silently prayed, *God, protect Gemma, General Havid, and Gabriella from Draven Cross's hands.*

John Barnes had been waiting at the Ayers Rock IEC for a direct attack from Christopher Barrett. What he didn't anticipate was multiple rockets followed by a helicopter crashing into the mock facility. The IEC was literally four walls only meant to lure Omega into his trap. While he survived the attack, Barnes was less sure he would survive the wrath of Draven. He squirmed from under the remnant of the front gate. Though alive, the pain in his left arm signaled he was not unscathed.

Barnes screamed out for anyone, any of his SAG operatives, but no one answered. He limped out to where a group of vehicles had been only to hear the rumble of the missing trucks leaving. Barnes knew Christopher Barrett had escaped, but he vowed to kill him no matter the cost.

Elated to share a message he had received from a man claiming to work for Barnes, Evan burst into Draven's office trailed by Gemma. "Sir, great news from our operation in Australia."

Draven responded, "Well, go on, Evan. I don't have all day."

Gemma had to stand by and watch as Evan attempted to be secretive about the capture of Gabriella. Evan stated, "We captured the spy. You know who I'm talking about, correct, sir? I don't want to say the person's name with Gemma present."

Gemma's heart was racing. Gabriella's old communicator had been vibrating in her jacket pocket, indicating Christopher was calling. Now, Evan was claiming to know who the spy was. She was trapped, hopelessly trapped.

God help me, she thought.

Draven rose from his desk, eager to cull the deception that had been festering in his staff. "Say the name, Evan. I'm sure Gemma is anxious to know how things are going in Australia."

Evan said with a smile of pride. "Gabriella was the spy; she will be brought to an IEC and prosecuted for her crimes against the UE. Additionally, the Americans from Omega Group were killed. A bonus gift is all reporting indicates that John Barnes died along with the Australian leader of the Christian resistance there. By all metrics, we've had a resounding success."

Gemma collapsed in front of Draven's desk at hearing the terrible news.

Evan rushed to her, only to be told to stop by Draven.

"Leave her, you fool. Are you daft enough to believe that she did not know her roommate and only friend at the UE was a spy? Gemma will have much to answer for. Have security take her to the headquarters detainment center. I need you to schedule a press briefing for an hour. I plan to share this victory with the world."

❧

Draven put on his most magnanimous smile as the red light above a television camera illuminated, announcing he was now live to the watching world.

"My fellow citizens, I am happy to announce that the UE has concluded an operation neutralizing a lingering terrorist threat affiliated with the late U.S. President Rodgers in Australia. However, the UE did lose several valiant soldiers in the process. Our thoughts and prayers go out to their families. I thank these brave men and women for their sacrifice to our unified world's peace and security."

Evan burst into the UE press, drawing the ire of Draven. "Have you lost your mind? I'm in the middle of a speech to the world."

Evan attempted to explain the situation, "That's the thing, sir."

The television monitor cut from the live feed of Draven to Jerusalem and Reuel and Eliyahu. Livid with attention drawn away from him, Draven turned to hear the announcement.

The two men of God proclaimed the word of God in unison, "*Then the seven angels who had the seven trumpets prepared to sound them. The first angel sounded his trumpet, and there came hail and fire mixed with blood, and it was hurled down on the Earth. A third of the Earth was burned up, a third of the trees were burned up, and all the green grass was burned up.*"

A UE officer entered the press room, urging Draven and Evan to the command center as multiple asteroids had been detected on a collision course with Earth.

Gabriella awoke in excruciating pain but grateful to be alive. She wasn't sure where she was but knew she was in some sort of prison cell. Her legs were bound to the chair she was sitting in, and her hands were tied behind her back. Gabriella's right eye was swollen shut and her mouth throbbed with deep pain. The taste of bile and blood lingered on her tongue from the attack. So here she was alone with only her newly found faith in God, a faith facing its first challenge.

How would she overcome this situation? She had to fulfill the promise of Samuel, one of God's 144,000 chosen, who had said in New York right after the Rapture, "Before the end of this time of tribulation, you will serve the Kingdom of God greatly."

Gabriella prayed aloud, "God, if You desire, You can remove me from the hands of my enemies, but if You don't, I pray You spare my friends that they might save others. Amen."